Praise for *Owl Island*

"*Owl Island* delivers the dual joys of a writer who wields a confident broad brush and has a sharp eye for tiny, perfect detail. . . . This book's plot has legs every bit as good as those of its heroine."
—*The Seattle Times*

"A rich story of human intersections, of secrets and family mysteries, scars and hope . . . [Coburn] moves a complex story with ease and loving attention to detail, mood and the senses."
—*Hartford Courant*

"Rich and poignant . . . Like a gem, *Owl Island* is brilliant, multifaceted and impossible not to enjoy."
—*Oklahoma Gazette*

"A subtle and well-developed story . . . compelling and realistic."
—*Seattle* magazine

Also by Randy Sue Coburn

Remembering Jody

Books published by The Random House Publishing Group are available at quantity discounts on bulk purchases for premium, educational, fund-raising, and special sales use. For details, please call 1-800-733-3000.

a novel

Owl Island

RANDY SUE COBURN

BALLANTINE BOOKS • NEW YORK

2007 Ballantine Books Mass Market Edition

Copyright © 2006 by Randy Sue Coburn

All rights reserved.

Published in the United States by Ballantine Books, an imprint of The Random House Publishing Group, a division of Random House, Inc., New York.

BALLANTINE and colophon are registered trademarks of Random House, Inc.

Originally published in hardcover in the United States by Ballantine Books, an imprint of The Random House Publishing Group, a division of Random House, Inc., in 2006.

ISBN 978-0-345-49871-7

Cover design: Carl Galian
Cover photograph: Jupiterimages

Printed in the United States of America

www.ballantinebooks.com

OPM 9 8 7 6 5 4 3 2 1

For Libby Burke
and in memory of my father,
Marvin Coburn
1919–2004

1

Obsessive love is always about rejection—always, always, always.

Phoebe Allen was old enough, experienced enough, and rejected enough to know this as fact. But before the night of her annual barbecue, she did not consider it a fact with much bearing on her present life, her present self. Self-employed, self-sufficient, self-assured—all those good, sturdy "self" words shoring up her place in the world, working like a charm, keeping her safe.

Phoebe always scheduled her barbecue for the second Sunday in August. Today, as she set out the last raspberry pie to cool, everything seemed under control. Through a kitchen window, she could see her neighbor Ivan clamping chinook salmon into wire racks, readying them for the coals. Another neighbor, Amelia, was in the garden, cutting cosmos, dahlias, delphiniums, and zinnias for buffet-table vases on the deck. With days of preparation nearly complete, not a finger had blistered or bled, nothing had burned or broken, Phoebe hadn't forgotten a single crucial ingredient for any of her recipes. Not one provoking incident had occurred to augur how troubled she soon would be. Or that she would look back on this year's barbecue as marking when everything began to change. Not only for her, but for nearly everyone living on Owl Island. Still, it would be easier getting a consensus about what caused the change than it was finding agreement on the topic of why the road they all lived on bore the name it did: Spit in the Wind.

Summer took its time coming here. Sandals and shorts were seldom seen in June. Fourth of July firecrackers had to be lit under cupped hands before being launched into wet, chilly air. August was the blessed month. In August it was warm enough in the afternoons to splash in the shallows of Little Pritchard Bay and cool enough in the evenings to wear a sweater while you sat outside cracking fresh-caught crab for dinner. Schools of spawning humpies—pink salmon best suited for canning—crossed the bay. Fledgling bald eagles swooped down from their aeries, learning to fish. Sunsets behind snowy westward mountain slopes occurred so late at night only the youngest of children surrendered to sleep before ten o'clock. Mornings brought the scent of blackberries warming in the sun, mingled with saltwater tang and alder smoke from woodstove fires. When a brief shower of rain hit, it reminded everyone they still lived in the Pacific Northwest, and nature required payment to sustain so many different shades of green in the landscape.

Not one of Phoebe's barbecues had ever been cancelled or moved indoors on account of weather. And by now she couldn't keep them all straight without looking at snapshots. Then she'd recall each event's details. When Ivan brought that frizzy-haired photographer who broke his heart, when Amelia made a pit for throwing horseshoes on the beach, when Laurienne, Phoebe's daughter, was caked pink with calamine for nettle stings. As the pictures revealed, these parties of hers were hardly exclusive affairs. The only requirement for invitation was residence along Spit in the Wind Road; the only purposes, good food and fellowship. Everyone regarded Phoebe's barbecues as their own equivalent of the Indian salmon feasts once held on these shores, occasions to celebrate the season's sumptuousness.

Although many years had passed since any Indians lived on Owl Island, the island still belonged to a local Salish tribe. In the thick of the Great Depression, the tribe's chief hired a Seattle surveyor to map the island, and it was the surveyor who gave Spit in the Wind Road its name. The chief's minions grumbled. If *they* didn't want to live on craggy Owl without plumbing or electricity, or dock their boats in Little Pritchard Bay, a body of water that drained to mud flats at low tide, why would anyone else? But just as the chief foresaw, plenty of white people felt otherwise—especially after a bridge got built linking Owl to Port Pritchard, allowing easy access to the mainland and the docks of Big Pritchard Bay. Power lines came, eventually. So did gas and water lines and telephone cables. But the rock-ridden, plow-resistant hills and moody waters were there to stay.

When Phoebe had first moved to Spit in the Wind, she'd asked Ivan about their address. Just what did the surveyor have in mind, giving this road the name he did? Ivan's only answer was another question: "What do you think?" Voiced in a curious, genial tone, as if the road were a poem open to interpretation, or a prediction that could only be borne out by the passage of time.

Standing on a hillside overlooking the bay, Phoebe's house was so solid and snug a structure, so replete with modern comforts, it hardly seemed possible that it had started out as the surveyor's rustic summer place. Willing as she'd been to alter the cabin—most notably with a new deck and second story—Phoebe led the resistance when more recent arrivals lobbied for a statelier address in keeping with their year-round homes. Like, say, Shoreline Drive. Or, even worse, Mountain View Way.

"If that's what you want," Phoebe would say, "why not move to the suburbs?"

"Not that there's anything wrong with people from the suburbs." This usually from some diplomat who had just fled them, and Phoebe would be obliged to respond.

"Hell no, it's sidewalks and cul de sacs I hate."

Phoebe had grown up sleeping beneath a large map of the Land of Make-Believe, a narrow island shaped much like Owl, and she preserved all the rips and frays acquired over the years by framing the map under glass. To her fairy-tale–tuned ear, "Spit in the Wind Road" sounded as if it would fit right in next to Breadcrumb Lane, Troll Alley, or Castaway Avenue. So, for that matter, did the name of her business—Westerly Webs. At community meetings, though, she sounded every inch the historian's daughter that she in fact was, defending her preference in the name of character, culture, continuity.

That was about as heated as arguments on Owl Island got, and a good thing, too, considering the differences that divided it. Except for Phoebe's barbecues, Spit in the Wind gatherings generally developed along geographical lines. On the north side, where the homes of Phoebe, Ivan, and Amelia sat strung out on cliffs among dozens of others, were those who tended to build their own dwellings and often bartered for the plumbing and wiring necessary to bring them up to code. They lived well but frugally, a collection of craftspeople, artists, and fishermen whose social affairs featured salsa, chips, and whatever jug wine was on sale in Port Pritchard at the Pioneer Market. On the south side people hired architects to design fancier places. More of a crowd that entertained with recipes out of gourmet magazines and bought wines that needed to breathe.

How the word "wind" got into the name of the road

they all lived on was obvious; Owl Island's firs and cedars grew at a slight tilt, shaped by southwesterly gusts, and could snap under the pressure of freak gales from the north. Some of Phoebe's neighbors contended the surveyor was punning with the word "spit," using it to mean not saliva but a point of land surrounded by water. Others believed "spit" referred to the gentle rains that in the wet months fell more frequently than major downpours, with drops so scattered it seemed possible to walk between them. Still others cited the old expression "Spit in the wind and it'll come back to you" as evidence the surveyor was dispensing cautionary advice, a karmic warning.

After tonight, Phoebe would be inclined to endorse this last definition, placing herself at the center of the causative chain.

Ivan stood over the brick barbecue checking coals as Phoebe brought out a bucket of her secret basting sauce. She was an unusual woman in her early forties who appeared youthful despite having hair streaked with gray. Except for bangs feathering across her high forehead, Phoebe's hair hung thick and glossy to her shoulders— silver threaded into coal-black strands—casting a glow on her olive skin, so smooth it seemed poreless. Tonight she wore a rust-colored rayon jumper over a gauzy white tee shirt, thin loose clothes offering only a suggestion of her body's shape.

"You look good," Ivan said as she emptied the bucket into a bowl by the grill.

This was nothing new, Ivan admiring Phoebe. He'd done it for years, expecting only friendship in exchange. But he'd been away for a while, in Japan on a Guggenheim to master slow-firing ceramic glazes. Over time, the postcards they sent each other had turned into long, revealing letters, and since his return she had felt him out on subjects they'd never before discussed. Touched him more. Invited him to extend their light, customary hugs and kisses into softer, longer, sweeter events.

"I know you like me in orange," she said.

She caught the pleasure in his smile and a bit of doubt, too, as though this shift in her was something he wanted, but couldn't quite count on yet.

He had come by yesterday to lure her away for lunch on Heron Island. Already at work in the kitchen for hours, she covered and stored the huge bowls of spiced hummus, black bean, and potato salads she'd been preparing, and just before the tide turned they set out in his dory, leaving Little Pritchard Bay for the far deeper waters beyond.

Because of its tiny size, Heron Island was untouched by developers. Although campers sometimes spent the night there, none were in evidence when Ivan and Phoebe arrived. After they built a fire on the beach and readied the clams Ivan had raked up that morning, Phoebe stripped down to her black Speedo and jumped from a red-skinned madrone bough into a salty slice of Puget Sound. Total immersion—the best way to go if you were set on swimming around here, even in August. Ivan stayed on shore with the bubbling steamer pot while she churned through lucent water, warm for a few inches on top but iced below with mountain snowmelt. Stepping out, she slashed her foot on a barnacle-covered rock. A shallow cut, but so much blood. Ivan rushed out in his wave walkers and carried her back to a padded blanket laid over a swatch of secluded beach. "I'm fine," Phoebe protested as he cleaned the wound and ripped off a strip of his tee shirt to bind it. "And I'm really starving."

They ate the clams, sopping up buttery lemon broth

with sourdough bread and drinking icy bottles of Anchor Steam.

Kayakers swung their paddles like slow-motion propellers in the distance, bobbing alongside crab-trap buoys in the foamy wakes of motorboats. Closer to shore a seal looked up from the water, craning its head as though taking bearings from Mount Baker's snowy steeple.

As dappled shade fell on their blanket, Ivan unwrapped and examined Phoebe's foot. "It stopped bleeding," he said.

"I told you it was nothing."

But it wasn't nothing. It was something, how glad she was to be scooped up and attended to by him. It was something, the loosening of pleasure his touch brought, coursing through her like heavy, hot liquid. It was something, how each of them seemed to realize at the same moment that they ought to make love. Something because of how this could not be reversed. It would either lead somewhere new, somewhere worth going, or spin them in circles—misspent energy better left behind, scattered over clamshells and heron nests. Phoebe felt her skin pulse, animated by the elements and their slow, sensual certainty. They went on. Together and alone. Lost and found. Strange and familiar. Surprised but in the end settled on their risk.

"I'm not sorry," he had said as she lay across his chest and he tipped out the last of his beer. "How about you?"

She rested a finger on the close-trimmed beard that covered his long, Nordic chin. "I'm glad."

When they got back to Owl Island, another question from him: "Stay with me?"

"Amelia's coming over to make some chutneys and piecrusts."

"Tonight?"

"She probably won't leave until late."

"What about afterwards?"

"You know how it can get around here. Let's keep our stuff private awhile. Wait for things to settle down."

Now, standing over the barbecue, Ivan squeezed Phoebe's shoulder. "Where's Judge?" he asked. Judge was the name Ivan had given Laurienne when she was very young and other children along the Road counted on her to settle disputes. "What do you think, Judge, where's the best place to drop our line?" he'd ask on their fishing trips, and he swore that her decisions, made only after pumping him for pertinent information, were better than his. Laurienne turned out to have too tender a heart for measuring matters on grown-up scales of justice, but "Judge" stuck anyway with everyone on Spit in the Wind. Everyone, that is, but her widowed mother. For Phoebe, Laurienne's name was necessary music.

She had only the foggiest notion of the work Laurienne did now in Seattle, writing programs in a language that could be understood only by computers and other people like herself. But maybe her talent for communicating in code made sense, on some invisible, cellular level. After all, she herself was a mystery, conceived under circumstances her mother had yet to figure out how to explain.

All afternoon, Phoebe had been listening for the sound of Laurienne's old Volvo crunching gravel out front. "Doesn't look like she's going to make it," she told Ivan. Her husky voice, suggestive of bourbon and cigarettes, was actually attributable to the jagged, puckered scar on her throat, centered above the delicate bones of her clavicle. "Laurienne's up to her eyeballs in work, has been all summer."

As Ivan slathered sauce on the fish, hissing splats and puffs of smoke rose off the coals below. "That's a shame.

You'll be busy playing hostess to the mob. If Judge doesn't come, I'll just be dodging people I don't really want to talk to all night."

"Well, there *is* an upside," Phoebe said. "If she doesn't come, I'll be free when it's over."

"Now that was a good thing to say."

Phoebe knew the people whom Ivan particularly wanted to avoid were south-side residents. Ivan himself was an unmistakable north-sider, an artist living in a home-cum-studio he had built himself, a place that in its early years had featured as clean and pleasant an outhouse as ever was made—but still, most south-siders found just the concept of an outhouse tragically déclassé. Phoebe herself didn't fit neatly into either camp, north or south. On the one hand, the work she did required that she be capable of figuring out how a medium-sized trawler might fish a bigger net without adding horsepower. Basic north-side material. On the other, she freely loaned items from her meticulously cataloged collection of books, music, and film videos up and down the Road with scholarly zeal. More like a culturally wired south-sider. Then there was her house. Simple enough to be friendly with all the others on the north, but so smartly designed and detailed it wouldn't have been out of place sitting on the south.

If Phoebe was a conundrum to her neighbors, she was transparent to Ivan, a close observer over the years. The men she had tested as lovers were kept, if at all, only as distant friends. While the first category held appeal for Ivan, the second did not. Long as he'd known and pondered Phoebe, he still couldn't quite nail all the origins of her wariness. What he understood was how the confusion she generated gave gifts, too. Privacy, and a considerable measure of control.

Ivan kept to himself differently, as if belonging to some

atavistic religion that mandated limited contact among adult creatures bereft of wings, gills, or fur. His leeriness of south-siders stemmed from knowing how many among them resented north-siders like him for getting there first and tying up all the prime sunset views, often with houses the south-siders considered downscale.

Such sentiments seemed petty to Phoebe on an evening fine as this, when Little Pritchard Bay bulged with a glistening high tide, pocked by jumping humpies, and the August splendors of Owl Island were ample enough to make her feel rich as anyone on earth, not just south-siders on Spit in the Wind Road. "They're perfectly decent people, Ivan," she chided. "Talk to them, you'll see."

No one on the island had a better sense than Ivan of where in the sky to look for a meteor shower, or of the exact day when wild yellow irises would burst into blossom on riverbanks. He knew all the best places to find chanterelle mushrooms in midsummer, morels in spring. The single can of cat food he lured crabs into his trap with worked better than any amount of the rotting chicken parts everyone else used. But Ivan shared such wisdom only with longtime familiars, and his unfortunate idea of social conversation meant re-creating episodes of a late-night radio show broadcast out of Idaho by a host obsessed with crop circles, alien abductions, and conspiracy theories. Phoebe had a hunch Ivan wasn't intrigued by the ideas expressed so much as by people's need to believe in them, their intolerance for ambiguity. But if *she* couldn't be positive about why such stuff intrigued him, what were south-siders who barely knew him supposed to think? Should one of them come to visit, interested in buying his pottery, Ivan wouldn't mention any of the museums or galleries that had exhibited his work, wouldn't encourage sales by dragging out catalogues featuring his pieces, wouldn't do anything to feed their need to know the significance of his reputation before settling on a price. Instead, he'd decide he wasn't ready to part with what they wanted, or describe, in stomach-turning detail, how it was made using the ground-up bones of mice he'd caught in his house over the winter.

He was an artist's artist, temperamentally unequipped for the schmooze of self-promotion. Only now, after his decades of monklike devotion, were curators and serious collectors taking notice. With the Guggenheim and a big show coming up, it looked as though before long he'd at last be able to live on his earnings from art alone—no more temporary fishing-boat, carpentry, or net-repair jobs to buy him time in the studio. Phoebe was ecstatic, but Ivan was, well, Ivan. So steady and sure of who he was that compared to him the more single-minded south-siders seemed like a bunch of hyperactive strivers. "I know what they'll all be buzzing about tonight," he said. "Some Californian wants to buy the Miller place."

Ivan was right. It had been such a long time since anyone on the island had put their house on the market that this news was bound to cause a stir. "Well," Phoebe said, "good for the Millers."

"And too bad for us."

Phoebe laughed. "Californians are not by definition evil, Ivan."

"He might come tonight."

"Who?"

"The Californian."

"What makes you think so?"

"Carl Brown invited him." Carl Brown, who had a streak of gray in his black beard that reminded Phoebe of a skunk, was a recent émigré from Boston and a real estate attorney for the tribe. He had hired a Seattle architect to design a screamingly modern boxy house on the south side, then set about establishing himself as the island's resident wine expert. This morning, when Phoebe ran into him at the Pioneer Market, all he mentioned bringing to the barbecue was a case of good pinot.

"Don't listen to Ivan," Amelia called down from the deck, where she was finishing up with the flower arrangements. "He got the news secondhand from me. Being from California is *not* the most interesting thing about this person."

"Spare me," Phoebe told her. She wasn't so pure as to abstain from gossip, but Amelia's flair for exaggeration was well known. Men initially attracted by the snap and energy in Amelia's sunny demeanor soon came to consider her a desperate divorcée reading soul-mate potential into such slender affinities as a shared taste for slack-key guitar or anchovy pizzas.

But Amelia was not to be deterred. "We're getting a celebrity in the neighborhood," she went on. "He's famous."

One liability of living on an island was that newcomers held an allure—or, as in Ivan's case, prompted an antipathy—way out of proportion to whatever might in fact be significant about them. Amelia's penchant only amplified the local one. "Someone famous" could be a maker of goat cheese who was well known in the region, a "celebrity," someone who inherited fragments of a family lumber fortune. As Amelia trotted down to the grill with bottles of beer and a bowl of chips, Phoebe teased, "I better get on the phone right now and invite the paparazzi."

"Go ahead, make fun, but he's a big cheese in Hollywood. Carl told me, but I can't remember his name."

"Right," Ivan said. "He must be really famous."

Phoebe's left eyebrow inched upward. "Why would

someone like that want the Miller place? Doesn't make sense. I mean, the site's fantastic." And it was—sitting on the western point that divided north from south, with views in three directions. "But the house isn't much."

"Come on, Phoebe," Amelia said. "Ever hear of renovation? Anyway, those people have houses everywhere." As a heron squawked overhead, she indicated the loveliness all around them with a sweep of her hand, like a game-show girl showing off a prize appliance. "Why not here?"

"I'll bet he just stopped off on his way to the San Juans," Phoebe said. "Once he gets there, he'll like the scenery even better. So high-priced, ordinary people can't afford it. That's where he belongs, with all the other billionaire actors and assholes. On land you own instead of lease. Something risk-free but sure to appreciate."

Amelia breathed an exasperated sigh. "It's a done deal—Carl says the guy paid a fortune for the place. And he's not an actor, he's a director. I saw one of his movies, something about an artist's model in Paris. Made me want to run right out to smoke and drink and be risqué."

Phoebe glanced at Amelia as though she had just spoken in tongues. Then she dropped the empty sauce bucket on Amelia's foot. Amelia yelped, more in surprise than pain. "What? What did I say?"

Phoebe's heart pounded; heat rose to her face. "I'm so sorry," she said, bending down for the bucket. Rising up, she knocked the beer from Amelia's hand. "Oh God, sorry, sorry again—I'll go get another."

In the kitchen, Phoebe leaned against the refrigerator, letting her pulse return to normal. While uncapping Amelia's beer, she tried to imagine a lighthearted comment to show Ivan and Amelia her disinterest in continuing their previous conversation. "It's not my policy to talk about neighbors until I've met them," she might say. But that lie could catch up with her fast as fire. She considered letting them know the movie Amelia mentioned came out an awfully long time ago, and it wasn't just Phoebe who felt no other film its director made since had been as good. That wasn't exactly lighthearted, though, and it begged the question of why Phoebe was so well informed about this still nameless man. She might actually have to *say* his name, something she had pretty much avoided for over twenty years. Best to keep it simple. And change the subject.

"I saw that movie, too," Phoebe told Amelia as she returned. "So, how do you think this guy's paying a fortune for the Miller place will affect the value of our houses?" Then, before anyone could answer, Phoebe checked her watch. "Look at the time—I've got to get dressed."

"Phoebe." Ivan spoke as though addressing an adorable but confused child. "You *are* dressed. You look fine." He was right, she did look fine. But not as fine as she suddenly wanted to look. No, it was worse than that. Not as fine as she needed to look.

Phoebe rifled through her closet, ignoring the half taken up by boiled-wool sweaters, overalls, gumboots, down vests—apparel that kept her warm whether she was working on the docks or in the largely unheated Port Pritchard warehouse she leased for her net-making business. Instead she went straight for the closet's other half, which contained clothes that might have belonged to a completely different woman, one whose taste ran to vintage velvet capes, cashmere jackets, long linen skirts, and decidedly feminine getups like the hand-painted chiffon dress that Phoebe pulled out on its hanger. Standing in front of the full-length mirror, she held it to her chest while wondering if it was possible to co-opt yourself with a secondhand garment already in your wardrobe.

Lily, Phoebe's aging wheaten terrier, had followed her upstairs. Now, head on paws, she dozed while Phoebe slipped out of her jumper and tee shirt. Phoebe's stretch bra and utilitarian underpants wouldn't do for the chiffon, so she shed them, too. After putting on a sexier, silkier set, the memory of getting underthings like this once for him—with him, actually—hit in a way that felt like having the wind knocked out of her.

A car door slammed outside. Lily pricked her ears, jumped off the bed, and ran downstairs like a puppy, whimpering with joy. Phoebe looked out the window to see Laurienne saying hello to the first flurry of arriving neighbors, who were carrying their own platters and bowls of food to the deck out back. When the front door opened, Phoebe called out, "I'm up here."

It took Laurienne a good five minutes of petting Lily before the dog would let her go upstairs. Reaching out to hug her daughter, Phoebe noticed that the pale, lightly freckled skin beneath Laurienne's green eyes was tinged blue, and her long, curly auburn hair hung limp, in need of washing. The old jeans she had on looked at least one size too big, gaping out around her hips. Her Pearl Jam tee shirt looked as though she might have worn it to bed several nights running. It wasn't hard to guess the explanation for all this. Where Laurienne worked in Seattle, twelve-hour days were such a given that Phoebe had only seen her in the city this summer. Laurienne had never been away from Spit in the Wind for so long.

"I cranked extra hard so I could make it," she said in her girlish, feathery voice—a voice that made it almost impossible for her to sound angry, even when she was. For Laurienne, barbecues had always been more enjoyable than birthdays (not so many people focused so exclusively on her, and whether she was having enough fun).

"I hope you didn't break any land-speed records."

"I drove the way you taught me, Mom. Like a little old lady." Laurienne took in Phoebe's half-clad state. "Why aren't you dressed?"

"Just running a bit late, sweetie."

Laurienne scratched Lily's belly while Phoebe pulled the dress over her head and sat to apply lipstick. Now that she was no longer alone, Phoebe felt ridiculous dolling herself up. And for what? To impress someone who might or might not appear tonight, to earn back his regard, to make him sorry he ever shoved her aside. All bad enough, but she'd forgotten until this moment how this someone, should he show, would no doubt meet her daughter—and who knew what would come of that?

Laurienne caught the change in Phoebe's face, but misinterpreted its cause. "Sorry I wasn't here to help," she said.

"Don't worry, everything's under control."

"Everything but you."

"I'm ready now." Phoebe fastened a suede belt around her waist and smoothed out the dress. "What do you think?"

Laurienne frowned. "Too fancy. You need to funk it up for a barbecue." She went down the hall to her own room and returned with a beaded cowgirl belt. "Much better," she said after Phoebe put it on. "Now you don't look like you're trying so hard."

Ivan hollered from the deck. "Judge! I got the telescope set up." Laurienne clambered downstairs to look at the eagles' nest she hadn't seen since this year's chicks hatched.

The longest dry spell of Phoebe's adult sexual life—

more of a Sahara, really, lasting almost three years—played a big part in how she began to consider Ivan differently. Laurienne's increasing absence was a factor, too. But now, with the island gossip fresh in her ears and Laurienne at home, it was a struggle not to slip back into her old way of regarding Ivan—as a good neighbor who required good fences, someone too close, too important, to risk wrecking things with an affair.

She had long favored men who were, in either geographic or emotional terms, remote. A few times she'd hit pay dirt, getting both in one package. When Laurienne was younger, Phoebe used another, more selfish reason for orchestrating her sex life this way: reluctance to share her daughter with someone who might press to adopt. Accustomed to having all the parental love and authority, she couldn't imagine ceding even a tiny piece of it away. Oh, she encouraged an uncle-like Ivan, or an aunt-like Amelia. But more than one lover had been dismissed for showing insufficient tenderness, sensitivity, or intelligence while stepping unawares into territory she reserved exclusively for herself. Territory where she had made herself impossible to please.

Once more, Phoebe assessed herself in the mirror. Turned out like this, only her hands, chapped and raw no matter what lotions she slathered on them—and she'd tried everything, from homemade comfrey balms to expensive department store concoctions to salves meant for softening cow teats and horse hooves—betrayed the years she'd spent knotting nets to heavy leaded lines and sewing mesh to mesh. For all her success in the net-making business, her involvement had begun in much the same way that she'd anchored herself on Spit in the Wind Road. By accident. An accident she could only recall as a flash, a car coming at her in the wrong lane and the swerve she took to avoid it. An accident that killed her husband and left her alone in this house with a child to support, turning a knack for knotting nets into a regular job, a regular business.

Now the accident's only visible trace was the scar on her neck, made plainly obvious by the cleavage-revealing chiffon. She decided a piece of jewelry was required—a good one. Her mother's single-pearl-drop necklace.

She connected the clasp behind her neck and the pearl fell into place just below her scar. The necklace emphasized not only the fullness of her breasts but the scar, too. Almost as if the pearl had been secreted from the place where she was once cut open, like a tear from an eye.

When the first batch of salmon was done Phoebe served all the children, using paper picnic plates so they could eat on the beach and be as rambunctious as they liked. Then she laid out ceramic plates Ivan had made and filled one of them for Laurienne, going heavy on the protein and starches, wanting to put some fullness back into her drawn cheeks.

All the while, Phoebe kept an eye out for Carl Brown. As Ivan took the last fish off the grill, Carl arrived carrying a case of wine. Only Carl's wife, Ellie, was with him, navigating the steps up to the deck on high-heeled sandals, and balancing a pewter tray filled with breads and cheeses sure to be unusual, imported, pricey. Phoebe met her halfway. "Here, let me help you with that."

"I'm the one who needs help," Carl grunted, heaving his case onto a table. He uncorked a bottle, poured a little for Phoebe, and waited for a reaction. When she said "Swell," he started shoving lesser wines aside.

"Sorry we're late," Ellie said, an edge of exasperation to her voice. "Carl thought we might have some company from out of town joining us tonight, but it wasn't to be."

It almost sounded as if she blamed Carl for blowing it with the Californian. If only things were that simple. Who knew? Maybe they were. Phoebe poured herself a full glass. "More for us, then." But, blending into the crowd, she kept chewing over why their new neighbor hadn't come, whether it had anything to do with her. Ivan had been right, lots of people *were* buzzing about him. But the information she craved was personal—how he looked, spoke, behaved—and all their gossip was about reputation and real estate. Before long, she'd drunk enough to giggle at the thought of Scarlett O'Hara at *her* fabled barbecue, complaining of how bored she was with everyone's talk of war, war, war. Now there was a girl who knew how to change the subject.

"What's so funny?" Amelia asked.

"You. Me. Scarlett O'Hara." Phoebe shrugged, her face falling, and folded onto the bench behind her.

Amelia took a stuffed mushroom from her hors d'oeuvre–filled napkin and popped it into Phoebe's mouth. "Drinking on an empty stomach—sure way to tears before bedtime. Stay here, I'll fix you a plate."

Phoebe ate, sobered up some, and started circulating again, too proud to ask for further details, to go fishing for information like some starstruck bumpkin and risk learning nothing more than what she'd known to begin with. Her rattled anticipation from earlier in the evening careened wildly from acceptance (*What I need to know will come to me*), to anger (*I'm not coming to him, he can damn well come to me*), to fear (*What the hell's coming at me?*). She was settling back into acceptance when Ivan caught her eye from across the deck where he sat eating pie with Laurienne, tilting his head in a way that asked everything from *Are you okay?* to *Can I help?*

I'm fine, Phoebe mouthed. But she wasn't. Even when conversation turned to topics her right-minded self found interesting, she couldn't concentrate long enough to contribute more than a scanty thought, idea, or experience. Luckily she was the hostess, with plenty of excuses for flitting from one group to the next, never staying in one place long enough for anyone to realize the intensity of her distraction.

As she lit candles and put out pots of coffee, Carl Brown crept up and grabbed her waist from behind. "I think I know what your secret is, Phoebe," he whispered.

She spun around, hand flying to her heart. "Jesus, Carl."

He went on, unperturbed. "It's taken me a while to figure this out, but now I bet I've got it. Will you tell me if I'm right?"

How to respond? Her best option: "Maybe."

"Okay. Here goes." Carl cocked his head and regarded her with a tipsy squint. "Rice vinegar."

"What?"

"Rice vinegar—that's the secret to your basting sauce, isn't it?"

No surprise there. Carl had been trying to wheedle the sauce ingredients out of her ever since last May's Copper River salmon run. So why this perverse twinge of disappointment? "Sorry," she told him.

"Okay," he said, waggling a finger, "but I'm not convinced you're telling me the truth."

She elbowed him in the ribs. "Why don't you just lay off the sauce, Carl."

"Ah, Phoebe," he sighed. "None of 'em around here is man enough for you. But if *I* were suddenly single—"

"If you were suddenly single, your wife would add years to her life." This from Margaret, a semiretired therapist who lived on the south side. "Providing, of course, she didn't get married again. You, on the other hand, would drop dead a whole hell of a lot quicker. It's true, they've done research."

"Once again you've saved my marriage. Margaret, I've got a question for you."

"Shoot."

"Rice vinegar, what do you think?" Then, without waiting for a response, Carl headed down to the beach crying out the *li-li-li* chorus from *The Boxer* in unison with several musically inclined Owl Islanders, who were playing guitars and singing around a bonfire.

"I'm off, Phoebe," Margaret said. "It was wonderful, you outdid yourself this year."

"I just made the same old things. You guys bring all the special stuff."

"You look gorgeous, too."

"It's the dress."

Margaret shook her head, bronze disc earrings swinging beneath a fringe of well-tended pale blonde hair. "We really have to talk sometime."

The biggest plus of having a therapist as a friend—especially one old enough to be your mother—was also the biggest drawback: She paid attention to everything you said. "What's the topic?" Phoebe asked.

"Why it's so hard for you to accept a compliment."

"That sounds like fun."

"You'd be surprised."

"It's against the rules, having friends as clients."

"I know." Margaret leaned in to kiss her once on each cheek. "But there's no rule against sharing tools with your neighbors."

Laurienne, Ivan, and Amelia helped clean up. So did

Sophie, Phoebe's office manager. Phoebe tried to hurry them all off, pleading fatigue when, really, she just couldn't wait to be alone. Only Sophie lingered on, labeling plastic bowls and bags of leftovers. "You're as compulsive in the kitchen as you are at work," Phoebe told her.

"I'm not compulsive," Sophie sniffed as she left. "I love organizing. People who don't just haven't given it enough of a chance."

After Laurienne went to bed, Phoebe poured a shot glass of homemade Himalayan blackberry cordial and opened the kitchen junk drawer to fish a long brown cigarette out of a flat, square box of Nat Shermans. Whenever she felt under siege, it comforted Phoebe to summon her dead mother's spirit by smoking her brand. She'd tried other, more common brands for this purpose, but they didn't work. So once a year she went to a specialty tobacco shop for cigarettes she kept on hand the way other people did seldom-used medications.

She sat at the kitchen table, the room dark except for a candle lit so her streams of cigarette smoke would be visible—a crucial part of the ritual. With the first slow exhale, she blew out her anger. With the second, her fear. With the third, she finally let herself form what she had learned tonight into a simple statement of fact:

Whitney Traynor bought a house on Spit in the Wind Road.

Darkness made it easier to conjure up what her own house was like when she and Mitchell first bought it— bats nesting in the ceiling, mice scrambling in the walls, only a woodstove for heat. They hadn't lived here for long when the accident happened.

Sometimes it seemed she went to sleep then and when she finally awoke she was in this room stringing nets.

She had a toddler instead of a baby. And Mitchell was dead. She knew there were still a few people in town with memories long enough to gossip. "Never quite herself again after the accident," they'd say. True, she didn't sing anymore, and singing had been one of the ways she once earned money. But singing for a paying audience was something she'd done more for the love of Whit than for the love of performing. Besides, her vocal chords were damaged when emergency medics intubated her at the accident scene, changing her register so much that after recovering, she sang for no one but her baby.

Awful things affected people—where was the surprise in that? And just what exactly did it mean, anyway, to say someone was never quite herself again? Whose self was it that Phoebe was supposed to be inhabiting if it wasn't her own? But now she felt compelled to examine that self for damage, like she would a net that had been working a while. Looking for frayed strands, places that had lost resilience. Spots Whit might rip apart.

Whit had never been inside Phoebe's house on Owl Island. It held no memories of him. One of its attractions, really. Only a few items remained in her possession that, when she came across them, brought him back to her with thrumming immediacy. A box full of letters, an old pink GE radio—both stored away on a high shelf in the garage, easily avoided. Not that she didn't think of Whit. Just that when she did, it was like silent conversation with a ghost, an imaginary person. *It's time for you and me to be imaginary friends.* Almost the first thing she ever heard him say, his voice coming out of the pink GE's sound holes. She wasn't ready for him to be real again.

Could she be such a grand magician at disappearing that Whit had no idea he was buying a house down the road from her? Or could Whit be such a one himself as to find her?

Once, when Laurienne was twelve and they were visiting Phoebe's father in Seattle, Lily bolted and couldn't be found. Three days later, when she appeared trotting down the Road, limping a little from her long journey, it seemed as if she were connected to Phoebe's house by an expandable band of invisible energy that pulled her back.

Maybe something like that could happen over far greater reaches of distance and time between humans, too. If they had once shared a great love. If traces of it still surfaced in their sleep. If they remained somewhere in each other's hearts.

Phoebe had made Laurienne promise not to leave in the morning without waking her, but it was so late when Phoebe finally went upstairs to bed that she considered reversing herself, writing a note to say goodbye. Laurienne was sure to be up at dawn, not so many hours away. But if Phoebe stayed in bed, Laurienne would head straight back to Seattle and work with nothing but coffee in her.

Phoebe was proud of Laurienne, more than holding her own among male fellow workers, all smart as whips. Her bosses were not much older than she, and they were so competitive, so driven. Phoebe wondered if lacking a father had anything to do with why her daughter would be drawn to prove herself to them, to perform for them— damaging herself in the process, judging by her appearance.

Phoebe had always been loath to discuss Life Before the Accident with Laurienne. The paralyzing questions she put to herself on the matter had evolved like this: Why spoil Laurienne's childhood, her adolescence, her supposedly carefree college years by giving her reason to think she needed to take care of Phoebe? Would Laurienne be embarrassed by her mother's past? Had Phoebe missed her moment to reveal the truth? Had too much time gone by to tell it?

Phoebe stopped by Laurienne's moonlit bedroom. Laurienne was sleeping on her stomach, splayed out like a wildly overgrown baby put down for the night. Phoebe unfolded an afghan at the bed's foot, pulled it up to Laurienne's shoulders, and kissed the top of her head. Hanging above the bed was the Land of Make-Believe map that Phoebe had first put in Laurienne's room when her daughter was still in diapers—a time when Phoebe thought she knew exactly what Laurienne needed, and how to give it, because of how enchanted her own earliest years had been. When the map of the Land of Make-Believe was new and whole and hanging over *her* bed.

2

When Phoebe was a little girl, her mother made an event out of bedtime. First Pearl let her decide what she wanted to wear over her freshly bathed skin. An adored only child, Phoebe had much to choose from—Annie Oakley cowgirl pajamas, lace-trimmed Lanz nighties, flannel sleepers with sewn-on feet. Once Pearl got her all zipped or buttoned up, she arranged a nest of pillows and sat holding the book so that her daughter, who was too young to read, could see the illustrations. Pearl always read from hardback books with color illustrations on slick, heavy paper. There were witches, fairies, ogres, and blissful water babies, all of whom could be found on the map of the Land of Make-Believe hanging on poster board over the bed.

After several stories, Phoebe would nod drowsily. Pearl encouraged this by gradually lowering the book from a position above her chest, nearly level with her face, to resting on her lap. Looking down put the force of gravity to work on Phoebe's eyes, making it harder to keep them open.

Then, Pearl sang. She often sang during the day, but those were songs in sunny major keys, different from the songs she sang after bedtime stories. At night, Pearl sang only in minor keys, soothing yet somehow mournful. She sang songs in another language that her grandma had once sung to her, lullabies and laments that for Phoebe added to the exotic allure of her mother's auburn hair, olive skin, and almond-shaped green eyes. Pearl sang folk songs, too, with a melancholy treble in her cigarette-husky voice. "I met her in Venezuela, with a basket on her head." Sometimes Phoebe, already showing signs of perfect pitch, would slumberously join in. "And if she loved others, she did not say, but I knew she'd do to pass away, to pass away the time in Venezuela . . ."

After the singing, after Pearl tucked her in, it was tempting to let go and tumble straight into dreams. But if she did, she would miss the best part of Pearl putting her to bed. And that was when she made the Magic Circle.

Phoebe lay in the dark, breathing in the scent of White Shoulders, the only perfume Pearl ever wore, a fragrance so similar to that of wisteria blossoming just outside the bedroom window that it seemed something she naturally exuded, like the vines. Lying in her childhood bed, inhaling Pearl, Phoebe was spellbound, watching every sweep of her mother's long, elegant fingers as she moved her hand through the air and intoned the words that never varied, night after night:

"Magic Circle, Magic Circle, keep my little girl safe. Keep her sleepy-bye and happy-bye all ni long. Don't let any bad dreams in, just let in good Don't let *anything* in except mommies and ties and bunnies and fairies and lambie

"And Peter Pan," Phoebe wou Pan, who lost his shadow and f with his own personal fairy make ordinary children lik definition of "magic." She her mother for the colo tures. Peter Pan was a

map, emerging from the hollow tree where he lived. No Magic Circle would be complete without him.

"And Peter Pan," Pearl would say just before the Magic Circle closed around the bed.

As Phoebe grew older, she never quite stopped believing that someone like him would land in her bedroom one night, searching for his shadow. And he *would* come to her.

Eventually.

He would come to her when she was no longer conscious of wishing for him.

He would come to her without a face, without a body.

He would come to her bedroom, not flying in through the window, as she had once expected, but over the airwaves, a voice out of the pink GE radio her parents bought for her sixth birthday.

The radio was a babyish thing by the time Phoebe was fifteen, when the map of the Land of Make-Believe hung incongruously alongside posters commemorating rock concerts and antiwar demonstrations. Her birthday present *that* year had been a made-to-order Martin 000-28, her first grown-up guitar. But the pink GE was still what Phoebe listened to while she did homework and her parents were downstairs in their studies, preparing classes for the next day. Phoebe always kept her radio tuned to KARP, the alternative Seattle station that broadcast out of an old doughnut shop north of the university district. Just about anyone who had enough albums to make up a playlist could get a show of their own on KARP, and the deejays had different specialties—blues, folk music, rock.

ry Sunday night in November when he time, not just to Phoebe in her bed- who happened to be listening within KARP's narrow broadcast range. "Good evening," the voice on Phoebe's radio intoned, "This is Whitney Traynor—you can call me Whit—saying it's time for you and me to be . . . imaginary friends."

If he had said he was Rags the Clown or Cowboy Bob, if his words had been delivered at a high pitch of forced glee, he could have been introducing a kiddy cartoon show. But this name had weight, this voice held mystery. Whit's words penetrated the Sunday gloom seeping through Seattle like fog, a dense vapor of stale sermons, forced family gatherings, and the distressing prospect of an entirely too predictable new week beginning tomorrow.

It was his accent that first took her—a thick, slow, southern syrup. Then came the tune that would be his theme, a crackly recording of Lucienne Boyer singing "Parlez-Moi d'Amour." The next song was Hank Williams doing "I'm So Lonesome I Could Cry." Phoebe laughed out loud at the segue, the goofy logic of putting those two songs together—like slapping grits down on a plate of coq au vin. Then she picked up her guitar. Even at fifteen, Phoebe was too petite to get her arms comfortably around a standard Martin D-28, but her 000-28, with its Brazilian rosewood back and spruce top, felt like a part of her. It had smaller proportions and a larger indent in the middle, giving a more feminine shape than the D-28, but the sound was every bit as full and gorgeous. Sitting on her bed, Phoebe effortlessly strummed all the right chords while singing harmony with Hank.

"Did you hear that, boys and girls?" Whit said, coming back on the air with a raspy sigh of appreciation. "Don't ever listen when they say you can't write a song without a bridge. One of the greatest songs ever written and no bridge in sight, not so much as a log thrown over the water. Nope, what we have here is a direct plunge into the drink. Let that be a lesson to you. If you want to be special, break the rules. And here's another little tip before we get back to the music. You know that thing they say is wrong with you? That thing you think you're supposed to be ashamed of? Don't try to hide it. Don't *ever* try to hide it. No, children, what you've got to do is make it bigger. Make it bigger so nobody can miss it. 'Cause chances are, that's the very thing that makes you worthwhile and sets you apart."

Oh, honey pouring into Phoebe's ears.

The chief criticism running through her young life was that when her mind was made up, she would not listen to what other people had to say, even if those other people were her loving parents who had only her best interests at heart. Phoebe's first sentence, as Pearl liked to remind her, was "Phoebe do it by *self*." She had demanded her own patch of garden to plant and weed, dressed her dolls in raggedy-stitched apparel she made from outgrown play clothes, and preferred taking tumbles to riding a bike with training wheels. By the time she was old enough to attend the exclusive private school in Seattle where Pearl taught English, she was used to doing things her way, by *self*. A trait her teachers did not find charming. Phoebe was too stubborn, they said, too intense to play well with others. She didn't seem to want friends so much as confidantes, one or two other girls happy to participate in games and fantasies of Phoebe's invention. She was an only child, that probably explained it. They just generally tended to be precocious when young, didn't they? She'd grow out of it.

But she didn't.

Now that Phoebe was in public high school, they said what was wrong with her was that she thought she was smart as her teachers. Well, wasn't she? Wasn't it some kind of proof that although she regularly skipped classes, running off to Ravenna Park with similarly inclined students to sing or flirt or smoke clove cigarettes (and the occasional joint), she still kept a nearly perfect grade point average?

There were no new songs for her to learn from Whit's first broadcast on KARP. She knew them all, even though his playlist could not have been more eclectic. Somehow, he found musical connections to cushion his leaps from Nina Simone's "I Want a Little Sugar in My Bowl," to a satirical Tom Lehrer piece advocating plagiarism, to "Hang On Sloopy," which Whit touted as the greatest rock-and-roll song of all time, prompting a half hour of angry calls from listeners. Phoebe was so smitten by then that she almost called in to agree with him. But she didn't want to make his acquaintance on the phone. She didn't want to risk sounding inarticulate or dumb. Instead, she took out a box of cream-colored Crane stationery that had been a present from Pearl and started writing a letter meant to make Whit realize how lost he would be without her. His shadow had been found, and she was it.

You don't know me, Phoebe began, *but I am your audience. I am the person your show is meant for.*

She included a photograph of herself singing at a high school talent show, the Martin slung over a sunflower print minidress with an empire waist that emphasized her bosom, already round and full. Although Phoebe measured only five foot three, her legs and arms were so long and lean that standing alone onstage, she looked much taller. The camera caught a three-quarter view of her face, with enormous violet eyes set off to startling effect by long black hair and thick, inky lashes. Her pillowy, high-bowed lips were pursed, as if kissing the note they held. It was easy to imagine each member of

Phoebe's invisible audience wearing an expression every bit as rapt as hers.

Whit's reply came within the week. *Do you know for a fact,* he wrote, *that you're only fifteen?*

Phoebe shrieked as though discovering a time bomb in the mailbox when she saw Whit's name on the envelope of that first letter. But she really wasn't surprised that he had replied. Letter writing was in her blood. Pearl and Jack, Phoebe's father, had fallen in love through the mail, writing countless letters while Pearl was earning her master's in comparative literature at the University of Washington and he was finishing his doctorate in American history at Berkeley.

If Phoebe had written three pages to Whit as though her life depended on eliciting a response, maybe that had something to do with the fact that if either of her parents had been boring on the page, Phoebe quite simply would not exist. She grew up taking their lively minds for granted, listening to them discuss art, music, movies, and politics over dinner, a congenial event that turned ugly only once, when six-year-old Phoebe announced that, like all her other classmates at Brookland Academy, she was going to vote for Richard Nixon.

Jack was a child of the Depression who had enshrined a bust of Franklin D. Roosevelt in his office at the university so that the former president's face could be seen in his window from the quad below, radiating New Deal spirit. Good-natured as he usually was, Jack failed to join Pearl in laughing at the absurdity of first-graders believing they could cast a ballot. "Leave the table this instant," Jack had bellowed at Phoebe. Then, to Pearl: "See what that fancy school of yours has done to her?" Phoebe had never before heard her father raise his voice in anger.

When she was very young, during the time Pearl was exclusively in charge of putting her to bed, Jack was hardly a negligent parent. On afternoons when Pearl drew the drapes and lay down with an ice pack for her migraines, Jack took Phoebe to the movies, holding her hand as they walked down the darkened theater aisle to their seats. Jack never learned how to drive a car, so they went together on the bus to musicals at the Neptune, revivals at the Ridgemont, and later, when Phoebe was old enough to read subtitles, foreign films at the Varsity. No matter what kind of movie they saw, Jack's tastes were so broad and so inclusive that he usually said the same thing afterwards: "Terrific picture." When it was a *really* terrific picture, they would see it twice before the venue changed. If they stumbled upon an out-and-out dog, he'd manage to find a performance or technical aspect to praise.

Jack could sing, too, though his ideas of songs to amuse a child were quite different from Pearl's. One of his favorites when Phoebe used to crawl onto his lap to be serenaded was "Don't Go in the Lion's Cage Tonight," about a girl whose mother is a lion tamer. The girl has a premonition and warns her mother not to go into the cage, but she does anyway and gets eaten.

Every Saturday, Jack took Phoebe to the record store, where she could pick whatever record she liked. As Phoebe progressed to music that was strange to his ears, music she knew from listening to pop rock stations on the pink GE, Jack never criticized or attempted to control her taste. Upon learning that his eleven-year-old daughter's entire happiness depended upon seeing the Beatles when they came to play the Coliseum, Jack bought tickets for Phoebe and her friend April.

"Do you really think that's a good idea," Pearl said,

"turning two little girls loose in the middle of that mob scene?"

"Nothing bad can come from going to a concert," Jack told her, though he found the musicians in question as lacking as Pearl did.

On the day of the concert, Phoebe threw a volleyball at April's head, knocking her down. April's mother angrily cancelled the concert date. Jack was angry, too. But after Phoebe told him she had beaned the girl for a racist remark, he offered to accompany Phoebe himself, so long as she promised not to scream. And when she did anyway, he stuffed his ears with cotton balls.

When Phoebe was thirteen, Jack moved into the spare bedroom while he recovered from gallbladder surgery. He never moved back. His given reason was Pearl's smoking—she lit a cigarette and read whenever she couldn't sleep, which was often, and he needed his rest. Jack was head of the history department now, a position that consumed all his free time. He had more meetings to attend, visiting dignitaries to entertain, the university's historical quarterly to write for and edit. Once or twice Phoebe caught sight of Pearl in her nightgown, stopping at Jack's door as though tempted to join him, then padding off to her own bed. She seemed to have migraines more often than ever and spent much of her time at home alone in her darkened bedroom, either recovering from an attack or trying to ward one off.

Phoebe wished it were possible for her parents to take up letter writing again. Maybe that would help bridge the distance that had developed between them. She imagined—not without reason—that a piece of what had come between Pearl and Jack was how to best handle their headstrong daughter. She tried for a while to compensate by behaving less like an adult trapped in a young girl's body and more like a happy-go-lucky teenager from some television sitcom. But no matter how good she was, the distance remained, and the main effect of Pearl and Jack's fading connection was to heighten Phoebe's appetite for intimacies of her own.

Phoebe knew her mother and father would be concerned if they learned she had received a letter from a grown man—which Whit presumably was—so she made sure they didn't find out. Easy to do, since Phoebe was the first to come home after school, the one who always got the mail.

Don't think you didn't charm the ice off the dog dish with that letter of yours, Whit's missive to Phoebe began. It was typewritten on a machine that punched holes through all the *o*'s, making the onionskin paper look, when held to the light, as though sprayed with buckshot. *Your mind is amazing for a girl who's been on the planet such a short time,* his letter went on. *There must be some logical explanation. An aging doppelganger in another dimension, maybe. A vampire's kiss. A busted reset button in the reincarnation cycle. Anything ring a bell?*

Whit wrote less than a page, and much of that was spent marveling at Phoebe's appearance in the photo she had sent. *Strange how familiar you seem. I can't decide if you remind me more of Kiki de Montparnasse (ever heard of her?) or Nema the Jungle Girl. For the price of six Coca-Cola bottle caps, I could see Nema in a serial every Saturday at the Volunteer Theater in Culleoka, Tennessee.*

Phoebe's first reaction was the same sense of triumph she felt after an intellectual challenge had been issued in class and hers was the first hand to pop into the air. She knew *exactly* who this Kiki person was, and couldn't wait to inform Whit. Still, there were other things to consider. It dated Whit, mentioning Nema the Jungle Girl; serials had been out of fashion for quite a while. But he didn't tell Phoebe how old he was, though she had asked specifically in her own letter. In response to her wondering what he did when he wasn't on the air, Whit had this to say for himself: *As for the air, if I'm not on it, I tend to be up in it.*

He clearly hoped to hear from her again, though. *What are your favorite books?*

After reading his letter enough times to memorize every word, Phoebe put it aside to ponder this request. She didn't want to mention anything with a whiff of childishness. What she wanted to write were love letters. If Whit couldn't see that her first letter had been one, he was a fool. And she felt certain, after listening to him and meeting him on the page, that he was much too clever to be a fool.

There was another part of Phoebe, separate from the places inside still enraptured with fairy tales and the Land of Make-Believe, that had prompted her, when only nine, to dance naked in front of the full-length mirror on the back of her closet door while imagining an audience of entranced men. Later this same part sent her digging through her parents' libraries when they weren't around, searching for sexually enlightening material. There, on Pearl's shelves of biographies, she first discovered Kiki de Montparnasse, queen of the Parisian demimonde—quite a different jungle than the one over which Nema reigned. And while Nema's looks were a mystery to Phoebe, she had a pretty good idea of the face Whit had in mind when he compared her to Kiki, the "scandalous" artists' model from the Twenties. Strong nose, dramatic eyes, generous mouth, all cosmetically enhanced to an almost Kabuki-like effect. At first, his comparison seemed ridiculous. Phoebe didn't pluck her eyebrows or line her eyes, much less her mouth. She barely wore makeup at all—just a touch of mascara and lipgloss for the features she knew were her best and was too vain to neglect entirely. As an experiment, though, she went to work with her mother's wands, powders, and pencils. When finished, she pulled on an old cloche hat of Pearl's. Her reflection in the mirror made her laugh out loud. *Il voit très clair,* she told herself. He sees what he's looking at.

And so, along with her second letter to Whit, she sent one of Pearl's copies of Kiki's memoirs, generously illustrated with Man Ray's nude photographs of his lover. Pearl owned the book in two different editions, one in English and one in French. Without Pearl's knowledge, Phoebe had used the French edition for a sixth-grade book report that outraged Madame Poiret. "Hardly suitable material for a child," Madame had informed Pearl in the teachers' lounge that day.

Pearl lit one of her slender brown Nat Sherman cigarettes and coolly exhaled a stream of smoke. "What am I supposed to do?" Pearl replied. "Lock up my books?"

"That might not be a bad idea," Madame said.

"I don't mean to be rude, Madame, but you've never raised a child like Phoebe. Do you know what a photographic memory is?"

"Of course."

"Well, my husband has one for text. Phoebe has something like it for music. She hears a song once, she knows it—every note, every word."

"An impressive gift."

"Yes, but she worries that singing's too selfish a thing to do when she grows up. Maybe she should work for world peace. Or go off to live in the woods alone like Thoreau. When her favorite friend calls, it's not to ask if Phoebe can come out and play, it's to ask if she can come out and picket. She's had her own library card since she was four. She's wanted to be a teenager since she was six. Are you getting the picture here? Hiding books wouldn't work."

Phoebe knew the English version of Kiki's memoirs had been banned in the United States; Madame Poiret had told her so, back in the sixth grade. Which meant there was a good chance Whit had never seen it. Of course she didn't tell Whit this was her mother's book— that would make her seem too juvenile. What she wrote was, *I'm afraid I can only send my copy to you on loan, as I can't bear to be without it for too many weeks.*

When Kiki's memoirs came back to Phoebe, another book was in the package—a worn copy of *Alice's Adventures in Wonderland.* Whit had stuck a brief typed note inside the cover.

> I am loath to part with Kiki, and am scheming to get her back. Meanwhile, this other book is yours to keep. It may not be a fair exchange, but then there are only two fairs in life—the state and the county. Remember, you heard it here first.

Phoebe was stung. Whit must be trying to change the direction of their correspondence. He had sent her not only a children's book, but one she already owned; a pristine volume had been on the shelf beside her bed for years. As her pique faded, though, she could see just how well *Alice's Adventures in Wonderland* fit Whit's on-air persona, his impatience with everything normal, everything adult. "They say you catch more flies with honey than vinegar," Whit had remarked on his show just the other night. "But what the hell would you do with more flies?" And so Phoebe began thinking of

Whit's offering to her in a different way. Surely there were segues linking Kiki and Alice. The first to occur was Kiki's real name—Alice, Alice Prin.

"Do you know much about Lewis Carroll?" Phoebe asked Pearl over dinner that night. This had been one of Pearl's good days, so Phoebe hoped her mother would take the bait and run.

"A reasonable amount, I'd say. Why?"

"The girl he wrote *Alice's Adventures in Wonderland* for—"

"Was Alice Liddell. The daughter of a professor Carroll knew."

"So she was a professor's daughter, too." Phoebe giggled.

"What's funny about that?" Jack asked.

"I don't know, it just tickled me. Was she much younger than Lewis Carroll?"

"She was a child," Pearl said. "He liked to entertain his friends' children. I believe the book began as letters to Alice."

"Interesting," Phoebe said, stifling her delight this time.

"Interesting how, honey?"

"Oh, I don't know. That his great work would start as letters to a kid. A girl. Someone like me. When I was younger, I mean."

Phoebe would be more eloquent than that in her reply to Whit.

After the first flurry of letters and books, Phoebe and Whit's correspondence established a lunar rhythm, with each of them writing once a month. Although love was never mentioned as something either felt for the other, the word was everywhere in their letters. He loved rain, Rilke, ripe Tennessee tomatoes, *Shoot the Piano Player,* and all the Northwest Mystic painters, but es-

pecially Morris Graves for his wispy, wounded-looking
birds. She loved the variations of gray in Seattle skies,
trumpeter Roy Eldridge's version of "Knock Me a Kiss,"
and *Children of Paradise,* a favorite film that turned out
to be one of Whit's, too.

Still, Whit's letters continued to be shorter and more
enigmatic than Phoebe's.

> I am currently absorbed in training fleas, catching
> them with chopsticks when they escape, and
> drinking cheap Tokay. All of which I understand to
> be ancient remedies for a broken heart. Although the
> best remedy of all, it seems, is hearing from you.
> That heart of <u>yours</u> is a pearl no swine deserves.

In emulation of Whit, Phoebe took to typing up
her letters on her mother's low-slung black portable
Underwood—the same machine on which Pearl had
composed all her letters to Jack. But Phoebe went to the
keyboard only after laboring over several drafts in long-
hand. With each draft, she added quotes from books she
had read, songs she knew, movies she had seen. The finished products were so natural and fluid no one would
ever guess that, from start to finish, the process took
hours, sometimes days.

When Whit played on-air one of the songs Phoebe had
mentioned in a letter, their secret life expanded in a far
more special way than if he had dedicated the song to
her outright. She smiled to herself whenever she imagined how worried her parents would be if they knew
about all this. How silly. What could be safer than writing Whit? He had already decided it was better for them
not to meet, something she had suggested after noticing
that *Children of Paradise* would be playing soon at the
Varsity. She liked the idea of squeezing Whit's hand

whenever something rare and special occurred in what to her was a film full of wonders.

Sophisticated as she was for her age, and as little as she needed subtitles to tell her what characters in the film were saying—either on or below the surface—Phoebe had just one very simple reason for wanting to see *Children of Paradise* with Whit. It was romantic. Like Whit's response to her proposed movie date.

Let's keep the mystery going in letters. We'll both see the film again and each wonder if the other is there in the dark with us. Or maybe I'll buy my popcorn, turn around, and walk right into you. What would happen then?

Phoebe took far greater risks than writing Whit when she made out with boys in Ravenna Park, or used a fake ID to shoot pool in a seedy waterfront tavern, or hitchhiked up to concerts in Bellingham. Even then, she felt protected. Actually, she felt protected no matter what she did, almost as if she believed that whether waking or dreaming, Pearl's Magic Circle continued to have the power of shielding her from all harm.

While never mentioning Whit's letters, Phoebe kept no secret from her parents of her enthusiasm for the newest, best deejay on KARP. At her urging, Pearl and Jack listened on the living room hi-fi one Sunday night in June, Jack working the *New York Times* crossword puzzle and Pearl ironing name labels into Phoebe's summer camp clothes. "I won't be able to do this many more times," Pearl said when Phoebe offered to perform the chore herself. Phoebe took this as one of her mother's my-little-baby-is-growing-up remarks and settled on the floor with a Mexican peasant blouse she was embroidering.

Every time Whit played a song that was in Pearl and Jack's record collection, Phoebe felt so sure her parents were impressed that she ignored their winces and flinches at his wilder selections. "Well?" Phoebe demanded at midnight, when Whit's show ended. "Isn't he wonderful?"

"I could have done without the Fugs," Pearl said, yawning as she reached for her box of Nat Shermans. "But that's just because I'm old."

"I could have done without the Chet Baker," said Jack.

"What's wrong with Chet Baker?" Phoebe demanded.

"I much prefer his studio recording of 'I Fall in Love Too Easily.' "

"I agree," Pearl said. "On this one, he was too obviously, well, altered."

"Altered?" Phoebe asked.

Jack capped his pen, raised his bushy eyebrows, and trained his piercing blue eyes directly at Phoebe over the rims of his reading glasses. "Stoned, I believe, is the current generation's preferred term."

"My generation, you mean," Phoebe said.

Jack pushed out of the armchair and tugged his favorite, fraying cardigan down around his protruding tummy. "I was thinking more about people my students' age."

"They're only four years older than I am."

"My *graduate* students' age."

Something like jealousy stung Phoebe, as if these PhD candidates of her father's were sibling rivals for his affection, the only children who mattered to him now. They were smarter than she was; maybe that's how they succeeded where so far she had failed, in figuring out the grown-up equivalent of crawling onto his lap to be petted and sung to.

"Stoned is when you smoke grass, Daddy," Phoebe informed her father. "Chet Baker gets strung out."

Now that she had her parents' full, surprised attention, Phoebe kissed them good night and went upstairs.

Pearl and Jack's lack of enthusiasm for Whit made Phoebe wish she had kept him to herself. Then Whit could have put her to bed, hypnotizing her with his voice much the way Pearl, invoking the Magic Circle, once had. Then, this very minute, she would be falling asleep with the sound of Whit fresh in her ears, enjoying the pressure of the pillow she now liked to keep clamped between her thighs. Maybe she'd even dream about him again. In these dreams—there had been several—all that mattered was being with someone who delighted in her completely, without reservation. Someone drawn by her intensity, instead of scared off by it like most boys her own age. This dream Whit was a fairly shadowy figure, since her only idea of what he looked like came from a stylized cartoon advertisement KARP ran in the weekly underground paper, showing a lanky guy with a big cowlick juggling record albums like a circus clown.

Whit's show had become popular—his following extended far beyond Phoebe. He was admired especially by the college students she had started hanging around with on University Way—called "the Avenue" or just "the Ave" by anyone considered cool, and nothing could be cooler to her than this crowd. She concealed from them not only her age but the fact that her father was chairman of the history department. That information would get her exactly nowhere, since Jack was part of an administration scorned by students as politically retrograde, an Establishment extension, a bunch of old-fashioned (read hypocritical, shortsighted, hopelessly compromised) liberals. Phoebe's connection to Whit was another matter entirely. *That* she used as a commodity with everyone on the Ave, shopping it to impress them. It was her way of following the first dictum of Whit's that she ever heard: Take your "defect" and blow it up, make it bigger. Whit was part of the secret life her parents and teachers would disapprove of, but in the outside world, the world bigger than these authority figures, she could enlarge what she hid from them.

Whit would be on the air only one more time before Phoebe left for camp—her last chance to perform private Whit rituals. Then she would be two months without him. Phoebe didn't see how she might write to Whit from camp in the way she was accustomed to, the way he seemed to like so much, if she couldn't use Pearl's Underwood, or hear the songs he played on the air as a springboard for her thoughts.

Not that she would be miserable at camp. Her brainy parents spent time with her outdoors only when they barbecued in the backyard. Camp was where she had learned to feel at home in the natural world. And apart from the books she'd loved as a child, camp was her only treasured link to girlhood, even though at first she didn't enjoy much about it besides singing around bonfires. At least she was warm then, and doing something she was good at, something people praised her for. But gradually, as the weeks passed, she began relishing everything that had once filled her with trepidation—sleeping in tents beneath giant firs, swimming in chilly glacier-fed lakes, hiking for hours up Mount Pilchuck on rocky trails. This year, she would be an assistant counselor, living unsupervised in a tent with other older girls.

Undressing for bed before Whit's show began, Phoebe wondered what he would think, not hearing from her for such a long time. She didn't want him to be hurt. Or worse, forget her. *I'm going to Europe this summer,* she scribbled to Whit on a postcard. *Don't get too lonesome while I'm gone.* That looked a little bare. *I'm writing you naked,* she added, and put the card in an envelope.

As Whit's theme song came over the radio, Phoebe turned off the light and got into bed. Later, while Whit introduced a Miles Davis cut with a dreamy story about hearing him play once in San Francisco, she pushed aside the pillow between her knees.

Willing Whit to go on and on, she touched the place at her core where all the sweet warmth seemed to come from, the place she used to raise her leg and show to the mirror when she imagined dancing naked for men, the place she had never quite imagined could produce sensations such as this, and saw in her mind a river and knew she needed to find a way across, though of course there was not a bridge in sight, only a direct plunge into the drink, which she took, following the sound of Whit's voice, and then fell back against her pillows, astonished to discover that another, even more delicious feeling would punctuate what she hadn't at all anticipated as this journey's end.

After tonight, Phoebe would always feel she'd lost her virginity to Whit.

3

When Laurienne got up at 6:00 a.m., she had every intention of heading back to the city after a shower and some coffee. She changed her mind when she checked the Norwegian fishermen's stove downstairs and found a pile of Nat Sherman butts. Her reason for opening the stove in the first place was the chill; every kitchen window was up, probably to air the room after all those cigarettes, and heat never got turned on before September. The Nats were not a good sign. She felt a twinge of guilt. Usually she could read her mother pretty well, as if one of those old-fashioned operator switchboards had been installed inside her head and all she had to do to discover Phoebe's state of mind was say, "One moment, please," then plug into the circuit labeled "Mother." But no time for that lately.

When she had first let on work might keep her from the barbecue, Phoebe wanted to cancel. "No," Laurienne yelped. "Everyone would be so disappointed." So she knocked herself out to get up here, but not in time to lend a hand, and even then, she barely saw Phoebe. Well, she couldn't help it. She hadn't been with anyone on the Road all summer. Not Ivan, who had taught her how to make pitchers and bowls on his pottery wheel. Not Amelia, who had taught her how to make potpourri from the wild roses that bloomed on the island in June.

Not *any* of the people whose houses she grew up running in and out of, learning how to do everything from gutting a fish to playing Dylan on an ocarina. Apart from Phoebe's father and his second wife, who'd died last winter, they were the only family she'd known.

Laurienne shut all the unscreened windows—even in August, bugs weren't enough of a problem to warrant screens—and loaded the woodstove's rear with crumpled newspaper and criss-crossed pieces of kindling. While they flamed she set out an enamelware carafe and heated enough water for a full pot of strong coffee. Then she called Seattle to check in at work.

One of her team members was already at his desk, or at his desk still. "What's up, Laur?" Cliff said, his voice heavy with sarcasm—or maybe fatigue, it was hard to tell. "Are you having a sleepover?"

"Yeah." Laurienne added a couple of short, thick alder logs to the fire.

"Lucky you."

"With my mom."

"Oh. For a minute there, I thought maybe you got laid."

"I am a computer programmer," Laurienne said in a flat voice, like Data on *Star Trek: The Next Generation*. "Computer programmers do not get laid."

"Despite the fact," Cliff continued in a similar monotone, "that all systems function within normal specifications." Then, in a regular voice: "Hey, got one for you. This guy finds a frog in a well, and the frog goes, 'If you kiss me, I'll turn into a beautiful princess and be yours forever.' The guy jumps back, like whooooa. Then he puts the frog in his pocket and leaves. After he gets home, he takes her out and, I'm telling you, this is one pissed-off frog. 'What's wrong with you?' she screams. 'Why won't you kiss me and turn me into a beautiful woman?' The guy says, 'I am a computer programmer. I do not need a girlfriend. But a talking frog is cool.' "

Fairy tales often disturbed Laurienne when she was little, listening to them at bedtime. How could Cinderella's father marry such a mean woman if he loved his daughter? Why was Little Red Riding Hood allowed to travel alone through a forest where wolves lived? Choices had consequences, that's what her mother had taught her, but the silly people from the map hanging over her bed just didn't get it. Instead of moving on with these stories, Laurienne had wanted to stop and correct all the poor judgment and injustices that made them possible. Now, as an adult, she seldom remembered jokes. But a joke applying logic to a fairy tale? That was something to stick in her brainpan. "I heard it before," she told Cliff. "Only the programmer was a feminist and the frog was a prince."

"Feminist humor," Cliff said, "is an oxymoron."

"Trust me, it's funnier." Fitting in with the guys was part of the job at BioIngenious, where so few women worked that Laurienne was pretty much resigned to the likelihood of never having anyone on her team who might slip her a tampon if she needed one, let alone share her sense of humor. Although in that department, Cliff came pretty close. "Cover for me till I get there?"

"What's my reward?"

"I'll bring you back some stuff from here."

"What kind of stuff?"

"Cool stuff. Juicy and slimy. You'll love it."

Laurienne hung up and tamped down the woodstove vents for a slow burn. Now there'd be time for her and Phoebe to walk the beach and have breakfast. When all the other kids she knew on the Road were watching Saturday-morning cartoons, she would be bundled up on the beach with her mother, perched on a log sipping hot chocolate while they named the birds flying over-head. Of course, on this particular morning, Phoebe might only want to say goodbye and go back to sleep. She had to work today, too. But if she did decide to drag herself out of bed, Laurienne would have the coffee made and herself squared away for a late arrival in Seattle.

She wasn't passive-aggressive, or whatever the popular term was for people who could only maneuver others into desired behaviors by indirect means. She just liked to prepare for things going her way. Also, she had been coding so intensely for such a long stretch that she approached just about everything as if it were an intricate problem to be solved, right down to what brand of toothpaste to buy. It was the hours that did it to you. Every project she worked on had rigid deadlines, but just when you thought you understood exactly what all the specifications and major themes were, you got zapped with scope creep. Programmers' shorthand for the urgent barrage of requests—no, demands—to add extra functions. Your program had to ring more bells, blow more whistles, but you didn't have an extra minute of time to invent them. And so what began as an amount of work you could barely get your mind around started multiplying wildly, like metastasizing cells. There was bound to be scope creep no matter where a programmer labored, but the problem worsened exponentially in a company with biological models at the heart. Exhausting, being so wired all the time. What she'd really like to do was crawl back into bed herself. Of course, if she did, her brain wouldn't let her sleep.

Not that she took her own complaints seriously. Everyone she worked with had the same ones, in addition to eyestrain, back strain, hand and wrist muscle pain, and the dreaded carpal tunnel syndrome.

Last night, Laurienne had spent most of the evening

with Ivan, catching up on their year apart. "After a few months in Japan," he had said, "I started seeing faces of the people I care about over here in the faces of people over there. Funny how that happens. Like you're seeing straight through to essence. One night in a Tokyo sushi bar, I saw a Japanese woman who looked just like Phoebe."

"Oh boy," Laurienne said, sensing the shift between him and her mother she'd hoped for ever since grade school. "Did she miss you, too?"

"I think so."

"Did she write letters?"

"Yep."

"Long ones?"

"Uh-huh."

"Sounds hot."

"We'll see."

"Oh no, Ivan. 'We'll see' is way too weak. With my mom you need a plan."

"Okay."

"Okay? What's that mean?"

"It means I believe in planning plans, Judge. What I don't believe in is planning results. Can't be done. Especially with someone smart as Phoebe."

Now, climbing back up the stairs, she wondered if Ivan had anything to do with the Nats.

Laurienne's seven hours of sleep had been enough to lighten the dark circles beneath her eyes. Showering had colored her cheeks; the blouse and khakis she wore were clean and pressed. Her hair hung heavy now only because it was still wet from washing. And she felt too fresh and revived to go directly to her computer. She probably wouldn't have paid so much attention to the Nats if she hadn't needed an excuse to stay longer. If she didn't need to feel connected to something other than work. Like herself. Like her mother.

"Gotta go, Mom," Laurienne whispered into Phoebe's ear. "You sleep." Lily, curled into a tight ball between Phoebe's bent knees and stomach, raised her head to whine and nuzzle Laurienne's face.

Phoebe stretched and yawned. "No, no, no. I'm getting up."

They sat together at the kitchen table that would always be covered for weeks after Christmases and Laurienne's birthdays with mating jigsaw puzzle pieces. As Phoebe slowly came to over her coffee cup, Laurienne frowned and spoke to her in an accusing voice. "You were smoking."

"I just needed to unwind from the party," Phoebe said.

"Why? Did someone say something to upset you?"

"Yes. As a matter of fact, someone *did* say something to upset me. They said, Phoebe, that daughter of yours is so thin a stiff wind would knock her over. Better make that girl something real fattening for breakfast. So how about a Dutch Baby, baby?"

Dutch Babies were their traditional special breakfast, something Phoebe's mother used to make. Laurienne felt cheated, never having known Pearl, the grandmother whose green almond-shaped eyes, long slender fingers, and auburn hair she had inherited. Whose cigarettes Phoebe had been smoking. In some ways, it seemed she knew more about Pearl than she did about her own mother. It was always easier to get Phoebe to tell Pearl stories than to tell her own. The Dutch Baby recipe was written in Pearl's hand on a yellowing two-by-three card. It was simple: a batter of eggs and flour poured into a skillet full of melted butter that got baked before being topped with sour cream and preserves. Laurienne wasn't hungry yet—she never was, this early in the morning. But she grinned and nodded at Phoebe's plan. Better to be hooking into Pearl through a Dutch Baby than through the Nats.

As Phoebe mixed the batter for their breakfast, sharp, insistent, watchdog barks came from the room she called her study. This was where her desk and floor-to-ceiling bookshelves were, the part of the house first struck by morning sun. "Lily, come," Laurienne called. But the dog's barking only rose to a more urgent pitch. Phoebe went to investigate and found Lily sitting on the red velvet fainting sofa with head raised toward something fluttering near the rafters, something that made a soft, whiny, whirring sound.

It was a hummingbird, come in through a cracked-open window, attracted by fuchsia flowers. Phoebe sent Lily away, shut the study door, opened the window wide as it would go, then tried to shoo the bird back outside. But it stayed high, flying backward to avoid her arms. Ivan said hummingbirds were the only bird capable of backward flight. She liked watching hummers hover and feed, and considered them less like birds than fairies, her favorite otherworldly creatures. One shelf in her study contained only fairy tales and books about fairies. Not because she believed in fairies. What was there to believe in or not? Fairies weren't about beliefs. Fairies were unfettered vessels of delight, about nothing but themselves. Meant to be embraced, not examined for existential evidence.

Well, there was no delight in the scared creature flying madly around the upper reaches of her study. All she had accomplished with her traffic-cop motions was frightening it further. Best to leave the bird alone for a while. If it was still here when she and Laurienne returned from the beach, she'd find a butterfly net and try that.

While their breakfast baked, Phoebe and Laurienne walked to the beach down a twisting path lined with blackberry bushes. Laurienne had brought a colander along, and when she stopped to pick, Phoebe helped.

"Did you hear about the Miller place?" Phoebe asked, working to keep her voice light.

"I got that it sold for a lot."

"That's all?"

"I was talking most of the night with your pen pal."

"Who? What?"

Laurienne turned to stare. "Ivan, Mom. Jeez, you're jumpy."

"Sorry," Phoebe said, concentrating on the berry hunt to calm herself. "When you were little, you liked picking better than eating."

"Please—not my blackberry ice cream again." Once, after harvesting far more blackberries than Phoebe knew what to do with, Laurienne made a batch of ice cream for the barbecue. If Laurienne had enjoyed blackberries then, she would have sampled the mixture and realized she'd used salt instead of sugar. Not even Lily would touch the stuff, and she loved salty things. "Anyway," Laurienne said, "you're just changing the subject. It's not fair, you know, the way you always do that."

"Only two fairs in life, honey. The state and the county." Phoebe mentally gave herself a little kick. On a morning when she wanted to banish every trace of Whit from her thoughts so as to not transmit any of her confusion to Laurienne, she was not only edgy on his account, but quoting him, too.

"You know what else isn't fair?" Laurienne set the colander down on a log and popped a berry into her mouth. Phoebe braced for something sad, something about growing up alone, something about having no father, no brother, no sister. But all Laurienne said was, "Now that I like blackberries, I never make ice cream."

They walked the pebbly beach, Lily at their heels. It was low tide and oysters were visible. Laurienne picked them, too, gathering a dozen to take to the city. "Summer's nearly over," she said, "and I've been so homesick."

"I wish you'd stay longer."

"I wish you'd come to Seattle more."

"But you're so busy."

"I'd squeeze you in. And you could go to movies with Gramps—he hardly gets out since Helen died."

"Now there's a choice piece of guilt to chew on." Laurienne was right. Jack's sorrow at losing Helen, the woman he'd married after Pearl's death, had hammered him back into a life of work and solitude. But Phoebe knew this mainly from weekly telephone calls. Being with her father now didn't seem to help so much as remind them both of that other, earlier loss.

"You could have some fun, too," Laurienne said. "Hit the clubs for live music. Have a real date with Ivan."

"Ivan doesn't like crowds."

"Come on, he'd do anything for you."

"Dating—that's what *you* should be doing. Getting out and meeting men."

"I am surrounded by men all day long."

"Darling, you are surrounded by nerds all day long."

"It's 1996, nerds are in now. I'm one, too, in case you haven't noticed. It's all your fault. If you hadn't sent me to Brookland, I might have turned out normal."

Brookland was the private school in Seattle that Phoebe had once attended herself, but only until ninth grade, when she rebelled and insisted on public high school. As a mother, she'd had different priorities. Afraid that Laurienne would be bored by public high school in Port Pritchard, where smart, pretty girls still played dumb to lure the guys they shook pom-poms for on the playing field, Phoebe had become the first and only north-side parent to send her child away to an expensive prep school. Not that she paid for Laurienne's board in Seattle; during the school week, the girl lived with her adoring grandfather and Helen, giving Gramps an experience his own daughter had denied him—the pleasure of having an unalienated female teenage creature living in his house who took after him. Someone happy to live by rules not of her own choosing, someone who actually enjoyed earning good grades, excelled at team sports (soccer, rowing, volleyball), and would never, ever consider going to class stoned. These days, bright Brookland graduates with college degrees and advanced computer skills easily slid into positions with firms owned and run by Brookland alums. Which wasn't quite the future Phoebe had imagined for her daughter during all those years of steep tuition.

She knew that when Laurienne said she might have turned out "normal," she wasn't referring to any of Phoebe's dreams for her of a flourishing social life or a stimulating creative career. She meant more like her parents. More like Phoebe, who had never held a "normal" job in her life—unless you counted a seasonal stint packing peas at the cannery when she was pregnant. Neither had Mitchell, the musician, freelance carpenter, and sometime fisherman she had married, whom Laurienne did not remember anyway.

Mitchell had been holding Laurienne in the passenger seat when the pickup Phoebe was driving went off the two-lane road between Port Pritchard and Mount Jensen. There was nowhere else for Phoebe to go, not with an approaching dairy tanker in the other lane and the red Impala that had been recklessly passing it dead ahead. In that agonizing, slowed-down second of choice, hers was clear: play chicken with a stupid, probably drunk driver, or get out of the way. The tanker driver used his CB to call for help, but the Impala had sped away, never to be caught. Mitchell's neck snapped as the pickup rolled down an embankment and threw him against the door— still holding Laurienne, his body protecting hers. Phoebe's memory of the accident ended before the pickup landed, but after she regained full consciousness in the Pritchard Valley Hospital, when she learned Mitchell was dead and Laurienne was alive and unharmed, she knew this was how it must have been.

Just before the accident, she and Mitchell had been squabbling. Over whether or not Phoebe ought to go by herself to Seattle for the *Kiki* premiere. The accident's lone witness as well as the police investigator laid all blame on the other driver. But Phoebe, with anguish unreachable by their opinions, would always question the quarrel's impact on her judgment.

At first, she wished that she had died, too—in place of Mitchell, or, if she couldn't have that, along with him. But her wish lasted no longer than it took to notice the pain in her milk-engorged breasts. It was Amelia who had brought Laurienne to her hospital room. Phoebe knew Amelia then only vaguely as someone else who lived on Owl Island, another new mother, and now here she stood with Laurienne on her hip and her own infant asleep in a quilted baby sling, snug against her chest. Phoebe was confused enough to ask if Amelia worked in the hospital.

"No," she said, putting Laurienne in Phoebe's arms. "Ivan brought me. I've been nursing your baby."

It was then, as Laurienne began to suckle, that Phoebe

felt the first hard tug of place, of community, that would work to keep her here. Jack helped as much as she would let him, but he and Helen were newlyweds and, like Pearl before her, Helen was in full charge of the domestic front; there were limits to what Jack felt he could offer. Phoebe couldn't imagine returning to the house of her childhood anyway, not with a baby, not with another woman married to her father. And now Laurienne was older than Phoebe had been then, when all she had to go by was instinct and intuition. Mitchell was present for Laurienne's birth. He loved her. He saved her.

He was the one, Phoebe had decided, who deserved to be remembered as her father.

On the beach, Laurienne stooped down to pick up a stick of driftwood and throw it for Lily. Phoebe reached out to touch her daughter's amber curls; dry and clean, they sprang out in rusty coils, a few shades darker and quite a bit looser than Mitchell's carroty kinks. How would he advise her on the job front? "You're still young," Phoebe said. "You've got plenty of time for other choices."

"I don't have time for *anything*. But if our stock flies, I might have some money. Maybe that'll buy me some time."

Later, as Laurienne was climbing up the hillside path, she turned around to give her mother a dead-serious measuring look. "Forty's not so old anymore. I mean, you're young, too."

But Phoebe didn't feel young, especially not with Whit moving into the neighborhood. She had changed so much since the time he knew her well. What had happened to her wildness, her impulsiveness, her attraction to risk? Well, the answer was perfectly evident, walking up the path right ahead of her, toting blackberries and oysters. A good thing to remember. Even now she could

conjure up a sense of creative valor around her early
mothering, in the discoveries she made alone, with no
help from a mother of her own. How to soothe her
baby's awful indigestion by propping pillows all around
so that she slept sitting up. How to defuse toddler tan-
trums with whispered words. How to pinch a six-year-
old's right arm with the right amount of playful pressure
so she'd be distracted from her terror of needles just before the pediatrician injected the left one.

Still. Straining to see herself through Whit's eyes, she
came up short and squat. How could she ever be smart
enough, funny enough, enticing enough, to be around
him again? She'd seen his press. Moving among famous
people for so long must have only heightened and refined his already considerable appetite to be stimulated,
to be amused. How could she ever keep up, much less
get ahead of him now? She was dull, with hands grown
raw from making nets that trapped and killed. Hands
that brought nothing to life now but her garden, and
that, too, would be mostly dead in a few months. Phoebe
stopped hiking uphill for a moment to catch her breath.
Laurienne's here, she reminded herself. That brought
her back, but not without a shudder at how special some
part of her still wanted to be for Whit.

After breakfast outside on the deck, Laurienne grabbed
her duffel bag and Phoebe waved her off down Spit in
the Wind Road. Once the Volvo slipped out of sight, she
tumbled again into the abyss with dizzying speed. Doing
the dishes thinking, *How many hours of my life have I
wasted like this?* Reproaching herself in the shower for
making such a mess, always doing things her way, by *self*.
Then, as needles of hot water pulsed against the knotted
muscles in her neck, she remembered the hummingbird
in her study. What if it hadn't gotten out?

Wet and naked, she raced downstairs and found the bird lying on the study floor, motionless, eyes closed and wings spread out wide. Another lovely thing dead? These birds burned up fuel so fast they needed to feed constantly; all that flying up in the rafters must have starved the life out of this one. It was a female, with a golden green throat. A headline flashed before Phoebe's eyes: *Woman Who Can't Sing Destroys Bird That Can Only Hum.* She stooped to touch the tiny creature's chest. Her wings pulsed, not with the rapid movement that rendered them invisible in flight but with a desperate, quaking shake.

Still naked, Phoebe ran into the kitchen to grab a saucer and custard dish out of the cupboard. She dumped some sugar in the dish, dissolved it in lukewarm water, and dashed into the bathroom for a Q-tip.

Back in the study, she lifted the bird, laid her on the saucer, and set it on the window ledge. "Okay, girl," she said. "Let's eat."

Phoebe soaked the Q-tip in sugar water before gently touching it to the bird's needle-like black beak, which stayed closed tight. Hoping some of the sweetness would seep in, she tried stroking the cotton up and down the beak until, finally, it cracked open for more. The hummingbird's throat pulsed as she swallowed. Phoebe kept soaking and swabbing. Eyes still closed, the bird rocked on the saucer and pulled in her wings.

"That's it," Phoebe crooned in her raspy voice. "Come on, girl. Come on, little Tinker Bell." The bird's beak opened wider. Out came a long, lashlike tongue to soak up more liquid. Never, not even in photographs, had Phoebe seen a hummingbird's tongue. The sight flushed her with a sense of privilege.

An hour passed like this—soak and swab, soak and swab, with Phoebe giving the bird more and more time between each bout of swallowing to assimilate the sugar. The phone rang—probably Sophie at the net shop, wondering where she was—but Phoebe didn't answer. She wouldn't leave the bird untended even for the few seconds it would take to fetch her robe. No one could see her; houses on Spit in the Wind were built so that none looked out directly on another. Still, she imagined how the sight of her, bent bare-breasted over a hummingbird, might startle anyone who wandered by.

When a bird flew into a house, Phoebe had heard, it was supposed to be an emissary of someone dead, a messenger of spirit. A tribal belief, or something more contemporary? Normally, she wouldn't dwell so long on the idea's origins. But last night she had smoked her mother's cigarettes and this morning made her favorite breakfast; ingesting Pearl in these ways and hand-feeding this creature did not seem entirely unrelated. If Pearl was sending a message, what could it be? A warning of danger, a reminder of love, or something altogether unfathomable by anyone still stuck inside a body? Having now spent more years without than with her mother, how was she supposed to know the answers to any of these questions?

At last, the hummingbird opened her eyes. When Phoebe offered the Q-tip again, she sucked hard, throat throbbing, and fluttered her wings. It lasted only a second, but her wings, moving faster, blurred. Then she wobbled under the window sash to the outside part of the ledge, wanting to leave but not yet strong enough. Phoebe captured her to administer two more Q-tip-fulls of liquid, and when she let go, the bird flew to the top of a nearby cedar tree, preening until she darted away, ready again to feed herself.

Phoebe smiled for a moment, then burst into tears,

aching for Pearl. Feeling the lack of her in everything. Wanting, for once, to be told what to do.

After Laurienne hit Seattle, she stopped at the Queen Anne Thriftway for things to go with oysters and blackberries. It was ten thirty when she pulled into the parking lot at BioIngenious.

The last time she had arrived so late in the day she was a junior at the University of Washington, clutching a written recommendation from the alumni office at Brookland, where she'd started down the coding path with eighth-grade computer literacy classes. Bradley Dunson, another Brookland graduate, interviewed her for a summer internship. "Why are you interested in working here, Laurienne?" he asked. Dunson looked to be in his early thirties, too young to have been in Phoebe's class, but maybe old enough to remember Pearl.

Laurienne was tempted to mention these women whose genes she carried, to fish for facts to fill her mother's informational gaps. Didn't jobs here have everything to do with genes? An answer to Dunson's question formed in her head, stripped of names and dressed up in personal-essay language. *Well, sir, I've pretty much worked it out that I was the shotgun in my parents' marriage, and since I see myself as being haphazardly conceived, I'm especially attracted to a business geared to taking all the chaos and guesswork out of biology. No, don't tell him that, he'll think you're whacked.* Laurienne cleared her throat, conscious of speaking like a beauty pageant contestant. "I'd like to be part of a field that's working to improve people's lives."

"You've got the grades," Dunson told her. "You've got the skills. And you've got the job—depending on your response to one more question."

Laurienne braced herself. "Yes?"

"Can you keep a secret?"

She exhaled a relieved sigh. "No problem there. I was trained by a master."

"Excuse me?"

"Yes, sir. I'm good at keeping secrets."

"You'll have to sign a piece of paper to that effect. Even in your limited programming role this summer, you'll be dealing with highly sensitive material. There's no textbook for what we do here, Laurienne. We're making history as we go. Our basic mission is isolating genes responsible for hereditary conditions and diseases. Once we put our finger on the right gene, we get a patent so nobody else can use the discovery without using us, so to speak. Discretion of the highest order is crucial to maintaining our competitive edge."

Laurienne performed so well that BioIngenious recruited her for a staff position in a year's time, after graduation. Even though one of the first corporate truisms she'd learned here was that a computer scientist could develop an understanding of biology far more easily than a biologist could pick up computer languages and database instructions, she loaded up on the sciences in her senior year. Now she was a team leader. But even if "they" tortured her for secrets, she doubted if anything she revealed would really ruin the company, or go beyond what any potential investor might uncover in cursory research. She worked just one corner of the jigsaw puzzle, without knowing precisely how it hooked into the big picture. Oh, she might hear from Dunson that a program she and her crew had sweated over was fetching good results. But it wasn't ever *her* finger that ended up pointing to the prize gene.

Laurienne stuck her head into Cliff's cubicle. "Did I miss anything important?"

He spoke without lifting his gaze from the screen. "Is your piece done?"

"Yeah, that's why I'm not standing here in a puddle of guilt."

"Okay, then. When I finish we'll put it all together and see how this baby flies." He shot his sleeves, hauled back his arms, attacked his keyboard like a concert pianist playing a showy cadenza, then pushed back from his desk and slumped dramatically over his chair. "I'm spent," he said. "I require nourishment. Where's that gloppy gooey stuff you promised?"

"Juicy and slimy," Laurienne corrected.

"Better yet."

In the snack room, Cliff watched as Laurienne cracked oysters and set out bottled sauce. "We ought to be having these with champagne," he said. "I mean, they're an aphrodisiac, aren't they?"

"That is not why I brought them."

Laurienne was determined to avoid sleeping with Cliff, who reminded her just a little too much of all the boys she was drawn to in college. Scruffy characters with distracted demeanors and goatees and thrift shop plaid shirts who regarded their computers as extensions of their bodies, the way less in-their-heads guys did their cars. Their idea of a date was watching unbelievably bad low-budget horror movies on video—an antidote to their advanced physics and math courses. They liked techno music. They liked comic books about mutant superheroes. They liked surviving on foods requiring less than ten minutes total to buy, prepare, and consume. And they liked counting on her for everything else they needed. Cliff was just an older, clean-shaven, twangier-talking (he came from Texas), somewhat better-dressed version. Also, he was nicer looking. Much nicer looking, as a matter of fact, with broad shoulders, narrow hips, and dark, soulful, wide-set eyes.

Another big difference was Cliff's design degree from Cal Arts; he'd picked up coding skills on the side. Still another was that he had created a mutant superhero of his own—a heroine, actually. A genetically twisted young woman capable of neutralizing the apocalyptic forces of shape-shifting demons, dark-side wizards, and vengeful, sexy witches. By day she's Lexie Shields, a shy, bespectacled, red-haired young scientist slumped round-shouldered over her computer keyboard; by night, a gorgeous, scantily clad savior of the planet. Sort of a Superboy with hair still wet from swimming across the gender divide—a grown-up, space-age Pippi Longstocking. And as much as Laurienne had resisted fairy tales when she was little, she'd loved Pippi. Not only for her red hair and freckles, but for being the strongest girl in the world. Which she had, come to think of it, once told Cliff.

Is Lexie Shields a tribute to her? Probably. But Cliff, who spends all his spare time designing a computer game with Lexie as its star, has never said so, and Laurienne's too nervous to ask.

Although Cliff has been at BioIngenious several years longer than she, he resists managing projects. What he cares about is retiring young and rich enough to start his own computer game company—like most of the other guys on her team, though none of them has the advantage of Cliff's art background. In the meantime they all keep their heads down coding, confident of eventually being rewarded well enough so that any deficient social or emotional skills will become quirky keys on the chain that led to success. Supersmart zoom brains operating under the assumption that they're cool. Lost boys, that's what they are. Laurienne has always been a sucker for them. Is still.

"Wow," Cliff said, devouring his oysters. "These are good."

"You've probably never had them fresher than this. They were sleeping on the shore this morning."

Laurienne unwrapped Thriftway shortcake shells, filled them with blackberries, and squirted some Dream Whip on top. Hardly an elegant presentation, but she felt sure this was the least processed food Cliff had consumed in some time.

"So," he said, "another day, another program. Just doing our small part to save the world."

Laurienne shrugged. "Who knows, maybe we are."

"Who knows, that's the operative statement. Will we protect humanity from some debilitating disease, or only the wealthy and well insured? Who knows. Will wowee new DNA tracers help catch criminals and free the innocent, or end up screening people for jobs, insurance, maybe even marriage? Who knows."

"You're so cynical," Laurienne told him.

"Picture this. Some high-flying female exec pays a fortune for her dandy little home chemistry set. Then while her date's off taking a leak, she swabs his wineglass."

"Why would she want to do that?"

"To see," Cliff said, "if he's got the loyalty gene."

"Why couldn't she just ask?"

"That's why you'll never be a high-flying female exec, Laur. You're too trusting. And this business we're in, it ain't all sweetness and light. I mean, say they isolate some gene for mental illness. Zap, it's gone. Manipulated out of existence. Disappeared from the gene pool. Only thirty years later, guess what? Whoops! Sorry folks, we just kind of accidentally along the way eliminated genius while we were busy wiping out psychosis."

"You read too much science fiction."

"I've just got an excellent imagination."

"Let's go put the program together."

"For instance, I can imagine that what you really want is for me to kiss you."

They were standing by the trash can, dumping their paper plates and plastic utensils, his blackberry-stained lips hovering near hers. Laurienne tried for a comradely arm jab that somehow turned into her fingers clutching his shirtsleeve. "You'll do anything to put off testing."

"Maybe it's just the oysters working."

"Hey!" Laurienne said sharply, but he didn't back off, just stood suspended as he was, and soon she found herself pulling him closer.

So many fishermen along the northwestern coast patronized Phoebe's shop that even in bad years, years when they pulled up her nets with scantier than usual catches and couldn't afford to order new gear for the next, she still did all right. Not only had she succeeded in a business dominated by men, her clients seemed to prefer dealing with a woman. She took pride in packing shimmery green nets hung for salmon fishermen so they unfolded on board smooth as silk, never wasting time with snags. For the shrimpers, she invented panels to exclude fin fish, increasing the shrimpers' catch. For the cod and pollock trawlers, she designed funnel-shaped nets that were black on the bottom, white on the top, red on one side, and green on the other, so that even if they came up in storms snarled and ripped, they were a lot easier than standard white trawl nets to untangle and repair on board. Word of her system spread to the big net shops in Seattle, which began copying her—without, of course, any attribution. She was used to that.

But there was a lot about her work that couldn't be

duplicated. Crews counted on the strength of her knots, the precision of her measurements. When a trawl net came back to her torn, she would ponder the damage like a puzzle until she figured out how to make an improvement along with the repair. That required understanding all the equipment a skipper used, so the net would fish again without ripping at sea in the same place. There were other, less practical reasons for her clients' fidelity. Why deal with a scruffy man much like yourself when you could go to Phoebe? Phoebe, who always smelled so nice—not doused in scent, but you could get a hit of something fresh as moonstruck sea air if you stood close enough. Phoebe, who had a way of making you feel worthwhile, as if what you did mattered, even when you weren't fishing.

She could usually lose herself in the work, in the satisfaction of seeing the mesh take shape, modeling it to form and function. Knowing it went from hands in her shop to hands at sea, lives depending on its integrity for safety, for sustenance. But this morning, with the hummingbird still so much on her mind, she drove to work over the bridge connecting Owl Island to Port Pritchard with an unsettling sense of her own murky depths.

Phoebe parked her Explorer in the big lot that ran between the Fishermen's Terminal docks and her net loft. The warehouse doors were open and Gabe had one of the god-awful CDs he played when she wasn't around blasting on the boom box. "I'm in no mood today for this angry-white-boy stuff," Phoebe snapped as she yanked out the disc.

Ivan looked up from the net he was working, taking in her irritation and swollen red eyes. "Hey," he said. "Are you okay?"

Remembering their lunch on Heron Island, his touch and the sun-warmed scent of his skin, she thought how nice it would be if he took her home and steadied her senses with some wild, imperative, indoor sex. But no matter how much she wanted him to comfort her, right now she couldn't let him. Not with everybody watching. Not with Whit in the air. So instead of answering his question, she just kept trashing the angry white boys. "I don't get what their problem is. They're rock stars and they're still not getting laid?"

"Please, Phoebe," Gabe groaned. "No more Bulgarian nuns. Or Armenian flutes." Gabe talked to Phoebe as if she were more of a parent than a boss—a result of being Amelia's son and growing up on Spit in the Wind Road. "The klezmer band needs a rest, too. I hear enough world music at my mother's house."

"I brought sea shanties," offered Brian, one of her regular part-timers. "The tape's out in my car."

Now Kristen groaned. She liked corny old classic radio stations best but wasn't about to say so because of her crush on Gabe, who was going back to Wharton soon and prided himself on being avant-garde in everything but his schooling. For Gabe, Kristen had forsaken her customary sweatshirts and baggy tees, wearing only clingy tank tops that revealed her full, firm, farm girl's flesh. She and Gabe were a team today, sewing repair panels to the same midwater trawl net.

Years ago, when Phoebe was pregnant and short on cash, it was Ivan who first put a net in her hands, paying to have her help him with one of his moonlighting jobs. Word spread fast. Phoebe tied perfect cloves, made perfect measurements, always hung a perfect drop. Now, as sometimes in the past, Ivan was working a short-term stint at the shop, his current goal being to earn extra money for a new kiln so he could turn out pieces faster for the big museum show he had coming up in the spring. "Why work?" she'd asked, confident the show would lead to all the money he needed. "I'll write you a check, you can pay me back later." But Ivan was a man whose only credit card was a plain green American Express that had to be paid in full each month; he didn't believe in debt.

Today he was doing the most skilled job in the shop: cleaning out holes in a bottom trawl hanging from a bar, knotting in new mesh. And he was so deft that he could do it without taking his eyes off Phoebe. "Our shuttles make a kind of music," Ivan said. "I like the shop when it's quiet." He also liked the sound of storytelling voices. If business was slow and he was working just with Phoebe, he might bring a book on tape. In winter, when they wore Polarfleece sweatshirts, down vests, thick socks, and fingerless gloves to stay warm in the shop, he chose novels with hot, lush locales. Good stuff, too— Graham Greene, Jamaica Kincaid, Gabriel García Márquez, Borges, Naipaul. Those were wonderful times. But at this moment, in the compassion of his gaze, she felt thankful not to be alone with Ivan. Why hurt him with her confusion?

"I want Irish," she said, and put on a Waterboys CD full of songs with strong, contagious beats. She liked goosing the crew with music like that. It improved mood as well as output. Instead of working just from the shoulder, arms pumping, nothing but muscle involved, a good rhythm got heads and hips into the act, wagging and swaying while shuttles leapt, strutted, bobbed, weaved. When you were chasing the tempo with your twine, it was hard to talk or get distracted.

Shuttles were clicking in counterpoint to "Fisherman's Blues" as Phoebe went upstairs to check in with Sophie. Born to a Port Pritchard fishing family, Sophie had lost her father in an accident at sea when she was young; his name, along with those of all the other lost local fishermen, was inscribed on a memorial that stood at the Terminal entrance. When things got hectic in the shop, Sophie stitched and strung with the same methodical zeal that she kept books. Phoebe had hoped to drain off some inner turmoil by telling what had happened with the hummingbird, getting the story into Sophie's ordering, organizing ears. But sitting upstairs in the office with her was Angus, a red-faced old skipper and one of Sophie's uncles.

"Hello, Angus," Phoebe said, wondering why he seemed so embarrassed. "What can we do for you?"

"Tried to get you on the phone," Sophie said with a sigh. "He won't tell me what he wants. He'll only talk to you."

"So leave us alone," Angus barked. Then, when Sophie was gone: "I sure am sorry I didn't get my new cod-end from you."

"It's not like you couldn't afford it," Phoebe said. Her best quality cod-ends—made of even more rugged material than the net itself—cost over twenty thousand dollars.

"I'm having bad dreams about it," Angus said.

"That's what you get," Phoebe teased, "for going to those guys in Seattle."

"It's the same dream every night, Phoebe. Everything's working great. We see the fish on sonar, spread the net out all nice and even, and pretty soon we got all the fish that cod-end'll hold socked in, and I'm so happy. But before we can pull 'em up, they escape. Every single one."

"Why do you suppose you had that dream?"

Angus fiddled with his hearing aid. "Goddamn salt air corrodes my batteries. Come again?"

"What do you think it means, Angus?"

He shrugged. "Well, maybe the fly mesh ain't right. Maybe they got it on too loose."

Margaret, Phoebe's therapist friend, believed every important element in a dream represented some aspect of yourself. If old Angus was his cod-end, he must be afraid of losing money. "Money bags"—that's what the fishermen called their cod-ends. But Angus hadn't come here to have Phoebe analyze his dream. He'd come because he was heading up to Alaska for the September season and wanted her to put his mind at ease. "Would you like us to redo your fly mesh?" she asked. It was a little like offering to retie someone's shoes. And exactly what Angus needed.

"Would you?" He grinned.

To show his gratitude, and maybe make amends for taking his business elsewhere, Angus added an order that would run his tab up to something worthwhile for Phoebe. "When I get back," he said, "you can change the hula skirting." Hula skirting was the fiber trim on the cod-end bottom that protected ropes from chafing. "They put on some real ugly colors down there, yellow and black. I like your blue and green lots better."

Waiting outside the office, Sophie heard everything. "You let him off too easy," she told Phoebe after Angus left. "His cod-end would have sure sweetened up our bonuses this year. You should've made him squirm more, locked him in for repairs. But why am I wasting my breath? You're no good at that."

"At what? Torturing?"

"No, confronting."

Phoebe narrowed her eyes. "Is that right?"

"See?" Sophie said. "A perfect example. 'Is that right?' instead of 'Quit meddling, Soph. Write up the order for Angus's net and go fetch the mail.' "

Sophie was good at *that*—getting cranky, crashing boundaries, then nailing them back up behind her. Usually Phoebe didn't mind. But today Sophie's casual criticism had struck a nerve and she didn't feel like pretending otherwise so she could describe what had happened to make her so thin-skinned, so stripped of her usual protective layering, so unwilling to be shut up inside an office, fending off the waves of busyness and chatter emanating from Sophie. "I'll go to the post office," Phoebe told her.

As she passed through the shop again, one of the only slow songs on the Waterboys album played—"The Stolen Child," a favorite Yeats poem of hers set to flute music. She stopped and listened to the next few lines, telling how a fairy steals a young boy, luring him away from a world of sorrow and weeping to one filled with charm and enchantment.

"Hey, Phoebe," Gabe said. "Think he's talking about drugs?"

Phoebe gave him a withering look, but before she could snap his head off Ivan jumped in. "He's not talking about drugs," Ivan said. "He's talking about fairies. Kidnapping fairies. Right now, Phoebe's wishing they'd climbed out of the bay twenty years ago and stolen you."

Gabe nodded thoughtfully. "Then it's probably not a good time to ask if she brought any leftovers from the barbecue."

At the post office, Phoebe picked up a package-notice slip along with her business and personal mail. Phoebe gave the slip to Sandra, the town's silver-haired postmistress, who sneezed three times and said "Beet pollen" before taking it to the back room where packages were kept. She returned with a neatly wrapped box marked "Fragile," big enough to hold a hat.

Phoebe signed for the package and carried it to a nearby counter. Her name and address were on a label, written by an unknown hand. There was no return address. The stamps were Mexican. Looked like another Mystery Package. Over the years, Phoebe had received quite a few—all addressed by different people, but Phoebe had pretty much convinced herself by now that they were sent by just one person, someone who wanted to remain anonymous. There was never a note inside. No two packages were from the same place, and many came from abroad. Sometimes she would receive a flurry, one every few months, then nothing for years. The first package contained a handful of unset rubies from Istanbul. From Canada, one spring, came a box full of live ladybugs. From Hawaii a pound of red-dirt salt that was actually quite tasty. There were child-sized clogs from Holland, a gold-plated teaspoon from England, a small goose-down pillow from Switzerland, and drawing sticks burned to charcoal from France. One package held a coffee mug the size of a fingernail, her name painted onto it in impossibly tiny letters, and another an old-fashioned alarm clock left out in the rain so that its face had rusted. Several items came from nature: a pair of Siamese sand dollars, a heart-shaped piece of petrified wood, laminated four-leaf clovers.

Phoebe couldn't be sure who was sending them. Maybe it was a troller she once had a fling with in Alaska back when she strung and mended nets for the Bristol Bay salmon runs—a high school science teacher in his regular life, fishing to finance a PhD in physics. Or maybe it was another short-term lover, the skipper who made a bundle on some bonanza cod runs, retired, and spent his time traveling. Both certainly possibilities. But all her suspicions centered on Whit. The contents of these packages were, well, unusual. And long as he'd been gone, she still thought of Whit—when she allowed herself to think of him at all—as the most unusual person in her life. The person who had given her the eyes to see these things, really see them. Plain, straightforward, direct, clear—Whit was none of these. But if metaphor were a language, he'd be fluent. Maybe sending packages was his way of apologizing, saying he was sorry for his part in the rupture eating at her again. But if it was Whit, he'd already know she lived here. He wouldn't have been mysteriously guided to Owl Island by his overwhelming feelings for her, the way she'd imagined last night. He'd be seeking her out. Can't have it both ways, she told herself.

What fragile item could be coming to her from Mexico? A piece of pottery? Some hand-painted tiles? She hefted the package again. No, not heavy enough for anything like that. She undid the packing tape and opened a box filled with tissue paper. In the center of the tissue was another, smaller box. She lifted the lid to reveal a delicate, cup-shaped object.

Phoebe gasped.

Could it be? In the dark post office, she couldn't tell for sure. She ran outside, crossed the street to bright sunlight to examine the intricate network of bark and twigs covered with lichen and spiderwebs. In her hands she held a fairy home. A hummingbird's nest, sprinkled now with tears.

4

Whit sat alone at a table in the dining room of the Blue
Heron Inn, drinking coffee while he waited for the tribal
attorney to bring a lease for him to sign. Jasmine was
still under the feather duvet in their room upstairs, probably asleep again. He was glad she hadn't wanted to join
him. Without her along, he could more easily discourage
the attorney from mistaking this for a social occasion
and get the exchange of papers over with quickly. The
less Carl Brown knew about him, the better. Carl wasn't
someone Whit needed to impress. Neither was anybody
else on Owl Island. The life Whit imagined for himself
there had nothing to do with his image, everything to do
with his work.

The only legacy Whit ever cared about having was the
films. He could even remember saying so to a journalist.
The one who had an annoying habit, while they were in
bed, of letting him know she had slept with directors far
more famous. "That idea came to François in a dream,"
she'd say. "He told me about it first thing in the morning, before we had our coffee."

Whit hated giving interviews, but he'd once done a lot
of them. That was when festivals vied to be the first to
show his work. That was when up-and-coming filmmakers always mentioned him as an inspiration. That
was a long time ago.

If one of the current crop of rising directors mentions Whit at all, it's as a footnote to the better-known talents he emerged with, lions long since kissed by the box office gods in the way Whit, for all his promise, never was. When Whit meets these acolytes at film festivals now, he can feel the fear behind their polite reverence. *Please God, don't make me have to keep struggling for money the way this guy does.*

"Oh honey," Jasmine tells him. "That's *your* fear. I've seen their faces. They are genuinely in awe of you."

He can't really argue with her. Whenever he feels low, it's his habit to exaggerate the depths to which he's fallen. He still gets films made. Still gives interviews. Still shows at most of the festivals that matter. And he's still famous, too, when it comes right down to it. Maybe not hot anymore, but hardly ice cold. If you took degree of difficulty into account, the way they did in scoring Olympic athletes, his survival was quite an achievement. "Yeah," Whit drawls, "bitter old goats are great at inspiring awe among the young."

"Stop that. You're an artist. You're ageless." She gives him an intimate squeeze. "And if you're a goat, you're a horny one."

"What can I tell you, kid? When you're right, you're right. And you're right." Whit does a very good Jack Nicholson, but Jasmine won't know the movie he's quoting if he doesn't name it for her, so he does. *"Chinatown."* And Jasmine smiles so lovingly that, once again, he forgives her limitations.

The way Whit works now, he can afford to live wherever he likes—providing that he leaves periodically to make a film. Which means shooting on a low budget in foreign cities where his financiers' dollars and deutsche marks go far, using actors who are either edgy, younger, and on the cusp of fame, or edgy, aging, and fast fading from the A-list. Then, when the film opens, after he's run around the country to preach his gospel in the presence of every critic and feature writer his publicist can wrangle, he'll be on Owl Island, living in secluded dream time. Jasmine will screen his calls. She'll cull reviews from the fax machine, destroying all but the raves. She'll get him in shape for another round, far away from anyone whose idea of conversation is discussing last weekend's grosses. And maybe, just maybe, he'll get lucky again. What better place to nurse a new start than your original training camp?

Of course, the town has changed. There used to be a sort of seedy distinction to Port Pritchard when most of the population worked on fishing boats or farmed the fertile valley on the outskirts of town. The people with whom Whit felt a kinship in his brief time here—outsiders, artists, political refugees—were drawn by the area's beauty and low cost of living. Now Port Pritchard was a bona fide, travel-guide-certified destination for all the tourists having breakfast at the dining room tables around Whit, getting ready to stroll down Main Street and patronize the Victorian-style shops, ice-cream parlors, espresso stands, and brew pubs that had sprung up to cater to them. Pleasure craft vied with working boats for space at the Fishermen's Terminal docks—another major difference—and from the window where he sat, Whit saw just a few utilitarian establishments: hardware shop, net-making loft, marine supply warehouse, feed and seed store. Apart from the Pioneer Market, the only place unchanged was the Tavern, where Phoebe used to sing. Even now, after all these years, Phoebe still shone for him. It probably wasn't fair, the way he kept comparing other women to her, gauging to see if their minds were as sharp, their empathy as great, their complexions as flawless. As though his memories were enough of a yardstick to measure such things by! He tried not to do it, he really did, but his time here with Phoebe had been so seminal, so unknown to anyone else, he just couldn't help himself.

Carl Brown had assured Whit that tourists disappeared when the rains came; nobody felt like clicking cameras or licking ice-cream cones then. Whit, on the other hand, was drawn by the rain. For him, the most attractive symbols on a weather map were hash marks. He liked to think rain matched the climate in his soul. But if the atmosphere or isolation ever became too much for him, he was getting such a deal on the Owl Island place that he could afford to escape for a spell. The price of a waterfront home on any of the trendier islands would have cleaned him out, forced him to go whoring for studio jobs or, even worse, TV movies. He congratulated himself on finding a little piece of paradise where none of his old neighbors in Santa Monica or Marin would ever think to look. Those showboat liberals who decorated their overpriced ranches in the hinterlands with indigenous baskets and blankets, then sent off checks to strangers in support of Native American causes. Could any of them, when it came right down to it, actually walk their talk? Would they ever do something as risky as he was about to do—sign a lease for tribal land, then buy a house on it and live there? Of course not. That would require guts. That would require a sense of poetry, not to mention justice. Qualities the business they were in—as distinct from the business Whit was in—didn't value.

As the waitress poured a refill for Whit, Carl entered the dining room wearing a red floral Hawaiian shirt, shorts, and sandals. The kind of clothes only a woman should ever wear. "Gorgeous day," Carl said, taking a seat across from Whit.

"If I wanted sunshine," Whit replied, "I would have stayed in California."

Carl laughed. "Don't worry. It won't last."

"I'm counting on that."

"Wonderful party you missed last night," Carl told Whit. "The neighbors are all excited about you moving in."

Whit was appalled. "You told them about me?"

"Nothing personal, only that you're a director."

"That's personal in my book."

"It's a small community. Everyone knows the Miller place just sold."

"I don't want everyone knowing my business."

"Of course not. Artists need their privacy. I respect that." Carl popped an Altoid into his mouth. He reminded Whit of an agent who once represented him, a portly, garrulous fellow who liked to say Whit was a European filmmaker born by accident to Baptists in the Bible Belt. (The Traynors of Culleoka, Tennessee, were actually all Church of Christers, so dour they made even hard-shell Baptists look frivolous, but their religion wasn't well-known enough to make a pithy punch line.) Where Carl had a stripe of white hair in his beard, this agent had one in his ponytail, and instead of Altoids, the agent irrigated his mouth with Binaca drops. Even beyond such particulars, agents were a lot like lawyers. They could help you only if you didn't need them.

Carl kept talking about last night's barbecue. "The woman who gives it every year, she's a real one-off. Smart as a whip, always knows what flick's playing at the art house in Mount Jensen."

"Is that her party trick? 'Thursday the sixth, *L'Avventura*'—no wonder everybody has such a ball."

"My point is, you and your girlfriend—"

"Wife."

"Well, the two of you have more than you might think in common with your new neighbors. Some of them, anyway. The north side's probably a little too scruffy for your taste, but we've gotten up a wine-tasting club on the south side. Going to Sonoma in the fall and France next spring. We'd love to have you and Jasmine join us."

"Yahz-meen," Whit said, "is the way they said it in Persia."

Carl frowned. "Is your wife Persian?"

"No."

"Is that the way *she* says it?"

"No."

"Okay, just checking. Well, you won't be sorry if you hook up with the wine club. These are all good people."

"There's just one problem, Carl."

"What's that?"

"I'm not interested in people."

Carl bent closer and spoke in confidential tones, as though dodging eavesdroppers. "I've watched some of your movies since the last time you were here, Whit."

"On video?" Then, when Carl nodded: "Too bad. You don't see the whole frame on video."

"I'll tell you what else you don't see," Carl said. "Car chases. Explosions. Violent deaths."

"No," Whit agreed. "Those all cost money."

"Man, your movies are deep. Important, too. They're about the human condition."

Whit recognized Carl's assessment from a quote on the back of a video box. "Compelling drama of the human condition." Another way of saying don't expect much plot.

"I'm no film buff," Carl continued, "but I can tell you this. You are most definitely interested in people. You don't make movies like yours if you aren't interested in people."

"Want to bet?"

Carl grinned at what he took to be Whit's self-deprecating humor. Those who didn't know Whit well often responded this way. No matter how cutting his words, Whit's still-boyish face and Tennessee accent erased the edge, eliciting solicitous feelings in people who instead ought to be shoving off in an insulted huff.

Carl signaled the waitress and ordered a full breakfast.

"I hope you don't mind eating alone," Whit told him. "I'm going out with Jasmine later."

"I know, I know—you want the lease." Carl unzipped his attaché case, then laid down a single sheet of paper and his Montblanc pen. "It's a standard contract, renewable every five years, just like we discussed. The jumps are a small percentage, basically cost-of-living increases."

Whit's sunglasses hid his widening eyes. Was Carl such a rube that he expected him to sign right now, on the spot? "My attorney has to go over this," Whit said.

"You tell him to call me if he has any questions." Carl lifted his latte with a toasting gesture. "To your health and happiness on Spit in the Wind Road."

But Whit wasn't listening to Carl. He was squinting out the window at a woman with long shining hair wearing black cargo pants and a crisp white shirt, sleeves cuffed at the elbow. She caught his eye while rushing out of the shadowed post office and crossing the street. Whit couldn't see her face very well—he needed a new prescription for distance and the sun was in his eyes. Her face didn't matter, though. What caught his attention was how, once she stepped into the light, this woman reacted as though the object she held in her hand had just come to life. He recognized in her movements a familiar quality of slow, distinct deliberation—

a childlike quality that had always drawn him to women, one he looked for and encouraged in actors. Standing very still, the woman outside gently turned the object, examining it from every angle. Then her shoulders started shaking. She was crying. Over something small and surprising. Maybe Great-grandma's tourmaline ring, mysteriously baked into the muffin she had for breakfast. A piece of flesh cut from the ear of a spurned lover. The key to a castle in Kilkenny. Whatever it was, Whit felt pretty sure he could imagine something better. Something that surpassed reality. Something preferable to reality. Something stripped of all reality's deadly daily details. That's the business *he* was in.

Whit grabbed Carl Brown's pen and sketched what he had just seen on the back of a napkin, in three separate frames. Why not? Movies had grown for him before out of less than this.

5

August 19, 1970
Clambake Heaven

My Dear Phoebe,

   Countless artifacts, visions, pieces of poetry and music reminded me of you over the summer. I wanted to share them. But a little nymph told me you were casting your shadow across Europe, with no fixed address. I hope you had a coffee for me at one of Kiki's haunts—the Dôme, the Rotonde, the Parnasse Bar. (All more vivid somehow than anywhere I've actually been.) Maybe you were even able to manage a glass of wine. Surely in Paris, a wise-beyond-her-years sixteen-year-old (Happy Birthday to you!) rates a *ballon de rouge, non*?

   I'm chasing across the Northwest landscape these days. Phoebe, I am making a film. No *Children of Paradise,* this. But it is about art. And truth. And beauty. Can't hire actors to play artists on account of how I can't afford 'em. This is a documentary, I'm forced to use the real things. Oh well, we works with what we gets. In this case, a small grant. How small is it (said the lady to the sailor)? So small I'm living out of car, suitcase, and sardine cans. I'll miss talking to you on the air. But I'll check the mailbox at KARP whenever I blow through town to see if there's anything in it for me (that's just the kind of guy I am).

It's all a little rough around the edges just now, but believe me when I say life is but a dream. So row, row, row your boat, my little friend, and don't forget to sing your songs. I feel happily insane in saying so impulsively, so unreasonably, so irrationally, I love you.

Whit

Phoebe had torn into the envelope at the mailbox and sat on the front porch to read it, going over the last sentence again and again. Whit actually said it—no, wrote it. Point blank, no doubt about it, on the same onion-skin paper with the same hole-punching typewriter as before. She felt a little badly now about telling him she'd gone to Europe, but refused to let remorse gnaw away at the bigger thrill, the thrill of being loved. Whit's letter was the best thing to happen since she came home from camp.

She folded the letter, tucked it into the bib pocket of her overalls, and went inside. Pearl lay sleeping on a hospital bed in the living room, face bloated from drugs, skin mottled from radiation treatments. Her beautiful red hair was gone, too—some of it shaved away for surgery, the rest cut short and falling out in clumps from the chemo. It felt like Pearl had died while Phoebe was away, and this frail stranger had taken up residence in her broken body. Just walking to the bathroom wore her out.

Pearl opened her eyes as Phoebe approached.

"Ready for lunch?" Phoebe asked. "There's chicken soup and cold cuts in the fridge."

"No, thanks, dear."

She tempted Pearl by offering to go get the kind of food they always liked best when they went out to eat together, just the two of them. A French dip from Manning's Cafeteria on the Ave, where ladies in hairnets and plastic gloves served them. Pizza from Harry's, where the owner threw dough up in the air. A burger from the Burgermaster, where they brought the food out on trays that attached to the car.

But Pearl just shook her head. "Really, I'm fine."

"You have to eat, Mother."

"I'll have something later. Don't wait for me."

Phoebe sat beside the bed and picked up her mother's worn old edition of *Pride and Prejudice*. Pearl saw double since her surgery. "How about some more Elizabeth and Mr. Darcy?"

"How about a song instead?"

Phoebe reached for her hand. She knew dozens of daytime songs that Pearl had once sung to her, songs that would have been happier, more cheering, than the only one that came out of her mouth—"Don't Go in the Lion's Cage Tonight," about the girl whose lion-tamer mother gets eaten by her beast. When Phoebe finished, she blinked back tears. "No wonder I'm warped. Daddy actually thought that was a great song for kids."

"You're not warped. You're a very special girl."

Now the tears were too many to catch. "You're not going to die, are you?"

Pearl squeezed her hand hard and didn't let up the pressure. "I'll do my best to stay alive, all right?"

Everything seemed backwards. Now, when Phoebe *wanted* her to lie, when she wanted her to promise that she'd live forever, Pearl was telling the truth. "I wouldn't have left if I'd known."

"I didn't want to spoil your summer."

What could she say that wouldn't make Pearl feel worse than she already did? She was probably just trying to keep Phoebe safe inside her Magic Circle, a place where mommies with cancer were unimaginable.

That Phoebe *had* enjoyed the summer only added to her present pain. How could she have been doing something so trivial as having fun while this was happening? Not until now, in retrospect, could she see the signs. Pearl hadn't sent as many postcards as usual. Birthday presents from Pearl and Jack last month were gift certificates for books and records; they usually went all out for this occasion, shunning anything so generic as a gift certificate. Phoebe hadn't heard from Jack at all. *Daddy's very busy,* Pearl had written. And so Phoebe came home to the shocking sight of Pearl, and Jack so distraught she knew he didn't have it in him to mislead her the way her mother had, letting her believe everything was fine. Nothing here was fine. Nothing here was the same. It was as if someone had detonated a bomb in her house.

Pearl's keeping the tumor on her brain a secret as long as she could seemed of a piece with another secret Phoebe had discovered while at camp. "Why didn't you ever tell me you were Jewish?" she asked now.

Pearl sighed, withdrawing her hand. "Your grandma didn't raise me Jewish, either."

"But at least you knew you were, didn't you?"

"It made life so much harder, Phoebe. I didn't want that for you."

"Harder how?"

Pearl picked up a glass of water and took a sip. "It's a long story, honey. You'll have it all someday, I promise. Who told you?"

Phoebe shrugged. "I just kind of figured it out."

Pearl lay back on her pillows and closed her eyes. "I need to be quiet now," she said.

* * *

It was really Bobby Shore, a counselor at camp, who figured it out about Pearl. Phoebe was drawn by Bobby's dark good looks as well as the fact that he knew all the verses to "Joe Hill," the old union song her grandmother Hannah had taught her. Hannah rarely came to Seattle, but sometimes Pearl would drive to Olympia with Phoebe to visit Hannah at her musty-smelling bookstore. One day in the barn with Bobby, Phoebe conjured Hannah, who died when Phoebe was five, by imitating her speech. "Come here my dollink leettle Pheebala, I'll put a reebon in your hair."

Bobby looked up from the horse he was currying. "I didn't know you were Jewish," he said.

"My grandmother was Russian, not Jewish."

"Maybe Russian, but definitely Jewish. So you are, too."

"I am?"

Bobby laughed, then saw she wasn't joking. "No question."

Phoebe sang to him from one of Pearl's lullabies. *"Shlof mayn tokhter, sheyne, fayne in dayn vigele . . ."* When she finished she asked Bobby, "Do you know what that means?"

"I can make out a little: Sleep my pretty daughter, I'll rock you in your cradle—that kind of thing. It's definitely Yiddish. Didn't your mother ever tell you?"

"No." But Pearl's omission didn't matter nearly so much then as Bobby's suddenly heightened interest in her. Someone who helped you discover a secret about yourself was nearly as exciting as someone like Whit, who had to *be* a secret. Upon reflection, she felt dense for not recognizing sooner what Bobby had revealed. After all, in seventh grade she had been plucked from her school choir to sing in a symphony performance of

Leonard Bernstein's *Kaddish Symphony* and, as a result, knew every syllable of the Jewish prayer for the dead by heart. At the time, this meant no more to her than memorizing the German words to Brahms's *Requiem* for a similar production the year before. But she knew the Kaddish was in Hebrew. Why didn't she notice its resemblance to the sounds with which Pearl once sang her to sleep?

Late Sunday night, during the very time Whit would be on the air back home, Phoebe sneaked off to meet Bobby by the river. He played the trumpet, like Chet Baker, and as a result was a very good kisser. Not once did teeth clank or tongues tangle, and instead of getting sloppy and slurpy the longer they went on this way, like a lot of others she'd necked with, he just seemed to get more serious somehow. Not pushy or insistent, just focused and as intent as a heavy-lidded boy too turned on to talk could be. She felt herself go all soft and fluid inside, as if the rising heat between them had melted their limbs, fused them together. His mouth never left Phoebe's while he unhooked her bra and helped her out of jeans and panties—so smoothly it was as if they were performers in some gorgeous horizontal pas de deux. When Bobby unbuttoned his own jeans and put her hand inside, her breath quickened in surprise. She had expected stiff from what she felt straining against the confines of his Levi's. But who knew it would have a pulse, a rhythm, a beat? Finally, she was going to get as close as she wanted, as close as she could possibly be to another human being, one who would see her for everything she was.

That was what she expected, anyway, based on how it began. But for all her inexperience, what came next seemed, well, clumsy. It wasn't just Bobby's fumbling with a condom. After he got it on, everything felt frantic, quick and fleeting as the pain of his first deep thrust. Even incestuous somehow, as if sharing this heretofore unknown Jewishness of hers—and if Bobby was right about the mother counting for everything in this department, then she *was* Jewish, she could become an Israeli citizen if she wanted—well, it made them more like brother and sister than lovers, magnets for feelings of failure and shame.

"Were you scared?" Bobby whispered as Phoebe tugged on her boots.

"No, not a bit." But she could tell *he* was. Not so much by what they'd done. But by her, by how ravenous she'd been to do it, and her disappointment now that they were finished.

It wasn't until later, after she crept back to the tent she shared with four other girls and crawled into her cot, that Phoebe felt a stab of fear. She wasn't worried about getting pregnant; she trusted the rubber. Really, it didn't seem to be her own fear so much as Pearl's, penetrating Phoebe's bones, her blood. But what was it that Pearl could be so afraid of? And how could Phoebe protect someone whose job it was to make *her* feel safe? Someone who had done that job so well that now she could be freely faulted—for not coming across with all the necessary information, for not fully aiding and abetting the grandest quest Phoebe had managed to define, that of being her most authentic self. Jack wasn't any more religious than Pearl, but the Bible he sometimes consulted for crossword puzzles was inscribed on the first page with his name and christening date. Surely he must have known. He was a historian, he understood the importance of the past. Why would he help Pearl keep her in the dark? Never mind all the things she hid from her parents, an ever-expanding list that now included Bobby Shore. Teenagers were supposed to hide information from parents. What kept her awake for hours, while the other girls breathed steadily in moon glow all around, was wondering what else she needed to know that these professional educators were concealing. Only after imagining Whit standing next to her cot and crawling in beside her did Phoebe finally fall asleep.

"I realize you're unhappy with your mother's choice," Jack told Phoebe. The two of them were in the dining room, eating Sunday dinner. Phoebe had made meat loaf at Pearl's request, carefully following the directions on her recipe card, but when it was done it seemed Pearl's only real appetite had been for inhaling the aroma while it baked. After a few bites, she excused herself and went back to bed. "I might not have made the same choice if I were in her circumstances," Jack went on, keeping his voice low so as not to disturb Pearl. "But she didn't want to burden you. It's her illness, her decision."

"I guess it was her religion, her decision, too."

"What?" He chewed for a long moment. "Oh. That. Yes, it was." More chewing. "We were older when we met."

"What's that got to do with anything?"

"After a certain age, it's not so much someone's circumstances or experiences that define them. It's the mental or moral attitude that makes them feel most alive. I'm probably mangling this a bit, but Emerson says discovering the secrets of your own mind reveals the secrets of all minds."

Phoebe blew out an exasperated sigh. She wanted outright declarations of feeling and here he was, cloaking himself in someone else's thoughts. "They're right about you. The students, I mean. You won't take a stand. You're as bad as . . . " It took Phoebe a while to think of what, to Jack, would be the most cutting comparison possible. "You're as bad as Nixon."

"Phoebe!" For a second, she thought he was going to send her from the dinner table, the way he had when she was six and said she was voting for Nixon. But all he did was get up and take his plate into the kitchen, where he finished eating alone. Which hurt even more than if he had yelled and sent her away.

"Phoebe?" Pearl called from the living room. Phoebe expected she wanted a glass of water, maybe something from her room upstairs. But when she got there, Pearl just patted the bed beside her and Phoebe went to sit. "Don't gonna be mad at me," Pearl said. It was a childhood locution of her daughter's that she'd always mention in Phoebe's short-tempered moments. "The meat loaf was wonderful, it'll be even better when I have it tomorrow."

"Okay."

"What's wrong?"

Hearing the question, Phoebe forgot about why she'd been contentious with Jack and dissolved into the complicity she hadn't felt with Pearl for so long—not since she started writing Whit. Here was her chance to say, I did it with a college student this summer I'll probably never see again; am I a woman now? Or, Daddy would be upset if he knew, wouldn't he? Or, how old were you the first time? Things she might not have wanted to say if Pearl were well. But Phoebe just shrugged. "I'm all right."

"There's a movie on tonight." Jack had brought the television up from the basement den for Pearl. "Want to watch it with me?"

The movie was *Bell, Book and Candle*, with Kim Novak and Jimmy Stewart. While the titles ran Jack came out to join them, looking relieved to see Phoebe lounging beside Pearl. The movie had none of the visual style that Jack usually enjoyed, or the play of language Pearl preferred. As for Phoebe, she couldn't help but hoot at Kim Novak's appearance ("Does anybody really have eyebrows that arch that much?") and Jack Lemmon's portrayal of a beatnik ("He makes Maynard G. Krebs look like Allen Ginsberg"). Even so, for a few hours they were once more a family, all absorbed in the same Technicolor world of witches, warlocks, and true love facilitated by a magical cat.

"Terrific picture," Jack said when it was over.

After Phoebe started school again, Pearl went into the hospital with a seizure that turned out to be a stroke. When she came home, she had difficulty speaking and could barely move the right side of her body. Other people were in the house all the time. Nurses, physical therapists, friends who came to leave casseroles, those who tended to Pearl when the nurses were off-duty. Pearl cried at most everything Phoebe had to say, from "I love you" to "I'm taking out the trash."

If only they could talk again. If only Phoebe had fairy dust to sprinkle over Pearl and fix everything that was wrong. But she didn't, which made her not just sad but angry, too. Angry at Pearl for not going to a doctor sooner, when the tumor was smaller. Angry at Pearl's surgeon and oncologist, for putting her through such agony. Angry at Jack for collaborating with Pearl to shut her out. But the anger just deepened her sadness and made her feel small.

"Life goes on," Jack said, encouraging Phoebe to study and see her friends. But life didn't seem to be going on for Jack. It was all he could do to keep up with his course load and faculty meetings. He had less time than ever for Phoebe.

No more father, no more mother, no more thrilling voice on the radio every week, either. The first thing she did to get on with her life was tear her room apart, keeping nothing as it was but her books and Land of Make-Believe map.

Gone were the poster bed, the tulip-sprigged drapes, and all the stuffed animals Pearl used to arrange around Phoebe's pillow forts. The mattress now sat on the floor, covered with an Indian-print bedspread Phoebe bought on the Ave. She hemmed up a set of muslin curtains and took out the regular lightbulbs in her room, replacing them with red and blue ones. Incense or candles burned whenever she was there.

A lot of people were like her, people who knew there was more to life than high school and homework. She listened to their music on her turntable, read their books, made posters for their protests, got high with them at concerts, played guitar and sang with them in the park, used their IDs to get everything from beer to birth control pills. None of them were her age. She had outgrown people her age. A powerful current flowed through the world away from her house, away from her classrooms, away from all the sorrow and tedium that filled her up in those places. All she had to do to swim in it was point her toes and dive.

Whit's last letter had upped the ante of their correspondence, and Phoebe's reply was taking months to develop. Her mother's cancer, her father's opposition to the demonstrations she marched in and his disappearance into grief, her actual (as opposed to imaginary) lost virginity—she could have written pages and pages about any one of those things. But not to Whit. "Writing Whit" was a place she went to in her mind to escape all that. Besides, she sensed it would be too much reality—or the wrong kind—for him. No, she would stay his fairy girl, only one foot ever on the ground, light as a feather, barely clothed, lips warm from the sun. A bubble of laughter, a bubble of light. The girl alive to all the mysteries, who could unravel the ravelings. That was the girl she dreamed of being for someone. That was the girl who got Whit to say *I love you.*

First she had to puzzle over the letter's clues to be sure what he was up to now. A documentary about art. What kind of art? She turned over the envelope to check the postmark; a little town north of Seattle where notable disciples of the Northwest Mystics, along with one or two surviving originals, still painted. He must have been up there traveling around, doing research, filming interviews and landscapes.

Finally, when she was ready, when she had filled nearly half a legal pad with alternate versions of what she would tell him, Phoebe hauled Pearl's Underwood upstairs and put it on her desk. She decided against the Crane stationery; she'd outgrown that, too. Instead, she used a piece of pale yellow paper, leaving a big blank space on top of the first page. When she was done, she pasted on an intricate collage—a lotus flower in the center of a rippling pool, shooting silver hearts out in all directions.

November 18, 1970
Here, There, and Everywhere

Dear Whit,
    This time I'm writing you by candlelight.
    And this is what I've got to say. If you're insane, then I'm crazy. Because sometimes I hear music when there's no music around. When that happens, I think maybe it's coming from you. It's almost like you're still doing your radio show. Only now, a year after your voice came on the air that first time (Happy

Anniversary to us!), I'm the only one who can hear it. I don't know how else to explain it, except there's this space around me where a part of you lives, and we're together even though we've never met.

Hey, it's not just Kiki I'm onto. Little Miss Know-It-All knows a little (but not all) about Northwest artists, too. The ones I'm guessing your film's about. 'Twas my mammy's doing. She was no spring chicken, as they say, when she married. And before that, she collected local artists. Artists were sort of like rock stars to her, I think. I saved the copy of *Life* magazine with the Beatles on the cover, she saved the one with the article about Mystic Painters of the Northwest. Well. If anyone can make a magical documentary about them, it's you. I hope this helps lead you to all the places alive in your heart. When you get there, those places will sing for you. They'll tell you secrets and giggle in your ear. They'll be like me.

Coming home hasn't been easy. I feel a little trapped, wings beating against bars. I'm all for truth and beauty. But a lot of what I've discovered is confusing. Can you tell me something about boys? When do they figure out body and soul are meant to go together? Do they ever? Or do I have to wait for a man?

I'm taking your advice and singing my songs. In fact, I'll be singing them next Sunday afternoon in Volunteer Park. Why don't you come if you're around? If you can't make it, don't worry. We'll meet when our fate is ripe for meeting. In the meantime, I'm here listening.

Oceans and skies full o' love,
Phoebe

Five months passed before Whit's reply arrived. By then, Pearl was dead. And Phoebe was gone.

There had been no funeral for Pearl, only a gathering at home. The dining room table was covered with platters of baked chicken and sliced ham, turkey casseroles made from Christmas leftovers, fruitcakes, bottles of Côtes du Rhône and Sémillon, a cut-glass bowl filled with fruit punch, a coffee urn. Arrangements of scentless gladiolas, anemones, red roses, and lilies filled the living room. Phoebe moved through the crowd, receiving mournful pats and hugs, saying hardly anything at all. No one here had known her well since she was a child. If, that is, they knew her at all. Adam, Pearl's older brother, was a virtual stranger. Phoebe always had a vague sense that her parents didn't approve of Adam, an Ivy League attorney who belonged to Chicago's most elite clubs and Episcopal church. He looked uncomfortable in his expensive business suit among all these elbow-patched academics. "I'm so sorry for your loss," he told Jack and Phoebe, saying nothing of his own. Phoebe would be damned if she was going to ask him anything about Pearl's past, or what reasons he had for not wanting to be Jewish (surely they were different than Pearl's). Instead she wandered, listening to conversations about her mother. How she had worked her way through college and graduate school, inspired her students, made such lovely dinner parties.

What was wrong with these people? Why weren't they wailing and tearing their clothes? Why weren't they more, well, Jewish? Why wasn't she?

An older woman whom Phoebe had never met sought her out by the stairway. "You look so much like her, you must be Pearl's daughter."

"Yes, I am."

"I read about your mother in the paper. If my son had lived, you might have been my granddaughter."

Phoebe shook her head, not comprehending. "His plane went down in the Pacific," the woman explained, "less than a month after the wedding. She still had some things of his; I was hoping I might get them."

"My mother was married before?"

"You didn't know?"

Phoebe shook her head.

"Oh dear," the woman said. "Never mind, then."

Unable to think of anything else to do, Phoebe reached out to hug this stranger, recognizing the heavy scent she wore as Youth Dew, almost synonymous with crepe-skinned ladies in orthopedic shoes and pastel wool suits. Still, it was a relief somehow, exerting herself to comfort someone. Someone much older but smaller than Phoebe—though who knew how tall she'd been in another time, when her son was alive. "I'm sorry," the woman said as she pulled back to dab her eyes with an embroidered hankie. "I'm so very sorry." Then, turning, she walked away.

First a secret religion, now a secret husband. What else did Pearl hide from her? As Phoebe gripped the banister, head reeling, someone took her by the hand. Carla, a former student of Pearl's. She used to babysit for Phoebe—though "babysitter" never seemed the right description for Carla, who taught her to play the chords she so quickly mastered on her first child-sized guitar and let her stay up as late as she pleased. Carla who, with her frosted lipsticks and swinging straight curtain of blonde hair, had added an extra measure of urgency to Phoebe's already substantial hurry to become a teenager.

"Let's go upstairs," Carla said. She led Phoebe to her room and sat down on the bed. "I got pregnant when I

was at Brookland," she said. "Your mother never told
you, did she?"

"No. She didn't tell me anything." And with that,
Phoebe pitched onto the pillows with huge, rib-rocking
sobs, weeping more for the mother who didn't live long
enough for her to understand than for the one she had
lost. Carla held her until she was quiet. "I just thought
it might be something you'd want to know. That she
helped girls like me who got in trouble."

"How did she help?"

"She knew about a good doctor, she arranged everything. It makes you wonder, doesn't it? I mean, I volunteer at the women's clinic because of what happened to
me. But I never had the nerve to ask if anything like that
ever happened to her."

Another unanswered question. But at least the parts
were fitting together a little bit better now.

Carla drew the curtains and lit candles. They spent
the rest of the afternoon in Phoebe's room, with Carla
bringing up plates of food. Phoebe remembered a line
from one of the songs she and Carla used to harmonize
on: "I see by your outfit that you are a cowboy." Well,
she could see by Carla's outfit—a granny dress made
from fabric much like Phoebe's bedspread—that they
were alike as any two cowboys. Gone was the makeup,
along with whatever she had once used to straighten her
hair; Carla now had the wavy-haired, wide-eyed, clean-
scrubbed, Pre-Raphaelite look that was the vogue among
hippie girls. She lived in Eugene, where she went to the
university and sang in a band. The four years between
them never seemed to matter much in the days when
Carla was supposed to be in charge of Phoebe, and now,
as she promised Carla to keep in touch, they felt nonex-
istent.

*   *   *

Since Pearl's illness, the yard had grown wild and jungly. Chrysanthemums that should have been deadheaded hung shriveled on their stems. Weeds filled flower beds, grass and moss overran the flagstone patio. Blackberry vines crept up from the ravine, wrapping around fence posts and choking shrubs. Birdfeeders were empty of seed, but a squirrel who used to eat out of Pearl's palm still tapped every morning on the sliding glass door to the dining room, begging for peanuts no one had the heart to offer.

Inside the house were other signs of neglect. Towels covered a living room windowsill to absorb water from a leak in the caulking. A burner was out on the stove, the one Jack always heated his morning kettle for tea on, but he still turned the knob and set the kettle there unless Phoebe was around to remind him it didn't work. Newspapers piled up on the breakfast nook table in such thick stacks it couldn't be used, but Jack insisted they stay, claiming he'd get to them eventually.

Every morning Jack wore bloody dots of tissue on his face, marking the spots where he'd cut himself shaving. At night, he buried himself in student papers. Phoebe could help only by driving him to the university after breakfast and picking him up in the evening, by taking him grocery shopping, by preparing food. By turning into a shadowy, inadequate version of Pearl when all she wanted in the world was to be *more* than her grief. The idea of living like this for another two years, until she graduated high school, was already difficult. Then it became unbearable.

In the den was a large box filled with Pearl's old lecture notes. Jack meant to donate them to the university library as meticulous records of her most distinguished professors' classes. One night, alone in the house, Phoebe went through the box. Her mother had been a serious student. There were no doodles, no shopping lists, no scribbling of boys' names encircled by hearts on these pages—just sheet after sheet of complex thoughts in a tight, efficient, well-formed hand. Amid all the drab, aging cardboard notebooks, a bright red binder caught her eye. She flipped it open and saw that it was filled with more words, only these were loopier, looser, more hurriedly written. "For Phoebe when she turns eighteen," it said on the first page, dated last summer.

My earliest and most often repeated lesson in life was that you can't count on the people you love to stay alive. I wanted to give you a life free of my troubles, free of my losses, free of my pain. The past was a thing to flee, to escape, in order to survive.

Phoebe shut the notebook. She couldn't read it here, breathing air still thick from Pearl's medicines, Pearl's death. But she wasn't about to wait until she was eighteen to find out what her mother wanted her to know.

Instead of going to school the next day, she drove Pearl's Buick downtown and caught the ferry to Bremerton, staying on board with her mother's journal as the boat went back and forth, an hour in each direction, the city and mountains by turns receding and looming, rain spiraling around the Sound as if chasing light.

You knew that my father died of a ruptured appendix before I was out of diapers. One result of losing a parent so young, I've read, is that it gives an imagination for disaster. Well justified in my case—which I'll try to put down for you as best I can between all these damn hospital tests and treatments. I'm not sure why it seems so important. Maybe because the death I've so often thought I deserved seems likely now.

*I let you think my father was a Russian immigrant,
like my mother. But he wasn't. He was Dutch. What
they both were was Jewish. Mother never spoke of my
father. I suppose she was angry at him for dying, for
failing her the way everyone she loved inevitably did.
But I used to imagine that had he lived, life would be
perfect and I'd be his favorite, the way my brother
Adam was Mother's.*

Pearl described the misery of her childhood in Olympia,
where Hannah supported the family by opening a used-
book shop. Whatever energy Hannah had left after
escaping the shtetl and surviving the Depression was reserved for Adam, whose success would affirm the wor-
thiness of all her struggles. Hannah made sure Adam got
into Harvard when he graduated from high school, quo-
tas be damned. When Pearl graduated in 1938, she got a
course in court stenography. But first she left to visit her
father's family in Amsterdam. So many aunts and uncles, all transferring their abiding affection for Leo Blume
onto his blossoming, sixteen-year-old American daughter. Her passage was their graduation gift.

Phoebe remembered how Pearl used to say that since
she had skipped an early grade, she was lucky that she
developed a figure young; it helped her fit in with the
older girls in high school, when fitting in was everything.

She read on. What was to be just a vacation, with a
week in the city and another at the beach in Zandvoort,
turned into an extended leave. Pearl got a job, typing
and filing for the import business owned by her Uncle
Abe. She lived in his and Aunt Mirjam's house, bunking
with their daughter Erika. Soon, Pearl's good high school
German had paved her way to passable Dutch.

It was the happiest I'd ever been. I decided to stay and work and save money and go to school there. I was in love with Amsterdam, the smell of spices in Uncle Abe's warehouse, my family and their Sephardic community. So different from Olympia, where Jews were an oddity. And before long, I was in love with Hans. He was a distant cousin, just a few years older and an art student at the university.

Curled up in her booth on the ferry, Phoebe laughed out loud at Hans's come-on line to Pearl: *Of what importance do you think it that Hemingway makes Jake Barnes impotent?* She wished there were more about their romance on the page, but instead of confirming her hunch that Hans was Pearl's first lover—was Phoebe genetically programmed to start having sex at sixteen?— Pearl went on to describe what her Dutch family called "Hannah's Chicken Little letters" ordering her to come home. The first one arrived after Czechoslovakia capitulated to Germany. More letters followed, addressed to the family at large, filled with dire newspaper clippings and warnings, urging them to put Pearl on a boat and book their own passage. But despite the family's monitoring of German broadcasts and debates on Hitler's designs, none of them could imagine uprooting themselves the way Leo and Hannah had. They were all in agreement, not only about this but about Hannah, too.

They thought their dear Leo had married down, choosing a shtetl Jew for his wife. They knew the type, and her dark, doleful nature was no more appealing to them than to me. This, too, shall pass, they said. We'll be safe, they said. The fever will spike and disappear. I wanted them to be right so that my mother would be wrong, wrong as she was in favoring Adam.

Russia and Germany's nonaggression pact sent Mother spinning into high gear. A telegram arrived, offering to pay my way to the University of Washington for one year. The most generous gift she ever promised. I hated leaving, but I couldn't refuse. What if this proof of love was all I ever got from her?

On the boat trip to New York, I attributed my nausea to seasickness. When it persisted on the train ride west and my period failed to arrive, I realized I was pregnant. I fantasized about returning to Amsterdam to become a wife, to become a mother. But not for long. Hans was still more romantic boy than budding man. And a dream of mine was about to come true. The dream of Pearl the college girl, striding across campus in her saddle shoes and twin-sweater set, recreating herself in an intellectual world where no one knew her as the Russian book lady's daughter who slept in the back of the store. So I promised the little girl inside me—I knew it was a girl, I just knew—I promised her she could come back later. And you see? She did.

Ink splotched that place on the page, as if from a tear.

Mother called me a whore and said "those people" had ruined me. But the thought of an illegitimate grandchild was even more awful to her than a promiscuous daughter. She found a nurse who did safe abortions and I went to Seattle for the start of winter term. In May, as I studied for final exams, Holland surrendered to Hitler. With open sea to the north and west, the Reich to the east, occupied Belgium to the south, my family couldn't escape now if they wanted to.

*After V-E Day, when I finally learned what hap-
pened in Holland, I heard voices in my head. Uncle
Abe saying it was fortunate there were so few Dutch
Nazis. Hans saying he supposed he could live without
going to the movies for a while. And then they would
be sewing stars on their clothes, Aunt Mirjam and
Erika debating whether the thread should match the
star or the garment itself. Then deciding it best to report for labor service, still praying for a quick Allied
victory. Then the transports to Auschwitz. Then dead.
Everyone, including Hans. All gassed or lost to ty-
phoid. And what did I do? Got married as fast as I
could. To a lovely boy who died, too.*

Phoebe closed the journal and went into the ferry
cafeteria for a wad of napkins to mop her face. So much
more grief to outrun.

There were only a few pages of Pearl's journal left to
read, and Phoebe put off finishing. Not so much as with
a novel she didn't want to end, but because she hated the
idea of having even more new questions that could never
be answered.

A memory surfaced, one from a hot summer day when
she couldn't have been more than three. She was digging
in the dirt while Pearl gardened, and before lunch they
took a bath together. Sitting in that deliciously cool water, she wondered what it was like being a baby and
drinking milk from her mother's full round breasts, the
way Pearl said she had. When she leaned over and put
her mouth on Pearl's nipple to see if it still held anything
for her, Pearl told her no in a strange, sharp voice. After
that, there were no more naps or baths together. Pearl
began working in her study and Phoebe learned, with
difficulty, she wasn't allowed to disturb her.

Just a rough spot from an otherwise happy time—that's

all it was. Still, strange how she could have the same sort of cast-out feeling now, from such different causes. Only later, standing outside on the ferry deck with wet wind whipping her braids, was she struck by the weight of all the hours Pearl had spent barricading herself, her slow surrender to everything she'd buried so deep.

In the weeks that followed, Phoebe rode the ferry nearly every day, ditching school to play her Martin and sing for other passengers, picking up a little extra money with everything from "It Wasn't God Who Made Honky Tonk Angels" to "Surabaya Johnny," a despairing Brecht and Weill song few would think to do in that context, much less on guitar. In February, when the sun split clouds and crocuses cracked the earth, she took to hanging out at the Fishermen's Terminal in Ballard, where she had loved going as a child on fish-buying expeditions. It was always a sweet experience—literally, since part of the drill was Pearl buying ice cream or hot chocolate for her, depending on the season. But now what she liked to do was spend time with the fishermen—and the rare fisherwoman—laying out and mending nets behind the Terminal docks. She liked their talk, vivid and direct. And it soothed her somehow, watching them weave integrity back into their nets.

Pearl had been on her own at sixteen. Now Phoebe was, too, with her mother's maps to guide her. The map of the Land of Make-Believe, still hanging by her bed, and the map of Pearl's sorrow, inhaled like air and burrowing into her heart.

Perfect grades no longer hid Phoebe's truancy. She was failing, deliberately failing—the ultimate act of rebellion for a daughter of academics. No plea, no bargain Jack offered had any effect. He sold the Buick, but that was too little, too late. She was already unreachable. Dropping out of high school doesn't have to be the end of the world. That's what Phoebe's adviser told Jack. Phoebe's such an unusual girl. So talented. So loving. So obstinate. Don't cut her off. Stay involved. Give her substance to scratch up against when she needs it. She's too smart to destroy herself. But if you fight her on this, she might destroy you.

Phoebe could have written the script herself.

Carla invited her to perform at a music festival in Eugene. It was spring break, and Jack had to go on a retreat with the university president and other department heads to thrash out a policy toward student dissidents. What he really needed was to formulate a policy toward his daughter. "Eugene's three hundred miles away," Jack said. "How would you get there?"

"By bus," Phoebe said. "I already have my ticket."

"I don't think so, Phoebe. I'd be worried about you."

"I'll be fine; Carla will take good care of me."

In the end, Jack gave reluctant permission. If he couldn't control Phoebe, he couldn't very well ask another adult, some friend of the family's, to do it for him. She was going whether he wanted her to or not.

On the Sunday she was to return, Phoebe called collect. "Your map is gone," Jack said, meaning the map of the Land of Make-Believe.

"I know. I've got it with me."

"Your curtains, too. I should have looked before you left."

"Please don't feel bad; it wouldn't have made any difference. There's an extra room in Carla's house. She and her roommates say I can rent it. I'm staying here."

There was a long pause on Jack's end. "Am I really as bad as all that? As bad as Nixon?"

"Daddy, I love you. I just can't live with you anymore."

*   *   *

Jack included an envelope containing Whit's next letter
with the check he sent to Eugene for Phoebe's expenses.

April 15, 1971
Station WHIT
(KWIT west of the Rockies)

Dear Phoebe,

There is no question about it: I am a rotten pen pal
and you deserve better. But please be assured—in the
pile of mail I found waiting for me at KARP, the only
piece that mattered was from you. Even before
tearing open the envelope, I felt bigger inside
somehow. Like your words were sure to open up
some secret space. You write with a peach blossom
beauty, you know. I stared at your collage with a
huge hunk of the intensity that made it. I read
somewhere that lotus flowers have their roots in
river-bottom muck. Don't we all? So wiggle your feet
in it, honey, and while you're at it, make a few mud
pies.

As for boys versus men, since I'm barely keeping
my own particular pieces of body and soul together, I
am probably not the best source of advice. But it
does seem that one thing all the ancient books of
wisdom agree on is the impossibility of finding "it" if
you're hunting "it" down. So just keep yourself in as
good shape as possible. And then let it come to you.
It will. When you're ready. Just like these letters of
ours. It's ALL in the hands of destiny. And I never
screw around with destiny.

Whatever little bird sang into your ear about my
little film sang true. She is slooooooowly taking
shape. I'm trying to be a good father and not force

her into finishing school. When the time comes, I'll let you know when and where to look. I have a feeling your response will mean more to me than that of any critic who might stumble upon it.

I lean out from this page and kiss your cheek.

Whit

Well. These were sentiments that called for an immediate reply—even though once again, like at camp, Phoebe was without Pearl's black portable Underwood. She shot back a postcard she'd been hoarding for Whit ever since she found it. On the front was a Man Ray photograph of Kiki's face, sideways next to an upright African mask. On the back Phoebe wrote a sentence she'd been honing for days: *Must be love that makes every heartbeat of mine echo yours.* Then she printed her Eugene address. *Here's where I live now—everybody's sister, nobody's daughter.* That looked kind of pathetic. *I like it fine,* she added. Not the honest-to-God truth, but so much of her took shape in letters to Whit, maybe just declaring this would go a long way toward magically making it so.

Phoebe's life soon settled into its minimalist Eugene routine. After paying rent, she banked most of what Jack sent every month. Another housemate at Carla's had taught her how to knit and tie macramé knots. "They're cool things to do when you're stoned," she said, but to this girl, everything was cool to do stoned, from flossing teeth to peeling an apple. Phoebe had other ideas. Soon she was knitting socks and mittens, spinning knots into plant holders and wall hangings, items she could barter at the Saturday Market, swapping for a leather jacket, used books, the occasional burrito. She worked at the farmers' co-op in exchange for locally grown foods, and could often be found among the hippie welfare mothers who showed up by the Dumpsters at Safeway and Albertsons when trucks arrived with fresh produce, knowing that enormous amounts of aging fruits and vegetables would soon be tossed, theirs for the taking, to make room for a new shipment. Phoebe transformed the stale stuff into tasty stews, soups, and pies that her housemates devoured. Before long, she'd bartered a deal with them, too: reduced rent in exchange for "shopping" and cooking.

What better proof could Jack want of the success of all his Emersonian theories on raising a self-reliant child? Here she was, daily defining herself as someone responsible, thrifty, nurturing—not some crazy kid who ran away from home, piling more pain on her already grieving father. But it didn't feel like that so much as it did that essential parts of her nature were surfacing, parts that needed to function autonomously and exercise authority. Even a treasured only girl-child like her—blessed with lessons for every talent she ever showed, weaned on carefully edited and expressed concepts of truth and beauty— could find authority, real authority, something difficult to discover at home, where adults had already carved most of it up among themselves.

She applied some of this new authority to her body. No more shaved legs or armpits. No more harsh, perfumed deodorants. No more sore, enlarged breasts from birth control pills; now, she had a diaphragm.

Meanwhile, she wasn't exactly turning into a drudge. She sometimes sang at a coffeehouse where the owner paid her in psilocybin mushrooms and allowed her to collect tips. Missing salt air, she bought a bus ticket for Yachats ("Yah-hots," the Greyhound clerk corrected

when she said it to rhyme with "hatchets") and spent a
sunny October afternoon tripping her brains out in a secluded cove. There was a TV game show host who always used to ask his housewife contestants, in a big
booming voice, "How would *you* like to be Queen for a
Day?" Alone on the beach, Phoebe giggled, imagining
herself draped in ermine, only instead of winning the
right to reign over a Maytag washer-dryer or freezer the
size of a closet, she had an empire of crashing waves,
scudding clouds, squawking seagulls, and mussels big
enough to pry off rocks for that night's soup. All she sur-
veyed seemed capable of cracking jokes, assuming independent identities, even falling in love. Everything was
new and original, like a play improvised especially for
her. Although later, coming down on the bus back to Eugene, she had difficulty imagining being always engaged
by such a performance. Now it made a new kind of sense
that most druggy communes, which she was far too
worldly to ever want to join, were located in isolated,
rural areas. Who could stand to be always alive that
way anywhere else? Better to absorb the awareness so it
became a kind of technique, there for the tapping. By
whom? By her chosen people, of course. By artists. If
time had all the dimensions she was beginning to suspect, maybe in some intrinsic sense she *was* that love
child Pearl had conceived with Hans, sent away but
invited to reappear later and discover her source like
this.

When Carla had a paper to write or an exam to study
for, Phoebe substituted with her band. It was amazingly
easy to end up having sex with somebody she found attractive, though rather more difficult to do it more than
once or twice; when told how old she really was, they
would either back off, nervous and embarrassed, or go

overboard in the opposite direction, as if she had suddenly become nothing but a piece of fine fresh pussy. Either way, it killed whatever fun she'd been having.

The Kiki postcard Phoebe sent to Whit came back to her in an envelope, with his additions printed in the margins around her original message.

Mine yours, too, praise the Lord and amen . . .
Checked the schedule down your way, so you are
hereby ordered to park your precious self in front of
Channel 7 on the 23rd, 9 o'clock.

Phoebe watched Whit's documentary alone, sitting inches away from a tiny black-and-white portable—the only television in the house. It didn't matter, not having color, since the film was in black and white, too. There was no narration, no explanation, no questioning voice coming out from behind the camera. Still, you knew exactly what was going on because of the deft, intuitive way Whit intercut images of Northwest Mystic paintings with interviews, archival footage, and long pans of shorelines, wetlands, mountainsides, and migrating geese. There was music, too. Smoky jazz, spare Satie, lush classical guitar. From start to finish, Phoebe sat in open-mouthed awe, much as she had spent her day in Yachats. He did it, he captured that awareness—in every object, every brushstroke, every leaf, every stone.

Again she wrote to him with pen and ink.

Nobody else but you could have made this film. You might not believe me, but I felt you in almost every frame. Terrific picture, absolutely terrific. It's going to change your life. I know it did mine. What's next?

Why not a movie-movie, about Kiki? I'll bet that
would sell a lot of popcorn.

When she'd been in Eugene for a little over a year,
Phoebe finally received a reply, typed on a sheet of doctors' notepaper advertising Valium.

I'm in trouble, and it's all your fault. My mouth
wrote a check on Kiki that my brain's having a tough
time cashing. Rented a house in a fishing village built
on stilts, far away from bill collectors and distracting
women. The Port Pritchard post office will be a
regular haunt, so come August please write me there,
in care of the blues. Do your books travel with you?
If so, I have a favor to beg. I've looked everywhere,
and I do mean everywhere (libraries, antiquarian
bookstores, behind refrigerators), but I can't find a
copy of Kiki's memoirs *en anglaise*. If you would be
so kind as to loan me your edition again, I promise
to treat it like fine bone china. Meanwhile, permit
me the cliché of observing how quickly time flies as
prelude to inquiring—are you eighteen yet?

Inside the envelope were newspaper clippings, three
different stories with underlined words in each.

"It happened all of a sudden, just like in a movie,"
Gomez said. "I went after him, got stabbed in the hand
but then knocked him out by throwing a chair at his
head."

It reads just like a movie script: a man convicted of a
crime nurses the sick officer whose testimony convicted him; a friendship builds, and on his deathbed

the officer clears his friend, thus bringing a happy ending to the story.

An Israeli soldier said, "I was standing next to a glass partition with dozens of other people when all of a sudden explosions erupted, <u>just like in a movie</u>."

Phoebe pieced it together pretty effortlessly: He was following her advice, trying to write a movie about Kiki. She sent back another Man Ray postcard, the one with an image of a violin superimposed on Kiki's nude back, as though the camera had caught her in the process of transforming into a stringed instrument.

Real life, just like in the movies. Who could ask for anything more?
    The book's in Seattle. Don't worry, I'll get it for you.

Carla was cramming for finals when Phoebe sang for her one Saturday night. The gig was at a tavern in Blue River, fifty miles outside Eugene but still in Lane County. Between sets, Phoebe sat with Robbie, the good-looking Vietnam vet who tended bar. Phoebe never drank liquor, but by evening's end she was looped on tequila shots and scrambling lyrics to an old Tina Turner song. "Do I love you, my oh my," she sang. "Mountain deep, river high."
    Phoebe was in no shape for the long ride back to town, so Robbie brought her home with him, to his trailer on the banks of the McKenzie River. She stood in a hot shower for five minutes at Robbie's insistence, then stumbled into his bed, naked and still drunk. He wouldn't touch her. Which was ironic, considering how they were awakened a few hours later by a county sheriff who

burst in to search for drugs; after failing to find any, he arrested Robbie for having sex with a minor. They'd been naked in the same bed—who would believe he hadn't? Certainly not this stern-eyed, silver-haired sheriff, in whose hands Phoebe's fake ID instantly fell apart.

"I'll tell you what," the sheriff said to Robbie. "You're awful goddamn lucky she's not *my* daughter."

"It's the truth," Phoebe said. "We didn't do anything. I was too drunk." Then, as if to prove it, she barfed all over the sheriff's shoes.

Robbie made his jailhouse call to a lawyer who got him off with a warning and a heavy fine. Phoebe wasn't allowed to place a call, but the sheriff made sure she heard every word of what he had to say when Jack got on the line.

"She's a beautiful girl, your Phoebe. Probably a nice one, too. But if you leave her down here, she'll be ruined forever. These people will turn her into trash. Is that what you want, Mr. Allen?"

Jack talked the sheriff into releasing Phoebe to Carla. Several days later, he arrived in Eugene by train and took Phoebe out for dinner in a Greek restaurant near the university. Neither one could meet the other's eyes. "Here's the book you asked for," Jack said, placing Pearl's copy of Kiki's memoirs on the table. "I hope she's not your role model."

"I'm not trash," Phoebe countered hotly. He didn't respond, but the waiter who had just set down a bowl of avgolemono soup in front of him flashed her a sympathetic smile.

Jack sampled the soup. "It's good," he said. "Nice and light—not too much lemon, just the way you like it. How about a taste?" Phoebe shook her head. Then, between spoonfuls, Jack continued. "I have a proposal I want you to give serious consideration. I think that instead of going back to high school, you'd be much happier signing up for a course to earn a high school equivalency certificate."

"I'm not coming home," Phoebe said.

"You can do it here. I'll be in Eugene this summer, too, teaching a labor seminar. Tomorrow I'll look for a rental close to campus."

"When did you arrange all this, Daddy?"

"A while ago."

"Before that sheriff took me in?"

Jack held her gaze steady for a long, convincing moment. "Yes." He pushed away his empty soup bowl and steepled his fingers with a sigh that said they need never speak again of that night, that sheriff, that phone call. "So. My idea is, we'll both have our classes and such during the day. Then in the evenings we can do things together."

"What kind of things?"

"Whatever we find appealing. Dinners, movies, plays, concerts."

"I like the sound of that," Phoebe said.

"In the fall," Jack went on, "you can start school."

"Start school? I can't even apply before I get the certificate, can I?"

"You don't even need to apply. A former student of mine is dean at a junior college in Mount Jensen. He's willing to take you on right now, so long as you commit to getting your equivalency. It's pretty up there, the school is small—a fine place to start. If your grades are good, and I see no reason why they won't be, you can transfer after a year or two to a school of your own choosing."

"Is Mount Jensen near Port Pritchard?"

"Yes, I believe it is."

Phoebe was growing weary of her Eugene routine, its

dearth of intellectual challenge. And it was nice, *very* nice, to feel looked after again, to anticipate sharing all the things that had once held her close to Jack. But none of that mattered anywhere near so much as her absolute certainty that his plan had the fingerprints of destiny, with a capital *D*, all over it. Not that she had dreams of being a college girl, like her mother did. All her fantasies about going to school in Mount Jensen centered on Whit. By the time she got there, she would indeed be eighteen, of legal age.

"Do you believe in fate, Daddy?"

"Only in Emerson's sense—'the soul contains the event that shall befall it.'"

What better way to have her ticket to Whit punched than by her own father?

In exchange for her agreement to everything Jack proposed for the summer, Phoebe asked only one thing: that he ship Pearl's Underwood down to her as soon as he got home. Her letter to let Whit know all this, the letter that would accompany Kiki's memoirs, had to be an especially good one.

6

Jasmine was still a bride, really. Whit bought the Owl Island house on their wedding trip. He did it impulsively, but that was his nature when it came to giving her presents, and the bungalow on Spit in the Wind Road was the best one yet. A new home, where no one else had ever slept with him. A new bed, too—she had insisted on that. Sweetly, but with a touch of wifely starch. Which was her privilege now, along with exercising all the domestic talent constrained by years of roommates, studio apartments, and necessary frugality. Jasmine LaFleur Traynor, née Donna Price, had a lot to keep her busy.

The structural changes Whit wanted for the house were at last complete, light and height transforming what had been a tumble of fusty, dark, low-ceiling rooms into bright, open sweeps of space with quartersawn oak floors. Custom-designed appliances were all in place, along with the cabinetry encasing them. While Whit traveled the film festival circuit, showing his new movie in Toronto, Chicago, Denver, Austin, and San Francisco, Jasmine drove north from Mill Valley for all the finishing touches—having the bathroom tiled and the interior painted, supervising the movers when their things arrived. Meanwhile she made do with a carton of kitchen supplies, a folding table and chairs, a portable stereo, and an air mattress.

Despite all the excitement of this new beginning, it wasn't long after Jasmine arrived on Owl Island that she felt her mood deflating. She had expected more of a welcome. Some casseroles, maybe, or offers of help, which of course she would politely decline. Instead, nothing but a case of wine from Carl Brown, the tribal attorney, who must have gone a little overboard in broadcasting Whit's privacy requirements to the community—requirements Whit had spelled out to Carl in a fax.

> *Under no circumstances will we welcome unexpected visitors, solicitors, envoys, or emissaries.*

"Do you really think that's necessary?" Jasmine had asked Whit.

"Trust me," Whit said. "You've got to hit this guy over the head."

Only a few days into the month she'd be spending here alone, Jasmine wasn't sleeping well. Disembodied voices, belonging to a man and a woman, kept her awake. Discussing what kind of curtains to put up in the bedroom, plain cotton or chintz. Worrying over whether the furnace needed to be replaced. Gossiping about their acquaintances, all dull as dishwater. Those who didn't possess the gift usually regarded ghosts as vaporous creatures who hung around pining for everything they'd left behind, or emanating evil intentions toward creatures occupying the space once theirs. But however much their first spectral words always made Jasmine's stomach quiver, she knew them to be annoyingly preoccupied with the mundane, like the majority of living creatures. Maybe these voices in her bedroom weren't from ghosts at all. Maybe they were conversations from the past that had bled into the present. Tonight they were weighing the pros and cons of double-glazed windows.

The Proton clock radio's glowing blue dial read 3:00 a.m. Jasmine got up and heated a cup of sake in the microwave. Then she went to her laptop and punched up two relocation charts, one for her and one for Whit, on Owl Island. Sipping sake, she studied the charts. His was a dream, with transiting and natal planets aligned so that they were practically blowing kisses at each other. But hers was a nightmare of hard angles presided over by stern, unforgiving Saturn. If Jasmine were reading for a client, she'd say opposition creates growth. She'd say friction, not harmony, produces pearls. She'd say progress never occurs without challenge. Blah blah blah. This chart was hers, goddammit, so she got depressed.

Normally, she knew better.

Charts were just a piece of the pie. A branch on the tree. A slough off the river. More valuable to her as a prop than anything else. It kept people from getting spooked if they thought something tangible, like an astrological chart, was telling her their secrets, when in fact Jasmine's best hits tended to come directly off someone new. Someone who, no matter how skeptical, arrived radiating information—the way Whit did when they first met. She had a terrible time reading anyone with whom she was on intimate terms, a category that included herself. Tougher still was trying to pinpoint an event yet to occur; even when clearly seen, it never floated up attached to a timetable. She could only fix it on the folds of something like accordion pleats that resisted flattening, then guess at whether the folds represented days, weeks, months, or years.

Was Jasmine a gifted medium or an inordinately skilled, sensitive observer? What a tired old question.

Thank God Whit didn't think in such black-and-white terms. What's more, he had no interest in testing her with predictions of his future. Mercury conjunct Jupiter in Aquarius—he would rather be surprised.

Finishing off her sake, Jasmine deleted the computer charts, rinsed her cup in the kitchen sink, set it on a towel to dry, and went back to bed. Maybe she was just going buggy. Her only company these days consisted of workmen and the collarless young white female cat Jasmine cuddled when she showed up, but only outside, since Whit was allergic to cats. Jasmine called the cat Katie, and learned from their wordless, picture-packed conversations that Katie lived in a new place with a swinging cat-door, but preferred mice and birds to the food she got at home. Whit phoned at least once, sometimes twice, every day, needing her encouragement. Still, she was lonely enough to ring up her mother in Chico and spend an hour talking to her.

Jasmine's mother, who still called her Donna, regarded Jasmine's professional skills as little more than a fancy version of her own ability to locate lost objects or know who was on the line before she picked up the phone. "It's something I can count on, Donna, but I surely wouldn't want to *bank* on it," she said now.

"I didn't call to be criticized, Mom."

"Well, I'm afraid you're not going to have much time for that kind of thing anyway, not after your husband gets there." She never referred to Whit by name, only as "your husband."

"Why? What are you talking about?"

"Nothing, honey. I didn't mean anything by it."

"Yes, you did."

"I just see you being . . . awfully busy, that's all. You're the young one, you have all the energy." Her way of noting that Whit was a little older than Jasmine's parents, who, when she was born, had been well into their twenties. But Jasmine's parents weren't artists, and the one time they had all been together, for the wedding at Whit's house, anyone could tell Whit looked like a kid compared to them. Still, in her present state of mind, her mother's comments were rattling, disturbing. Did she really see something?

That night, Jasmine was awakened not by ghost voices but by loud, plaintive cat yowls. The next morning she went outside to take Katie onto her lap and saw red, raw-looking marks through the flattened blood-flecked fur on her neck. My God, what was wrong with these people? Why didn't they keep their cats inside? Hadn't they ever heard of feline AIDS?

The phone rang and Jasmine ran inside to answer. Instead of saying hello, she burst into tears. "Katie's been raped!"

Whit was pretty upset, too. He peppered her with questions, not giving her time to answer. Who was she talking about? Where did it happen? Was Jasmine remembering to lock up at night? Could she get someone out today to install an alarm system?

Then he found out Katie was just a cat.

"Jesus, Jas," he said, expelling a huge sigh of relief. "I hope you didn't let her into the house."

Jasmine sat in her new kitchen with its honed black granite counters and bird's-eye maple cabinets making drawings of all the rooms in the house, deciding where their things would go. When the van arrived, she was ready to direct the movers: the Chinese cabinet, French armoire, and art deco sofa went together over there; the Japanese chest of drawers, African mask, and abstract American landscape over here. Whit had a talent for combining disparate styles in a spare, effortless way. Whatever he chose was for itself, not because it would work with everything else, but his eye was so good that somehow, it always did. Jasmine had grown up surrounded by the typical suburban hodgepodge of stuff, objects chosen less out of feeling than necessity and compromise. But Whit was incapable of compromise when it came to anything visual. A quality she imagined as a kind of shield, protecting her from shabbiness, from ordinariness, from predictability. All the things she had so intentionally left behind in Chico.

When the rest of the house was squared away she unpacked the boxes in Whit's study, putting all his books and scripts on built-in birch shelves. The old Remington on which Whit had written his first script went atop an Ashanti stool, like sculpture on its stand. He never used the machine—he wrote his scripts now on an aging Selectric—but he kept the Remington around as some kind of icon. Whit was hopeless when it came to assembling electronics, so Jasmine hooked up the computer he had yet to master, along with the phone, fax machine, and printer, then tucked the wires together behind the long waxed mahogany table he used as a desk.

Finally, the house began to seem like home. Her new domain. Lovelier than anywhere she'd ever lived before, with views of mountains and sparkling water from nearly every room. The house was small, with only two bedrooms and one bath, but after a few more movies, they'd build an addition. She liked the area, too. Not so clogged and snooty as Santa Monica or Marin. Jasmine felt silly, letting herself be unnerved by the voices, her mother, the charts, the cat. The voices could be tuned out. So could her mother. As for the charts, now her mistake was ridiculously obvious; what she should have done was configure her and Whit's birth data into a single, composite chart before casting for relocation. As for the sweet little cat, well, Katie wasn't Jasmine's responsibility. None of it mattered. What mattered was that here, far away from anyone who knew other women in Whit's life, she would be the undisputed queen. Taking care of Whit, of course, but hardly at her own expense. He had already shown her the world in a way none of the actors, bartenders, or baristas whom she used to see could afford. Before Whit, she'd needed her passport only for occasional trips to Mexico; now she'd experienced powerful past-life recollections in film festival cities like Cannes, Berlin, Venice.

Jasmine's chores took on a more pleasurable, sensual flavor. She went to the Co-op in Mount Jensen to stock up on basics for the Mediterranean-style meals she intended to prepare. It was her first trip there—one of the housepainters had told her about it. At last, all the stuff she had grown accustomed to that you couldn't find at the Pioneer Market in Port Pritchard: organic produce, imported cheeses, chicken and meat free of hormones and antibiotics. A lot like Wild Oats, where she went in Santa Monica, minus the atmosphere of status and ambition.

Even though Jasmine had a list, she found herself distracted by other shoppers. Might this one be a client someday? Would that one turn out to be her new yoga teacher? She noticed a striking woman who pushed through the aisles with an air of curiosity that belied her obvious familiarity with the place. *That's how I'd like to look when I'm forty,* Jasmine thought. *Still pretty, but not surgically altered—not so you'd notice, anyway. I'd stop coloring my hair, too, if the gray came in that gorgeous, if my skin was still so nice.*

Other people were also noticing this woman. They knew her. They liked her. They attended to her, too, calling out her name, leaning over counters for long chats.

Trailing along in her wake, Jasmine felt a kind of contact high. This was the good part of small-town life, the part she missed and wouldn't mind having again. Another shopper, a snappily dressed older woman with silky blonde hair, was especially glad to see the woman Jasmine was watching. "Phoebe!" she cried. "Where have you been keeping yourself?"

Phoebe—a pillowy name. It suited her. Jasmine studied cheeses while the women talked. It was always so easy, plugging into strangers—telling if some couple is married or having an affair, divining the preoccupations hiding behind social chitchat. Phoebe's friend was saying they ought to get together soon for a movie or dinner. "Sounds great, Margaret—I'll call." But Jasmine could tell Phoebe wouldn't, not anytime soon; this Margaret was someone she loved, but wanted to avoid. Interesting.

As Phoebe moved along, Jasmine followed at what she hoped was a discreet distance, investigating every display, every shelf, that drew Phoebe's attention, surprised to discover that she, too, needed pine nuts. And lemon verbena soap. And one of those clear plastic thingies that you stick onto the kitchen sink to hold your sponge. Putting these items in her cart made Jasmine so happy she could hardly believe she hadn't thought of them herself. Then Phoebe turned and looked at Jasmine, brows raised over exquisite violet eyes.

"My first time here," Jasmine explained.

"Do you plan on coming back?"

"I guess so. I mean, yes. Why wouldn't I?"

Phoebe laughed. "Don't forget to join when you check out. Member's discount, it really adds up."

Jasmine flashed her brightest, most dazzling smile. "Thanks, I won't forget." Then she pulled out her list and shoved off. Maybe next time they ran into each other, she would introduce herself. Even then, Jasmine would not let Phoebe know about the momentous pulse of change she'd picked up following her around the Co-op. Too bad she couldn't tell her sooner; beneath all the brightness, this was one very worried lady. But prematurely spilling such psychic beans would send all the wrong signals. It would make Jasmine seem like some wacky fortune-teller, a goofy gypsy too unscrupulous to use her real name, instead of the sophisticated, accomplished intuitive Jasmine knew herself to be.

Jasmine went to Seattle to have her hair cut and colored (not to cover gray, but to darken her natural nondescript brown) and her legs waxed. A regular client for whom Jasmine did telephone readings was an advertising executive in the city, and she had suggested a salon on Seventh Avenue.

Afterwards, Jasmine went on an even more personal, private mission, inspecting five different piercing parlors before finding one on Capitol Hill that met her standards. Much as she wanted to surprise Whit with an unexpected piece of jewelry, Jasmine wasn't about to go just anywhere, or let just anyone pierce such a delicate portion of her anatomy as she had in mind. The place on Capitol Hill featured a clean, private room and a refined female operator. Well, relatively refined. Layla looked like some wild, Ecstasy-induced, white-girl version of Topsy, with short platinum hair done up in dozens of little braids that stuck out from her head and a fistful of jewelry puncturing her eyebrows, nose, and ears. But Layla knew her stuff. She had not only pierced many labia, but had experienced the procedure herself.

Layla consulted with Jasmine in a backroom office, where no other operators or customers could overhear. "I had a woman do mine, too," Layla said. "It's just like going to a gynecologist. You want someone who's actually felt everything you'll be feeling. And this is really a breeze. The lidocaine shot is just a little pinch. That's it—then you're numb, you don't even feel it when the needle goes in. Believe me, not *one* of my ear pierces was so quick and painless."

Layla showed Jasmine all the instruments she'd be using and went through the aftercare protocol, which included abstinence from sex for a while. "That's not a problem," Jasmine said. "My husband is away."

"Cool." Layla looked at Jasmine as though taking inventory: no visible tattoos; only one dainty pair of earrings; simple, elegant clothes. Hardly Layla's standard client. "Your husband's tongue isn't pierced," she asked, "is it?"

"No, he's not the type."

"Good. My boyfriend's is, and that can lead to trouble."

"Really?"

"Yeah. His stud got caught in my ring."

"Ouch."

"You said it. Wanna pick out your jewelry?"

Jasmine chose a sexy little silver hoop with a small onyx bead. Layla directed her to a curtained-off area where Jasmine removed her panties and skirt and put on a smock. In the private room, after she lay down on an examining table covered with paper, Layla gave her a handheld mirror.

"What's that for?" Jasmine asked.

"So you can show me where you want the piercing."

Jasmine positioned the mirror in front of her crotch and pointed. "How about right there?"

"Excellent. Exactly where I've got mine." Layla marked the spot with an indelible felt-tip pen and swabbed Jasmine's vulva orange with Betadine. "You have the perfect physiognomy for this procedure," Layla said as she clamped the area with triangular-shaped forceps. Then, reaching for her long, thick hollow needle: "Some women are so small they're really hard to do."

As the needle went in, Jasmine turned queasy. She put the mirror down on her stomach, closed her eyes, and didn't look again until the hoop was in place.

"What do you think?" Layla asked.

In addition to being orange between the legs, Jasmine was swollen now, too. The glistening ring of silver looked strange, as if someone perverse had tried to make a nasty bruise or an overripe piece of fruit look festive. Jasmine had to close her eyes again to envision the eventual results. "Perfect," she said. "Just what I wanted."

Then she got dressed and drove back to Owl Island sitting on a bag of ice.

Two weeks later, the unveiling in their bedroom thrilled Whit every bit as much as Jasmine had hoped. His fingers found it first. For once, Whit was speechless. Or nearly, anyway. All he could say was, "My oh my." So much more erotic, piercing a secret tender spot rather than a public piece of flesh.

"I knew you'd love it," she told him.

"Oh you did, did you?"

"Has anyone ever done anything like this for you before?"

"You're the psychic, what do you think?"

"I don't think so."

"What can I tell you, kid?"

She'd heard the *Chinatown* line enough to paraphrase and finish it for him. "When I'm right, I'm right. And I'm right."

They knew each other's bodies well by now, but he'd never been more excited to have her. Even so, they made love slowly, getting reacquainted with their repertoire of kisses, from lengthy and deep to light and glancing, necking for so long that Jasmine nearly forgot they were two adults in their marital bed. This reminded her of how it had been when she was in high school, steaming up windows in parked cars. So lovely, combining that swoony old illicit thrill with plenty of room to maneuver and the plush feel of Egyptian cotton sheets. Whit paid attention to all the best, subtle places—her toes, the backs of her knees, the inside of her thighs—while she lingered along the ridges of his collarbone, the sweet smooth skin along his flanks and belly. Unlike the younger men she'd been with, Whit never confused passion with being in a hurry. That wasn't the only difference. When Whit was born in Culleoka, Tennessee, it was not the custom to slice the foreskin off baby-boy penises. Before Whit, Jasmine had never seen, much less caressed, one that was uncut. It was like a gift to unwrap. Sheathed sword, concealed weapon—these were the sort of phallic terms that came to mind and made her giggle.

"Want to tell me what's so funny?" Whit asked. Then he put his tongue to her hoop, pressing the bead against her with such exquisite pressure that she moaned and shook while pulling him inside.

"Directing is like making love," Whit said afterward, as they lay with legs still scissored together. "You never know how the other guy does it."

Jasmine laughed, but she recognized a cue when she heard one. "You might never know *that,* but you sure do seem to know how everything you do to me is going to feel. It's amazing, but not so surprising, I guess. All your movies are about women."

"I'm only going to ask you one more time. Did you ever see any of my films before we met?"

She answered with a line from *Kiki,* his first. "You ask a lot of questions for an artist."

"Tell the truth."

"Okay, then. Truth. No."

"Insensitive girl, what am I going to do with you?"

"Well," she said, straddling Whit, giving him a glimpse of hoop before brushing his chest with her small firm breasts, each shaped as though molded by the same champagne glass. "I guess you'll just have to teach me a lesson."

7

"His wife came to my yoga class," Amelia told Phoebe. "Have you seen her?"

"He just got up here," Carl Brown told Phoebe. "Have you seen him?"

"Looks like we got another one of those goddamn SUVs on the road," Ivan told Phoebe. "California plates. Have you seen it?"

No, no, and no again. Still, Phoebe lived in a constant state of anticipation, the volume knob on every sensitivity turned up to full blast. Exhausting. Five pounds had melted off her body, just disappeared. Where did they go? Maybe nosy little Phoebe particles shimmied through cracked windows at Whit's house in the dead of night, escaping the tight diurnal rein she kept on her curiosity.

So he had a wife. All the more reason to maintain distance. What would be worse, liking this woman or despising her? Discovering she already knew lots about Phoebe, or had no inkling of her existence? There must be better choices. What clogged her mind? Some scientist, one of that bunch Laurienne worked for, could probably assess her fevered anxiety's chemical composition, break it down into a formula of neurons and peptides, a map of jangled synapses. What she imagined, though, were frenzied lab workers in red sponge clown noses extracting her juices with bendy straws instead of glass pipettes, sloshing them into candy jars. *Great Love, Horrible Heartbreak, Surgical Cut*—that's what the jar labels said, every one of them punctuated with a big fat question mark.

Ah, that felt better—cartooning her time with Whit. No twists of the knife with absurdity, just a brisk immunizing sting.

Phoebe rattled around Westerly Webs pulling together material for her exhibition booth at the Fish Expo in Seattle, a sure sign of autumn. As was the end of this sluggish spell in business. She'd had to let Kristen go, hoping to get her back when things picked up, after all the boats were home from Alaska and everybody started getting ready for winter fishing. With Gabe in school again, that left Brian as the only seasoned employee on the floor. "It's just temporary," Phoebe reminded Sophie, who'd been fretting.

"But it's why we never get very far ahead. You can't grow on slack times."

Sophie thumped down on Phoebe's desk a catalogue from an outfit up the coast in British Columbia. Phoebe knew the firm. A prosperous one, with flume tanks for testing the drag on trawl nets and computer programs to solve problems Phoebe sussed out by eye and handheld calculator. "See for yourself," Sophie said. "These guys still make all the traditional stuff. But they're doing nets for athletics, too."

Sophie had bugged Phoebe before about sport nets, but with the catalog as ammunition, she was relentless; if they didn't start making batting cages for baseball players, driving nets for golfers, and every other kind of web for people to slap, throw, and shoot balls and pucks over, through, and against, they'd be forever at the mercy of erratic seasons and an aging, shrinking fleet.

As the printer whirred out a letter to Fish Expo, Phoebe turned to Sophie, affecting a sneer. "Sport nets are for sissies."

"Hey, I know you're tough, Phoebe. Like a marshmallow."

"I mean it, Soph. They are so frigging mindless, nothing but a bunch of square-cut mesh. No turns, no panels, no form. Besides, what do I know about sports?"

"What do you know about fishing?"

At that, Phoebe's spine stiffened. She had done her share of working the docks, studying on board action. "I know what the guys need—lots of times before even they do. It was hard enough making *them* get it; I won't convince another woman."

"Okay, okay. But this is about business, not sisterhood. And when you ship out sport nets, you never have to worry about people dying when they use them. Remember how low you got after the *Arctic Queen* went down? Nightmares for months."

"That wasn't the worst part." Phoebe shuddered, recalling the visions spawned by Coast Guard reports of the *Queen*'s accident, how she'd tipped with an unreeled cod-end on board and two crew members were trapped in its mesh. "I could see their faces."

"Well, there's no heartache like that with sports."

"If you think there's no heartache there, you ought to talk to a Cubs fan."

"I thought you didn't know anything about sports."

"I like to keep abreast of lost causes." Phoebe took her letter out of the printer tray and swiveled around to sit in front of Pearl's old Underwood. She told herself that she kept the machine so well cleaned and maintained because of its fine design and how it once belonged to her mother, reasons that had nothing to do with Whit. The Underwood's only flaw now was how the letter x stuck after striking paper and had to be retracted by hand—an easy enough problem to have fixed next time Phoebe went to the city. She rolled a business envelope in and typed out the Fish Expo address.

As Phoebe picked off the x, Sophie said, "It's a snap to do envelopes on the computer."

"I prefer this way. Anyhow, the Cubs aren't sports, they're tragedy. That's why Ivan's such a soulful guy, his daddy raised him on the Cubs."

"Fine, Phoebe, talk about the Cubs."

"I thought sports was the subject."

"You don't have to do everything the hard way. There's nothing wrong with making nets for kids who're just having fun. Or for celebrities earning tons of money."

"You know what ungrateful bastards celebrities are; you read the *Enquirer*."

"Only in the checkout line," Sophie said. "And people who say they don't aren't telling the truth. What we need is a net distributor, someone to bring in the jobs. And we ought to have a Web site, too."

"What do you mean? We *are* a web site."

"On the Internet, silly. Phoebe, I want to stay with you, but I can't keep coasting along with the way things are. Both my boys got Charlie's big rabbity teeth crammed into my squirrelly little jaw—they're going to need braces soon, and college after that."

"All right. I'll think about it."

"Think hard this time, okay?"

Outside, the sky looked splotched with squid ink. Rain hit windowpanes in wind-tossed splats, rattling the glass. "Go home, Sophie," Phoebe said. "It's late."

* * *

Phoebe was alone, waiting for price lists to print, when Ivan came for his last part-time paycheck. His new kiln was now on the way, paid for in advance. She knew the return of her comradely distance had him hurt and angry, but he'd countered her withdrawal with his own silence and retreat into preparations for his show. Now he wore the air of someone ready to call a truce. "It's Friday night," he said. "I'm flush. How about I take you out for dinner?"

"I'm kind of tired, Ivan."

"We'll make it an early night, then." He walked over to the cedar shelf where Phoebe kept the most displayable objects that she'd received over the years in her Mystery Packages. "This one's new," he said, picking up the hummingbird's nest.

"It came a few months ago." Phoebe went to join him. "From Mexico."

"In Mexico, hummingbirds are a symbol of love."

"Really?"

"Yeah." He set the nest down. "There's a self-portrait Frida Kahlo made. She's wearing a necklace of thorns and there's a hummingbird, too. Right here," he said, extending his fingertips to the scar above Phoebe's clavicle, "on her throat." Phoebe swallowed beneath his touch, her body recognizing its invitation with an involuntary rush of pelvic heat, a reminder of their lovemaking on Heron Island. But instead of raising her face to his she just kept looking at the nest until, finally, Ivan dropped his hand.

Was it possible that Whit had somehow discovered what happened to her? Frida Kahlo, oh my God. Now there was a woman defined by obsessive love. Sanctified by it, really. Who cared about Diego Rivera anymore? Kahlo was the one who mattered, and she was a feminist icon. Not a sucker, not a smart Jewish girl who should have known better than to subordinate herself to a fat, philandering genius. An icon! She'd probably be on a stamp someday, gazing out serenely below that single long eyebrow. And for what? For embodying love based on ideals so towering they dwarfed anything so ordinary, so unimaginative, as mere fidelity. For mythologizing her pain. For expressing all the romantic notions and emotions Phoebe herself had once embraced, and had been tamping down inside herself for years. Who knew, maybe Frida would have done the same if she'd been able to have a baby, if giving birth hadn't been another shattered dream to splash onto canvas. Or would Frida have subordinated another life, that of an actual child, to the man she loved? There were, after all, women who'd done that—who do that still.

Glancing at Ivan, Phoebe caught a questioning look. "I've seen that painting," she said.

"It's a good thing, getting a hummingbird's nest. Probably means somebody loves you. But I guess that's not surprising. That somebody would love you, I mean."

"Do you really think so?"

"Sure."

It dawned on Phoebe much too slowly how unfair it was, that she heard these words only in terms of Whit. "Oh, Ivan, I'm sorry. I've been kind of confused."

"How long have you known me, Phoebe?" Ivan almost always spoke so slowly, so deliberately, that Phoebe had learned to hold her tongue to avoid interrupting. She could spit out at least three different ideas in the pauses it took him to express just one. Usually the wait was well worth it, but now she grew impatient. "Do you really want me to do the math?"

"Longer than you've been getting these packages, right?"

A tiny nerve snapped—behind her right eye, it felt like.

Pain shot through her clenched jaw, her knotted neck. Nothing serious, just tension, though whenever this happened Phoebe feared falling prey to her mother's migraines, her mother's tumor, her mother's early death. Trudging an overgrown trail on Pearl's map of misery. She opened her mouth wide to pop her jaw and tilted her head from side to side, easing the tightness. "Jesus, Ivan. What is it with you and redundant questions today?"

He shrugged and stuck his hands in the pockets of his jeans. His beard was gone, his fading tan a reminder of its borders. On a man with softer features the effect would be downright silly, embarrassing even, like private parts that ought not to be publicly exposed, but his appearance seemed only faintly odd. While Phoebe suspected Carl Brown of growing a beard to hide a weak jaw, Ivan's problem was just the opposite; he claimed the deep cleft in his prominent chin made shaving a particularly bothersome ritual. Did men ditch their beards the way women cut their hair—when they were disappointed in love? Phoebe had plenty of time to ponder all this before Ivan responded.

"You ought to know by now," he said. "Women have told me a lot worse things than 'I'm confused.' "

"Oh yeah? Like what?"

"Like 'You don't make enough money.' 'Have you ever considered therapy?' 'I met another guy.' Let's see, what else? 'It's not too much in this day and age to expect flush toilets.' But that was before I went modern."

Phoebe had not only known some of these women but, as Ivan's closest female friend, had tried to convince a few that they were making a mistake—confusing his calm steadiness with lack of interest or joie de vivre, looking for someone to change their lives instead of share them. They never listened. Phoebe understood. If you wanted to know the best way to cook a Thanksgiving turkey, she was the person to ask, and what you got was not only advice but an education, a thorough rundown of all the pluses and minuses of the buttered brown bag, brining, basted cheesecloth, and outdoor-smoker methods. But if what you wanted to know was the best way to be happy in love, well, you talked to somebody else. Somebody with a better track record.

"Look," Ivan went on, "you don't have to be afraid of saying you're confused. You're *allowed* to be confused. You're also allowed a plate of fish and chips at the Tavern."

Phoebe was wearing a baggy red sweater and old jeans torn out at the knees, but nobody dressed for the Tavern, not even on a Friday night. And she was so hungry that a plate of deep-fried Tavern food sounded good. She'd missed Ivan's company, too—missed their beach walks, impromptu dinners, gazing at nets of stars through his telescope. At least when Ivan gossiped about the newcomers, he only talked about their vehicle. He wouldn't press her over dinner, either. Didactic he wasn't.

She imagined him fresh out of Cranbrook, when he came to Seattle as an MFA candidate in the university's art department, teaching freshman studio courses. They must have adored him, like all the graduate students who sought him out now to learn exotic glazes and firing techniques. But Ivan, driven by contemplation and intuition more than structure or defining principles, found formal teaching a drain and quit rather than complete the degree he needed for tenure. Phoebe hadn't known him then, but she knew the conviction with which he must have acted. The same sort that led him to get a vasectomy years ago, after a girlfriend's abortion. "I love kids," he once told Phoebe, "but I'm the kind of guy who'd shortchange them to make art." Self-fulfilling prophecy—that was her verdict. But he had insisted it was something he'd always felt, like his attraction to nature and women. "On the days when I believe in reincarnation," he'd said, "I think I had a whole bunch of lives with a whole bunch of kids, but the only stuff I got to make was plates and bowls and pitchers."

Phoebe pulled on her anorak. As she threw a wool scarf around her neck, her hand unconsciously went to the place on her throat that Ivan had touched. Since Mitchell died, no one's fingers but hers had ever lingered there without some kind of clinical intention.

"Come on," she said, "let's go."

There were no rules against sleeping with a fellow employee at BioIngenious, but still, Laurienne held firm to keeping her affair with Cliff a secret. Why? Cliff kept asking. "Because it would wreck my credibility as a team leader," she said. "Dunson wouldn't like it."

"What you mean," he said, "is you wouldn't like it if Dunson knew. Geez, Laur, he's not your father. What's he going to do? Take away your birthday?"

They were in bed at Cliff's studio apartment. Or rather, lying atop a mattress that sat directly on the floor, all the bedding shoved down to the foot, their bodies beaded with perspiration even though, outside, it was a cold, rainy October night. It wasn't just the heat of passion that had them sweating. There was hardly any room for furniture in Cliff's place because it was jammed with computers, six of them: one reserved exclusively for wandering on the Internet, two for coding, another with sophisticated graphic capabilities, and a couple of Macs to feed the anarchistic tendencies that made Cliff take such pleasure in slandering Microsoft. He kept all the computers constantly humming, generating so much warmth that even though he never turned on the heat, the thermostat now registered in the mid-eighties. Laurienne thought longingly of the icy landscapes in *The Thing from Outer Space*. That was the sci-fi movie Cliff had rented on what turned out to be the first night they made love. His idea of romance, watching a movie about a nasty alien who freezes a bunch of scientists out of their arctic shelter by turning off the heat. Almost the reverse of what was going on here. And now, feeding the temperature spike in Cliff's place were computerized battles the two of them had devised between a whole raft of menacing aliens and superscientist Lexie Shields.

"It's like a sauna," Laurienne said.

Cliff claimed the heat made him feel at home, reminded him of Texas. "It's not that hot," he said. "Anyway, saunas are healthy. You sweat out toxins. That's the trouble with you Northwest girls. Your blood's too thin; you don't sweat enough."

"You're the one with all the toxins. Open the window."

"It's open."

"Then open the door."

"We'll have to put on clothes."

"I don't care."

"We could go to your place."

"No, we can't." Another firm rule, along with never spending an entire night together. In Cliff's place, it was easy to ignore the pile of dirty clothes, the metal pans beneath stove-top burners lined with crusted, baked-on grease, the tub that drained too slowly, the floors that needed cleaning. But she imagined that if she let him into her sweeter, tidier, roomier apartment, in no time at all evidence of his domestic neglect would follow him there, like some abandoned creature, and if she wanted anything done about it, the job would be hers. No thanks. Maybe she'd fallen into the same old trap again, but only partway, which kept them equals. She wasn't really taking care of him, unless you counted elevating his usual diet with take-out cartons of the foods he loved—Szechuan, Mexican, Thai—and ate spiked with so much hot sauce that they could make you sweat, too. That was the upside. The downside: She got less sleep than ever. Lexie Shields kept them both awake deep into the night; soon, they'd have a prototype ready for potential backers. "Besides, we can't work on Lexie at my place."

During their first night of pillow talk Cliff had mapped out the game for her. She told him that to broaden its appeal, Lexie needed a bigger motive driving her battle against the evil apocalyptic hordes. "Saving the world isn't a big enough motive?" Cliff had asked.

"It needs to be more personal."

"Well, Lexie can't fall in love with one of the creatures. They're monsters."

"That's how much you know," she said. "Girls fall in love with monsters all the time."

"Don't go all philosophical on me. Anyway, girls aren't into games the way guys are."

"They would be, if you gave them a story they could care about. The way you have it, Lexie got these superpowers because she was with her father when his supercollider accident killed him. Some kind of atomic backwash rearranged her genes, right?"

"I'm not changing that."

"Okay, okay, I don't think you should. But what if instead of dying, her father's accident created a huge glop of antimatter that sucked him into an alternate universe? What if the accident wasn't really an accident at all, but a plot engineered by the evil aliens?"

"What's *their* motive?"

"He was on the brink of some big discovery they need

to conquer Earth. The aliens keep him trapped in this parallel universe so they can boost his brain. See how that would give Lexie extra drive? She would not only have to battle these creatures to save the world, she'd have to crack the problem her father was working on when he disappeared. What she wants is to win and to save him at the same time."

"Two for one," Cliff said. "I like it."

When Laurienne was little, she didn't understand her mother's enthusiasm for *Peter Pan*. Wendy was such a wimp, happy to just be sewing make-believe buttons and bringing bedtime stories to the table, getting nothing for her trouble but being kidnapped by pirates when she could have been out there swashbuckling with the boys. But Lexie was no wimp. And once Laurienne invested in Lexie's story, it was fun helping Cliff write the game engine, working out the confrontations and battles in code, seeing how he slipped it all into a sci-fi graphic skin. First she had to study other successful games, from Castle Wolfenstein to Zombie Nazis. She also had to learn new coding. But these were her kind of puzzles. Now she understood why guys were so hooked on this stuff. You got to be in control of the whole picture, not just a little piece. You got to twist DNA without fetching the numbers. You got to kick chaos in the ass.

Laurienne knew she was the inspiration for Lexie, even though initally Cliff would admit to nothing more than having a thing for voluptuous, freckle-faced, red-haired girls. "Voluptuous" being a word that automatically excluded Laurienne, with her far-from-ample bosom. Now he wasn't so cautious. After blotting her chest with a cool, damp cloth, he circled her nipples with a fingertip. "I don't want you covering them up. They're perfect."

"They're little-girly. Just like my voice."

"Well, I love them. I love your voice. I love you, too." She looked at him, surprised but silent. "Help me out here," he said. "I feel genetically altered just saying that."

She took his face in her hands. "Look at me. What do you see?"

"A red-hot mama?"

She shook her head.

"Repulsion?"

"Be serious."

"Love?"

She smiled at him and nodded, but didn't say a word.

"Is that all I'm going to get? Confirmation of a guess?" She nodded again and kissed him.

"Okay," he said, his lips moving on hers. "I'll take it."

It was a typical Friday night at the Port Pritchard Tavern, with butts parked on all the bar stools, every booth full, the place raucous with jukebox music, kitchen bells signaling orders up, smacking pool balls, players' shrieks echoing the shouts of patrons watching the Supersonics game on a soundless television set hanging over the bar, and conversation pitched loudly enough to be heard above it all. A Western swing–style band from Mount Jensen would be playing soon at the rear of the main dining room, and the only free tables were on either side of the bandstand. As Phoebe and Ivan claimed one, the jukebox, stuffed with most of the same old vinyl records as when Phoebe used to sing here, thumped out "Hang On Sloopy."

"I used to know someone who thought 'Sloopy' was the greatest rock-and-roll song of all time," Phoebe said.

Ivan pondered, then shook his head. "In my book, it's a sloppy second to 'Down in the Boondocks.' "

"Well, they're both about being from the wrong side of the tracks."

"But 'Sloopy' is a guy singing for a girl who's supposed to be trash."

"So? Nothing wrong with that."

"Yeah, but it's like he's doing her some huge favor."

"Well, he is," she said, "by standing up for her."

"By screwing her, is probably more like it. 'Boondocks' is better because the guy's singing for himself. He's the one who doesn't fit in. He's the one in a world of hurt, not congratulating himself for being able to feel hers. He's crazy about this girl, but she can only see him on the side and he understands. It's not fair, he's going to have to do something about it. But meanwhile, he's not whining."

"So you think it's more poignant?"

"More honest. More interesting, too—more chords."

"Remember *American Bandstand*? There's a reason why 'Sloopy' is on the jukebox and 'Boondocks' isn't. It has a better beat for dancing."

"Maybe. In a go-go, do-the-pony kind of way. But I like to hold a girl when I dance with her." This being a conversation with Ivan, the song was long over and a slow, smoky Sam Cooke platter played now.

"Prove it," Phoebe said.

"Sure." Ivan guided her onto the empty floor with his palm in the small of her back and kept it there as she turned into him. "I'll lead," he said. "I heard you're kind of confused these days."

Phoebe winced. "I just didn't want you to think the way I've been has anything to do with you."

"Gee, that makes me feel better."

"I mean it's not your fault."

"I didn't think it was."

"I'm just worried about some things."

"Such as?"

"Sophie's on me about doing sport nets again."

"What else?"

"Laurienne." She flushed a little at these evasions, but Ivan, looking over the top of her head, just nodded.

"She's worried about you, too. Thinks you're lost without her. Says you don't have enough fun."

"What do you say?"

"I say what does she know, you could be having *lots* of fun. In secret." He spun her out in a twirl and after he pulled her back in, laughing, someone tapped Phoebe's back. Even dancing, Phoebe's edginess was such that a touch as light as that gave her a start. She jerked her head around and there was Amelia, standing akimbo in her green-checked Tavern waitress uniform. Phoebe gave her a one-armed hug, keeping the other arm around Ivan's shoulders. Amelia's wide mouth, high cheekbones, crinkly eyes, and sandy hair were the same as Gabe's. Phoebe thought it must be strange, having your own features so perfectly duplicated in a child of the opposite gender—a chance to see what you'd look like if you'd been born with a Y chromosome instead of two Xs, an endocrine system that pumped more testosterone than estrogen.

"Are you cutting in?" Phoebe asked Amelia.

"I wish. Crazier than usual here tonight, and wouldn't you know? There's a really good-looking guy over at the bar."

Phoebe looked where Amelia indicated and saw a black-haired, handsome man bent over a draft. "His name's Dennis," Amelia said. "Out here for the Bureau of Indian Affairs. Doing some business with the tribe."

"Uh-oh," Ivan said. "I've got a bad feeling about that."

"Oh, you're just jealous," Amelia said.

"Forget jealous," Ivan told her.

"Then what?"

"I don't know," Ivan said. "Maybe it's got something to do with that director coming, paying so much for the Miller place."

"What's wrong with our home values going up?" Amelia asked.

"It's our land leases I'm worried about."

Amelia shrugged and launched into her version of the patter required of waitrons by the town's fancier restaurants, the ones patronized more by their neighbors on the island's south side. "My name is Amelia and I'll be annoying you tonight. Reciting your menu, grinding your pepper, asking questions when your mouth's full." Then, in her regular voice: "Came for your orders. Once the band starts, you'll have to give them in sign language."

"Is the halibut fresh tonight?" Ivan asked.

"Yep."

"Two fish-and-chips, then. Phoebe's hungry enough to take frozen, but not me, I'm discriminating."

Phoebe punched his arm. "A couple Hefeweizen drafts, too."

"Got it." Amelia reached up to pat Ivan's shaved cheek. "You look heaps younger without the fuzz. Isn't it funny how some men get gray in the beard before any goes to their head?"

"I guess," Ivan said. "If you think old is funny."

Amelia waved a dismissive hand. "Oh, please. Guys get all the breaks in that department." She nodded at a newly arrived couple cruising for a table. "Exhibit A at two o'clock, in case you don't believe me. Which of course you never do. But I'll tell you something, Ivan. If you really put your mind to it, you could probably snag some sweet young thing, too. And don't roll your eyes at me, that was a compliment."

The woman Amelia had pointed out looked to be still in her twenties, though barely. A little bit hippy but tall enough so that only another woman picking her apart would consider it a flaw; a man would call her lush. She had short, coal-black hair, luminous skin, plummy cheeks, and full, rose-colored lips parted over radiant white teeth. Phoebe recognized her as the girl at the Co-op, the eager little duckling who tailed her through the aisles.

The man had a cowlick of thick, fair, barely graying hair hanging over his high, handsome forehead.

The man was slim-hipped and rangy in black jeans and a chambray shirt.

The man, of course, was Whit.

Amelia was right, Whit must be considerably older than his wife. But even more notable was that he didn't look the least bit out of place beside her.

Despite all the time Phoebe had spent getting used to the idea of seeing Whit again, she felt the bottom fall out of her stomach. Her heart raced and her hands went clammy, taking orders from the part of her brain beyond reason. Slowly, she realized the sensation overwhelming her had a name. Fight or flight. Amazing, how all that electricity could be coursing through her body without stopping everyone around her dead in their tracks.

Ivan spoke to Amelia as if nothing had happened, nothing at all. "Thanks," he was saying, "but I'm not interested in fucking babies."

Amelia laughed. "Hang on to this one, toots," she told Phoebe, and leaned in to whisper. "Maybe *I* ought to figure out how to sleep with some guy I've known forever." Then, to them both: "Anyway, that's the woman I met at yoga—the director's wife. Said she'd swap me some teas for a reading."

Phoebe shook her head, wondering if she had misunderstood. "A reading?"

"Yeah, she's an astrologer."

"You're kidding."

"That stuff's no joke to me. When Gabe was born, I took one look at all the Capricorn in his chart and just *knew* he'd go into business."

The jukebox cut off in mid-song. "Whoops," Amelia said, "better scoot."

As the swing band picked up their instruments, Whit and his wife took the last remaining table, on the opposite side of the dance floor from Phoebe and Ivan's. Whit would have a hard time spotting Phoebe through all the couples crowding onto the floor now, two-stepping to an old Bob Wills song. Phoebe focused on the musicians until Amelia came with food, and then, while dipping halibut in tartar sauce and dragging french fries through Dijon mustard, the way they do in France, the voices of Fight and Flight screamed in her ears.

Blow Ivan off and get the hell out of here before Whit recognizes you, said Flight. *You're kidding yourself that he still cares, and if you talk to him, he might say something awful, something that hurts really bad, the way he did before.*

Oh, fuck being hurt, said Fight. *Get over there in your red sweater, Loretta—make the man squirm.*

The swing-band singer was begging to be taken back to Tulsa, standing in the same spot where Phoebe had once strummed her Martin 000-28, a set list in Whit's handwriting taped to the curved rosewood side of her guitar. Whit had also given Phoebe a stage name for her Tavern debut—Dolores con Cuervos. Which translated literally into a nonsense phrase—Sorrows with Crows. To suit Dolores, the first song was a country-and-western rendition of an old Gene Pitney song, "I'm Gonna Be

Strong," sung in Spanish that she learned off a foreign
language album. At the time, the name Whit gave her
had seemed amusing and bold—two things that, along
with playful, seductive, and smart, she was always trying to be for him. She doubted anyone at the Tavern
tonight, apart from her and Whit, would remember Dolores con Cuervos's gigs. There weren't that many, for
one thing, and for another, they'd all fallen on sparsely
attended weeknights. She hadn't exactly been a star.
"You can pay me back when you're a star," he told her
once. Obviously, she never became one. Did that mean
she didn't owe him anything anymore? And what did
she owe herself? An even tougher question, a thicket of
brambles and briars.

Despite the relative anonymity in which Phoebe had
entertained at the Tavern, word of her performances
had circulated around Port Pritchard after the accident.
Still, even a neighbor who'd heard her sing back then
would be too tactful to bring it up now. Why remind
Phoebe of the catastrophe that took her lovely voice,
that would be the thinking. Having this part of her life
so widely understood, with nobody needing to receive
the information directly from her, was one of the benefits of staying here. The biggest, maybe. Somewhere
else—somewhere large and hectic—she would always be
explaining her voice, her scar.

The dictates of normal, linear time would have thrown
Whit in her path at a more neutral, nondescript place,
like a gas station or bank. That's what she would have
preferred. But the sense of time she once lived by and
shared with Whit was not at all normal. It was theatrical. You fell in love to theatrical time; linear time paid
the bills. In theatrical time, he had the upper hand. Even
so, she saw the advantages of her position. Since Whit
hadn't noticed her yet, the stage was hers to take. And

how could he not be thinking of her tonight? How could he have come here without her in mind?—especially if he was the one responsible for all those Mystery Packages?

Ivan didn't seem to notice Phoebe's meandering, probably because of the swing band's fast, loud music. When the band took a tuning break and Whit's wife headed off for the ladies' room, Phoebe asked Ivan to get more drafts from the bar. Then she dabbed on some lip gloss, ran fingers through bangs, and walked across the dance floor.

Whit looked up at her, his face a question mark melting by degrees as she sank into the chair across from him. His eyes narrowed like the aperture of a camera—blurring the background, tightening the focus, framing her.

No more fight-or-flight for Phoebe. Instead, a flood of emotion from the place he first touched in her. Did he see her now the way she could him, as if nothing so bad could really have happened if they were face-to-face again? "I'm here," she blurted.

"Can't argue with that." Oh, that old sweet southern syrup, pouring into her ears again.

"Did you know I was here?"

Whit flashed his crooked grin at her—a moment she'd certainly imagined enough, but now she felt incapable of enacting preconceived scenarios, of taking the time for a knowing smile, a rueful head shake, or humming the first notes of "Who's Sorry Now?" "Here, there, and everywhere," Whit said. "Isn't that your address?"

"No. Not for a long time."

"I feel like I conjured you."

"I knew you'd say that."

"Yeah, well, the same guy still writes all my material.

Do you have a cold?" Phoebe shook her head. "What's wrong with your voice?"

"This is how I sound."

"Oh." His eyes went to her throat, her scar, but he didn't touch her there, much less ask what had happened. Because he already knew somehow? "It's kind of sexy, that rasp. Especially for a singer."

"I don't sing anymore."

"I guess there's a lot I don't know about you now."

"And vice versa."

"Details. Not necessarily the most important things." As the band started up again, he shoved the remains of his burger and fries aside, took a swallow of beer, and stood. "Let's dance."

That surprised her; they'd never danced before. "Why start now?"

"Because I'm sorry for how things ended? Would have said so sooner, but we weren't speaking. Come on, Dolores. A dance for auld lang syne."

She rose with a glance at Ivan, still waiting at the crowded bar, his back turned, and a sharp twinge of guilt told her to sit right back down again. But she didn't, she couldn't. Instead, she put her hand in Whit's. Maybe now he'd make a prettier apology.

"This will be strange," he said as they started stepping to the beat of a semislow cowboy lament. "Introducing you to my wife."

He held her lightly, with space between them, but even so, he was close enough for her to tell he still smelled the same. Lovely, like melon and clove. "You finally got married," she said.

He shrugged. Another twisted little grin. "I finally found another Phoebe."

His words clamped onto her gut like red-hot pincers. "I didn't know you were looking for me."

"Oh, I quit that a long time ago." What did he mean? That he had succeeded in locating her, and therefore stopped trying, or gave up after a few failed attempts? From his tone, it could have been either. Another glance at the bar told Phoebe Ivan was watching them now. "Hey," Whit said, corralling her attention. "The smart-as-a-whip woman who gives the barbecue every year—that's you, isn't it?"

She shrugged and nodded. "I guess."

"I think I must have seen you."

"When?"

"One morning. Coming out of the post office, some little treasure in your hands."

She studied him closely, but his look gave nothing away. "Yes, it was a treasure. You didn't recognize me?"

"The light was in my eyes. I never thought you'd come back here to stay."

"I never thought you'd come back here at all."

"I drew you on a napkin. Didn't know it was you, of course. But that got me going on another movie. It's just about the only thing that's holding me together now. Guess I ought to thank you."

Phoebe swallowed hard, feeling as if something was going down her throat. An old emotion, shaped like a hook. All he had to do was reel her in. But just then the woman whom Phoebe presumed to be a younger, less damaged version of herself landed on Whit's shoulder, freshly combed, lipsticked, and perfumed. "See, honey?" the woman said as she kissed Whit's ear and cut in on them. Then, turning to Phoebe: "I told him he was bound to run into someone he knew, sooner or later." She extended a hand for two firm, solid shakes. "Hi, Jasmine Traynor. And you're Phoebe."

"My bride is physic," Whit said.

"He means psychic." Jasmine smiled, explaining the

obvious to Phoebe, who tried not to laugh too weakly. Jasmine wrinkled her nose at Whit. "But that's not how I know her name, sweetheart. I heard people calling her that at the Co-op."

Ivan had dropped the drafts at their table and was heading for Phoebe now. Good. She didn't have to just stand there while Whit canoodled with the new, improved Phoebe. "Our neighbors from California," she told Ivan, looping her arm through his to make introductions.

Ivan was so modest, so reserved, it was easy to forget the solid first impression he made. No need to be embarrassed about being seen with him, or giving Whit just enough information to let him wonder if they were married or living together. Ivan's aversion to social chitchat dovetailed with Whit's, guaranteeing a quick escape. If Jasmine blathered on, Phoebe might die before getting away.

"Well," Phoebe said as the band began a ballad. "See you around."

It felt all wrong, just walking away to nurse another beer, so she reached up to hold Ivan around the neck and started dancing with him, pulling him closer and closer as they moved, if not leading with her pelvis in fact, coming awfully close in theory. Her body in charge—remembering his, requiring its comfort and desire. All around, couples showed off tricky steps and complicated turns, but Phoebe's and Ivan's feet hardly moved as they swayed together, less like dancers than reeds blown by the same breeze. Ivan pressed closer still and she felt not just the warmth of his breath but the appetite in it, too.

"I'm ready to go," she said.

*   *   *

Outside, the sky was spitting rain. Under a parking lot light Ivan stopped and turned to her. "I knew that wasn't for me," he said. "And now I know why."

"You're wrong."

"There's big stuff between you and him. Why didn't you tell me?"

"I told you I was confused!"

"It's not just that you didn't say anything today, or since the barbecue. How about in all the time you've known me?"

"I didn't think you'd find my past so fascinating."

Ivan shook his head, an angry look on his face. "There's just no getting your trust—not as a friend, much less a lover."

"You sound like you're sorry about that now."

"Yeah? Well, that's because I am."

He turned to walk away from her.

"Don't," she said, but by then he was already behind the wheel of his old black Saab.

Phoebe pulled up the hood of her anorak as Whit and Jasmine emerged from the Tavern. She went to her car, not wanting to be seen, but opening the Explorer door she heard Jasmine's voice caroling across the parking lot. "Good night, Phoebe."

She sped out of town well ahead of them.

Strange how quickly an argument had come on the heels of seeing Whit again. Worse was the way it reminded her of what she and Mitchell had fought over the day he died—her wanting to go without him to the *Kiki* premiere, where Whit was sure to be. Touching on the accident even so lightly as that sent a panicked surge of energy through her body. Lightening her foot on the accelerator. Focusing her attention on the road. And cutting the memory dead.

Driving not a hair over the speed limit of thirty, she

crossed the bridge connecting Port Pritchard to Owl, turned onto Spit in the Wind, and braked when she reached the drive to Ivan's place. She considered going in to apologize, but that only put her back on the Tavern dance floor, hearing Whit's apology again, and sent her down the road to her house instead.

Later, when sleep wouldn't come, Phoebe got up, threw on a robe, and went downstairs to enter the garage through a door off the foyer. One side of the airtight space was taken up with high, deep, industrial-style storage racks. All the lower shelves held paint buckets, drop cloths, brushes, rollers, and rafts of bulk products from Costco. She got a stepladder to reach the top shelf, the front of which was jammed with tents, kerosene lamps, emergency candles, air mattresses, beach mats, and a big Coleman cooler. Behind all that was where her dusty old pink GE sat beside a big blue hatbox from the Bon.

She hauled down the hatbox, took it to the fainting sofa in her study, removed the lid, and sifted through stacks of twine-tied letters she'd written her parents from camp. At the bottom of the box was another packet, wrapped in purple grosgrain ribbon. All the letters and postcards she had ever received from Whit, in order by date. With Lily curled against her hip she started reading, slowly because of how much they brought back to her after such a long time. It was hours before she slipped the last letter back into its envelope, which bore a date stamp from the Port Pritchard post office.

8

When Phoebe came face-to-face with Whit for the first time ever, it was at a place of his choosing—in front of the Port Pritchard post office. She didn't mind finding her own way to him. Wasn't that what she'd been doing all along? Besides, it felt like part of the romance, meeting where his letter setting their date had been mailed. He had no phone in his rented house—amazing, really, how they'd never once spoken on the phone—so even if one of them needed to cancel or postpone at the last minute there was no way to do it. But she felt convinced enough of her importance to Whit that she could more easily conceive of him kidnapped by aliens than not showing up. How could he possibly have any more choice in the matter than she?

Phoebe thumbed a ride into Port Pritchard from Mount Jensen, the county seat, where for fifty dollars a month she'd found a room above a music store close to a campus so small, with a compact student body so local, that it had no dormitories. Her entire wardrobe, which fit into a single modest suitcase, was in earth tones. For this late-afternoon appointment on a sun-stippled September day, she had put together an outfit that was to her the very definition of counterculture chic. A long gold velour skirt with an elastic waistband that she had run up on a foot-treadled sewing machine especially for meet-

ing Whit, her best green cotton turtleneck, and over that
a brown-print smock that had once belonged to Pearl—
basically a zippered Fifties apron with unintended iconoclast appeal. On her feet she wore heavy, waffle-soled
army-surplus boots that required thick hiking socks to
prevent blisters. An orange bandanna, knotted at the
nape of her neck, held back her shoulder-skimming
braids. Altogether it was an ordinary enough look in
Eugene, but standing in front of the post office in Port
Pritchard, where most passersby were fishermen or
farmers or their wives, Phoebe drew stares.

She saw him first, coming down rickety hillside steps
that connected Main Street to the residential bluff above.
Never before had she been with anyone so tall, so long-
waisted, so, well, nervous looking. The closer he drew,
the more difficult it was to think of Whit as being much
older than she, not with that dense cowlicked thatch of
dirty-blonde hair and smooth boyish face. He had a fair
complexion, the kind of skin that burned in the sun, but
hearty color in his cheeks kept him from appearing ane-
mic. It was his eyes that really took her breath away—
wide, deep-set, brooding, and thickly lashed. He walked
with a distracted gait, as though marching orders got
lost somewhere along the length of his legs, and only
when he came within a few feet of her did it seem that
an absence of alternatives—nobody else was waiting on
the street—convinced him of her identity. She might have
been disappointed, or even offended, but already he'd
invoked her protection. It wasn't every day you encountered your secret life, got to take it in through all
your senses instead of just your eyes and ears and
imagination—how could the prospect of animating the
persona he'd created on the page for her *not* be daunt-
ing? Having a similar task made her edgy, too. And so it

happened that before they even touched, she had already forgiven him.

Whit had a crescent-shaped freckle on his earlobe, like a painted-on piece of jewelry, and when Phoebe reached up to embrace him, she caught a faint whiff of what she felt certain must be his natural scent, not unlike her father's favorite imported fruit tea. Then he spoke, the first words of his intended specifically for her and her alone.

"You're so short," he said. "I didn't think from your picture that you'd be so short."

She froze for a second, gripped by an unexpected fear of saying the wrong thing. Then she gave a shrug, less like an indifferent "so what" than an irrepressible shiver of delight. "That's probably because I've got the arms and legs of a much taller person."

Whit smiled. Or rather, the right side of his generous mouth curved in the direction of a smile. Phoebe felt relieved, finding in his expression the flash of intrigue, the glimmer of respect that she wanted.

"I'll take you up," Whit told her, "so you can see where you live now."

The most southern thing about Whit, apart from his accent, were his manners. He walked Phoebe to his fire-engine-red Econoline van so that he was closest to the lightly trafficked street, guaranteeing that he'd be the first hit in the unlikely event of some vehicle jumping the curb or splattering mud. After opening the van's passenger-side door, he handed her in like a railroad conductor. But he clearly felt no need to fill the air between them with conversation. For someone who had once wielded a radio mike, Whit didn't talk much. He was more like a living letter, saying mainly what popped and sizzled, preferring silence to the meaningless filler everyone else used for social lubrication. "I'll take you up so you can see where you live now"—it was almost like a poem. So was Mount Erie, where Whit parked the van, walked her out to a clearing, spread a blanket, and took a couple of Pilsner Urquells from a six-pack. "The favorite beer of Czech filmmakers," Whit said.

It tasted light and hoppy, not a bit like American brews. "It's good."

"Stick with me, kid," he said, wiggling his eyebrows and tapping the ash of an imaginary cigar, "and you'll get stuck."

Taking this as a cue, Phoebe sang her first song for him, a comic tune she'd heard Groucho Marx perform once (once was enough for her) on television: "Show Me a Rose or Leave Me Alone." Whit got the segue without requiring any explanation. Another big relief. She was tired of reining in all her references, of having them met with blank, puzzled stares.

"How many other songs about roses do you know?" Whit asked. Plenty, as it turned out. Enough for a set on somebody's radio show, if somebody hadn't forsaken the airwaves for film. But now it seemed as if the radio show had come to life, and they were it. Imaginary Friends in the flesh.

Phoebe bent both knees and wrapped her arms around them, a move that revealed the swell of her calves. "A pretty girl ought not to hide legs like that," Whit said.

"I bet you'd like them better shaved, too."

"I'm not big on the mountain mama look. But I do like how you're wearing that scarf. Reminds me of the Italian farmer women in *Bitter Rice*."

"Do you like lingerie, too?" A pointed question; Phoebe hadn't worn underwear since leaving home.

"No, I don't like lingerie, Phoebe. I love it."

There was too much admiration in his eyes, too much affection in his tone for her to feel criticized. Instead, she filled up on the sense of being with someone who understood how rich the life inside her was. Someone who could help her find a way to share it, express it, and could guide her through it, because it was so big she couldn't conceive of how she'd ever be able to negotiate it on her own. Someone, at last, who could match the intensity of her feelings. Disappointed? Not Phoebe. Whit was everything she had wanted him to be ever since his show became the sound track for her expanding existence. How to explain, then, her lingering apprehension over saying the wrong thing, the thing that might hurt him or, worse, make him think less of her? Oh, well. What he could nurture had to do with vision and ways of seeing, not girlish little whim-whams. And she knew coming in, from their letters, what his vision of her was. Adventurous, uninhibited, unexpected. Everything she *wanted* to be.

Whit pointed out the treacherous stretch of water directly below, torn by crosscurrents and churning eddies. "Deception Pass," he said. "Which I guess would make the spot where we're sitting the perfect place for a Lover's Leap."

"Dying for love is silly."

"But dramatic."

"Which has led to trouble more than once." Not used to beer and lightheaded already, she covered her mouth for what she hoped was a dainty burp.

From here, the farmland and dikes of Pritchard Valley spread out like a lush cultivated quilt, a Van Gogh landscape banked by sumi-style mountains. Shoots of low light filtered through nested clouds, bounced off snow-capped peaks, shimmied down fir-covered slopes, glanced across fields of beans, lettuce, cabbage, and squash. On the water, beyond Deception Pass, Phoebe saw trawlers returning from the sea, a tugboat with a freighter in tow.

Shiny ebony seals sunned themselves on rocky outcrops shaped by water and wind. There couldn't possibly be a view more full or various than this. "I'm going to enjoy where I live now," she said.

"You will if I've got anything to do with it. Your going to school here—that's for real?"

"'The secret of the world,'" she said, "'is the tie between person and event.'"

"Yeah? Sez who?"

"Emerson. My father's always quoting him."

She looked up at Whit, ready for the kiss that seemed to come at her in slow motion from a great height, uncertain whether she should part her lips or keep them closed, the way his were until at last they lit. It was a kiss that started out soft and friendly, then, with her encouragement, gradually turned into a long, lingering exploration—an expedition, really, into the myriad possibilities of Phoebe and Whit kissing, or as many as could be discovered still sitting upright and fully clothed. "Sweet," she said when they drew back from each other. And that was the end of it, for now. Their first time together would not be on a scratchy blanket over scrub and stone.

They got back into the van and Whit drove north till they reached Chuckanut Drive, a twisting road that hugged the shore. As the sun began to set, they stopped at a hillside restaurant called Oyster Cove Inn. Whit stashed the last two Pilsner Urquells in Phoebe's canvas shoulder bag so they could be taken inside, where the waitress knew Whit's ways well enough to supply empty glasses and remind him to pour beneath the table before taking his order for a dozen raw oysters. Phoebe had never eaten an oyster raw before, only cooked in scrambled eggs or on a barbecue grill, and the thought of one sliming down her throat turned her stomach queasy. But

when Whit presented her with a Quilcene dressed with
what he assured her was the perfect combination of
lemon juice, cocktail sauce, and cracker, she gave it a try.

"What do you think?" he asked.

"I think it tastes like tears . . . like ocean . . . like sex."

"Good answer."

"This seems like a great place to write."

"It *ought* to be."

"Still having trouble?"

"Only when they have to talk."

"The book didn't help?"

"It's all in my head," Whit said. "I just can't get it
down right on paper."

"Maybe you should go to Paris."

"Joe sent me in June."

"Joe?"

"Joe Zaglan, my producer. Well, you've been there,
you know how amazing it is."

Phoebe squirmed a little, at his omission and her own
lie, but wasn't prepared to correct her story. "Why don't
you just tell this producer you need more time?"

"That's a little dicey. See, how all this happened was,
Joe saw the documentary and said I should call next
time I was in L.A. Seemed like that ought to be pretty
soon, so I flew down and he took me out to lunch at this
restaurant where you could throw a napkin in the air
and be sure it would land on some hotshot actor or
agent. He asked if I had a feature film in me, and even
though I hadn't put down a word, I told him I was
working on a script about Kiki de Montparnasse. By
dessert, he'd pretty much cast every principal part and
written out a check for my advance."

"Don't worry, you'll do it."

"That's what he says. When he can get me on the

phone, anyway. But enough about me. Let's talk about what you can do for me."

He was joking, but she decided to take him seriously. "I can help you."

"Can you type with more than two fingers?"

"By touch. I'm fast, too."

Another lopsided smile. "Maybe you're my secret weapon."

Phoebe liked the sound of that. She even believed there might be something to it. During the summer in Eugene, she had developed the habit of studying in the university library and waiting there to meet Jack when he was done with his classes and tutorials. Homework didn't take long; Brookland had been so demanding she probably could have passed the high school equivalency exam straight out of ninth grade. So Phoebe dove into the card catalog files, finding books from the two categories that interested her most: Victorian fairy tales and Paris in the Twenties. It was a funny combination. Still, the common thread was perfectly apparent to Phoebe. In one world, she encountered the Light Princess, Lilith, orphaned girl children, loving grandmothers, wisewomen; in the other, Sylvia Beach and her Left Bank bookstore, Gertrude Stein and her salon, Natalie Barney and her lesbian lovers. Even men who wrote about Paris said it was a female city. And just like the world of fairy tales, Paris had no use for anything puffed up or stuck on itself, anything ordinary or established. What it wanted was transformation.

No conscious purpose guided Phoebe's reading. Not an undergraduate program in existence would have encouraged the indulgence of her dual passions. She was just spending time with what magnetized her, trusting that the solace she got from her reading meant it was good for her, too. Maybe now what she knew would also be good for Whit.

He drove her back to Mount Jensen, walked her to the door beside the music store that led to her room, and gave her a twenty-dollar bill. "What's that for?"

"We're fifteen miles apart," he said. "That's a little far for smoke signals. One of us ought to have a telephone."

"I feel funny taking money from you."

"Funny how?"

"Funny uncool."

"Don't worry about it. You can pay me back when you're a star."

When she returned from her first day of classes he was parked outside the music store, waiting for her. There hadn't been time to get sexier new clothes, but she'd bought a razor so at least her legs and armpits were shaved. They went to the docks at the Port Pritchard Fishermen's Terminal, where Whit bought a huge live Dungeness crab straight off the boat for only three dollars. Driving the short uphill distance to Whit's place, she asked him to stop at an overgrown lawn full of shaggy-mane mushrooms. "Those'll be good with the crab," Phoebe said, and picked until she'd filled the pockets of her smock.

The kitchen in Whit's tiny house had two small windows, both rounded like portholes, and a pair of antique kerosene lamps hung on swinging gimbals to prevent spillage. Phoebe ran her hand over the highly varnished oak counters, rimmed and trimmed with brass rails. The stove was a narrow gas model, the refrigerator resembled an old-fashioned icebox. With his height, Whit seemed a giant in this room, but it was sized perfectly for Phoebe. "It's like a boat galley," she said.

"The original owner made wooden yachts and dories. He did most of the work here himself."

Whit lifted the crab by the edges of its shell, placed it in a Dutch oven he'd filled with cold salted water, and turned on the burner. Phoebe was appalled. "So now it's going to slowly cook to death?"

"Basically."

"But that's cruel!"

"What's cruel is throwing crabs in after the water comes to a boil."

"That's how my mother did it."

"That's how most people do it, but if you're really listening, you can hear them scream on contact. This way, the warming water puts them to sleep. Then they die unconscious."

"Ooooh," Phoebe said, wrinkling her nose. "I wish I didn't know that."

While the cooked crab chilled, Phoebe wiped the shaggy-manes with a damp cloth, sautéed them in garlic and butter, and made a dipping sauce out of mayonnaise, lemon juice, horseradish, ketchup, and Tabasco—a sauce much like the one Pearl had prepared for crabs from the Seattle Terminal. Then, as they ate, and drank more Pilsner Urquells, Phoebe told Whit some of her secrets. How she'd written him on the same typewriter that her mother wooed her father on. How her mother had died. And something else that really seemed to captivate him.

"One night when I was alone in my room listening to the radio," she said, "I had my first orgasm to the sound of your voice."

"You're kidding."

"I didn't know what to call it then, but that's what it was."

"Nobody's ever told me *that* before."

"Feel flattered?"

"Kind of cheated, if you want to know the truth. Like I wasn't around when something thrilling happened to me." He leaned over the bowl on the kitchen table that they'd tossed their crab shells into and kissed her nose. "What if I don't live up to myself?"

Whit's bed was in a loft at the top of a narrow teak staircase, overlooking the A-framed living room that held an old horsehair sofa and rolltop desk. A portable Remington typewriter sat empty atop the desk, beside it a wire wastebasket filled with a few pieces of crumpled paper, and a tidy stack of books, including the one Phoebe had sent. The Kiki postcards from her were also there, tacked to the wall near a series of snapshots panoramically arranged into Left Bank cityscapes. It looked like Whit was stuck. The wastebasket should be full to overflowing, the books scattered all around, opened to pertinent pages, the Remington loaded and ready to fire away. Or so Phoebe thought before Whit began nuzzling her throat, pulling her toward his bed.

Later, as he rocked gently inside her, she remembered stop-action footage she'd once seen of a flowering peony. Something like that seemed to be happening to her now, a sensation the exact opposite of menstrual cramps, with everything releasing instead of contracting, going into orbit around her pelvis as if it were the sun. No wonder they called it the solar plexus! What a difference there was between the thrill of romance-in-the-head, born of yearning for someone to touch your soul, and the honest-to-God complete and utter helplessness of locking onto that actual person, of having it seem, even while he sets your insides wheeling around, as though he's more like an extension of your own body than someone separate. It certainly wasn't anything like what she was used to. None of the short, quick thrusting that was exciting enough while it lasted, but left her feeling unfinished afterward. With Whit she glided, traveling wherever it was they were going together. Still, she didn't expect to have with him, or any other man, anything like what happened when she touched herself. When she did, she nearly screamed with the surprise of it.

"I reckon that's what you get," Whit said, "after two years of foreplay."

When he sat up to pull the quilt over them, she got her first good look at him and wondered out loud if how good he felt inside her had to do with his being uncut. Or, as Whit put it, with a droll inflection, *anatomically complete*. "I hope you're right," he said. "There ought to be at least one advantage to being born in Culleoka, Tennessee."

She fingered the quilt, its intricate pattern of flowers. Some of the petals were frayed, as though from years of wear. "My grandmother made it," Whit said.

"Is she alive?"

"No. She's probably spinning in her grave right now."

"Why?"

"Are you mocking the afflicted? Because let me tell you, if there's a God, it was a rotten joke He played, getting me born to a bunch of Church of Christers."

"I've never known any Church of Christers."

"Well, let's just say Granny would not approve of you and me lying here, nekkid fornicators that we are, underneath all these scraps from her old housedresses."

"Guess it's a good thing she won't be seeing your movie."

"If I ever make it, you mean."

"Oh, you'll make it." She kissed sleepy butterflies on

his eyelids, then his lips. "I promise you will. Just think of Kiki like a fairy tale. There she was, queen of Montparnasse, when a bastard child like her should have grown up to be a scrub maid or a prostitute. She turned into something the people she came from never could have imagined. Her life was enchanted." Phoebe yawned and snuggled against him. "A country girl on her own in the great big city. An orphan in the storm, finding her true home. Rags to riches. Alice Prin in Wonderland."

They spent Saturday together in Seattle, combing used record stores for Twenties jazz. Their last stop, where Whit pounced on a recording by the Original Memphis Five with Miff Mole on trombone, was at a shop tucked into the warren of hardwood hallways that ran beneath the Pike Place Market. Next door was a tiny barbershop with a single chair. On an impulse, Phoebe stuck her head in and spoke to the dapper little mustachioed proprietor. "Do you cut women's hair?" Soon her braids were on the floor and she had a Kiki-like bob.

"I like it," Whit said over a shared shrimp Louie at the Athenian, where they sat at a table overlooking Elliott Bay. "Suits your sassy side."

"Now I really need some new clothes, right?"

"Well, you're delectable in earth tones. But you'd be absolutely irresistible in a short leather skirt."

Phoebe blew some of her Eugene savings on one they found at a shop on the Ave, along with red cowgirl boots and a tight blue sweater that brought out her eyes. "Why don't you keep all your new things on?" Whit suggested.

"Can't. No underwear."

"Kiki never wore any."

"Kiki didn't wear miniskirts."

"Okay, we'll fix that."

Phoebe had never gone shopping for underwear at the Bon with anyone but her mother, and that had been some time ago. She expected Whit to be at least a little embarrassed entering this traditional, if not downright stuffy, female domain, but he surprised her by behaving as if this were some kind of surreal adventure they ought to be enjoying and laughing at, in a sly, silent, conspiratorial way. Maybe that was good. After all, if things went according to plan, before too very long he'd be deciding what actresses ought to wear. Or not wear. Phoebe felt a small flash of jealousy, something Whit would surely chide her for if she ever admitted to it.

Without even a hint of a blush, Whit stated his preferences to the matronly saleslady who came forward to help Phoebe: lacy, black, bikini-style, cleavage-revealing. The saleslady, however, was flummoxed, especially after Phoebe turned to Whit and said, "I won't wear panties without cotton crotches. That's how a girl gets yeast infections."

"I believe we have what you want in the Olga line," the saleslady managed, studiously ignoring Whit. "I'm so glad to see someone like you coming back to good brassieres."

"It wasn't my idea."

"That's right," Whit said. "She's here under protest. But it's for her own good. Someday she'll thank me for it, don't you think?"

"Absolutely," the saleslady agreed, still addressing Phoebe as she gathered up garments from a wall of shelves behind the counter. "It's terrible what you young girls are doing to yourselves, going without. Not that it matters for the ones who haven't got much on top. But you, you could do yourself real damage. Now, if you'll just come with me to try these on?"

"Oh no," Phoebe said, "we don't need to do that. I'm a thirty-two C."

"How can you be sure? When was the last time you were fitted by a professional?" Phoebe glanced at Whit and giggled, but the saleslady held her ground. "I won't sell a brassiere to someone new without a fitting. You'd be surprised how many women are out there, walking around in something they have no business wearing."

"Let's go across the street," Phoebe pleaded with Whit. "The customer's always right at Nordstrom."

"It's okay darlin', I don't mind waiting." Whit spoke in his most southern-gentlemanly tone, as if Phoebe's sole concern was his comfort.

In the dressing room, the saleslady snapped Phoebe into a 32 C and had her bend over to fill the cups. Straightening up, Phoebe looked at herself in the mirror. When she was little, she used to imagine growing breasts that would be long and thin, like sausages, and rolling them up into a brassiere. She'd taken plenty of baths with her mother, but only when too young to realize she'd most likely end up with breasts much like Pearl's—wide, rounded, full. She had to admit, they looked wonderful in this bra, which was far more delicate and sexy-looking than anything she had ever worn before.

"I'll take it," Phoebe said.

"No you won't," was the saleslady's brisk reply. She raised Phoebe's right arm and tapped beneath it. "The cup stops here but your breast doesn't, it goes right on out to the middle of your armpit."

By the time they were done, the saleslady was ready to acknowledge Whit as her only true ally here in the cause of maintaining firm, fully supported breasts. "Just as I thought," she told him with a triumphant smile. "She's a thirty-*four* C."

* * *

Phoebe's course load was light—American history, second-year French (which she could ace without cracking a book), English literature, and Introduction to Filmmaking, her only elective, which Whit promised to help her with. On one of the last summery days in September, Phoebe went out with him to make her required ten-minute silent movie—*Phoebe Comes to Pritchard Valley.* They started out the morning standing by a muddy field recently harvested for cow silage, Whit holding Phoebe's hand while they sipped hot coffee from a thermos, waiting patiently until wind-whipped hoots sounded in the distance. Hundreds and hundreds of snow geese soon appeared, wings struck blindingly white by spears of morning sun. Harsh honks shifted from steady, recurrent, cracked-key bleats to more of a sustained foghorn blare as the geese passed the field, then swung back, their tight V formation melting. With a Super 8 camera from school, Phoebe shot them swooping in to land, then turned the camera on Whit, who, à la Bob Dylan in *Don't Look Back,* held up a sign that Phoebe had filled with big, double-thick Magic Markered letters: Geesey Come, Geesey Go. After that, they packed up and moved into town, where she shot Whit inside the post office, removing an oversized postcard from his mailbox that had a big pair of red lips painted on one side, and on the other, more words: I'm Coming. At the Greyhound station, Whit took over to capture Phoebe in her long gold pioneer-woman skirt, carrying a suitcase in front of a parked bus with "Mount Jensen" in the destination slot above the windshield. At Deception Pass, he shot her in a bumblebee-print baby-doll dress and her new red cowboy boots, pretending to sip juice from an oyster shell, smiling her love at him with a sign between her knees:

Buzz, Buzz, Buzz. At Fishermen's Terminal, they found a crab-boat captain willing to film them sharing a kiss.

Phoebe brought the developed film back to her rented room along with a viewer, splicing tape, and an editing machine. Nothing was at stake for Phoebe but a pass-fail grade. She would have to steal equipment or shoot dirt in order to flunk. Still, the exercise felt exciting, like a warm-up for them having fun with *Kiki*—especially when Whit saw the footage of him at his desk that she'd shot to use up the last of her film, a montage with both Whit and the room growing more and more disheveled and messily creative-looking. "Brilliant," he said. "We can use that for *Kiki*."

Whit had never been in her rented room until he came over for the editing. Among all her things, he was most drawn to the Land of Make-Believe map. "That's how I found all the places in my mother's bedtime stories," she told him.

"My mother never read me anything but Bible stories," Whit said, still studying the map. "Maybe we should get in bed so you can educate me."

She laughed and clasped hands. " 'Don't go, Peter. I know such a lot of stories.' " For once, Whit didn't get the reference. "Wendy," she told him. "In *Peter Pan*, right before he teaches her to fly. Peter Pan was the first person I ever fell in love with."

"You fell in love with a cartoon?"

"No, first came the TV play with Mary Martin."

"Even kinkier. You fell in love with a woman pretending to be a boy."

"I didn't see the cartoon till I was six. Daddy took me to the Varsity when Disney brought the movie out again."

"I always had to sneak off to movies."

"Why?"

"Because the baby Jesus never watched them? Because they're graven images? Who knows. We're talking about people who put on the Monkey Trial."

"No wonder you're blocked. I'll tell you what. When you need a childhood, you can borrow mine."

He held out his arms, looking too moved to speak, and when he released her from a long hug, she saw that his eyes were glistening.

Soon their time together developed a regular rhythm. Whit wrote while she was in class and studying at the library, then he picked her up and she retyped that day's edited, pasted-together pages on his Remington (which, as it turned out, only punched through o's on very thin paper). After that, they shopped for the dinner that she would make, and after that, Phoebe sang and played her Martin. One night she sang a Maybelle Carter bluegrass song, "Keep on the Sunny Side," then "Marieke," her favorite Jacques Brel ballad, followed by Slim Gaillard's "Flat Foot Floogie (with the Floy Floy)"—and was able, when Whit asked, to translate the title's Forties jive into plain English for him: prostitute with venereal disease. She jumped from late-Romantic German lieder to "Mack the Knife," from "Da Do Ron Ron" to "Do Wah Diddy Diddy," from Judy Garland to Patsy Cline. If Whit hadn't fully understood before how she could believe his radio show was meant especially for her, he did now.

Phoebe's work at the Remington was never just a matter of simple transcription, since once she got familiar with the screenplay format, she often ended up with two or three pages for his one. When the clattering Remington keys fell silent, Whit would go to the stereo and lift the needle off whatever music from Kiki's era he was playing. "What is it?" he'd ask.

"Oh, nothing," Phoebe answered one day when the drill was new. "Just an idea."

"Spill."

"Well, why is he asking her here what other artists she's posed for?"

"Isn't it obvious?" He sounded miffed. "Because she's naked and posing for *him*."

"But what he really wants to know," Phoebe said, "is how many other artists she's fucked."

"Such language out of that luscious little schoolgirl mouth." He frowned, considering. "You're right, it's better if she's onto what he's after."

"Maybe she even shoots him down."

"How?"

"She could say something."

"What?"

"I don't know."

"Okay," Whit said, "let's try. How many other painters have you taken off your clothes for?"

Phoebe gave him her idea of a Gallic moue. "You ask an awful lot of questions for an artist."

"Put it in," Whit said, "put it in. But write it so she's vamping. Have her coming on to him."

"What if she makes him change places with her?"

"What do you mean?"

Phoebe grinned. "She could put on her robe—"

"Nah, let her stay naked."

"Okay, she walks naked from one side of the canvas to the other and orders him to go sit for her."

"With his clothes on?"

"That's what he can say. 'With my clothes on?'"

Whit came over and kissed the top of her head. "I love a good curtain line. Our movie will have lots of them."

Our movie? Phoebe felt such a thrill that if she hadn't already been convinced they'd taken up residence together inside the Magic Circle, that would have been the clincher.

"I've been trying to get you for weeks," Jack said when Phoebe called. "Are you sure you sent me the right phone number? You are going to school, aren't you?"

"Of course. But I'm spending most of my time in Port Pritchard. I've got a boyfriend there; he's making a film."

The more she tried to reassure Jack, the more questions he asked. Phoebe not only had to disabuse him of his first notion—of her boyfriend as a kid in her college intro course—but bring Whit to life for Jack so he would believe this person he knew only as a deejay could pull off directing a film about Kiki. She purposely bypassed all the things she couldn't possibly explain, like the seductive spell Whit cast with his enthusiasm for whatever captured his attention. Instead she talked of his background. How he fled the South with an art scholarship at a midwestern university, where he happened to see the Man Ray film in which Kiki does nothing but open and close her eyes, with another pair of eyes painted on her lids—the same surreal image that would begin Whit's film. How he'd designed sets for the theater department, which led to acting and a stint in the San Francisco Mime Troupe, where he met the founders of a Seattle theater company who insisted that the Pacific Northwest was the place where a visionary like him could really find his legs. It wouldn't further Phoebe's cause to mention the odd array of paying jobs Whit had worked since arriving in Seattle (movie theater manager, art gallery director, newspaper ad solicitor), so she didn't. The crowning achievement in Phoebe's biography of Whit was, of course, his documentary about Northwest

Mystic painters. Which, as it turned out, Jack had not only seen but admired.

"How old is this fellow?" Jack asked.

"Twenty-eight," Phoebe lied. She felt funny about saying "He's ageless," which was how Whit had directed her to respond if anyone inquired. Thirty-four might be considered getting on for a first-time film director, but that was nothing compared to how it sounded in connection with your eighteen-year-old daughter. No, twenty-eight would be plenty old enough to Jack's ears. And Whit looked plenty young enough to pull it off.

All this data about Whit was not easy for Phoebe to acquire. He didn't believe in the past; what mattered, he said, was the present. So to keep him from clamming up she muffled her interest when out slipped detailed bits of Whit's life that she found particularly intriguing. Such as the death of an adored older sister when he was six. Or how he couldn't eat red meat after watching his father slit the throat of a cow Whit had raised for 4-H. Or the fact that Whit had been named for a grandfather who was a Church of Christ preacher and pretty much disowned him when he went to art school.

No wonder Whit had such an imagination for disaster. No wonder he not only elicited Phoebe's protection but was so protective of her, panicking in the grip of some imagined calamity if she was ten minutes late to meet him. She was just about the only family he had. All the more reason to share her father. Surely Jack, movie maven that he was, would appreciate Whit's plans for *Kiki*. And with his scholarly background, Jack might even be able to address some of the issues troubling Whit.

Jack had another woman in his life these days—Helen, a fellow professor whose work he'd edited in the historical quarterly. But he arrived alone to meet Phoebe and Whit at Le Tastevin, his favorite French restaurant in Seattle. "So," Jack said to Whit after they ordered aperitifs, "I understand you're making a film about Kiki."

"Well," Whit said, "thanks to your daughter, the script's laying out in my head well enough for me to give you some highlights." Phoebe sipped her red Dubonnet with a lemon twist while Whit took Jack through scenes showing Kiki's bastard girlhood and how she became the avant-garde's muse, posing nude for Montparnasse artists, beginning her love affair with Man Ray, singing her risqué songs for the demimonde at their favorite nightclub. The trip to New York for a screen test that led nowhere but straight back to Paris. American dollars turning shadowy, low-rent Montparnasse into everything anathema to its pioneer bohemians—a prosperous, brightly lit tourist destination, with only Kiki enduring as before.

"I wonder what your vision of her is," Jack said. "Do you see her more as an object of interest for these artists, or as an artist in her own right?"

"Great question," Whit said, and pulled a tiny notebook out of his jacket pocket to record it. Then it was as if Whit had crested the peak of an unseen roller coaster, because down he went, making Jack aware of all the obstacles he faced. Period movies were expensive. Costumes, sets, cars—they all cost more money. There wouldn't be the budget to shoot in France, they'd have to make do in Old Montreal, which could pass for Paris only through the lens of a cinematographer so extraordinary they probably wouldn't be able to afford him. Also, Kiki wasn't exactly famous anymore, but this liability, Whit hoped, would be balanced by the titillation of what he referred to as "her modern attitude toward sex." Then he fretted about whether he'd be sued for invasion of privacy if he fictionalized Kiki—an issue that Jack could address with some authority.

"Dead people have no rights of privacy," Jack said. With a glance at Phoebe he added, "I'd say that, basically, she's there for the taking."

"It's such a relief," Whit said, "talking to somebody in the know on this, not having to explain who Kiki is."

After they studied their menus and ordered, Whit turned back to Jack. "Did you know Phoebe was born right after Kiki died? If I believed in reincarnation, I'd be spooked. She even looks like her."

"Well," Jack said dryly, "the hairdo helps."

Phoebe caught a pleat of disapproval in his voice. "I got in trouble using Mother's French edition of Kiki's book for a sixth-grade book report," she said. "Did you know?" Jack shook his head. "I guess that was one of *our* little secrets," Phoebe said.

"Yes, your mother was a great one for secrets. So are you." He looked at her sharply, then reached under his glasses to rub his eyes as if they were tired. Phoebe could tell he was tearing up, but she could no more question his emotion than she could Whit's. "Pearl had that book when we met," Jack went on. "It was one of her treasures. She read fluently in French, even though she never felt comfortable speaking it. I gave her the American edition so she could compare the two, see how all Kiki's colorful language translated into English."

Phoebe nodded. "*The Education of a French Model*—that's the copy we're using for the script. We're working on it together."

Whit put his arm around Phoebe. "She's my partner in crime."

"I guessed as much," Jack said, "when she first mentioned the film."

If he guessed that, then he must have also guessed by

now that Phoebe was in touch with Whit before she left Eugene, maybe even why Phoebe was so agreeable to school in Mount Jensen. But she didn't ask and he didn't say—as was their custom. In all the time they enjoyed together in Eugene, dining out and attending cultural events, never once did Jack inquire about his daughter's experiences or venture into any territory that might turn charged or unpleasant. Phoebe had followed his lead, figuring it wasn't that he had anything against strong feelings, just that he preferred getting at them from a distance, through his books, his movies, his music.

"That book is bootlegged, you know," Jack said. "A renegade American publisher put it out, Samuel Roth. He was famous for that sort of thing. Went to prison for printing *Ulysses* when it was banned. So he had nerve, in a slimy sort of way. But his specialty was exploiting authors. He didn't pay them, and they were in no position to stop him. I doubt Kiki ever saw a sou from that man. Although by then, I believe she had just about drunk and drugged herself to death."

"That's something Phoebe and I have been debating," Whit said. "I say absinthe, she says cocaine."

"Most likely cocaine." Jack gave an expressionless chuckle. "I don't suppose you plan to dwell on *that* in your movie."

"No, no, no. It's the larger-than-life Kiki I care about. I'm just nervous. Probably because of the documentary. You wouldn't believe all the legal hoops I had to jump through. The network was so afraid of being sued. I imagine my producer will be, too."

Jack gave a small harrumph. "I doubt you'll have any trouble at all basing a U.S. movie on a pirated book written by a dead woman with no heirs."

Phoebe wondered for a second if Jack was putting Whit into the same boat as that Roth character he'd been talking about. But Whit, who had a far sharper instinct for insult than she, was unruffled. "Another relief," he said, raising a glass of the Pomerol Jack had ordered. "Here's to you, Professor Allen."

Jack raised his glass to Phoebe. "And here's to the education of an American young lady. I'd be so pleased to see your name on the screen, Phoebe. If the movie comes to pass. If that's Whit's intention." Phoebe turned to Whit, who nodded at her father. "Yes, that would be exciting," Jack went on. "And you've always liked learning on your own. By *self*," he added with a small, almost sorrowful smile. "But I hope you're not neglecting your classes."

"Haven't missed one. Whit won't let me."

Whit shrugged, nonchalant, poker-faced. "That's what she's there for, isn't it?"

Now both of her men looked relieved. Mission accomplished. Still, it bothered her a little, how easily Jack seemed to cede the matter of her well-being. She guessed why when she went inside the house with him at the end of the evening to borrow a few of his books about Bohemian Paris. "Before you go," he said, "I've got news. Helen and I are marrying at the end of spring quarter."

On the drive back to Port Pritchard with Whit, as Phoebe pretended to sleep, tears slipped down her cheeks. Jack could find another wife, but the only way she could duplicate what she'd lost with Pearl was to become a mother herself. *Not now,* she thought as actual sleep overtook her. *But someday.*

After Whit sent off a rough draft of the script, his mood swung wildly between believing that he was about to make the most important film in cinematic history and that he was blowing his last chance at significance in the world. Out of the manic energy generated by these fluctuations, Dolores con Cuervos was conceived, costumed, and given her debut at the Tavern. She was a country girl at heart, Dolores was, but with an edge so raucous, so worldly, that she sang French verses to "Black Denim Trousers (and Motorcycle Boots)" while wearing a beret. For her Spanish rendition of "I'm Gonna Be Strong," she swapped the beret for a tinsel-fringed cowgirl hat. Whit was the only audience Phoebe cared about pleasing, but the pool players, waitresses, and just about everybody who wandered in for a draft or a burger on the weeknights she sang, loggers and longhairs alike, applauded for her like mad.

"You could take your act on the road," Whit said after one of her gigs. He was in bed while Phoebe toweled off after her shower and slathered on vanilla-scented skin lotion. "You're good enough."

"And leave you?"

"I'll be your manager. Just like Loretta Lynn and What's-His-Name."

"Not if you make your movie."

"This'll be my fallback career. After the movie goes belly-up."

"Oh, right." But something in his voice made her turn to look at him. "What did you hear?"

"Can't fool you, can I?"

She pounced onto the bed and took his hands in hers. "You talked to him! What did he say?"

"We're on."

"So he liked the script?"

"Well, Joe understands the script is only a blueprint—"

"Ooooh, I love it when you talk like a director."

"He kept asking me about how I'd shoot the ménage à trois scene. You can bet he'll be on the set if that day ever comes." Whit laced his fingers behind his head and gave Phoebe a penetrating look. "It's one thing to put it in the script, and another to know what it's like. How women go about it, I mean."

"I wouldn't know."

"But you could guess, right?"

"Well, sure."

"Maybe we'll have to do some research."

On the surface, his tone was light and teasing. Phoebe could only counter with banter of her own. "What about you? Do you ever guess about being with another man and a woman?"

"Please—one naked man is plenty. I mean, I'm really grateful there are women who disagree, but men are so . . . ugly."

"A lot of women feel that way about their bodies. The hidden parts, anyway."

"What can I say? They're wrong. Wrong, wrong, wrong."

Phoebe wriggled beneath the covers, perplexed by their conversation but more excited about the movie. To celebrate, she made long, elaborate love to Whit, leading him on the route he best liked taking her—to the edge and back repeatedly, prolonging the thrill, which for her now included a heady new sense of command, of dominion over bodily territory almost as familiar as her own.

"Hey, little schoolgirl, you really ought to be getting credits for *that*," he said afterward as she lay against him, thigh flung over his stomach. When he spoke again, though, he sounded a little frightened. "If this thing actually does get rolling, I'll need you with me. Maybe you could take a semester off—come down to California, work on *Kiki*. And I'll bet they go for Dolores at the Troubadour. What do you say?"

"I'll think about it," Phoebe said, and she meant it—there was a lot to consider. Ditching school, disappointing her father, the prospect of performing, in so many ways, in such a big arena. But already her heart was racing with the answer he wanted.

9

After staying up late reading Whit's letters, Phoebe awoke before dawn and rattled around the house. Going through stacks of *Fishermen's Journals* and *New Yorkers*. Simmering up a winter's worth of chicken stock out of frozen necks and backbones. Watching an old Barbara Stanwyck movie, hoping all that tough girl dialogue would act as some sort of inoculation.

When the sky lightened to a dull nacreous hue, she emerged from the house wrapped in Gore-Tex for a wet walk with Lily. On her way to the beach, she crossed a broad stand of cedars between her house and Ivan's. Trills of music bled beyond his studio walls—cranked-up Philip Glass—and the windows shone with fluorescent work lights. No surprise in his not running out to join her given how she'd behaved at the Tavern, but something unexpected in how punished she felt. Impossible to trust him the way he wanted, not now, with so much slippery stuff resisting her grip. And reading Whit's old letters hadn't helped, just delivered a blinding one-two punch, resurrecting first the thrill stirred by their arrival, then the anguish of losing all that love.

She continued down to the water, where the air smelled of seaweed. Herons fished the shallows, slow-stepping between rocks hung with shiny black mussels. An extreme full-moon minus tide had hit its nadir, sucking huge drafts of Little Pritchard Bay through Deception Pass and then out to sea. Dories and cruisers hooked to far-out anchors tilted at odd, undignified angles, with a look of insult at being forced to sit their bottoms down in mud. Phoebe threw a stick for Lily and lost her footing on an algae-covered rock. Landing hard on her ass, she just sat there and cried. She ought to burn the letters. Light a match to the bunch and see if anything resembling confidence and good sense rose from the ashes. She couldn't imagine Whit hanging on to every single letter *she* had written, tied up in ribbon for all her successors to find. It was pathetic, keeping an archive like that. But what about the Mystery Packages? What about the new script she'd inspired? Things that might mean it all was alive inside him, too.

Phoebe blew her nose, dried her eyes, stood up, and kept walking west, past Whit's house and around the bend to the south side. Now the wind was in her face instead of at her back. She felt cold, tired, hungry. Spotting smoke from Margaret's chimney, she climbed the hill to her place, heading for comfort—and maybe just a little enlightenment.

Ever since the barbecue, Phoebe had been brooding over Margaret's observation about how difficult it was for her to accept a compliment, wondering what that meant in the broader scheme of things. She had also been avoiding Margaret. Margaret had to know something was up. They usually saw each other several times a month, for movies and dinners and weekend junking trips. Margaret was a master at sifting through piles of domestic dross to find the gold, and Phoebe, whose senses overloaded early in the hunt, relied on her eye. They liked the same sort of chewy psychological novels; the same sort of slow, dense films; the same sort of probing, nuanced conversation. No question about it, Margaret's nurturing energy and twenty years' seniority were an enormous draw, and Phoebe imagined she played an opposite role, since Margaret's only child, a son, had died from an AIDS-related illness. If there was anyone she ought to confide in, it was Margaret, who would guard her secrets just as she did the privacy of her clients.

"Finally," Margaret said when she came to the door, face streaked with flour and smelling of cumin. *"Entrez vous."*

"Are you sure? You look busy."

"I'm talented enough to talk and cook. Grab some logs—I'll dry off Lily."

Even in her weekend grubbies, Margaret looked stylish. Not for her the loose, flowing clothes worn by most older women. She still had a waist and she liked to show it. For reasons Margaret insisted were more professional than vain, she dyed her hair and even had a plastic surgeon take some tiny tucks to tighten the skin around her eyes and neck. "Maternal's great," she'd told Phoebe, "but my clients are young and nobody wants Grandma for a therapist." Her kitchen was more like a living room, with a fireplace, comfy chairs, and overflowing bookshelves. As Phoebe fed the fire, Margaret finished searing lamb cubes in a blue enamel pot.

"Having a party without me?" Phoebe asked.

"Just making a stew for freezing. But I ought to have a party *for* you, long as you've been gone." Margaret tipped wine into the pot, then poured coffee and put out a plate of fruit with some sliced Emmenthaler. "You look tired. What's going on?"

And so she told her. Not everything—not about Ivan's becoming her lover, not about the Mystery Packages or Laurienne's conception. Those were stories she didn't know how to begin. She spoke only of Whit—how they had met, how *Kiki* came from their time together, how she had seen him at the Tavern. That was enough for now, and it wouldn't make her cry.

"Well," Margaret said when she finished. "You sure have been sitting with a lot."

Phoebe nodded. It wasn't advice she wanted so much as soothing.

"I met him, you know," Margaret said. "At a little dinner the Browns gave. His wife, too. What's her name, Iris?"

"No, Jasmine. Another Phoebe. That's what he called her."

Margaret looked astonished. "Interesting," she said.

"It really pissed me off, that he could think I was replaceable. Is that what you mean?"

"Well, I guess there are a few physical similarities. Pretty smile, gorgeous skin. And she's got black hair, like you did, only hers is colored, I bet. But if you want my opinion, it's a competition he's set up—with him in the middle."

Phoebe felt a rush of anger, as if she'd been slapped, though it came on so hard and fast it had to be all out of proportion to what Margaret had said. "You're giving him bad motive, aren't you? Maybe he just missed me and didn't know how to fix it."

"Maybe. But you don't have to stick around, watching him take little honeys and call them Phoebe. Jasmine is certainly darling about it, but my sense is, all her power comes through her husband. And believe me, she knows him like an ant knows an aphid."

Long divorced, a woman who'd had better luck with lovers than husbands, Margaret preferred solitude to a man who wanted a traditional wife and couldn't keep up with her. It was a choice that had always made sense to Phoebe, who used it as justification for her own choices. But now she resisted Margaret's snap judgment and its implicit put-down of Whit. She'd rather fault Jasmine—for being an astrologer, for lacking an intellectual edge, for having too-perfect teeth. But mainly for perfecting her own old unconscious role with Whit, doing by design what she had done only for love, and getting to enjoy all the benefits of his success into the bargain—the prestige, the travel, the easy life that let her pursue work divorced from necessity, like an interesting hobby. A favorite villainous line of Captain Hook's rose to mind: *That's* the canker that gnaws. And it was all much too shameful and unfair to admit. Especially with Margaret being so negative about Whit. In Phoebe's behalf, no doubt, but this wasn't the consolation she'd come here hungering for.

"I'm sorry," Margaret said, reaching over to pat her cheek. "You weren't ready for that."

Late in the afternoon, Phoebe went to the woodstove with Pearl's old blue Bon box in hand, but her determination to burn Whit's letters vanished just as impulsively as it arose. She was on the garage stepladder again, returning the box and its painful evidence to exile, when the phone rang. She dashed inside to answer.

"Dollies are running," Laurienne said by way of greeting.

"Dollies are running," Phoebe repeated into the receiver, stumped until she realized Laurienne meant Dolly Vardens—wildly colored spotted trout named for a flashy-dressing Dickens character. "Oh, *those* Dollies." Her daughter and Ivan had a long-standing tradition of catching Dollies on the river together. Much as Phoebe appreciated a flamboyant fish with literary lineage, she only once managed to get out at the crack of dawn to catch them.

"We're going out in the morning," Laurienne said. "I'll be home in time for dinner tonight, if that's okay."

"Sure. I'll ask Amelia over."

"How about Ivan?"

"I don't think so." Phoebe pulled a container of pesto made from last summer's basil out of the freezer to thaw. "We're taking a little break from each other."

"I thought something was wrong with him."

"We're grown-ups. Whatever's between us won't get on you."

"I know," Laurienne said. "I'm just disappointed."

"Me, too."

"What are you going to do about it?"

"If I knew, I wouldn't need a break, would I?"

"What are you so afraid of?"

A good question, but it just made Phoebe feel cornered and snarly. "Keep it up, Laurienne, and I'll need a break from you, too."

Laurienne must have been ready to leave that instant, because she blazed the seventy-five miles from Seattle and breezed through the front door in little more than an hour. Before releasing her from a long hug, Phoebe had to stifle another surge of tears. *No more crying,* she commanded herself, then went back to assembling ingredients for a pesto risotto.

"What can I do?" Laurienne asked.

Preparing food together, they moved with the ease of old dance partners. While Phoebe sliced smoked salmon, diced shallots, and soaked morels dried last spring, Laurienne threw a salad together and told her about work, the comprehensive new database her team was designing to isolate disease-causing genes. Exciting science, maybe. But hardly personal enough to account for Laurienne's flushed, hectic exhilaration. Phoebe dug further for the buried lead: Cliff and the Lexie Shields game.

"Sounds great," Phoebe said. She had her doubts, though. Laurienne's braininess and achievements used to seem like good preventive medicine, fortifying the self-esteem all the experts now claimed girls lost their grip on in early adolescence. But maybe her daughter's drive was just a cover, like Lexie's costume, and underneath she was still wide open to attack. Even though Phoebe had never played a computer game more complicated than Pong, this seemed such a guy thing, creating worlds where you could win big and blow things up at the same time. What was Laurienne doing, playing with the boys in that arena? Must be fatherlessness that made males so fascinating and mysterious, magnetizing her to them for definition. That superheroine of hers even had a missing father—one she would kill for to save.

"Do you have a contract with Cliff?" Phoebe asked.

"A contract? No. Why?"

"Because you're doing so much work on the game."

"He'll be fair."

"You can't count on that."

"I know him a whole lot better than you do."

"I just don't want to see you making the same mistakes I did."

"Mother," Laurienne said, drawing out the syllables in the age-old tone of aggrieved daughters. "I'm making a game with him, not a baby."

"That's not what I meant."

"You were pregnant when you got married, though, weren't you?"

"Me and lots of other women."

"But you never flat-out told me."

"The important thing was, I wanted you to be born. So did Mitchell."

"Would you still be together if he hadn't died?" Laurienne asked.

"That's hard to say." And it was. Not only because of how Mitchell died, with Phoebe at the wheel, but because of the untold story living just down the road now. Still, simple to infer an answer for Laurienne's question from the fact that not one couple from the days when she and Mitchell first moved onto the Road had stayed intact, not one. Their youth, the times, the drugs—hardly great guarantors of marital longevity. Maybe Mitchell had what it took to last, but what about her? "We might have made it through all the stuff that wrecked everybody else," Phoebe qualified. "He was pretty special."

"Doesn't mean Ivan can't be special, too," Laurienne said.

Phoebe sighed. "I know."

For all her reluctance to supply fully fleshed stories from the past, Phoebe had never stinted on describing Mitchell for Laurienne. A sweet, smart man from a mean, dumb background. With a violent, alcoholic father, a mother who died too young (another lost grandmother), a brother killed in Vietnam, a sister married to a Mormon deacon with five kids of her own. That was the biography Laurienne already knew. Mitchell Gentry had been a dog in a family of cats, a cowbird in a nest of jays, which only made him all the more exceptional. And so he remained the dead but otherwise perfect father, the grinning red-headed mannish boy in snapshots who played the Gibson guitar Laurienne inherited and built the cradle she first slept in. Who was tall and athletic, like her; who loved jigsaw puzzles, like her; and who had saved her life. So now she kept knocking herself out to prove worthy of his sacrifice. Hard for Phoebe to reconcile such a dire thought with the girl now flipping on a World Party CD and bopping around the kitchen table, holding Lily's front paws. A whole new reason emerged for not saddling Laurienne with any disturbing new information about how she came to be: she was in love.

Laurienne yawned her way through dinner and went to bed after clearing the table. While Amelia loaded the dishwasher, Phoebe poured blackberry cordial into Pearl's delicate cut-glass cups and got out the Scrabble board.

"I saw Ivan," Amelia said, picking wooden letters out of the old sock Phoebe kept them in. "Want to talk about it?"

"Now here's a pretty word," Phoebe said. "'Herald.' Double word score, double letter on the *h*, let's see— twenty-eight points. Look out, Amelia, I'm cleaning your clock."

"As usual. I have five consonants and two vowels, both *i*'s."

"Don't tell me; make a word."

"Can it be in Welsh? Okay, okay—'bill,' six whole points. Did you know Jasmine's husband used to hang out around here a long time ago?"

Phoebe just nodded, as if pulling six new letters from the sock required absolute concentration.

"She read my chart today," Amelia went on. "It was amazing—she totally tapped into me."

Phoebe's heart fluttered and she reached for the cordial. "Did you go to her place?"

"No," Amelia said. "She's got a little office at Fishermen's Terminal. Says her husband doesn't like her doing readings at home. It's a neat setup, real Zen. I'm such a ditz, though. She gave me this great reading and I forgot to bring the teas we swapped for."

Phoebe went to the kitchen drawer for a Nat. "What did she say?"

"Do you have to smoke?"

"Not if it bothers you."

"You're the one it's going to bother someday."

Phoebe replaced the pack and folded her arms. "Well?" she said, giving Amelia a go-ahead nod.

"Well," Amelia said, "she zoomed right in on my afflicted Jupiter."

"Whatever that means." Reductive little recipes, that's what they seemed like whenever Amelia laid any astrology on her. *Your Virgo Venus is so persnickety when it comes to men.* Or: *No wonder you do the work you do, all that water in your chart.*

"For one thing," Amelia said, "it means that I shouldn't be allowed to pick out my own sweeties."

Sound advice, actually. In the grip of a crush, Amelia went straight to intimacy, skipping all the usual preliminaries. No movies, no dinners, no long revealing talks. When it came to men, a girl like Amelia never got the growl for the grin. Margaret chalked it up to Amelia having attention deficit disorder, but then ADD was one of Margaret's specialties and she tended to see its symptoms everywhere. Amelia must have told Jasmine about Dennis—the guy from the Bureau of Indian Affairs, her latest romantic disaster-in-the-making. When Phoebe had called to ask Amelia to dinner, she'd heard the abridged version. How Amelia finagled to get off her shift early last night, chatted up Dennis and discovered that he had just quit smoking, so she took the bit in her teeth and ran, showing up at his motel room in the wee hours with a basketful of lung-restoring teas and then, as though that were foreplay, hopping into bed with him. Be careful, Phoebe had cautioned, but Amelia swore she and Dennis were both washed clean to the elbows, which made it sound as if they'd engaged in surgery instead of sex, then rhapsodized about how soulful southwestern Indians were. Phoebe could count on the fingers of both hands similar exchanges over the years. So now it was annoying, hearing Amelia sound so bowled over by Jasmine's advice.

"What does Jasmine propose?" Phoebe asked. "That she inspect guys before you sleep with them?"

"No." Amelia leveled a dead-serious look. "She says *you* should."

"What? How did she make that leap?"

"Well, we were talking about all the planets in my eleventh house of friends, and she did this incredible riff on best friends. How they know our hearts and show us things about ourselves and we always trust their judgment. She says she married her best friend."

"Good for her. What did you tell her about me?"

"Just that we're good friends. Why are you so paranoid? I saw you talking to them at the Tavern. Jasmine and her husband—what's his name?"

"Whit Traynor."

"I must not have lived here when he was around before. I wouldn't forget a guy like that. Ivan remembers him, though."

Phoebe was sure Ivan had moved to the island after her time in town with Whit, but since Amelia always got little details like that wrong, the point didn't seem worth disputing. "Okay, my turn," Phoebe said, dropping back into her chair. "Are we going to play or gossip?"

"You sound like a man. It's not gossip, Phoebe, it's sharing information. It's what girlfriends do. It's what *we* used to do."

"Okay, okay. I knew Whit once, but so what? I used to know a lot of people."

"Why didn't you say so sooner?"

"He's a very private person and so am I, Amelia. So am I." She spelled out "quest" on a triple-score square and recorded her points.

Amelia dumped a fistful of consonants with "crown" and addressed the ceiling. "Some people are great at listening to all *your* problems. But they won't admit to having any of their own."

"Oh," Phoebe said. "I read about someone like that once."

In a burst of laughter, Amelia sprayed her mouthful of cordial down her sweater. She rushed for the dish towel, wet it, and dabbed at the purple stains. "Damn, I shouldn't be allowed to wear white," she said, then turned back to Phoebe. "For your information, there are actual health benefits to women talking things over."

"Is this the gospel according to Oprah, or more of Jasmine's amazing riff on friendship?"

"No, smart-ass. An article in one of my homeopathy magazines, about how stressed women produce some brain chemical men can't make, and this chemical makes women want to nurture and be nurtured. Which produces even more of the chemical, and that extra amount is what calms you down."

"What do you know, the old wives beat another bum rap."

"So talk to me."

"Come on, we talk. We were talking. We will be talking. That's almost the full conjugation—what else do you want?"

Amelia shook her head. "You can dish it out, Phoebe, but you can't take it. You've got to ask for help when you need some."

Tried that, Phoebe thought. *Didn't work.* Either her brain had forgotten how to produce this soothing chemical of Amelia's, or was burning through it the way a damaged engine did oil. She plunked down three letters in front of an *s* for "nets," then changed her mind and switched the order to spell "nest." Nest. As in the thing she mustn't foul.

On Sunday, after Laurienne returned with her Dollies and Phoebe fried up the biggest of them for lunch, they drove to Mount Jensen together. First stop was the bookstore, for some serious browsing and early Christmas shopping. Next, a new movie at the art house. Phoebe would have seen anything, just for two hours of escape, but had she checked reviews first, she might have thought twice about going with Laurienne to *Secrets and Lies*. A British film, about a black girl who tracks down her white biological mother. Later, over Coronas and carnitas at the Crying Pig, Laurienne said, "If I were the girl in the movie, I wouldn't have been so positive that woman was my mother. I'd have made sure the hospital didn't screw up."

"Well," Phoebe said, clearing her throat, "movies have their own reality."

"That's what you used to say about fairy tales."

"Good, I still agree with myself. Besides, those characters had plenty of conflicts. They didn't need more."

"Hey, I enjoyed it. In fact, it made me want to find relatives on my father's side."

Phoebe nodded as if she understood. But later, as she lay in bed, this wish of Laurienne's kept her awake with its time bomb's tick. Just where should her daughter go to track down blood kin, to the Gentrys or the Traynors?

Monday morning's routine tasks and duties came as a relief. When Phoebe went downstairs, Laurienne's coffee cup was rinsed and on the drain board. She had al-

ready left for Seattle. Ridiculous for Phoebe to feel
slighted by this, but she did. It was her own fault, for not
being happier over Cliff and the game. And especially for
not showing more confidence in Laurienne's judgment—
the same behavior she'd found so irksome when Margaret used it on her. She picked up the phone and left a
cheerful message at Laurienne's office, inviting her out
to dinner in Seattle next week, when she'd be there for
Fish Expo. "Ask Cliff to come," she added. "I'd love to
meet him." There, that felt better.

Phoebe showered, dressed, and drove to town. A crowd
of Indians were walking toward the Tribal Center, and
as she passed in the Explorer, a few hid their faces behind arms and hats. One little girl crouched to the
ground and pulled a poncho over her head. It happened
every year, this daylong celebration of sacred singing,
dancing, and drumming, and for its duration, strict ob-
servers avoided eye contact with white people. Which
always seemed the wrong way around to Phoebe. Whenever someone hid from her she wanted to say, No, don't—
I'll hide *my* face, okay? Difficult to convey, though,
especially from behind the wheel, and besides, she appreciated the need to be the one who does the rejecting.

For all her Monday-morning fresh-start determination, Phoebe took a circuitous route into Port Pritchard,
driving past the house where she had once lived with
Whit. No longer a rental, it had been sold to an architect
who added on a residential wing and used the old structure as his office. When Phoebe went there years ago
to contract improvements for her own house, she cataloged differences with detached interest. A large wooden
flat file in the old sleeping loft, drawing tables where the
desk had stood, a new skylight. The only unchanged
space was the galleylike kitchen, with wood and brass
polished to a high gloss. She had felt good coming here

then—wielding a checkbook, controlling a clear-cut transaction. Not like now, crawling by so addle-brained that it took a friendly toot from Sandra the postmistress to get her moving again.

More coffee—that would clear her head. Pulling into the lot by Westerly Webs, she noticed a handful of fishermen, early returns from Alaska, throwing down nets. She bought a double latte at the Terminal espresso stand and walked among them, looking for crazy renditions of repairs made at sea. First stop: waves of uneven mesh sewn into a zigzagging hole. "Hmmm," she said in earshot of the skipper.

He looked up in a flash. "What?"

"Nothing," she said, sipping her coffee. "I just hope you're going to fix that."

"Why?" He sounded like a nervous kid afraid she was going to tell on him. "You don't think this is okay?"

"Maybe you'll get it right next time it tears."

She moved on to another net. "You're lucky I came by. Those bar cuts are angled the wrong way."

One more stop before going inside. "You're going to clean those knots, aren't you?"

Phoebe liked tweaking them, liked having them hang on her every word. Good for business, too. Although they weren't exactly putty in her hands, these men. Part of what drew her to water folk in the first place was how many free spirits could be counted among them— musicians, raconteurs, practical jokers, serious readers. Not unlike the movie world, in her experience, with one huge exception. Fishermen rarely screwed each other over. They couldn't afford that kind of ego. A fatal movie set accident made headlines, but fishermen died all the time. Just last year, nineteen drowned in the Alaskan waters where her fleet fished, and the risk made them seem to get something extra out of being alive.

Mitchell had fit right in, felt like he'd found a much sweeter way to make good money than build movie sets, which he'd been doing when they met. But then Mitchell had started fishing in the bonanza days. When Port Pritchard skippers were getting their first taste of Alaskan beauty and bounty. When fortunes were made. When she worried about Mitchell dying young at sea, not by her side in a flipped-over pickup.

As Phoebe settled in at her desk, Sophie returned from the post office with the morning mail. Phoebe noticed an envelope with no stamp or postal mark, just her name. Typed manually, in a Courier style so quaint and familiar she knew right away who had sent it.

P.O. Box 923
Port Pritchard

My Dear Phoebe,
   My not-so-long list of enduring things includes your place in my heart and the Remington I'm typing on right now. What about you? Still got yours? Kindly reply to my new secret post office box.

   Love,
   W.T.

Short as Whit's message was, Phoebe wasted time pondering it like a cryptic crossword clue. So he got a secret post office box where he could hide her. Nothing to get so flattered and flustered over. Especially since he still hadn't answered any of the questions that made her so crazed. She knew what Margaret would make of it all. He was married now. His note didn't change a thing.
   Phoebe grabbed a piece of stationery, scooted over to

the Underwood, and rattled out her response, stopping three times to peel off the errant *x*.

Westerly Webs
P.O. Box 367
Port Pritchard, WA 98246
(360) 692-5158; fax (360) 692-5159

Whit,
   Right from the start, we were postal. Who knew what <u>that</u> would end up meaning?
   Still got mine (as you can see). It's stuck in the key of X. Tempting to interpret. But all things considered, I think it's best to just let X equal X.

   Be well and happy,
   P.A.

10

Laurienne was taking a shortcut from Owl Island to Interstate 5 when the Volvo's engine coughed, sputtered, then went dead. A lousy spot for mechanical failure—not on a busy highway where there'd be plenty of people to stop and help, but on a farmer's back road, with no one in sight. Steamy tongues of river fog licked at furrows of freshly turned soil, dotted with foraging gulls. Even inside the car, with windows up, she could smell the manure from a dairy farm miles away. With that odor in her nose, just the idea of eating the cranberry scone she'd bought in Port Pritchard was nauseating. Her only choice was to wait, a long while, with nothing to do but stew over how irresponsibly late she'd be for work. If she had to just sit, she'd rather have a fishing pole in her hand.

On the river yesterday with Ivan, pulling up Dollies, time had dissolved back into the old spaciousness of her childhood, when long, unmonitored hours of spontaneous diversion were the norm. Then came high school in Seattle and a whole other sense of time, as a rationed commodity. Living by the watch for bus schedules, team practices, study hours, sleep—especially sleep. And as she jumped into bigger ponds with even more fish, time continued shrinking. "You're just paying dues, Judge," Ivan told her. "You'll write your own ticket when you're ready." She wasn't so sure. Unlike Ivan or her mother, she didn't think of herself as stand-out smart. She'd discussed this with Gabe, the one other kid she grew up with on the Road who understood; you might be a brainiac to everyone back home, but people smarter than you not only exist, they're a dime a dozen, waiting to take your place.

In Seattle, her only time-melts were Cliff and Lexie. Lately, she and Cliff had been staying up so late, finishing the Lexie Shields prototype in his hyperheated apartment, that they would leave for BioIngenious after just a few hours of sweaty sleep in each other's arms. It is only in this way, working on Lexie until sliding into a stupor, that Laurienne ever ended up spending the entire night with Cliff. It's happened often enough in the home stretch of Lexie's showcase battle against the mad scientists from an alternate universe, those alien demons holding Lexie's father hostage, that Laurienne had stashed a change of clothes in Cliff's closet, a bag of her favorite French Roast in his cupboard, and, in his refrigerator, cartons of cherry yogurt shaped like tiny nuclear power plants. Cliff said they should be ashamed of their wastefulness, keeping identical office hours yet never driving to or from work together, but there she won't yield. Her Dijon-mustard-colored Volvo has to be parked in her designated spot, Cliff's cream-of-tomato-soup Datsun in his, or she would really feel as if she were back in school, enthralled by another Lost Boy.

Ivan, unlike her mother, seemed to understand about Cliff. His caution was the opposite of Phoebe's. "It's fine to go slow," he had told her on the river, "so long as you don't cheat your real feelings."

"Like my mom with you?" she'd asked.

"A whole other ballpark," he said. "Closed for the season."

That was all she could get out of him on the subject—
a stupid sports metaphor. Not nearly enough for a verdict, though hearing much more would have made her
squirm like the night crawler on the end of her hook.
Phoebe's stinginess with information was one thing, but
who wanted the skinny on their mother's sex life?

Laurienne checked her rearview mirror as a pair of
headlights crept up from behind. Finally! She jumped
out to wave over a black Range Rover with California
plates.

The man driving parked behind her car, switched on
emergency flashers, and leaned out the window. "What's
the problem?"

"My battery must've died," Laurienne told him.

"Wait a second." He turned down the smoky trumpet
blaring on his car stereo. "What did you say?"

"I think it's the battery."

"Need a ride?" he asked.

"Just a jump."

"Sorry, I don't have cables."

"I do. Pull around to face my car, I'll get them."

He looked confused. "Wait, maybe we should push it
off the road. Someone might hit us."

"Nobody goes fast along here."

"But the fog."

He spoke slowly, with a southern accent. She always
had to override her automatic equation of accent with
dimwittedness, a prejudice that this guy, with his wide-
eyed lag time, was only reinforcing. "You saw me," Laurienne reminded him. "It's not that thick."

At last he swung the Range Rover in a wide arc, like
he was driving a Peterbilt. It took forever for him to figure out how to pop the hood on his car, and then he just
stood there, useless, watching while she attached cables

and raindrops stained his buttery leather bomber jacket. "Looks like you know what you're doing," he said.

"It's easy. Positive to positive, negative to ground."

"I can barely change a lightbulb." He said it as though his ability to admit such pedestrian incompetence was something quite remarkable. Or so it seemed, in her impatience. Normally she would have slowed down, shown appreciation for his time, taught him how to attach the cables himself. But with seconds ticking away in her head, she couldn't wait to get rid of him, couldn't wait to find a phone and call the office.

She hopped back into the Volvo, started the engine, and, letting it thrum, jumped out again to remove the cables. "Thanks, that ought to do it. Unless you have a phone."

"Nope. Driving is dream time for me. I hate those things. What you really should do is have a mechanic look at your car."

"I will," she said.

"I'll follow you, just in case."

"Really, I'll be fine." She didn't try to hide her exasperation—not that he seemed to notice.

"I insist."

."Suit yourself."

He kept his emergency lights flashing as he trailed her. What did he think he was, a police escort? And then the Volvo died again, this time with enough phlegm in its warning cough that she managed to pull off onto the shoulder before it ended. She beat the steering wheel with her fists, but already it was starting to strike her as payback, how fast she got shut down for trashing her Good Samaritan. She locked the car and walked back to him. "Must be the grounding wire."

"Can we fix it?"

We? She couldn't help laughing. "Nope, it's under the

car somewhere. I know a mechanic in Mount Jensen. If you could drop me off at the highway, I'll call from the gas station."

"I was just on my way to Mount Jensen for a Washington driver's license. How's that for a coincidence? Not that I believe in coincidence. Hop in."

Inside the car, she stuck out her hand. "Laurienne Gentry," she said. "Thanks for stopping."

"Whit Traynor. No problem." He waited until she buckled her seat belt before checking the road—with such prolonged wariness that Laurienne craned around for a look of her own. No other cars in sight. Still, he switched on his left-turn signal before pulling out again.

"Are you always so careful?" she asked. "Or just practicing in case they make you take a road test?"

"To be perfectly honest, Laurienne, I'm the tiniest bit stoned, therefore paranoid."

That explained a lot. The Range Rover's musky scent, the loud jazz, the molasses-like speed of his responses, his amazement at the most ordinary stuff. He wasn't so much creepy as, well, kind of goofy—and in a familiar way. It was the car that threw her off. Now that she stopped to really take him in, he wasn't even dressed like the regular older guy she'd mistaken him for. Regular older guys didn't wear nubby silk shirts with colored tees and jeans. These were the kind of clothes Ivan and his art buddies put on for openings and parties. Though she didn't expect Whit shopped for his at hands-of-the-World–type places or thrift stores, like they did. He could afford the upscale versions. "Are you some sort of artist?" she asked Whit.

"Why do you ask?"

"You just seem like the type."

"I make films," he said. "If that qualifies."

"A director?" He nodded. "Cool. Anything I've seen?"

"That depends," Whit said. "Are you a cinemaniac?"

"A little bit, yeah."

"Does your favorite theater put real butter on the popcorn?"

"Not just butter, but organic."

"Then you might have caught a few."

Was he famous enough that pressing for titles would be tacky? Something in his voice told her so. The rain stopped and Whit turned off his wipers. Laurienne rolled down her window for a blast of fresh air.

"Want to throw some glass in that blowhole?" he asked.

Glass in the blowhole? Now she was the one scrambling to keep up.

"I'll open the vents if it's the smoke smell bothering you," he clarified.

"Oh. Okay."

"Laurienne—pretty name. Never heard it before."

"My mom made it up."

"So what's *your* line?"

"Bioinformatics."

"Never heard of that, either," Whit said.

"Computer programming, with a biotech company."

"Companies like that are up here?"

"I just come from around here. My job's in Seattle."

"Sounds exciting," he said.

Instead of taking the Interstate turnoff, Whit stayed on the poplar-lined two-lane to Mount Jensen. Longer this way, but she'd forgotten her hurry. "Stressful is more like it."

"Pretty interesting, though, to someone like me. Dealing with all the stuff that makes us human. A lot of poetry there."

"A lot of greed, too—according to my boyfriend, anyway. He says biotech businessmen are the new robber barons."

"Yeah, well, robber barons getting rich off the gene that makes them robber barons. Big surprise. I'll bet this is your first real job, right?"

"Right."

"You're just figuring out who you are. It's always a mistake to take your first real job too seriously. No matter how hard it is."

"It's challenging, that's for sure. But what's fun is the computer game we're designing."

" 'We' meaning you and the boyfriend?"

"Yeah, Cliff."

"Do those games have a story? Plot, characters—things like that?"

"Ours does."

"Well, then," he said, turning to her with a big, boyish, off-kilter grin, "we have something in common. I'm in the making-up-shit business, too."

"I thought you had to live in L.A. to make movies."

"The trouble with L.A. is it doesn't give you anything back. You're what, twenty-one?"

"Twenty-two."

"Well, if I stopped to help a twenty-two-year-old woman on the side of the road in L.A., she'd either look like a soap opera actress or want to be one. But here I get to meet someone like you. A smart person from a whole other world."

Essentially the same assessment of her specialness that seemed so wrongheaded before he showed up. But that was coming from her mother, Ivan, Amelia. People who had always known and loved her. Coming from an experienced, sophisticated, maybe even celebrated stranger, being a smart person from a whole other world sounded pretty good. In fact, it sounded great.

By the time they reached the mechanic's shop in Mount Jensen, Laurienne had told him enough about herself to get advice on everything from whether or not she ought to cut her hair to look more adult for work (no, just wear it up—the length suited her height) to making the Lexie game ripe for sequels (Lexie contacts her father, but doesn't free him). "But what's really interesting," Whit told her, "is if the aliens have turned the father, and Lexie finds out she's really battling him."

"No," Laurienne said, her feathery voice as forceful as she could make it. "Her father has to be good. He's got to be worth saving."

"If you say so," Whit told her. "But don't discount contradictions. The spice of life. Remember, you heard it here first."

Before saying goodbye, she tried to talk Whit into letting her give him a pair of jumper cables by way of thanks. "Forget it," he said. "That's why God invented triple A. But maybe you know someone around here who can help me out with my computer."

"Why, what's wrong?"

"Don't know. Haven't turned it on yet. Too scary."

"Not any better with computers than cars, huh?"

He shook a finger at her. "Mocking the afflicted—not nice, Laurienne."

"Ever get to Seattle?"

"Got some business there soon."

"Then I can do it." Laurienne wrote down her contact information at work. "Bring it to my office, and don't forget the installation discs. I'll get it up. I can maybe even get you a lab tour."

"No, no—you're a busy girl."

"I insist," she said.

"Hey, that's *my* line."

"Hey, you really saved my life today."

But once Laurienne reached her whole other world, the glow Whit had given it was fading. Dulled by the lie she'd phoned in to Dunson's office from Mount Jensen—she woke up sick this morning, but might make it in by afternoon. Dimmed by the steep mechanic's bill in her wallet. Then extinguished by an interoffice e-mail message ordering her to report to Dunson's office "ASAP, or whenever your recovery permits, Ms. Gentry."

"The new program tests out fine," Dunson said as Laurienne settled into an armchair near his desk.

"That's good news." She tried to hold eye contact while he paced, but sparkly things began dancing in her peripheral vision as she tracked him around the room.

"And now here's the bad news," Dunson said. "I expect we'll be announcing our patent approval any day now, so results from this database have to be even more exact."

Laurienne shook her head a little to see if the sparklies might disperse. They didn't.

"You don't agree?" Dunson asked.

"Oh, I do. Completely."

"We need a thorough rundown of all the research out there concerning this gene. And we can't nail it without more programming modifications, without repurposing the code. Think you're up to it?"

A bolt of white-hot pain sliced through the back of Laurienne's head and traveled down her neck. Holy shit. One little white lie, not even a whole bogus sick day, and this was what she got—sick for real. She clutched the chair arms, knuckles whitening as breath hissed down the back of her throat. "I think so," she told Dunson. "We've got a good group."

"I'm talking about you, specifically. Don't tell me you're having personal problems."

"No. I mean, nothing I can't handle. Nothing out of the ordinary." As the pain mutated into a viselike grip on her forehead she fought down a wave of nausea.

"Because I can put someone else in charge if you're tapped out."

"No sir, I'm not tapped out."

"Okay, but if anything ever does come up, remember, my door is always open." He came close to give her shoulder a squeeze that was somewhere between solicitous and sexual. "I enjoy taking a certain amount of credit for your performance here. Wouldn't want you falling short at an important time like this."

She focused on the top button of his black knit shirt as he half sat, half perched on his desk above her, the posture of a pedagogue flavoring authority with youthful verve. "I won't fall short," she said.

Taking notes, she somehow made it through Dunson's explanation of all the new program functions that had to be created. When they were done, she walked down the hall until she was sure of being out of sight, then raced around the corner to the women's bathroom, punched in the entry code, and barely reached a toilet before vomiting.

Laurienne stayed in the stall for what seemed a long time while her body rocked and heaved. It wasn't at all like what she remembered from being sick as a kid, when she lost everything in one big purge while her mother held a damp washcloth to her forehead. Whatever had hold of her now seized and wrung her out once, twice, then three times, with a round of dry heaves for good measure. She slumped against the stall to catch her breath, her balance. The root of her tongue ached from all that retching, but now her headache felt more manageable, more normal. She was wet with sweat and shaky but okay—okay enough to call a meeting in an hour, then dash home, shower, change clothes, and return before it started.

"Are you all right?" Cliff asked before the team assembled.

Laurienne nodded. "I've just got a headache. The Advil ought to kick in soon."

"I'll get you a Coke." She made a face, but Cliff, who drank Coca-Cola every morning for breakfast—always poured out of bottles and only over ice that was crushed, never cubed, so as to maximize contact between his elixir of choice and the stuff that chilled it into perfection; another one of his Texas things—Cliff swore that the caffeine in Coke would give ibuprofen an extra medicinal kick. "Besides," he said, "you could use the calories."

As expected, Dunson's demands elicited groans and moans and bitching from all the guys on her team.

"There goes my vacation," said one.

"A new high in scope creep," groused another.

"This isn't scope creep," said a third, "this is starting over from scratch."

Afterwards, while Laurienne suspected everyone of nursing mutinous thoughts in their individual office cubicles, Cliff came into hers, distinguished from the others only by a few extra square feet and a corner window looking out on Lake Union. "Don't worry," he said, "I'll back you up."

And over the next few days he did—taking on some of the most difficult coding tasks himself, organizing a late-night dart-throwing contest to blow off steam and build esprit, pumping his contacts in the lab for information about how far they might stretch the deadline without running afoul of Dunson. "You think *we're* stressed,"

Cliff told Laurienne while they ate pizza in her office one night. "Lyle says they're going batshit upstairs."

"Must be a mighty important gene they've got."

"I told Lyle how anal this program's getting, and he said, 'It's kind of ironic, when you think about it. Being so anal over the Peter Pan gene.' "

"What do you think he meant by that?"

"No fucking idea. When I asked, he changed the subject real quick. It's all a bunch of bullshit anyway. I mean, how can they patent genes that took us millions of years of evolution to develop? They're *our* genes, goddammit, they belong to us."

"Yeah, but we can't figure out how to manipulate them to cure diseases and feed people. Besides, once a gene's isolated and purified, it's not natural anymore, it's man-made. Patents are better than a situation where all these companies keep discoveries secret from one another."

"That's what Daddy Dunson says."

She picked a mushroom off her pizza and threw it at him. "Stop. Anyway, he's not old enough to be my father."

"Even worse. He's sweet on you."

"You're jealous."

"Wait till he sees Lexie."

"You're not going to show him Lexie!"

"I meant later. After we're out of here."

"Whoa," she said. "We can't just quit, not without a buyer for Lexie lined up."

"That's why I'm setting up meetings. With game company execs."

"You took the initiative? Cliff, that is so great." She looked around to make sure no one was out in the hallway, then pasted him with a long, juicy kiss.

"I can put them off until we start testing again," Cliff

said, his hands on her butt, pressing her closer. "Then you'll have to cover for me."

A couple of sparklies were encroaching from the right. Laurienne eased away from Cliff to pop open another can of Coke and slug some down. His prescription worked. Caffeine on top of Advil could twinkle away the sparklies to wherever they came from in a flash, and the cola syrup helped settle her tummy.

"Believe it or not," she said, "there are some people who think what we do here is poetic."

"Really?" Cliff stretched and yawned. "They must be nuts."

"Not nuts. Just really smart." She told him about meeting the director, and after Cliff went back to his computer, she hopped onto the Internet to scan the titles of Whit's movies, some of which she'd seen. There were also lots of stories about him—too many to investigate now. Still, it jazzed her just to see them.

11

Jasmine set out to walk in misting morning rain along Owl Island's north shore beach. The air, fragrant with chimney smoke, reminded her of bacon and kindled a longing for the coffee she'd given up a few years ago, after getting expensive new porcelain facings for her teeth.

Back in her other life, as Donna Price, she had mottled teeth, brown and yellow like tiger's-eye quartz—the result of taking tetracycline when she was four. At age twelve, she cultivated a tight-lipped little Mona Lisa smile to hide them. Her parents anted up to have her teeth bonded with plastic resin for her sixteenth birthday, a definite improvement even though the bonding soon chipped and took on a dingy gray cast. When she dropped out of Chico State to leave for L.A., her drama instructor had given her the gimlet eye and his assessment of her chances. "You could actually be somebody," he said, "if you got your teeth fixed." But she would have to do it the hard way—turn herself into somebody first, *then* get her teeth fixed.

Every so often Jasmine stopped along the beach to pick up flattened river rocks she wanted for rooting paperwhite narcissus bulbs. If she got them nestled in and watered by month's end, she'd have fragrant blossoms come Christmas. Whit hated traditional Christmas trees, but he didn't mind lights on an entryway cactus or the scent of tall narcissi from lacquered Chinese bowls. Soon her pockets bulged with enough stones to sink someone bent on watery suicide. Not something she would ever be morbid enough to do, but the thought did occur. Anyway, with this tide, you'd have to walk pretty far out to get wet above the knees.

Before long, Phoebe ought to appear on the beach, throwing sticks for a bearded blonde dog, just as she'd done the last few mornings. Jasmine had caught sight of them through binoculars, too far away to warrant scampering down for a chat. Getting Phoebe into her office wasn't going to be near so easy as snagging Amelia. But then she had learned just about everything she needed to know about Amelia while hanging upside down beside her in yoga class, and it was Amelia who had suggested they make a trade: Jasmine's rundown of her transiting planets for a full set of Amelia's therapeutic teas. Peppermint for tummy aches, valerian for sleep, ginger for flu and fever, slippery elm for chest congestion, mugwort to sharpen intuition. Amelia even had a special cache of dried Indonesian jasmine leaves. "Oh, I'd love some of that," Jasmine had said.

"Jasmine's great," Amelia told her, "but it's tricky."

"I figured there must be a reason why the tea's so spendy."

"Oh yeah. You've got to trust your source when it comes to jasmine. False jasmine smells just like true jasmine, but tea from the false stuff will kill you. I probably don't have to tell a California girl like you what the true kind's good for."

"Mom's favorite aphrodisiac," Jasmine lied. "I was conceived on it." Nobody here needed to know about Donna Price from Chico.

Teas for a reading—hardly a fair exchange considering her customary fee, but Jasmine had been quick to agree. Her skills were getting rusty. No more voices in the night disturbing her sleep, but maybe she just couldn't hear them because Whit tied up so much of her energy. Some womanly conversation would be nice, too—all those lovely complicit murmurs of understanding and interest that you just couldn't get from a man. Good enough reasons at the time of Amelia's proposition. But now, walking across damp pebbled sand pocked with holes from squirting clams, the real appeal of reading Amelia was perfectly obvious: her proximity to Phoebe.

In a natal chart, the moon meant instinctive emotional needs. That's how Jasmine's attraction to Phoebe felt, like lunar tidal pull. More so now, since she'd sneaked a look at the screenplay Whit had been holed up writing on the Selectric all week. There was a detective, his assistant on the case—a funny sweet young thing who was some kind of DNA expert—and the detective's old girlfriend, a net maker in a small northwestern fishing village. Clearly grown from Phoebe.

"I knew her when I was starting out" was all the information she could get out of Whit. It would take more than that for Jasmine to know how much of a threat, and what particular kind, Phoebe posed, and the best way to neutralize her. If only Jasmine could travel backward through time to the Co-op, when she first saw Phoebe—before any personal stakes were involved—and do a more thorough scope. A useless idea. If she went back in time, she still wouldn't know what to probe for.

Jasmine quickened her pace when a stick came sailing around the bend, landing at the foot of a red-skinned madrone tree. As the dog bounded toward her, she picked up the stick, tossed it farther, and waved down the beach at Phoebe. "That was pathetic," Jasmine shouted. "I throw like a girl."

Phoebe's face was obscured by a yellow slicker hood, but it didn't take a psychic to sense that she would rather turn and walk the other way than continue approaching Jasmine. The dog was another story. It sat, shook hands, and rolled over for her, all without being asked, after Jasmine flashed a specially bought treat.

"I hope that was something low-fat," Phoebe said. "Pancreatitis is a thousand-dollar vet bill."

And good morning to you, too. "Oh, it was," Jasmine said. "Does that happen often?"

"No," Phoebe admitted. "Once was enough."

The dog squatted to pee. "What's her name?"

"Lily."

"Oh," Jasmine cooed, scratching under the dog's muzzle, "glad to meet you, Lily—I'm a flower, too." Once, a divorced client of hers had claimed that a dog and a vibrator were all the domestic companionship she required. If only the same were true of Phoebe. Then they could be easy, uncomplicated friends. Jasmine smiled up at her. "My new office is in the Terminal building. That makes us neighbors twice over—on the island, in town. We really ought to get together."

"Sounds good," Phoebe said. "But this is such a busy time of year."

"Yeah, a lot's going on with the holidays coming. But it's so beautiful and peaceful up here, all I want to do is fluff up my nest and snuggle in with my sweetie."

"I meant it's busy at work."

"Oh, for me, too. You wouldn't believe all the people who can't face the new year without a reading. They start lining up right about now."

The outer edge of Phoebe's left eyebrow lifted. "Do you tell them what's going to happen?"

"Mostly I just connect them with their own intuition."

"That's what I told Amelia," Phoebe said. "She talked about your reading like you were pulling stuff out of the air. But the way I see it is, we're all pretty big inside. We know more than we think."

Less of a kiss than a slap in that assessment, but Jasmine nodded her head in avid agreement. "Literally. Thinking can even get in the way of knowing. Especially when it comes to ourselves." Lily bumped up against Jasmine's hip for more attention. "Oh, this dog's such a lover, isn't she?"

"Shameless," Phoebe said. "I'm jealous. I mean, she can just sniff another dog's butt and find out everything she needs to know."

"Guess I'd be out of business if people were like dogs."

Phoebe let go with a husky, full-throated laugh. Jasmine grinned, wondering if Phoebe had decided to be sophisticated and above it all, or was just willing to smoke Jasmine's roaches for a little hit of Whit. Not that it mattered. Either way would do.

They walked together, companionable now, Jasmine asking Phoebe for tips on where to buy cords of firewood, getting much more information than she'd bargained for—the kind of wood to specify, how much to order for the winter, the conditions under which burnban regulations went into effect. As they approached the zigzagging steps that led up to her house, Jasmine came to the point and offered Phoebe a reading.

"What do you charge?" Phoebe asked.

"Usually? Four hundred dollars. But this would be on the house. Just let me call on you for more advice on how to get stuff done around here."

"You can have the advice," Phoebe said, "but I'm really not into that sort of thing."

"I won't bog you down in jargon and woo-woo spiels, if that's what you're worried about."

"I just can't imagine you're going to tell me anything about myself that I don't already know."

"You might be surprised."

Phoebe laughed again. "I'm not so big on surprises, either."

"Surprises can be wonderful," Jasmine insisted. "What have you got to lose?"

"You're not going to give up, are you?"

"I'm really good. Want references?"

"Oh, what the hell," Phoebe said. "It might be interesting." She wrote her birth data down on one of the business cards Jasmine had brought along. When she handed it back, Jasmine glanced at the date and hid her sense of victory behind a trusty old Mona Lisa smile.

Interesting that someone so skeptical about astrology knew down to the minute when she was born. Jasmine would have been shocked if Phoebe had turned out to have her sun in a ballsy, exuberant fire sign, or cerebral, intellectualizing air. That left only earth and water, and just as she'd suspected, Phoebe's was in water— emotional, secretive, sensitive, internalizing water. Cancer, ruled by the moon. And now Jasmine had everything she needed to connect all the other planetary dots. "Great," she said, giving Phoebe one of her cards to keep. "Call my office; we'll set something up."

Damp chill in her bones, Jasmine returned to lay a fire in the living room with the last of her little Co-op-bought bundles. The muffled click of sporadically struck Selectric keys came from behind Whit's study door. She put on a CD of Scarlatti guitar sonatas and went into the kitchen to toast an onion bagel and make a pot of peppery tisane, knowing full well that as soon as she calculated Phoebe's chart she'd be working it for hours like a rank beginner. She was even giving it away like a beginner, despite having learned from watching her mother what a risk freebies were, how they could backfire and burn, causing some people to regard you as a kind of psychic Mother Teresa and turn up on your doorstep at all hours, crying for counsel, and others to dismiss you as a deluded nut-bag or worse, a fraud. But Jasmine's mother, for all her native ability, never had the patience or discipline to pour her vision into a container system like astrology, to learn its psychological language and symbols, to charge professional fees for her insights. Not that anyone ever encouraged Jasmine.

"Put that much time into schoolbooks and you might get better grades," her father said when she was a teenager poring over her first serious texts. Well, what could you expect with a hard-angled moon like his? Zero scope for imagination.

While the tisane steeped, Jasmine slipped a cozy over the pot and ate her bagel standing over the sink. It had been a while since she felt pressure to pull off dazzling coups of cognition—like when she nailed a big-shot network producer's confusion over whether her first priority should be adopting a Chinese baby girl or putting *Crime and Punishment* into development as a miniseries. "Amazing," the woman had marveled. "It hasn't even made the trades." That was when she was seeing clients several days a week at Kitano Hot Springs, the desert spa where people came to her wrapped in sumptuous Yves Delorme robes, buzzing with pleasure after long soaks and shiatsu massages. Whit had been such a one, sitting still for a consultation only because his actress girlfriend, flying high on her own reading, had made an appointment for him and insisted he keep it.

For most hot-springs clients, hearing her recount trau-

mas from their childhood was like a day at Disneyland.
But after slamming up against Whit's resistance, she
attended only to the present, throwing curveballs and
changeups, clipping the darker corners of his psyche.
She had just finished describing the ideal woman for
him, borrowing liberally from parts of her own personality, when he stopped her. "You're not getting all this
stuff from that drawing, are you, Donna?"

"Charts can be very helpful," she told him.

"Show me which one of those little lines says I had a
kidney stone last year."

As Donna Price, she really had to knock them out. As
Jasmine Traynor, exotic wife of an esoteric film director,
she had only to be her own lovely, curious, sociable self.
She had only to be . . . impressive.

It was probably nothing, Phoebe's living down the
road from them. But Jasmine would feel a whole lot better if she could be sure those tremors of change she'd felt
around Phoebe in the Co-op wouldn't rock her, too. If it
were somebody else's problem, somebody else's husband,
Jasmine would know in a flash. She wasn't unique.
Every other psychic she'd ever discussed this with said
emotional involvement acted like kryptonite on Super-
man. Warped their wavelengths, leached the insight right
out of them. No wonder so many professionals wound
up old, alone, eccentric—a fate Jasmine had long ago
determined would not be hers.

She went back to her desk with a steaming hand-
painted Italian mug, turned on the computer, entered
Phoebe's data, and, within seconds, up popped the chart.
It was always stimulating to see where someone's planets landed on the ecliptic, and never more so than now.
Jasmine contemplated all the angles of ease and opposition, all the promises and threats, all the talents and lia-
bilities in this chart. Now it seemed flat-out funny that

Phoebe had resisted a reading; with her intuition, her eye for the big picture, her zeal for analysis, she would have made a first-rate astrologer. Although some nasty aspects to the moon suggested pain and conflict through the mother, compared to Jasmine, Phoebe was born on Easy Street. Probably had all the tutus, dolls, and dentistry money could buy. Another click of the computer mouse showed current planetary pressures. Phoebe's fourth house was under attack by Saturn and Mars. No wonder she was so rattled. The fourth house represented home, family, safety, and hers had frayed, faulty wiring, foggy windows, a foundation in desperate need of re-footing. But this was a woman perfectly capable of assembling everything she needed for an overhaul. Lucky her. Providing, of course, that Whit wasn't what she needed. Which brought Jasmine to the most ominous calculation of all—seeing how Phoebe's chart plugged into his.

More mouse clicks and there it was, the two charts juxtaposed. It was spooky how well they went together. Hand in glove. All kinds of potential for intimacy, and the sort of heavy-duty astral connections that suggested lifelong ties.

Jasmine's stomach quivered a little, the way it did when she heard ghosts.

12

After kicking cocaine, Whit's old producing partner Joe Zaglan had packed on so many pounds that he never wore shirts that required tucking, only ones made from expensive material and cut to fit loosely over his ample paunch. Nothing if not a realist, Joe had developed over the years a preemptive habit of describing himself as a fat, rich Hollywood Jew. He didn't seem bothered by his bulk, either physically or aesthetically, and the first thing he did after checking into his Seattle hotel was head out to eat. Two days, five restaurants—these were the kind of numbers Joe most enjoyed crunching now.

Whit, on the other hand, prided himself on wearing the same size jeans as when they first got together over *Kiki*. He sat across from Joe in a booth at McCormick & Schmick's, where the dining rooms and counter stools were filled to capacity and people without reservations were being turned away at the door. "I was lucky to get us in," Joe said. "Some sort of fish festival's going on."

"Fish Expo," Whit corrected.

"Guess you gotta be local to know shit like that."

"Big news up where I live. Half the town's here for it."

"Yeah, well, the fish *I* came for are on the menu."

Whenever Joe had news, he liked to deliver it only after settling into a Zagat-rated theater of food and drink. If it was good news, you could indulge to celebrate; if bad, to compensate. A win-win situation—for Joe, any-how. Today's news had to do with Whit's latest film, the one he'd just been flogging at the fall festivals.

"The trade reviews out of Toronto killed us," Joe told Whit. "There's no way a studio's going to pick us up for distribution."

Whit nodded. It wasn't as if he didn't understand what he was up against. Not only did the prick who covered Toronto for *Variety* predict a limited art house audience for his new movie, he suggested the director's friends perform an intervention to keep him from making another. Even worse was the *Hollywood Reporter*'s damning treacle: "Although wonderfully acted, beautifully shot, and sure to delight Traynor's diehard audience, it's doubtful his latest endeavor will win him new fans." In order for anything Whit made to succeed, which was to say get released, new fans were a must.

The film was another period piece, with a Toronto location doubling for New York in the Fifties. Slap them back in time, knock them off balance, and then, if you can grab them before they fall, they're yours—that had been his thinking. But with this one, what he wanted was a contemporary spin on the kind of urban romantic comedies they used to make, with Judy Holliday, Jack Lemmon, Shirley MacLaine—hell, even Doris Day and Rock Hudson. Keeping it fast, fractured, funny, but supplying all the sexual complexity that could only be suggested back then.

"If we do our job right," he told everyone in preproduction, "this will be *Pillow Talk* as made by Eric Rohmer." He wasn't an idiot, he knew such a hybrid didn't exactly spell big box office. But it used to be that getting an interesting movie made was the whole battle; now the toughest part was getting it into theaters. He had enough of a built-in audience to earn everybody a little money, no sweat. The trouble was, nobody wanted a *little* money anymore, not since that goddamn shark movie. Which pissed him off so much he forgot how terrific he thought that goddamn shark movie was after seeing the director's rough cut, when he could still enjoy it as a hip horror ride, not resent it as a minting machine. Just Whit's luck, making his own first movie in that monster's shadow. A friendly critic once suggested over a drink that, given his talent, the arc of Whit's career could only be explained by the presence of a black Tennessee crow perched on his crib. Sometimes—now being one of them—he thought that critic had it right. Maybe it was just another piece of bad luck, premiering in the same city where he shot the film. They probably should have waited for Sundance, where he was a favorite with parka-clad, chukka-boot-shod audiences.

Yes, the trade reviews were horrible, but trade critics were dumber than boxes of hair when it came to appreciating anything out of the ordinary. Besides, the film had played great at all the other festivals he schlepped it to after Toronto, and Joe had made end runs around worse before. What's more, Whit still believed he'd pulled it off, still believed he'd made the movie he set out to make, and so he had let himself imagine right up until this moment that Joe would announce a promising new game plan—the real purpose of his trip to Seattle.

"I was only going to get a glass of wine," Whit said. "But maybe we should order a bottle."

"Sure," Joe agreed.

"So you can't hook us up with one of the independents?"

"Independent studios, don't make me laugh. There *are* no independents—everybody's dependent on the money." Joe scanned the list of the day's specials. "The oysters look good, let's get a sampler. Then I'll have the Canadian salmon or the Alaskan halibut, so how about some Sancerre or pinot grigio?"

"It's going straight to video then?"

"Yep."

"Jesus. Kiss of death."

"I tried. Told these guys, if it's my money, I'd do a limited release, generate a few positive reviews, build some momentum. But they don't want to risk another nickel on a distribution deal, they're happy with the profit from cable and cassettes. And there's nothing I can do except keep the news under wraps for a while."

Whit folded his arms and leaned back against the booth. "You could have told me this on the phone."

"The oysters are fresher up here."

"You've gone from thinking with your prick to thinking with your gut."

"My idea of maturity, you should try it."

"If you wanted maturity, you asked the wrong guy to lunch."

"Come on, don't take it personally."

"How am I supposed to take it? Like a *group*?"

"Why not? It's a collaborative art."

"Really? Stop the presses. Joe Zaglan reveals film-making is a collaborative art."

"Before you take any more of this out on me, let me tell you something. My heart is pure. Lots of mega-rich guys itching for new hobbies up here. Got a few lined up who want to play mogul. Think just because they're loaded, they can score big in movies. Think they can do it from Seattle, too—like that'll keep them clean. Anyway, you're the star. They need to meet you."

"When you said we were meeting executives, I thought you meant real people."

"Their dough's real enough. There's another reason I came—to cattle-prod your ass. Your next one's the lure, so finish it off." Joe reached for a shopping bag and tossed it on the table. "And use this to do it." Whit opened the bag and removed a box of screenwriting software. "The best program out there," Joe said, "everybody loves it. Makes production a hell of a lot more efficient. Get rid of the Selectric, Whit. It'll go faster, you'll see, and we'll save time."

"Except for the time I'll waste learning how to use the goddamn thing and retyping pages." Whit glanced at the back of the box. "Looks like they got a testimonial from every paint-by-numbers hack in town. This is why you wanted me to bring the laptop?"

"After you check in we'll go to your room, install it together."

"I can see it now. *The Farkle Family Writes a Movie*."

"I should've hired another producer to give it to you. Any idea of mine automatically sucks."

"All right, all right—I'll keep it. But I don't need your help."

They'd been sniping at each other this way for years, like an old married couple. The key to their longevity, Joe thought. So many of Whit's behind-the-camera collaborations were like short-lived little love affairs, the infatuation spoiled by project's end from the kind of spats Joe ignored when they involved him and smoothed over when they didn't. And still Whit complained. Complained about how he never had the luxury of working with the same key crew members. Complained about the rampant ingratitude of people he'd given breaks to, how he spotted their talent and taught them so much, and they just used him as a stepping stone. Complained about everything, really—never blaming himself, always Joe. And Joe put up with it, for the highs of working with Whit in his mesmerizing mode. Close as he could come these days to a cocaine rush.

Only later, full of wine at the end of their meal, did Whit really begin to rage. "Final cut doesn't mean shit without final control, does it? The problem is, these fucking cretins can't sell anything but the same old soup in the same old cans. And what really pisses me off are those suckers out there, paying good money to see crap they've already seen before."

"Like a Fifties-style romantic comedy?"

"Thanks."

"Can't resist fish," Joe said, finishing off his halibut. "I shot that one in a barrel."

"Nobody wants to think, nobody wants to finance films. What they want are McMovies, what they want—"

"Please. Get a megaphone and tell the guys from the fish festival."

"The only reason anybody puts money into one of mine is *Kiki,* but who's got the balls to finance a *Kiki* today?"

"As I've been saying for how long?" Joe raised his Rolex to Whit's eye level and tapped the face, as though inviting him to read it. "Four years, maybe? Now do you believe me?"

"Your credibility requires years of evidence, Irving."

"Years of pain, you mean, Meyer." It was a signal, using their old joke names for each other, like jocks slapping each other's rumps to break a huddle.

"And you keep coming back for more," Whit said. "What's that make you?"

"Diversified. You're not the only director around, pal. So how's the script coming?"

"Not bad. This one is writing itself. I could be done in a week."

"Tell me more."

"It's about this big-city detective who's hit the skids. A

juicy case comes along, his last chance to play in the big leagues again."

"What kind of case?"

"Something to do with fishing boats."

"Naturally, since we're surrounded here by fishing-boat guys."

Whit shrugged. "That's how it works when I've got a movie going in my head. Everything filters in."

"What's the boat angle?"

"That's just the McGuffin. What counts is how evidence comes down to DNA, and the way our story spins on this piece of the natural world that's going to hell. It's the layers I love. Our guy's a fish out of water. Everything depends on whether he can pull off this one case. Only right at the center of it, he finds a woman from his past. The one who slipped away. Losing her's a big part of why he's sunk so low. So now he's got two mysteries to solve, he's got two shots at redemption, and one won't work without the other."

"Love and corruption—that's good."

"What's great is I'm so excited. In spite of every-thing."

Joe leaned across the table. "Okay, Whit," he said, ca-joling. "Who are you fucking?"

"I'm a newlywed; you've seen my bride. Who do you think?"

"Oh, she's lovely, all right."

"Also incredibly sweet."

"And a mind reader, too. Just what you've always needed. But I know you. If there's not something new on the side, the juices don't flow."

"What's new is living up here," Whit said. "I put this story in a drawer a long time ago, couldn't make it work. Now I know exactly what to do. This could be the best thing I've ever done. If you don't want it, I'll go somewhere else."

"No, no—sounds great. Castable, too. Go on; finish it off. Write it in blood; I don't care. Plenty of names want to work with you, no problem there. But we need more than a pitch. I can't take the lid off your head and show them your brain."

"After *Kiki* we could cast without a script. Everything changes with the camera. Anyway, I'm not a screenwriter. Why would I want to be a screenwriter? Screenwriters are just first drafts of human beings."

"That's exactly the kind of talk that helped kill us in Toronto. Don't laugh, I'm serious. These critics now, they mostly all want to write movies; they ain't in love with auteurs. But you, you have a couple of drinks with them in some bar and start mouthing off—scripts don't matter, it's the vision that counts, all that blueprint crap. Sticking it to them where they live. So then they file it away and nail you in a review. Besides, those days are over, my friend—actors signing on for peanuts if you just promise to write them a good part. Now I need something on paper."

"I gave you something on paper."

"That's right, you gave me something on paper. But I need to show them more than a bunch of pictures on a napkin."

Laurienne expected to have only two or three testers looking for bugs in the repurposed program code. That's what she was used to, that's what she had prepared herself for. But this time, Dunson saddled her with six testers—as many people as she had programming. In the usual scheme of things, programmers hated testers because they discovered every flaw in your code, but were compelled to love them for the same reason. Better to

have testers find glitches than the scientists upstairs.
This bunch of testers, though, was impossible to love.
They were like a herd of evil children who whooped and
high-fived every time they discovered a new way to
crash the program.

It was a terrible week for Cliff to be off playing hooky
with Lexie, slipping away for meetings with potential
backers, and Laurienne was beginning to think it was
something Cliff was terrible at doing, too—schmoozing
with executives who were only a few years older but had
already made the envied leap to play-for-pay. So far, no
takers. Nobody willing yet to finance the game's completion. She itched to grab the reins herself, to whip on
her version of Lexie's supersuit—she'd started to read
fashion magazines; Dolce & Gabbana would work—
then accomplish the mission for them both. Now that
BioIngenious had approval for its new gene patent, the
stock price was rising. Her idea, which practically made
Cliff twitch with fear, was to cash in their options and
jump into a pond all their own. Meanwhile she'd have
to keep swimming along like a good little fish in this
one.

Covering for Cliff meant Laurienne not only had to
debug the program pieces she'd coded; she had to fumi-
gate his, too. It almost never happened that two programmers arrived at the same destination by the same
methods. Everybody had their own puzzle-solving style—
their own quirks and idiosyncrasies, signature shortcuts,
gymnastic leaps of logic. Working on Cliff's pieces felt
like trying to become another person. It wasn't like the
merging of sex, so insistent and intuitive. This felt more
like blowing fuses while you mind-melded. She hated
fixing Cliff's problems because she almost had to re-
create the faults from scratch, and once she did, it was

harder than ever to see her way out, she was so blinded by the reasoning behind his errors.

A yell came from the room where testers were working. "All *right*!" Shit. Another program crash. She popped a couple of Advil. The headaches were controllable now, but still they made her nervous. What if they were a symptom of something terrible? What if brain tumors were in her DNA and she had one, just like Grandma Pearl? If there were time to see a doctor, maybe she'd know the answers.

Laurienne left her office to record the erring sequence, feeling less like a project manager than a nanny. The testers were performing for each other, that was the problem, so she split them up, herding testers into her programmers' cubicles and programmers to the testers' open work area. Now it was her team high-fiving. "That's what I call solutionizing," one of them said, slapping Laurienne on the back.

It turned out that this time, it was a piece of hers that the testers broke. Looked like another night at her desk—no dining out with Phoebe. Laurienne had made reservations and was hoping she'd have not only Cliff to introduce but good news about the Lexie game, too. Which seemed to put Cliff over the edge when she mentioned it this morning. "What if things don't work out that way?" he'd said. "Do I have to stay home?"

While Laurienne looked up the number for Phoebe's hotel, her phone rang. This was something that happened all the time, one of them calling at the very moment the other was about to, so without thinking, she picked up the receiver saying, "Hi, Mom."

A long pause at the other end. She braced for Dunson's disapproving voice, but instead there came a velvety drawl. "Sorry to disappoint you, Laurienne, but this is not your momma."

"Oh, hi," she said. "How are you?"

"The better question is, Where am I? Downstairs, in the lobby. Got some time for my computer today?"

It couldn't be more clear what she ought to do. Offer Whit a rain check and get back to work. But having him arrive so unexpectedly made her feel special, like a kid plucked from the audience to be the magician's assistant.

Laurienne called Lyle in the lab to arrange a tour for Whit, then went down to fetch him and vouch for his visitor's pass. In the elevator, she peered into a mirrored panel and tucked a stray strand into the tortoiseshell clip that held a twisted rope of hair on top of her head. They dropped Whit's laptop off in her office, then waited for Lyle in the lab lunchroom, which smelled of old coffee grounds and microwaved popcorn.

Whit stood at the bulletin board, reading a recent article from the *Seattle Times* business section about the gene patent. "I figured you were a happening girl, Laurienne," he said, "but it looks like you work at a happening place, too." He turned to her with a smile. "Wow, you even know how to blush."

Lyle opened the cafeteria door and motioned for them to follow as he raced down the long hall. Lyle was such a social klutz that when he opened his mouth, out popped a toad. "Laurienne says you're a hot film director."

"Geez, Lyle." Laurienne could feel her cheeks flame again. "I did not say hot."

"Good," Whit said. "Because if you asked me, I'd say tepid."

"Usually," Lyle said, "we only give tours to potential investors."

Whit shrugged. "Who knows? That might be exactly what I am."

"Now's a good time to get on board." Lyle flashed his

security card over a door scanner and led them into the lab, where his white-jacketed colleagues huddled over microscopes, pipettes, and computers of their own. "This is where we test DNA and check the databases to see if we're onto something new."

"Then you get a patent?" Laurienne liked the way Whit spoke—not sounding so much like a self-important old fart, the way Dunson did, as like someone genuinely curious, accustomed to having his interest stimulated.

"Eventually," Lyle said.

"Can you splice and edit DNA?" Whit asked.

"If you know what you're doing," Laurienne said. "You can copy the edits, too. It's a lot like film."

Whit smiled. "Not too much, I hope. Film lies at a rate of twenty-four frames per second."

"A limited analogy," Lyle said. "DNA might let you down, but it never lies."

"If someone brought you a waterlogged body part, could you figure out who it was?" Whit asked.

"Is this for a movie?" Lyle looked hopeful.

"Could be."

"Well, I'm not a forensic scientist, but yeah, you could pull DNA off the body part, especially if it was in cold water. You'd need another sample for comparison, though. A cheek swab's always best."

"Might be kind of difficult if his head was still out at sea somewhere."

"A piece of gum, cigarette butt, beard stubble—those'll do in a pinch. Then you'd look for matching DNA patterns."

Lyle pulled slides from a bank of narrow, sterile-looking drawers, putting them under a microscope to show how much patterns could vary. It wasn't often that Laurienne got so close to the target of all her work. Forget scope creep and annoying testers—this was why sweating over the code mattered.

"That was terrific," Whit told Laurienne afterward, in her office. "Thank you, Madame Curie."

"Hope it helps. Your movie sounds exciting."

"I don't know about that. But if it is, you'll be a big reason why."

She was so lost in looking at her world through his eyes that it rattled her when the phone rang and this time it *was* Phoebe, calling from the Convention Center. "Sorry," Laurienne told her. "We're crunched; can't make it tonight. I was just going to leave a message at your hotel."

"Oh."

Phoebe sounded so letdown that Laurienne scrambled for an alternative. "I'll call you later; I can probably make it over for a nightcap. Just block your phone if you go to bed early so I won't wake you up."

Laurienne hung up and sighed. "I'm a bad daughter," she told Whit.

"Parents—can't always please them."

"You said it."

"But I'll bet yours are busting buttons all the time over you."

"Well, that's kind of a problem. I mean, I wish my mom had more to make her happy."

Just as Laurienne expected, Whit owned a Mac. He was too much of a maverick iconoclast for a PC. While she clicked on a couple of program icons, he watched, leaning over her shoulder. "What are you doing?"

"Not much. Looks like everything's set up, registered, and ready to go."

"Really? Must have come that way." He pulled a box

from the laptop carrying case and handed it to her. "But I just got this, for writing screenplays."

She broke the box open, scanned the instructions, popped in the program CD, and had the thing running in five minutes flat. After clicking her way through a short demo, she showed Whit how to press the tab button once or twice to make the proper spacing for dialogue and character names.

"Amazing," Whit said, as though *she* were the magician. "Are you sure you've never written a script before?"

Her fingers flew on the keyboard and Whit watched as words appeared on-screen.

WHIT
Are you sure you've never written a script before?

LAURIENNE
Yeah. I only write in code.

"Now you try," she said, motioning him into her chair. Staring at the keyboard, he used two fingers to hunt-and-peck another exchange.

WHIT
What's code for "you are a pearl
any oyster would treasure"?

LAURIENNE
Plant that one in Kansas, mister,
you'd grow ten ears of corn.

It was fun playing with Whit, the way working out the Lexie story was with Cliff. What was it Whit had told her when they met? "We have something in common;

we're both in the making-up-shit business." She wished Cliff would get back to the office so he could have a little romp with him, too.

When he finally did arrive, Laurienne was finishing up with Whit, showing him how to start the program tutorial. Cliff wore rumpled chinos and a worn brown corduroy jacket over a white Cal Arts tee shirt—his version of businesslike. He glanced at the laptop screen, where an animated movie camera was hopping around, eager to start helping someone write a script. "Oh," Cliff said. "You must be that guy."

"And you must be that other guy," Whit said. "The lucky one, with the beautiful brainy girlfriend."

"Lucky?" Cliff said. "I don't know about that."

What? Yet again, Laurienne's cheeks flushed with embarrassment.

Although Cliff's manners were better than Lyle's, he went straight from a handshake to spinning on Laurienne with "What's a tester doing at my desk?" Not exactly the meeting of minds Laurienne had hoped for, but maybe that was the problem—her expectations pressuring Cliff, the way Phoebe's did her.

"Hold on," Laurienne said. "What happened? How'd it go?"

"They love the game."

"They do? How sweet is that?"

"Not very. They won't put up money to finish it right."

"Well, fuck 'em," Whit said. He pulled a cigar from an expensive-looking container and clipped the end into a wastebasket. "Don't put all your eggs in one bastard."

"It's a no-smoke building," Cliff told him.

Laurienne pressed her lips together. He sounded like a dorky hall monitor.

"Relax," Whit said, "this is for the road. What I'm

saying is, you've got to play hardball with these people."

"Do I?" Cliff took off his jacket, and for a second Laurienne thought he was going to ask her to hold it while he took a swing at Whit. But all he did was grab a Coke from her fridge and leave.

"Sorry," Laurienne said.

Whit waved his hand in a minimizing gesture. "You don't have to apologize. He's just got a lot to learn."

While Whit packed up his things, Laurienne noticed an envelope from Dunson in her in-box. As she flipped through his lengthy weekly memo, there fluttered out from between the pages an unattached proposal that appeared to concern the very gene that had everybody cranked into overdrive.

This particular BioIngenious invention is a human 9-transmembrane receptor which, for application purposes, has been putatively identified as a phenalokine receptor. Based on the binding, blocking, or stimulation of other homologous phenalokines, this patent covers its use in the prevention and/or treatment of such age-related disorders as cancer, Parkinson's disease, heart disease, arthritis, Alzheimer's, adult-onset asthma and diabetes, and osteoporosis. The potential benefits of the aforementioned invention are evident to those skilled in the diagnostic implications and arts which it encompasses.

Now she understood the Peter Pan handle. Phenalokine—that had to be the gene's active protein. And this document? The gene patent application. The thing responsible for BioIngenious's stock starting to climb. How could it have been approved? They had no idea what this gene's function was. They had no idea how to use it. But they wanted a patent to guarantee profits in case another researcher came along who could figure it out and invent some kind of therapeutic application. And that's what the program they were debugging was designed to do—track down anybody working with the gene so they'd have to pay to use it. Madame Curie—funny Whit had called her that. She flashed on a high school paper she'd written about Marie Curie, who refused to patent any of her discoveries, refused to limit their benefit by cost. Maybe Cliff had the right idea about this business they were in after all.

She supposed it was all legal, since nothing about the patent-application language was newsworthy enough to make it into reporters' accounts. But the little-girl judge still alive inside Laurienne cleared her throat and reached for the gavel. "That is just not fair," she said aloud in her wispy voice.

Whit put on his jacket and spoke to her in commiserating tones. "I don't know what's bothering you, but I can tell you this. There are only two fairs in life—the state and the county."

Laurienne slid the application into a drawer. "I know," she told him. "That's what my mother says."

13

Phoebe sat in a darkened auditorium at the Seattle Convention Center, mind adrift. If only she could rewind the other week's Tavern scene and play it like an adult. Letting Whit rattle her the way he did must mean she'd regressed. Too old when younger, too immature when older—maybe Jasmine would claim to see this story in her stars, though if you threw the messy stuff of her life up against a net so huge, you were bound to catch something. At least that's how Phoebe saw it.

Or did she? Her surroundings surely shaped these thoughts, the way ambient sound seeps into dreams. At this Fish Expo event, nets were the topic. Phoebe crossed her legs and focused on the screen in front of her. It was filled with images of snagged nets billowing beneath the water—cast-off gear that still caught, still trapped, still killed. Ghost nets. A hazard of the trade. Only straight curtains of net, the kind gill netters and purse seiners used, could be killer ghosts; even worse threats were enormous drift nets from factory boats. Phoebe didn't equip factory boats, but she'd worked on just enough curtains so that these derelict nets did what ghostly things were supposed to do. They haunted.

Dead-eyed, entwined creatures appeared next on the screen—porpoises, seals, orcas, gulls, otters. Phoebe drew a shallow, shuddering breath. "What you're looking at are killing fields," the Net Relief director said. "That's what we'd call them if they were on dry land, if there was the kind of public outcry there ought to be about this. But it's hard to get people upset about something they can't see happening."

As the auditorium lights came up, the director wound up his pitch. "We need your help if we're going to do everything that needs doing. Like tracking and removing lost gear. Like funding our recycling program." He gestured in Phoebe's direction. "Right here in the Pacific Northwest, Phoebe Allen's Port Pritchard net loft is one of our flagship recycling centers. Phoebe, would you say a few words?"

She bobbed up to nod at the audience. "It's way past time for the industry to step up to the plate on this one," she said. Everybody still looked a little queasy from what they'd just seen, like they needed help to change gears and do something about it. "And I don't know about you," Phoebe added, "but I just hate the thought that a net of mine might have abandonment issues." Applause and a smattering of laughter, mainly from the men who already knew her. Those who didn't laugh wore sympathetic expressions, as though she'd walked into a wall instead of cracked a joke, but she could already predict how many would come trailing by her booth later for a private exchange. A familiar dance. First she caught them off guard, then they decided to investigate.

Phoebe set an example by being first in line to write out a check. "Free for dinner tonight?" the director asked. He was attractive in the way of many northwest men—studiously casual, lean runner's body, features shaped less by angst than ease. He wore a wedding band, too. Married men were obvious items on the menu when you hungered for the kind of distance Phoebe had long required, but such a messy entrée. Yes, she was flattered. And now, she also happened to be free. But she said, "Thanks, I'm already booked," and left.

Riding the escalator down to her booth on the exhibition floor, Phoebe wondered whether Whit was a ghost net in her life, a twisted thing never properly severed or disposed of. Trapping not just her, but him, too. Why else had he written to her after their Tavern dance but to undo the tangles, set things straight? If that were even possible. Net-caught creatures seldom escaped without fatal damage, minus a claw, a wing, a foot.

What a dreary way to see things, especially if you still wanted to believe in the possibilities of love. She could neither divine Whit's intentions nor expect him to come right out and state them. Mysterious, charming, hypnotic—that had always been his style. But he was married now. To ditzy baggage, maybe, but married still. And who was she to judge Jasmine? More than anything, it was the sting of hearing her called "another Phoebe" that made it so tempting to dismiss her. Anyway, getting a secret post office box to write the original Phoebe must have been Whit's way of protecting that piece of his life. And what about her? She had plenty of her own to protect, especially when it came to him. Difficult to forget about Whit, though, when he was so much in the air.

At lunchtime today, caught in a snarl of Pine Street traffic, Phoebe had flipped on the radio and heard the last notes of a familiar instrumental tune. "Kiki's Theme," from the movie. Then a prerecorded message: "My name is Whit Traynor, and you're tuned to listener-supported station KARP."

Phoebe jumped as if he'd materialized in the seat beside her, where the newly repaired Underwood sat. The deejay came back on to say, "If you're old enough to re-

member Whit's *Imaginary Friends* show on KARP, you're
old enough to make a generous contribution to our annual fall fund-raising drive."

Well. That was one way to calculate the cost of remembering Whit. It struck her as being so Old Seattle
for the deejay not to tout Whit any more than he did,
not to dwell on his celebrity by naming movies or linking him up to the sound track cut. That would be New
Seattle style, crass and obvious, whereas the intention
here felt different, more like letting people already in on
the connections savor them, along with their own implied coolness—let everybody else figure it out.

This year the Fish Expo organizers had put Phoebe on
the same aisle with a trawl outfit from the Faroe Islands
and a seine shop out of Le Guilvenec, France. Which was
good; they hardly competed for the same customers. But
one aisle over was the fancy company from British Columbia, the one with sport nets that Sophie wanted
Westerly Webs to take on, and their proximity had only
accelerated her annoying campaign.

As Phoebe approached her booth, the guy from Le
Guilvenec called out. *"Arrêtez, mademoiselle, s'il vous
plaît."* Waving a one-sheet guide to Seattle restaurants,
he asked for recommendations. Since establishing that
she spoke French—creaky now, but serviceable enough
for his harmless flirting—he'd cornered her every day
for elementary repartee. Accustomed as Phoebe was to
being Queen of the Hop at Fish Expos, this year felt different, more like the way it had back in junior high
when you got boobs and suddenly all the boys paid attention. Maybe raising her antennae for Whit's latest
broadcasts meant everybody else's signals came through
louder, too.

Sophie was in the booth with Angus, who wanted to

know when his hula skirting would be ready. When Sophie left on her break, Phoebe sat him down for a piece of banana bread and some orange spice tea from her thermos. "What's the word?" she asked.

"Gonna be a good winter, they're saying. Pulling down top prices. I'll be out for a major cod catch and a pollock roe bonus. On the inside waters this time."

"Great. I'll look forward to seeing your nets." Fishing grounds closer to shore were tougher on gear, more likely to trash nets than the open sea—a boon for Phoebe's business.

"You never think about the muscle you need just to stand up out there till it hurts," Angus said. "I'm too old for fishing in the open anymore. Would've quit a long time ago, but for my divorce."

"I don't believe you."

He reached up to tweak a hearing aid. "Come again?"

"They're going to have to beat you off that boat like ice."

"Well, it's thick in my blood, no question."

"I know some guys in their seventies still fishing on the inside."

"Yeah, but I don't want to press my luck. Time to let the son take over. Plus, at my age, you've lost too many friends to the water. The odds get spooky. Got to take it easy on my last trip."

"Your last trip? No wonder you want to hit it big." Phoebe did the figures in her head. With a boat like the *Moonraker,* able to pack seventy tons, Angus and his crew could clear up to ninety thousand for the cod alone. There wasn't enough pollock roe in the world to satisfy the Japanese market, and the bonus for a slew of fat females could easily tack on another fifteen. "Are they paying much for the milt?" she asked.

Angus shook his head. "Not even worth mentioning."

"Humans aren't so different," she said. "Sperm is cheap, but eggs are expensive."

Angus laughed and years melted away, reminding her of how good-looking he'd once been. Old Angus, that was how she usually thought of him. Barrel-chested and muscular, white-haired, wind-whipped, aged by the same salt air that corroded his hearing aid batteries. But enough of the other Angus survived that within a certain stratum of divorced, never married, or widowed women in Pritchard Valley, he still had his pick.

"When I'm not having nightmares," Angus said, "I dream about you, Phoebe. So don't take this wrong, but where I come from, humans don't eat their own eggs."

"They're expensive, though. Infertile women pay doctors gobs of money for goosing eggs from their ovaries. But think about the peanuts guys get for jacking off into bottles at a sperm bank."

"I'd rather not." It wasn't Angus who said this but Whit. Again, Phoebe felt her spine twang to the sound of his voice. She turned to see him standing by the booth counter, pocketing her brochure. "Too late now, though. You threw that image in my head and it's stuck there."

"We were just discussing what sperm's got to do with the price of eggs," Angus said. "What the hell are you doing here, Traynor?"

"Same as you, I'll bet. Stalking Phoebe."

"I better get back to work," she said, though that meant nothing but waiting till someone else stopped by.

"Me, too," Angus said. "Got a man to see about water pumps."

Angus left and Whit came around to Phoebe's side of the booth. "You were right," he said. "We shouldn't have danced. It got us off on the wrong foot."

Phoebe winced at the pun. "How do you know Angus?" she asked.

"Ran into him on the docks, doing a little research. According to Angus, you're the best. Which is hardly a surprise. You've always been the best, Phoebe. Anyway, since we're both down here on business, I thought we ought to have dinner."

"Does 'we' include your wife?"

"Just us. I've got reservations. Somewhere quieter than the Tavern, a better place to talk."

Dinner. Not a quick, caffeinated breakfast, not a bustling businesslike lunch, not anything in the light of day. And what made him so sure she'd be available? "Bad idea, Whit."

"Why not? Two old friends reminiscing—what could be more ordinary than that? We'll be good. A photographer could come take pictures and nothing would make the front page. We need to clear the air, don't you think? It's an environmental thing—the Clean Air Act of 1996."

Phoebe shook her head, and Whit dropped his smile. "Things are different for me now," he said, "being married. I'd stop a bullet for Jasmine, swear to God. And you've got someone special in your life, too. We don't want to hurt anybody else. But we did hurt each other, didn't we? And we ought to set that right. Come on, Phoebe. You don't just throw away a story like ours."

He still knew how to make her say yes.

For past Fish Expos, Phoebe had either stayed with her father or driven back and forth between Seattle and Owl Island. This year, though, she had reserved a suite at the Inn at the Market, justifying the extravagance to herself with how she rarely traveled and so deserved a little pampering. Also, traffic on I-5 had become impossible. She didn't want to put herself through the morning commute, and since Helen's death, she couldn't stay at her father's without spending more time than she'd have to spare with him. Poor Jack, outliving two wives younger than he—both of whom were expected to outlive him, to take care of Jack when *his* end came. And his only female descendent was too busy doing things her way, by *self,* to check in on anything other than a spotty, erratic basis.

She supposed Whit must also have a hotel room somewhere, but he didn't say and she didn't ask. If you're going to be good, you don't talk about where you're sleeping. Besides, he'd been noble about his marriage today. He might have been noble with her, too, if she hadn't blown it. Still, what did it mean that he'd tracked her down to the Convention Center? If he could do that, surely he could have mailed the Mystery Packages and known that she lived on Owl Island when he moved there. And she had to admit it wouldn't have taken a great detective—much less a magician—to trace her steps from the film set in Montreal. All Whit had to do was call her father. Maybe that was exactly what he'd done.

Her plan for the night was to step out completely neutral, a fortress of nonreactive equilibrium—the best way, it seemed, to cut loose the ghost. In showering off the day, she made an effort to cleanse herself of worries as well as excitement. Then she selected clothes that gave no indication of wanting to perform: a white, scoop-necked jersey tee, black jeans, boxy black cashmere jacket, black stack-heeled boots. The ensemble of a hip, secular nun, with a titillating touch of cleavage, maybe, but just about as far as she could get from what she'd worn for the barbecue. No hopeful chiffon, no mournful pearl from the past tonight. Just your basic black and white.

Whit was waiting when she arrived at Place Pigalle, seated at a small table with a view of Elliott Bay and ferry-boats crossing in the dark distance, shining like giant oblong, mobile wedding cakes. It was his kind of restaurant, all right: checkered floor tiles, mahogany bar, good paintings along the walls, and packed with discerning customers. You'd need a name as recognizable as Whit's to snare a last-minute reservation tonight—if that was what he'd done. She used to come here a long time ago when this was a run-down dive where a teenager could get beer with a fake ID. Should all else fail, she could talk about that.

Whit stood and kissed her lightly on the cheek, then held out the chair across from his. "Thought I'd get the jump on *you* this time," he said.

A young woman wearing tight pants and a cropped sweater came to their table with a Pernod and water on the side for Whit, a red Dubonnet with a twist for Phoebe. "Did I get that right?" he asked while pouring a small amount of water into the Pernod, clouding up the glass like a lab experiment.

"Right enough. I don't drink Dubonnet much anymore."

"So. Westerly Webs—you're a spider now."

"Yes." She sipped her drink. "A black widow."

"I know a little something about spiders. The only reason they started spinning webs was that bugs figured out how to fly."

Effortlessly as it fell from his tongue, this was the kind of line he would have prepared in advance. Phoebe couldn't help it, she felt a little ripple of happiness from knowing he'd gone to the bother for her. "They adapted, you mean. I guess that's what I did, too."

"I never would have predicted you'd be doing what you're doing."

"Join the club."

"But then, unpredictability was always part of your charm."

Phoebe shrugged. "I like working by the water. I like being the boss. I'm good at it, too."

"You're so definite now. But are you sure you've got the right metaphor? Spiders catch bugs, not fish."

"Nothing's stronger than spider silk—not even steel."

"What makes you a black widow?"

"What do you think?"

"You had a husband; he died?"

She nodded, waiting to see what his response would reveal. "I'm sorry," he said, his words slow and low-pitched, his expression so sympathetic she had to avert her eyes to keep from crying.

"Yeah. Me, too. Could we change the subject?"

"Sure." Whit squeezed her arm, took a pull on his drink, and just sat there awhile before speaking again. "I might not know much about the business you're in now, but I'll tell you this—you were smart, getting out of the business I'm in."

"I was never in it. You must be thinking of Dolores con Cuervos." That was whom the *Kiki* credits listed as having coauthored the story with Whit, while he took sole credit for writing the screenplay. Her punishment, Phoebe had long supposed, for getting involved with Mitchell.

"I can change the credit," Whit said. "Set the record straight. Probably should have done it a long time ago. Would you like that?"

Somewhere in the corner of her mind she heard Margaret's voice, asking who in the world would ever find out about that. *Oh, shut up, Margaret,* she thought, and met Whit's eyes with a curt nod. "Seems fair," she told him.

"People still ask about Dolores," he said, his voice

fond and fey. " 'Who is she really?' 'What else has she done?' "

"What do you say?"

"That she broke my heart and ran off with the circus." He knocked off the Pernod. "Truer than I ever knew, eh, Dolores? Only I was picturing you in fishnet stockings—not making fishnets." Then, shaking his head, a smile sliding up one corner of his mouth: "Ah, Phoebe. The movies I could have made if you hadn't left me."

Just like that, he yanked away her fortress, her bulwark, the floor she had planned to stand on all night, serene and two-footed. "Is that how you've worked it out? *I* rejected *you*?"

"You did leave me."

"You can't really believe—"

"I don't want to argue—"

"Because that is just ridiculous!" Her next slug of Dubonnet went down the wrong way. Coughing, she flagged their waitress to ask for a glass of water. "Here," Whit said, holding out the remainder of his Pernod water for her. "No thanks," she told him. "I want my own."

Avoiding his gaze, she stared after the waitress as she went to a corner cabinet, stooping to remove glasses from a low shelf and place them on top. Her pants slid down her hips a little, revealing a few inches of bare skin. On either side of her spine were dark curving lines, the bottom edges of a tattoo. Seeing tattooed young women was so common that Phoebe had devised a cautionary maternal theory for Laurienne: no pale, freckled, red-haired person had ever improved her appearance with multiple piercing or tattoos. Still, this waitress's tattoo shocked her.

Before the waitress could stand up again, Phoebe grabbed Whit's hand and pointed to her back. "Do you think?" she asked him, still staring at the girl.

"Huh?" he said, but caught on in an instant. "Ohhh. Could be."

That's all it took to spin her out into sharing with him the same second in the same minute in the same hour of theatrical time. "A hundred bucks says it is," Phoebe whispered as the waitress approached.

"Darlin'," Whit said, "I won't bet against you on this one."

"Can I get you anything else?" the waitress asked. "Ready to hear the specials?"

No doubt about it now, this girl was definitely American.

"We couldn't help noticing," Phoebe said. "It looks as though you have a tattoo on your back."

"Uh-huh." The waitress sidled closer and pulled up her sweater so that only Phoebe and Whit could see. And there it was: a tattoo that resembled the *f*-holes on a violin, so that this girl's back mimicked Kiki's in the Man Ray photograph. "I'm a big Kiki fan. Know who she is?"

"I do believe we've heard of her before," Whit said.

"That old movie about her is what got me started with everything *a la française*."

"Oh," Phoebe said. Whit had a tight grin on his face, damming back laughter. "I didn't think *Kiki* would be big with people your age," she went on.

"It's huge with people my age. The ones who aren't total tech-heads or too, you know, *roturier*."

"*Roturier?*" Whit asked when they were alone again.

"Bourgeois, I think," Phoebe told him.

"Jesus. If I were that girl's father, I'd shoot us."

If he were that girl's father? What an opening. She could ask all kinds of questions—"Have you ever wanted children?" "Do you know I have a daughter?" "How good is your math?" But she wasn't going to show her hand before seeing his. And lively though their talk over dinner was, it didn't go deep enough to uncover anything unknown or clean up how they'd parted.

Whit had just begun relating his professional troubles when the waitress brought their check. "I'm sorry," she said, "but people are waiting for your table."

No bar stools were available, not there or at the two other places they tried. "Fucking fish festival," Whit grumbled, so Phoebe suggested her hotel, which had no bar but did offer room service. A bad idea, hatched by too much alcohol? No, no—prior occupants of her suite must have held business meetings in the living-room-like area where they settled with a bottle of Chartreuse. While Whit described his latest film's stillbirth, his hurry to make another before the stink of failure landed on his head, Phoebe glanced over her shoulder, measuring safety in the considerable distance between where they sat and the bedroom, telling herself that Whit's hypothetical photographer could still barge in and fire away, with no incriminating results. Anyway, Whit was noble now.

"Sounds like you're on the same old roller coaster," Phoebe said.

Whit stood and paced the room, glass in hand, orbiting her chair. "Not the same. It was the kiddy ride back then." He stopped for a swallow of the pale green liqueur. "At my stage, you strap yourself in and lose your stomach."

"Maybe you need a break. Go somewhere you can relax and don't have to play the director."

"But I *like* playing the director." He sounded a little miffed.

There was a water view from Phoebe's room, too. She watched another ferry cross, letting the silence stand. Though to do so she had to fight herself, had to resist all her old instincts to run the maze of his dilemma, scrambling for the only reward lever that ever mattered: proof of his regard.

"What was it like for you when you saw *Kiki*?" he asked. "I always wondered."

"Well, the first time was after this." She indicated her scar.

He lit on the couch again and studied her in his old riveting way, as if what he saw would reveal more than anything she might say. "How did that happen?"

"An accident. I don't want to talk about it."

"So very definite now," he said, pouring more Chartreuse.

"Does that bother you?"

"No, I like it. It's good."

For all Phoebe's fabled cinema savvy on Spit in the Wind Road, *Kiki* had put her off movies for years. She didn't come back to them until Laurienne started school and VCRs came along. Jack gave her one for Christmas and began mailing tapes of movies pulled off his cable-wired TV—classics they'd seen together, more contemporary films she'd missed. To love movies again after Whit, she had needed to go cold turkey for a while. Even so, the initial effect of seeing something new and special was to spin her off into imaginary conversations with him.

"*Kiki* had been playing for months when I finally caught up with it," Phoebe said. "All I could see was what wasn't there, like negative space in a sculpture. I thought it was awful."

"Don't sugarcoat it on my account."

"You asked."

"No, I get it. That's what it's always like for me the first time. I only see the budget, the cuts, the compromises."

"I figured it was my problem," she said. "So I went again, with my father."

"Your father," Whit said, flinching. "He must hate me."

"He doesn't hate anyone. But he does hate messes. I never told him what happened between us. He thinks Dolores con Cuervos was my bright idea. Whenever he mentions you, he always calls you my friend." A painful habit she had never figured out how to break him of, but she didn't admit that to Whit. " 'There's an article in *Film Comment* about your friend,' he'll say, or, 'I saw your friend's new movie.' He hasn't missed one, I don't think."

"What about you? Have you seen all your friend's movies?"

"Some, not all."

"And?"

Part of her wanted to scream, or maybe just gloat. *It's been all downhill for you since me, mister.* But that wasn't quite true—maybe *Kiki* was Whit's peak, but he'd had a few successes since, mostly working with other writers—so she tried instead for kindness, for tact. "It seems like you're ready to begin a new cycle."

"That's why I came back up here."

"Is that the only reason?"

"There's never just one reason, Phoebe. There are almost always at least two, and the first contradicts the second." He looked at her as though he'd just told a marvelous secret.

"I don't know if that's the truth or bullshit."

"I don't know if there's any difference." Whit clicked off the lamp. "It's a better view without lights."

As Phoebe watched a necklace of stars float out from behind a cumulus cushion, she felt woozy, as though spinning off into space herself. When she leaned over to set her Chartreuse on the coffee table, Whit took her hand in both of his. "It would have been a better film if you hadn't left me," he said.

That pulled her a little closer to Earth. "Now you've said it twice."

"Must believe it, then."

He still had her hand. She wasn't sure how to get it back—with a yank, a ladylike demurral?—or even if she wanted to. "It's just so strange, your seeing things that way. Don't you remember what happened?"

"What I remember is how sad it was, finishing the movie alone. Kind of like being a single parent. But I'm proud of how she turned out. I kept hoping you'd be, too."

Don't answer a question you haven't been asked—wasn't that how trial attorneys coached their clients? She'd rather find out if he already knew about *her* life as a single parent than risk mentioning it herself. "Oh," she said. "I think I understand how you feel."

"No surprise there. I could always talk to you like nobody else."

"Not even the new Phoebe?" She couldn't resist.

"Oh, my bride is sweet and lovely, there's no denying that. Not an awful lot of trained muscle to her brain, maybe, but then it's probably not possible, finding all the things you need in one lover." As he reached out to graze her throat with a fingertip, his eyes welled with tears. "You and I came mighty close, though. Closer than I've ever been. Or expect to be again."

He drew her to him and her back stiffened. Then he stroked her hair, murmuring into her neck, "Guess I just didn't realize how much you mattered. How much losing you would hurt then. Still hurt now."

In the flattering free fall from there to here, from then to now, she melted onto his shoulder and went mute. His hands seemed everywhere at once, letting her know just how well he remembered all the specifics of her body, how to flood it with pleasure. It was like being inside a circle of fire, fueled by the feeling of being bright and shiny enough for him to want again, and the flaming tongues spoke as her clothes slipped away, saying, *Stay where you are, you need this heat, it comes from love, and love is all that matters.*

He pulled her down to the bloodred Persian carpet, and when he took her face in his hands to look into her eyes the swoon deepened, intensifying everything from the sensation of carpet beneath her back to the surflike whoosh of traffic from the Alaska Way viaduct. Was this how it used to be, what she wanted now? She couldn't tell. The part of her able to decide such things didn't function. Her body was following his silent orders, and if he wanted her to put her coat on backward or tie her shoes together she would, though if someone asked why, she'd say she just felt like doing it. As it finally dawned on her that the fever driving him was one of possession, it hardly seemed to matter because he was quaking inside her and the flames still warmed her flesh.

Only afterward, when Whit dragged a pillow off the couch to rest against, did the spell completely shatter. She felt inexplicably awful. Too soon for a hangover, but it was that kind of dull, persistent ache.

"Did you move up here because of me?" she asked.

"You know, I'm beginning to think I did." As he emptied his glass, watching her, Phoebe felt a cold wet trickle running down her thigh and reached for her clothes. "If only I'd known," he said.

She snapped her jeans together. "Known what?"

"That it could be this way again. That you were so unhappy."

How could he speak as if one thought flowed logically

from the other? "Unhappy?" Phoebe turned on the light. "I didn't say I was unhappy."

"You didn't have to." He was getting dressed now, too, buttoning his shirt. "Phoebe," he said, "I don't want to fuck up your life another time. I don't want to be another thing that makes you sad."

She knew of people who turned their backs on the ocean and got swept out to sea. Something similar had just happened here, and once again, it was nobody's fault but her own. Her throat tightened with the sense of how far beyond rescue she was, the gulf between happiness and everything Whit had stirred up inside her. "I think you should go now," she managed.

Whit walked over to where she stood, kissed the top of her head, and regarded her in a proprietary way. "You'll be all right?"

She avoided his eyes and nodded, kneading her icy fingers.

After Whit left Phoebe flopped across the king-sized bed and lay there numb, waiting for a call from Laurienne that never came. She fell asleep fully clothed, not between the sheets but rolled into the duvet like some larval insect.

She dreamed of rushing off in a taxi, late for her flight to a faraway, unspecified place. After an Olympic sprint through the airport to her gate, she encountered a smiling flight attendant who held out a hand for her ticket, and though Phoebe tore through every one of her bags, she couldn't find it anywhere. When she awoke in the morning, it was to the sound of her own moans.

Light filled the hotel room and now she had a hangover for real. The last day of Fish Expo lay ahead. Mechanically, she dragged herself off the bed to shower, to cleanse the body that felt like nothing so much as an endless pit of unmet demands, and the only things she could think to give it were fresh air and food.

A high-pressure front had blown in overnight, whisking away the city's wooly gray blanket of autumnal clouds and crisping the briny air. Sunshine climbed over the backs of skyscrapers and hit Elliott Bay's stippled water, turning foamy boat-wakes into a snow-white cruciform. Phoebe walked through the Public Market to buy an orange from her favorite stall, breathing in along the way aromas of baking boreks from a Turkish shop, pirogi from a Russian one, and simmering adobo from a Filipino lunch stand. Shivering, she buttoned her thin leather jacket. She hadn't thought to dress for the chill. A golden retriever sat outside a patisserie tied to a wrought-iron rail and Phoebe, missing Lily, stopped to scritch his ears before stepping inside for a coffee and croissant to go.

"Phoebe?" someone at one of the tables said as she paid.

She turned to see a large man in a billowing brown moleskin shirt hunkered over a big bowl of coffee and a plate of three *pains au chocolat*. Must be someone she had met at Fish Expo. "Yes?"

"It's Joe," he said. "Joe Zaglan. You've gone gray and I've gone fat."

No argument there, though the difference between the lanky Joe she remembered and the man before her now seemed less the result of aging than balloon gas. He stood to embrace Phoebe, ignoring the hand she'd stuck out. "Makes you easier to recognize than me," he added. "What happened to the voice?"

"Oh, cigarettes and whiskey."

"You expect me to believe that, the way you look? What the hell are you doing here?"

"I live up north a ways."

"Yeah? So does Whit. My nothing-new-on-the-side guy."

"Excuse me?"

"It's so great to see you."

"I'm in Seattle on business," she clarified.

"Same here. Business with Whit."

He fixed her with a knowing gaze, but she stayed cool. "So you guys are still an item," she said. "You certainly outlasted me."

"And a few other women, too."

"Must be a successful partnership."

"Let's just call it an enduring one. Sit, sit," he told her. "I've got to eat these things while the coffee's still hot or else they're no fun." He shoved his plate of pastries in her direction. "Be my guest; have one."

"Thanks, but I really have to run."

"You're not still mad at me, are you?" he asked through a mouthful.

"Why would I be mad?"

"Over how we, you know, parted."

"I got what I wanted," she said.

"The money, you mean."

"What else was there?"

"The credit."

"A losing battle. I was a nobody; who would have listened to me?"

"You ran away too fast to find out, didn't you?" Joe gave her arm a placating pat. "I'll let you in on a little secret, though, in case you've got regrets. Nobody ever profited from a long-term association with Whit. And I'm not referring to gross here. I'm talking real numbers. I'm talking at the end of the day. I'm talking *net*. Know what I mean?"

Bland as milk she said, "I assume you mean that net is what matters."

"Doesn't net matter in your business?"

"Oh yes, net's the one that counts in my business, all right."

"You're lucky. In mine, net's the one you never see."

Instead of going back to her hotel to eat and pack, Phoebe left the patisserie and headed for the waterfront, wanting just one thing now—as much distance as possible between herself and Joe, between herself and all the bad decisions that he reminded her of. By the time her forced march brought her to a bench by the bay, she was warm from exertion. But her coffee had gone stone cold.

14

As it turned out, the best time for Phoebe to join Whit in California was after she finished spring semester. He sent her a plane ticket a month in advance. Meanwhile, it kept her from minding the wait that he sent frequent love notes, often tucked around a check meant for her to spend on something special for herself. He also called often—sometimes just to hear about her day, sometimes to chew over the latest pre-production snafu. "You're the only one I can talk to about these things," he said. "With everybody else, I have to always look like I know exactly what I'm doing. And all this is just preliminary. I need you here for when it gets real."

"Well," she told him, "I hope I can help."

"There's no doubt in *my* mind. Look how far you've brought us already."

When Whit picked her up at the L.A. airport in his rented black Camaro convertible, she got a look at the script, which was out to actors by then—without, she noticed, her name anywhere on it. This wasn't final, Whit explained while they sped down the freeway, just a temporary measure to fatten his credentials that Joe, his producer, had insisted upon. To get the most money, the best actors, the tightest crew. He laid out for Phoebe how Joe had put the argument to him:

"Sure, you got a film to your name, Whit, but it's an

obscure little black-and-white documentary for PBS—
not enough to make studio executives cough up the
dough for *Kiki*. You got a background in theater, too,
but not in New York, with productions that matter.
Which is to say, made money. Your stint with the
San Francisco Mime Troupe? If your average jaboni in
the business gets them at all, it's as a bunch of freaks
plundering two equally obnoxious traditions—Marcel
Marceau and that Punch and Judy horseshit. Whaddaya
call it, commedia dell' artsy-fartsy? Most of your hot
young directors—your Coppola, your Spielberg—they're
film school graduates, another distinction you lack. A
first-time director needs every ounce of authority he can
get, or nobody takes him seriously. Not seriously enough,
anyway, to get *Kiki* produced, reviewed, and into theaters where civilians pay to park their butts."

Whit was such an on-target mimic that Phoebe felt she
knew Joe Zaglan before they met. This phantom Joe of
Whit's, for all his crudeness, made sense to her. In her
own way, she'd been grooming Whit, too. Now it was
Joe's turn to take everybody the distance.

"It's not about ego," Whit said. "It's about going to
the whorehouse."

"I'm confused," she said. "Who's the whore here?"

"Joe's my pimp; I'm the one they think they're buying."

"Who cares what they think?"

"Joe, for one. My agent, too. Did I tell you I got an
agent? But not me. I don't care."

"Me neither, then. Not one little whit."

In honor of Phoebe's first trip to Los Angeles, Whit
played hooky to give her a tour. First came lunch at
Musso & Frank's, where they ate corned beef and cabbage in a high-sided mahogany booth, attended by a
waiter in a snappy red jacket whose creased, worry-

worn face said he was old enough to have served Raymond Chandler when he was hanging out here, working on *The Big Sleep*. Plenty of other famous writers doing time in Hollywood had pickled their mogul-punctured egos over at the bar. All of which made the meal monumental for Phoebe, who couldn't say exactly how all her pertinent information had been acquired. Even though she'd regularly marauded her father's personal library, filled with books about every conceivable wrinkle of contemporary popular culture save rock-and-roll, sometimes she knew *so* much it seemed possible that information entered through her skin.

"Are you this at home wherever you go?" Whit marveled. She hadn't been so many different places, but she was struck anyway by what he'd said. Her map, her books, her Underwood, her other treasured possessions inappropriate for temporary transport—they were all back in Mount Jensen, in the room that her landlord had given her for free until school began again in the fall. Privately, Phoebe wasn't so sure she'd be going back. But since navigating the map of her spirit had led her there, that room was more of a home than her father's house. Which meant she really didn't have a home. Maybe she didn't need one. Maybe as long as there was enough for her mind to grab hold of, she could root in anywhere. Be the sort of person who thrives wherever she goes. Who carries her home inside.

Phoebe had a secret desire, fueled by years of watching *Gidget* and listening to surfer music on her pink GE, to put on a bikini and splash in ocean water that was actually warm enough to swim in. Secret because she couldn't imagine Whit's long, pale, elegant body in swim shorts, so she didn't even mention it. Still, after stopping by Grauman's Chinese and the tar pits, then driving through Beverly Hills and Santa Monica, they *did* walk the shore in Malibu at sunset, which was just about as gratifying. They even parked on Mulholland Drive and necked like horny teenagers before going to the Chateau Marmont, where Whit had a one-bedroom bungalow by the pool and a bottle of champagne on ice waiting for them. On her pillow, there was a gift-wrapped box—a beautiful heart-shaped art deco lipstick mirror. "Now that you're here," he told her, "everything finally feels real."

The next morning, Whit introduced Phoebe to Joe at Left Bank Productions, the newly christened company established on Larchmont Avenue in honor of *Kiki*. Joe's office was decorated with posters from the three productions that made up *his* professional résumé—schlocky horror movies featuring no-name actors and drugged-out, demented killers all apparently inspired by Charles Manson. These bloodbaths of Joe's not only earned out their budgets but made a little profit, too, so he was proud despite their sideshow tackiness.

"Ah, the famous Phoebe," Joe said, sounding much more impressed and approving than she had expected. "You didn't tell me she was Jewish, Whit."

Of course, Joe was, too. But how could he have known about her? Nobody in Seattle ever so much as guessed at the truth of her heritage from Pearl, not even when she sang Bernstein's *Kaddish*. Whit, who'd had to leave Tennessee before meeting anyone Jewish, must have been thinking something similar. "What is it with you people, Irving?" he asked Joe. "I just don't see what looks Jewish about Phoebe. How can you tell these things?"

"I don't know, Meyer," Joe shrugged, "we just can."

"Phoebe's a half-breed, Irving. On her mother's side."

"That's the right half, Meyer. Enough to help out a redneck like you."

"Think so, Irving?"

"Absolutely, Meyer."

"Stop," Phoebe screeched. "What is going *on*?"

"We're Irving and Meyer," Joe explained.

"Meyer and Irving," Whit added. Then, in unison with dirty-blonde and dark-brown-haired noggins tipped together: "The Gevalt Brothers."

Being around them felt to Phoebe like breathing helium, giddy and fun. "*Gevalt* means help, right?"

"Get her." Joe jerked a thumb in Phoebe's direction. "Seattle really *is* a hick town, isn't it?"

"Okay, okay. How is it I'm supposed to help Whit?"

"By adding to his air of Meyer-ness," Joe said.

"Does anybody else find this amusing?" Phoebe asked him.

"You'd be surprised. Sprinkle some Yiddishkeit on Whit's corn pone, everybody wants a little nibble."

Barely out of his twenties, Joe had grown up in the business, the son of a man who had produced a string of successful TV sitcoms. Phoebe found it puzzling at first that Joe, whose previous movies looked so awful even Jack would be hard-pressed to find something to like about them, was regarded down here as the one with pedigree and lineage. No matter how different his taste or style, everyone assumed Joe had inherited his father's nose for thoroughbreds. Whit was every bit as much a vehicle for Joe as *Kiki,* and all the joshing and silliness of the Gevalt Brothers couldn't conceal Joe's ambition, or the fact that his tall, wiry body ran on a manic, jaw-grinding energy that owed much to regular lines of coke.

It was time for one of the endless meetings set up to cast secondary roles and sign up the remaining crew. Film editor, set designer, sound man—one by one they came on board and began assembling their own little fiefdoms.

"I can't hire people," Whit said. "I'm too much of a slut."

And it was true, he had a terrible time rejecting anyone who seemed excited about working with him. Especially actors, who could, of course, display a fuller, more nuanced range of excitement than, say, a prospective gaffer or grip. Phoebe sat in on these sessions, worrying about Whit's being so suggestible, so easily swayed. She supposed it all stemmed from fear of looking like a first-time idiot.

Before leaving Port Pritchard for Los Angeles, Whit had positioned Phoebe on the couch at one end of the room. There she stayed for most of the day, reading while Whit focused on her with a viewfinder, changing focal lengths and switching lenses and making dozens of sketches to record how her image changed with each adjustment. He wanted a reference chart so that when he started working with a cinematographer, he'd feel a little less stupid. Though when Whit showed his chart to Ludvik, the cigar-chomping, teetotaling, Pilsner Urquell–loathing Czech cinematographer he and Joe ended up hiring, Ludvik laughed himself silly.

"Don't be afraid," Ludvik said. "You are not my first virgin."

A strange thing happened once all the hires were made, once people started coming to Whit for decisions—and he had to make decisions all day long, about everything from schedules to haircuts. Now that they were all constructing the same dream, he was more enthused than frightened.

Phoebe's job was to assemble a "bible" for the actors, notebooks full of photocopied passages from Kiki's memoirs and excerpts from books written by or about Kiki's intimates. Phoebe gathered up information to create a detailed time line of the Twenties, highlighting achievements in art, fashion, politics, literature, music, theater, science. It was a big, consuming task and, apart from *Phoebe Comes to Pritchard Valley,* more interesting to her than any of the projects she'd completed in her first year of college, although she *was* proud of all the poetic allusions she'd managed in a biology term paper on the life cycle of salmon, turning it into a journey of Homeric proportions. *You're awfully fuzzy on the specifics of spawning,* her professor had written on the back page, *but here's an A for bringing a tear to my eye.*

Phoebe went with Whit and Joe to a prerelease screening of a film in which Dinah Loftis, the actress playing Kiki, had a supporting role that was impressive, career-making. It was a second viewing for the Gevalt Brothers, who'd seen a rough cut, and a first for Phoebe, who sat between them. Dinah wasn't beautiful, not in the conventional way, but she had the look, the intelligence, the humor, the warmth for Kiki. "Whit will have to be tough with her," Joe told Phoebe. "They say she's already a ballbuster."

Phoebe gave a derisive snort. "Probably just means she's smart."

Joe chuckled. "You'll see," he said. "You'll see."

Just when she'd see was the open question. Most days Phoebe was busy in the office, or running down material in libraries and bookstores. Some nights Whit spent just with Phoebe, taking her to dinner, usually at an Italian restaurant that was lined with mirrors, like almost every place in L.A. It was just about her favorite thing to do with him now; except for in bed, they were most alone in restaurants—away from phones, meetings, decisions. And Joe. Oh, Whit's leg might jiggle beneath the table until wine arrived, but he soon settled down and focused on Phoebe as if nothing was more vital than his delight in being with her. After dinner they would move on to a coffeehouse or record store, looking for still more film music, then drift back to their Chateau Marmont bungalow, passing through the lobby so Whit might catch a glimpse of Mick Jagger, whom Phoebe had spotted checking in. But more often Whit's evenings required working with Joe or Dinah, and he worried about Phoebe getting bored, being on her own so much.

"Why don't you try the Troubadour on open mike night?" he suggested.

But even though she had brought along her guitar and performance clothes, wrangling a gig seemed like a frivolous diversion when she felt so indispensable to Whit, to *Kiki*. Whit must have seen the sense of this, since he never brought it up again. And so Phoebe stayed in the bungalow, where she wanted to be—playing music on the stereo Whit had set up in the bedroom, eating takeout food, and all the while working like a demon on the "bible" and the script. One night while Whit was out, she wrote a new scene on his Remington to replace one that was troubling him, and left the pages on his pillow. He read them sipping coffee in bed the next morning.

"Wow," he said. "It's so great, how you've envisioned this. I can shoot it just the way you wrote it. *Incroyable*, Dolores."

Later that day, Dinah showed up at the Larchmont office in a halter top, low-slung jeans, and pink platform sandals, her long curls still damp from the shower. She looked so completely contemporary it came as a surprise to catch a flash of hair when she raised an arm to flip back her sunglasses.

"Did you grow out your pits for Kiki?" Phoebe asked. Dinah just stared at her. "I'm so glad you got the part," Phoebe added, but Dinah flinched and pulled back, as if she had bad breath. Well. "I'm Phoebe, Whit's girlfriend."

Whit came out of Joe's office and hugged Dinah.

"Oh, do you have a *girlfriend,* Whit?" Dinah asked.

Phoebe hated the way Dinah made her sound—stodgy and uptight instead of special and exclusive. "Of course he has a girlfriend," Phoebe said. "I gave him Kiki's memoirs. That's how this whole thing got started."

"I told you about Phoebe," Whit said. "She came down to help us out."

Dinah folded her arms. "I purposely haven't read the memoirs."

Phoebe looked from Dinah to Whit. "She's kidding, right?"

"Is she calling me a liar?" Dinah said.

Whit stepped between them and flung his arms around their shoulders. "Ladies, ladies," he said. "You just listen here, now. I understand the first requirement of a director is that he have the bladder control of a camel, and I've been practicing. Which means I'll be taking such a long leak that you two will have plenty of time to kiss, make up, and start speaking to each other directly. Then we can go to lunch."

Disappointed as Phoebe was in Dinah, she set about charming her. For love. For art. For Whit. "I want to show you something," Phoebe said, taking Dinah by the hand. She led her into an empty closet and closed the door. Quickly, before Dinah's eyes could adjust, Phoebe grabbed a wintergreen LifeSaver from her skirt pocket and bit down on it, hard. Sparks flew off her teeth in the dark.

"How'd you do that?" Dinah demanded.

"Magic. Now it's your turn."

"For what?"

"To surprise me."

"Okay." Dinah groped for Phoebe's hand, skittered fingers across her palm, then reached up and touched her face, repeating the whole procedure until Phoebe realized that she was doing the scene in *The Miracle Worker* where a triumphant Helen Keller spells "water" in her teacher's hand.

Whit found them still inside the closet, slumped on the floor, hooting and holding their sides. "I told you to make up," Whit said. "Not regress."

With Whit seated between them at a corner table in Chez Hélène, a quiet, unpretentious French restaurant in Beverly Hills, Phoebe peppered Dinah with revelations and questions that uncovered all they had in common. Complete collections of the Mrs. Piggle-Wiggle and Mary Poppins books. Ricky Nelson scrapbooks. Longstanding weaknesses for canned Hormel chili con carne and A-1 steak sauce. Even Jewish grandmothers who'd predicted ulcers before they turned sixteen.

Dinah was trying to put on ten pounds to play Kiki, hoping most of it would go to her chest. "So what's the big deal with the memoirs?" she asked Phoebe as the remains of her sand dabs, chèvre-spread bread, and *pommes frites avec béarnaise,* along with everybody's thrice-filled wineglasses, were cleared away.

"I didn't say it's a big deal—just hard to find in English, and Whit had never seen it till I sent him my copy."

"Your *mother's* copy," Whit corrected.

"Your mom a little know-it-all like you, Phoebe?"

"Maybe I take after her, I don't know. She's dead. Two years next Christmas."

"I'm sorry." Dinah's eyes widened as she reached across the table to touch Phoebe's hand. "But honestly, I have a good reason for not reading her memoirs. I want her coming from here"—Dinah thumped first her chest, then the top of her head—"not here. I keep waiting for your boyfriend to bust me on it. I mean, I know how di-

rectors are supposed to behave. It's just like improv. If I
say black, they're supposed to say white. But this one, he
keeps trying to figure out a way for me to get what I
want. Plus, he's enthusiastic, and enthusiastic people are
usually such idiots. So I'm kind of frustrated, like, 'When
is he going to start manipulating me so I can get pissed
off and use it in my work?' That's the only thing I can
figure out these fuckers are good for. But so far, no luck."

Phoebe, suspecting Dinah's perfomance was meant
more for Whit than her, paraphrased a line of Kiki's
from the script. "You're not losing any weight over it,
though, right?"

"I told you, Dinah," Whit said, "I'm not worried.
You're going to *be* Kiki—you don't have to write a trea-
tise on her. I just wish you'd decide whether or not
you're using an accent. We've got to get you started with
a language coach if you are."

"I'm already working with one."

"Oh. Okay. I mean, swell."

Phoebe stared at her napkin, folding it like an elaborate piece of origami. "I don't know what I expected. I
guess I just thought you'd act her the way we—I mean
Whit—wrote her."

"I do believe you were right the first time," Dinah
said.

Whit nodded his assent. "I couldn't have done it without her," he said, and Phoebe felt a small thrill that
made her realize just how hungry she'd been for ac-
knowledgment. But that evaporated into concern when
Dinah wrinkled her nose at Whit and said, "*Now* you're
acting like a director."

"No, no," Phoebe objected, "it's just better if the studio doesn't find out till later."

"If you say so." Dinah shrugged. "I guess he can't
fuck you if he's already fucking you, right? Anyway,

they won't let you into the Directors Guild unless you swear on a stack of Bibles that the screenplay doesn't matter because it's only a blueprint."

"Can you tell her momma's a screenwriter?" Whit drawled. "It's kind of like being a red-diaper baby, only you're brought up to hate directors instead of capitalists."

"Your mother's a screenwriter?" Phoebe asked.

"She started out in TV," Dinah said. "On a series Joe's father did."

"Did you know Joe before *Kiki*?"

"How do you think I got the script? Anyway, Mom's big claim to fame was fourth credit on the Tarzan movie where he goes to outer space. She did all Jane's lines." Dinah picked up a spoon to crack the crust on the crème brûlée that had just been put down in front of her. "So how *did* you two write *Kiki*?"

"Scarfed up all the research and shoved it aside," Whit said. "Let it filter into behavior."

"That was the idea, anyway," Phoebe added.

"So if all the important behavior's in the script, why do I need to retrace your steps?"

"You don't," Phoebe and Whit said at the same time.

Dinah tipped back her head and laughed in a way so natural it was almost impossible to tell this gut-rumbling guffaw belonged not to her but Kiki.

Lunch lasted four hours and when it was over, Dinah, the hands-down winner of the memoirs flap, leaned over Phoebe's way, gave her a kiss on the lips, and said it probably would be a good idea for her to read Kiki's book after all.

"It was amazing how you turned Dinah around," Whit told Phoebe that night. "She loves you."

"Come on, she barely knows me."

"All the more impressive. She practically went down

on you in that restaurant. I'll bet you could get her to do anything. Maybe we ought to think about making you first assistant director."

A now-familiar note of expectation in his voice kept her from laughing with him.

Joe was the first to fly off to Montreal, setting up shop in the hotel where everyone would be staying while on location. Whit would follow soon, then Phoebe in his wake. On their last night together at the bungalow, Dinah came for dinner. Phoebe made an asparagus salad and used the two-burner stove to prepare chicken breasts in mustard cream sauce and crusty new potatoes with plenty of garlic and fresh thyme. Whit supplied several bottles of Taittinger—all empty by the time Phoebe served slices of store-bought lemon tart for dessert.

"I am officially, unequivocally *visage de merde*," Phoebe pronounced as she cleared away the dishes.

"Let's go for a swim," Dinah said. "No one's around, we can skinny-dip." Before Phoebe could answer, Dinah was out of her clothes and in the water.

"You go on," Whit told Phoebe. "I don't believe in skinny-dipping."

When the women returned, wet-headed and wrapped in towels, the bungalow was dark except for two votive candles lit in the bedroom. Fully dressed except for his shoes, Whit lay atop the covers, puffing on a joint and listening to *Kind of Blue*.

"Want to share that thing?" Dinah asked as she and Phoebe plopped down beside him.

"Careful," Whit told her as she took in a big lungful. "Potent stuff."

He was right. When it hit, the high was actually more like mushrooms than any dope Phoebe had ever smoked. Everything around her took on a kind of visual shine,

especially Whit and Dinah. "Look at her feet," Phoebe
marveled to Whit. "Hasn't she got beautiful feet?"

"Absolutely," Whit said.

While Dinah flexed and spread her toes in the candlelight as if she'd never before noticed them, Phoebe focused on Whit. "Look at his mouth. Golly. I mean to
say, gee. Did you ever in your entire life meet a man with
lips like that?"

And then, for the first time, Phoebe could see herself
doing what Whit wanted. Pleasing another woman
couldn't be so very different from pleasing herself, she
thought as her hand traveled up the length of Dinah's
leg. And this was no stranger, this was Dinah, the
medium now for Kiki, or the Kiki that she and Whit had
imagined—an instrument already accustomed to their
music, already tuned to their touch. Dinah looked at
Whit, dropped her towel, and leaned over him to kiss
Phoebe. As their kiss deepened, Whit rolled out from between them and propped on an elbow, watching.

Phoebe's stomach fluttered.

What was she doing, inviting Dinah into their bed?

She was tempted to laugh, to make the kiss into some
kind of joke and leave it at that. Instead she closed her
eyes, letting the scent of swimming pool chlorine on her
skin, on Dinah's skin, conjure a childlike sense of play
and safety, which somehow, with her and Whit, was
essential to the erotic, and then there grew a different
feeling, almost like being part of some primal family,
cushioned by the flesh of both parents, connected to them
only by sensation and desire. Another pair of breasts,
these more peaked than pillowed; another bottom, this
one a perfect dimpled Valentine; another pubic triangle,
stiffer and thicker than her own, but crowning a place
every bit as moist and familiar. Phoebe let herself be
swept away by the welcoming softness of Dinah's body

as it opened, first to her, then to Whit, and as she slowly slid back into her separate self, now she was the one watching, amazed at nothing more than the magnitude of her own generosity, her own patience, because surely he was going to finish with her, his bountiful lover, the giver of this extraordinary gift.

But he didn't, he shuddered and came instead inside Dinah while Phoebe tasted her on his lips. Phoebe couldn't help it; she started to cry.

Whit eased away from Dinah to draw Phoebe closer. "What's wrong, honey chile?"

"Aunt Dora's box," Phoebe said.

He caught a trickling tear with his tongue. "Aunt Dora's box?"

Phoebe swiped at her eyes. "That's what I thought my mother was saying. When she told me not to go opening Pandora's box."

Dinah raised up and kissed Phoebe's neck. "I am not Aunt Dora," she said.

But oh, she was.

15

"It's better if I go alone," Whit had told Jasmine before he left for Seattle. "You'd just be bored." That made sense to her, since she had arranged most of the schedule for his three-day trip—appointments with Joe, with an ophthalmologist, a dentist, a masseuse, a stockbroker, and the radio station that wanted Whit to record a plug. Jasmine actually relished the idea of a few days alone.

Whit would return tonight, and she had a full afternoon schedule of telephone consultations in her office: two solar-return charts, one compatibility chart, and a natal reading for a three-day-old baby. Not for the baby's ears, of course, but his mother's. His mother being a famous stick-thin actress who had engaged the services of a surrogate to carry her lab-fertilized embryo to term and now, with the baby born, wanted to know if any future trauma from that arrangement could be discerned in his planets. This reading came first.

Jasmine slipped a disc of Chopin nocturnes into the CD player and sat down at her desk to study the infant's chart. So many planets stacked one on top of the other in the second house of finances. No wonder: so many monetary transactions required to bring this baby to life while maintaining his mother's figure.

Jasmine never discussed the content of her readings with Whit. Professional confidentiality was the reason she gave when clients inquired. Truth be told, her husband wasn't interested in their problems, not even if the clients were famous. Especially if they were famous, it sometimes seemed. It brought out his competitive streak. But Jasmine's receptors were wide open for anything to do with babies these days, and this client happened to be Trudy, Whit's old girlfriend. Which called up her own competitive streak.

It was Trudy who had accompanied Whit to Kitano Hot Springs and insisted he keep the appointment she made for him to have an astrological reading. That was when Jasmine was still Donna Price. When Trudy was still ravenous for the recognition Donna assured her the stars promised. When Donna stole Whit from Trudy.

"Trudy's not much older than me," Jasmine had told Whit on the phone when he called this morning, "but her husband's nearly sixty." "So?" he said. So. Tonight was probably not the best time to whip out all the photos of happy-looking younger woman–older man couples with babies that she'd snipped out of *People, Premiere,* and *Vogue,* building her case. Before getting married, she had agreed with Whit that children weren't the important thing. It seemed romantic then, a guarantee of rare and lasting passion. Anybody could have children. Almost anybody. Probably not her. No matter how loudly her body screamed *baby, want one!* Not if she wished to stay married.

A leaden feeling clung to her today, the backwash of a disturbing dream. In it, she was a passenger on a cruise ship pulling into some lush tropical harbor. Lounge chairs and umbrellas dotted a sugary white-sand beach where muscular bronzed young men waited to serve drinks. But as she raced down the gangplank with all the other pleasure seekers, the ship's captain threw out an arm to stop her. "What's wrong with you?" he yelled.

"There are sick people on this boat. You have to stay here and take care of them; that's your job."

On waking she had taken the dream as referring to her clients, especially Trudy; how bizarre to be paid for reassuring someone so frightened of a few extra pounds, a little stretched flesh—especially when you considered that the payoff was a baby. But now the dream seemed to be about Whit. He needed her attention. Was Phoebe the reason why? The awful thought occurred that whatever ran now between Whit and Phoebe was her reward for swiping him from Trudy. She considered offering a belated apology as prelude to the baby's reading, but when the phone rang and she heard the bubbling ecstasy in Trudy's voice, her compunction shrank.

"This is the man I've been waiting for," Trudy cooed. "First one ever who's all mine. I'll send you pictures, Jasmine. You won't believe how perfect he is."

Maybe Trudy knew about Whit's aversion to fatherhood and was just rubbing it in. No, no, no—she wasn't that good an actress. "Congratulations," Jasmine said. Time to turn off the fear and plunge into spirit. Time to get to work.

Jasmine clamped on her telephone headset, took a sip of bottled water, and attached a little black suction cup to the receiver so she could tape the reading. But then another call came in for Trudy. "Sorry sweetie, it's my press agent; I have to take this," Trudy said.

"Don't be long," Jasmine warned. "I've got a full day." But really, she just didn't want to be alone with her thoughts.

After his Kitano Hot Springs reading, Whit had gone home to San Francisco with Donna Price's phone number tucked into his wallet. It didn't take long for him to call. He said Trudy was away—on the East Coast, acting in another director's film. It was clear from his tone that this was not so bad as sleeping with another man, but almost. A few more late-night conversations, a little light phone sex, and Whit was FedEx-ing her a ticket to fly up for dinner at his favorite restaurant, a northern Italian place near Union Square where everybody knew him. Walking back to his car, he turned to her in a narrow alley and spread his hands beneath her face, as though framing her for the camera in this setting. Then, angle established, they had their first kiss.

A strange emotion flooded her then, and she recognized it as one described in all the acting manuals—the sense of connecting with a role you were born to play, something she had never before experienced. Certainly not in the meager parts she got hired to do before giving up to become an astrologer: standing in a doorway for an earthquake-preparedness film, performing her single scene as a prostitute in *Death of a Salesman* in shadowy light behind a scrim. Neither role required smiling. Her drama teacher at Chico State had been right—her stupid teeth held her back. She'd been silly, thinking some mogul would see how easily her flaw could be repaired, like the bulbous tip of Marilyn Monroe's natural nose had been, and invest in her glamour. Things didn't work that way, not anymore. She had charisma, no problem there. But where this really shone, it turned out, was in intimate consultation, when all her lines were like one long, brilliant improvisation.

She didn't need her part with Whit written out; she had it down cold. She would be his sorceress, his wolf-eyed witch. She wouldn't fight him for the spotlight; she'd be happy to sit in the audience. Somehow, she conveyed all that from her end of their first kiss.

When Trudy came home from location, Whit gave her the news—he was in love with somebody else. He coddled Trudy's ego with assurances that the woman in question was not an actress. Technically the truth. Metaphorically a lie. Actually, kind of sweet. Trudy raged, she cried, she flung accusations and crockery. Still, as breakups went, theirs in the end was a civilized production. No sloppy endings, no bridges burned. Just the way Whit wanted, without him ever having to utter an instructive word. And in a few weeks, Trudy called to ask for another reading.

Jasmine LaFleur was Whit's pet name for her, but she liked it well enough to file for a legal change. An outward indication of how her life was unfolding, like tiny, tightly furled jasmine tea leaves steeping into long, fragrant threads. According to her calculations, it shouldn't have taken nearly so long for her name to change again to Traynor. For that to happen, though, more transformations had to occur.

Whit sent her to a cosmetic dentist who examined her skin tones to determine the exact complementary shade of white her new teeth should be, then huddled over her Novocain-numb mouth, stripped the bonding off her awful old teeth, and took "before" photographs she made him promise never to show her. She had to wear thick temporary veneers that made her mouth feel full of Chiclets before she got the real things—the real artificial things, to be precise. Dazzling ice-thin porcelain facings, sculpted for dimension and imbedded with a few tiny flaws so they wouldn't look fake. Sixteen teeth, eighteen thousand dollars. And worth every penny. At last she had a smile as enticing as her lips. If this had been done before she tried to launch her acting career, she might have had some success. But what mattered was Whit caring enough to want her appearance in synch with his conception of her.

There were other improvements. He never asked her

to change this or change that, but she knew how to respond when he made observations like "I don't think
your eyebrows look quite the way you want" or "Darker
hair would really set off your skin." Her boots were of
softer leather, her jackets better tailored, her lingerie less
sporty—no more girl-style Jockey panties. One day he
remarked on the flecks of violet in her eyes, edging the
iris, saying it seemed as if this was the color they had
once tried, and failed, to become—had she ever considered tinted contacts? But there Jasmine balked. She drew
the line at sticking foreign objects into her everyday
Donna Price hazel eyes, changing them to another color
that she now realized would match Phoebe's.

"Well," Trudy said when she clicked back to Jasmine,
"tell me everything. Is he going to hate me someday for
how I got him?"

"Relax," Jasmine said. "His moon's in Gemini, sign of
the twins. Duality's part of his emotional equipment; he
wants two of everything. But better make sure he finds
out the truth from you."

Jasmine looked at the baby's chart one last time, sipped
more water, punched the record button, and closed her
eyes. Pretty soon she was cranking, pulling full-fleshed
scenarios and sparkling analogies from the air. Trudy
barely spoke, and hissed like a cat when her assistant in-
terrupted; that's how riveted she was. "Thanks," she
said at the end of her hour. "I can't tell you how much it
helps, knowing what he needs from me."

Jasmine hung up and stretched out her back. Not a
small thing, easing the way for this baby's happiness.
Surely that had bought her a little grace, a little expiation.

Next came the compatibility chart—lesbian interior
designers at odds over whose taste would prevail in their

new Pacific Heights home. She dazzled them, too. Then
everything went sour again.

Her first solar-return client was a real estate agent
who rushed her to jam his reading into the time it took
to drive from a house in Rancho Park to one in Santa
Clarita, all the while yelling at other drivers on the freeway.

The next client canceled.

Jasmine grabbed her tote bag and sticky mat. Might
as well squeeze in another round of yoga. An advanced
class was on the schedule for this afternoon. Only fifteen
minutes into it, sweat poured off her face and plopped
onto her purple mat. The studio was packed with people, Amelia among them, and their collective body heat
steamed every inch of the floor-to-ceiling windows.
Near the end of class, as Jasmine lay resting on her back
in Shavasana, an intuitive thunderbolt struck.

"How about I follow you home?" she whispered to
Amelia after the last round of *ohm*s. "You can put together those teas for me."

Inside Amelia's house, Jasmine marveled at the cozy
clutter—gardening books piled up on the floor, thriving
plants in every corner, an embroidered shawl flung over
the sofa, baskets filled with balled yarns, collections
of everything from old English tea tins to hand-tinted
roller-coaster postcards. Jasmine had collections, too.
Seashells, Victorian dolls, tiny glass animals, ink stamps—
all in boxes since she started living with Whit.

Phoebe's dog lay on a cushion in the kitchen, a white
cat nestled against her flank. "Did Lily run away?" Jasmine asked, rubbing the dog's head.

"I've been keeping her while Phoebe's in Seattle."

"Phoebe's in Seattle?"

"Just got back, actually. Ought to be here any minute for Lily."

"She has family in Seattle, right?" Jasmine asked.

Amelia nodded. "This was business, though."

Unfinished business was probably more like it. But at least Jasmine now knew why she'd been compelled to come here, and asking more questions would be a tactical error. With expiation out the window, she could only stall for time.

The cat rose to rub against Jasmine's legs, letting her know this was Katie, the raped kitten who used to visit, grown bigger and fatter now, wearing a thick, belled collar. "You remember me," Jasmine said, picking her up, "don't you, Katie?"

"That's Smudge," Amelia said. "She was a stray. Came in through the cat door covered with soot the very same day my old cat died. It was weeks before she'd sit still for a collar, and then all the birds and mice could hear her coming. Couldn't hunt anymore, so she stayed closer to home. Drove you crazy, didn't it, Smudge?"

"All is forgiven," Jasmine said, "especially since you upgraded her food."

"Yeah, she wouldn't touch anything out of a can. Now she gets salmon. What, did she tell you that?"

"When I was little, I used to think everybody could get what animals had to say."

"God, you're spooky good! I'm going to have to listen to that tape of yours again."

Amelia led her to a room with shelves that were filled with glass jars of tea, arranged by type. While Amelia packaged her teas Jasmine went to the bathroom for a pee, determined not to leave before Phoebe arrived. What would she do if that didn't happen soon? Offer to take Lily over herself? "Hi, Phoebe, your dog's rash is all better now and by the way, did you fuck my husband?"

Oh, never mind, she thought, pulling up her panties. Whit would be home soon and she had a pork roast marinating in the fridge that needed to be brought to room temperature soon.

In the hallway she heard Phoebe arrive and the sound of Lily going nuts, barking and whimpering all at once. "Hey there, silly girl," Phoebe said, her scratchy voice pitched high and happy for the dog. "What's with the eczema, huh?"

"I rubbed in some aloe gel and comfrey every night," Amelia said. "That cleared it right up. So how was Seattle?"

"Exhausting. Felt more like a month than four days."

Jasmine backed up and strode into the kitchen, taking Phoebe by surprise. "Hi," Jasmine said. "About time we set a date for your reading, don't you think?"

"Sure," Phoebe said. "Sounds good."

Oh, Phoebe seemed friendly enough. But Jasmine could almost hear steel doors clanking, deflecting her probe. No reason for a fortress where a simple boundary will do.

Phoebe hugged Amelia goodbye and spoke to the dog. "Want to go home for dinner?" Lily went off like a firecracker again, whimpering and pawing at the door. As Phoebe had to know she would.

16

Phoebe's bedroom glowed, lit by the moon hanging over Little Pritchard Bay like a giant klieg light. Exhausted though she was, when Phoebe closed her eyes up came images from the night before. Whit pulling her down, his hand slipping under the waistband of her jeans, her clothes and resistance coming undone. Her first reckless sex in so long, and not so different from her first sex ever. In the dark, disappointing, with big missing pieces. But the images remained, burned into her brain. She thumped her pillow and flipped over in bed, knocking Lily's head off her leg. The dog snorted, shook herself, jumped gingerly to the floor, then slouched halfway down the hall, turning back with a baleful glare before heading into Laurienne's room.

Phoebe got up, too. She turned on the light, opened the mahogany jewelry box on her dresser, and slipped the simple gold wedding band Mitchell had given her onto the chain of her mother's necklace. It was something she had never done before, calling on the dead for help, for protection, for signs. She imagined that the dead, being dead, wouldn't judge her ill. They'd smile and shake their heads as if to say, *Humans on earth— such a shame, how tough it is for them to love each other.* But she had to admit, on the scale of defensible actions, manufacturing forgiveness for herself from the other side fell pretty low. "We're bigger than we think," she'd told Jasmine. Maybe this was nothing more than pulling the dead up from inside herself, not summoning their spirits from the heavens or the ether or wherever it was they were supposed to hang out. Only the comfort of it mattered, having the gold and the pearl against her skin, these things their hands once touched touching her. And still, it felt as if the scar on her throat had turned into some kind of tumor, grabbing her in a choke hold. Maybe it *was* a tumor and she would die, leaving everyone to piece together the puzzle without her. Or not. Whatever was best. She wouldn't write a journal like the one left to her, that was certain. Passing on grief for someone else to carry. No, she would leave her loved ones in peace.

How mawkish, thinking this way. Especially since she had always skipped over the impact of Pearl's past and clung to its drama—how it set her mother apart, made her special, put her inside her own enchanted compass, only this one so cursed almost everyone within it died too soon. Including Pearl. Pearl, who ought to have put a gate on Phoebe's Magic Circle, who ought to have made it a place to leave and enter at will, as needed. Maybe then the Magic Circle really would have kept her safe, taught her to awaken from perilous dreams. But Pearl had failed to protect her. Not just because she died, but because she withheld herself while she was alive. At least she withheld the truth about herself, and wasn't that the same thing? And Phoebe, never intending to, had carried on the tradition, giving Laurienne just as poor a role model for revelation.

Not the sort of insights she'd expected this jewelry to bring. They made her palms sweat, her pulse race. She needed a Nat, right away.

After pulling Levi's and a sweatshirt over her thin,

flower-sprigged flannel pj's, Phoebe slipped bare feet into plastic gardening clogs, clomped down to the kitchen, grabbed a cigarette, and went outside. It was so cold she couldn't tell the smoke from her exhale of frosty air. Half the pleasure gone right there. She walked down the deck steps and prowled through the cedars between her place and Ivan's. His studio lights were on.

Ivan always worked late nights ramping up to a show, and this one was major. There he'd be, in the Valley's Northwest Museum, wall to wall with the great Mystic painters, and all she could think about was how the museum gift shop sold videos of Whit's old documentary. She wouldn't have knitted these things so tightly together before last August, before Whit was everywhere once more. Before she messed everything up with him. Again. And now she'd have to sit through a reading with Jasmine. Not just a woman she'd befriended and wronged, which was bad enough, but a psychic to boot. And for all Phoebe's suspicions of someone who'd go pro in that department, she was frightened by the prospect of Jasmine's scrutiny.

Phoebe walked on, twigs snapping beneath her feet. She heard the staccato hoot of a great horned owl and saw the bird's snowy throat before it swooped overhead. The only other sounds were of tidal waters lapping the shore and muffled voices from Ivan's radio—Art Bell's show, no doubt.

She stamped out her half-smoked cigarette, stripped the tobacco, stashed the butt in her pocket, and went to the studio window. Ivan, in a down vest and blue Cubs cap, was dabbing pigment at a textured conical vessel, the mouth lined with tiny mouse teeth. It looked alive, like part of some strange gorgeous creature from the underworld, pared down to skeleton and skin. She waited until Ivan changed brushes to crack open the studio door. "Sorry, it's just me."

Ivan glanced her way only for a second. "Well, that sure did sound pathetic."

"Couldn't sleep. Can I blame it on the harvest moon?"

"Nope. Harvest moon's around the equinox. What we have here is the full hunter's moon—or what's left from last night."

"I'm sorry to bother you—"

"Stop apologizing and you can stay."

"Okay." He was still upset with her, she could tell by the way he held back his smile. But sweet as it would be to feel the glow of his affection again, she sensed no imperative to work for Ivan's esteem. In that way, he reminded her of Mitchell. "Anybody good on Art tonight?"

"Yeah, this guy who believes in backwards speech. Says if you play recordings of someone lying backwards, you can hear them tell the truth. He just played something O.J. said in reverse. Sounded like, 'She made me kill her.' "

"Why do you like this stuff?"

Ivan met her eyes with a shrug. "It's pretty interesting, what people decide to believe."

"But backwards talking? That's crazy, he's a con artist."

"Can't con anyone who doesn't want to be. Anyway, everybody's got their own version of crazy going on. I'll bet I've done a bunch of things today that I think are important and somebody else would call nuts. Like, for instance, polishing mouse teeth."

She felt an urge to grab the belt loop on his jeans and pull him to her for a simple, self-evident kiss, but there was too much dirt on her heart for that.

Ivan set the mouse-teeth vessel aside to measure and mark a swath of cured beaver skin, translucent and textured like a piece of medieval parchment. He used such skins as wrappings, firing them into the form of a piece, secured with bits of polished bone. With the exception of mice trapped in his house, Ivan never destroyed the animals whose parts he used. He either came upon a carcass himself or found it left on his doorstep, much like the kill a cat brings its master. Locals who knew nothing of art but plenty about nature appreciated the spirit of his work enough to think of him whenever they came across a dead animal they had no interest in eating. Ivan handled the skin as if performing a sacred ritual he'd rather conduct in silence, if not privacy.

"Ivan?" An unfamiliar female voice traveled through the house and into the studio.

"Back here," he called out. Then, to Phoebe: "I seem to have acquired an assistant."

"You're paying an assistant?"

"I don't. The museum does."

She was tall, young, blonde, and lanky, dressed in art-student black and paint-spattered work boots. No older than Laurienne, but heaps more worldly looking, with a sassy, unrepentant swagger. In her arms, a bottle of merlot and clear plastic carryout dishes from the Co-op—sesame noodles and chicken drumettes.

"Hi, Marieke," Ivan said. "This is Phoebe."

"Marieke?" Phoebe said. "Like the Jacques Brel song?"

"So I've been told."

Marieke spoke with an Australian accent. She shook Phoebe's hand with a killer grip before addressing Ivan again. "Just thought you might be getting peckish 'round now. Don't forget about your statement. Catalog copy is due tomorrow."

"It's done," Ivan said, gesturing toward a yellow legal pad on his worktable, covered with scratched-out lines down to the bottom third, where a solid paragraph stood.

The sight of his sloped, skinny scrawl gave Phoebe a pang, recalling all the letters he'd written from Japan, back when everything was still clean between them. Or was it? As much of herself as she'd poured out to him, she hadn't dived deeply enough into the past to uncover Whit.

Marieke picked up Ivan's legal pad. "Better make sure I can decipher this." She read aloud over the radio voices:

"I could list the materials used to make these vessels in concrete terms, but I would rather tell you they are composed of life and death. Life in natural clay and pigments, death in the bones of mice and beavers, the skins of deer and rabbits. This is not what makes them beautiful to me. But it is what makes them matter."

Marieke tore off the sheet of paper, then folded and pocketed it. "Bravo," she said. "That's perfect."

"Nah, it's just something I can live with," Ivan said.

His words sounded nonchalant, but his grin looked plenty flattered to Phoebe. She worked to unclench her jaw. "Marieke's right, Ivan. I know how much you hate writing those things, but this is the best one yet."

"All right, then," Marieke said. "I'll be off. See you tomorrow with the kiln."

"That was weird," Phoebe said when they were alone again. "The museum pays her to get groceries?"

"No, but she has plenty of initiative. Plus, Daddy's rich and Marieke wants to learn glazes."

"Is she really helping you?"

"Lots. Doing all the paperwork for the catalog. Pulling in pieces for the show, cleaning brushes, running errands—"

"And picking up your kiln. Looks like she has a crush on you."

"Comes with the territory, I guess. Not a bad little ego boost, though, considering."

"Considering us?"

"I meant it's nice being appreciated for what you've got to give. Maybe the problem with us is you've known me too long." He pulled a Swiss Army knife from his pocket to uncork the merlot, then poured two glasses.

"No, that's not it." Now Art Bell had somebody on hawking oil lamps and powdered food, survival gear for what was shaping up to be an event made to order for his conspiracy-loving listeners, Y2K. "Mind if I turn this down?"

"Only if you tell me what the problem really is."

"It's complicated." She adjusted the radio and dropped into a white Adirondack chair. "It's like I opened a door and my whole life came screaming out and knocked me over. I don't know what to do."

"Wonder what I'd hear if you said that backward."

"What's that supposed to mean?"

"I thought I understood the situation, why getting close was so hard for you. It was because of Mitchell, I figured—what a stand-up guy he was, how he died. Plenty of tough stuff to get past there. I still have a hunch that's the real deal. But now, looking back, I'm seeing signs. Some things I heard from Mitchell, others you let slip."

"It's not all problems on my end, Ivan. If you hadn't gotten the Guggenheim and gone away, if I hadn't written you that first long letter, nothing would have happened with us. Maybe it's like having kids—you were afraid of the distraction and responsibility."

Ivan didn't speak for a while as he took a blade and cut the skin into a broad swath. Then he looked up and said, "I can see why you think so."

"And speaking of letting things slip, Amelia says you

remember Whit from a long time ago. Why didn't you ever mention that to me?"

"It took me awhile to place him."

"I didn't know you were around back then."

"I was student teaching at the U, coming up north to sit at the masters' feet. One day I'm stretching canvases for a painter who used to hang out with Tobey and Graves when in comes this character with his film crew. Asks me to hold a light while he does an interview. My name got in the credits, on the thank-you list."

Phoebe shook her head. "Jesus."

"Small world. But like Kinky Friedman says, I wouldn't want to paint it. The time I heard you sing at the Tavern— he was there then, too."

"You never told me that either."

"About hearing you sing? Did too. You said that part of your life was over, and I said that was a shame because you were good. Really good. Terrific, even."

"Was this before the accident?"

"Yeah," he said, his expression asking just how well did she know him if she could imagine anything else. "You had a lot going on. Guess you forgot."

Phoebe backtracked then, like an old lady driving miles out of her way to avoid a left-hand turn. "It just hit me funny, hearing something like that from Amelia."

"Did I mention to Amelia that I didn't like him? Because I didn't. Didn't like him then, don't like him now— way too squirrelly for me. That sounds like jealousy, but it isn't. Not more than a little, anyway. I just wish you could have been straight about it."

"I told you, it's complicated."

"Here we are again, back at complicated."

"How simple do you need this, Ivan? You want me to talk straight? I can't even think straight."

"Then do us both a favor, babe. Go home."

Those were his words, but the impact was more as if he'd said, Nobody wants you, you're too unhappy, too confused, you don't even know how to be honest with yourself. And it made her scream: "That's the choice? I can dumb my life down for you or go home? Fine, I'm leaving."

She took a last gulp of wine and stomped out of the studio. Never before had she raised her voice with him. It seemed necessary, though, as if it gave her more room to breathe. But only for a few seconds, because her anger was just a cork, a stopper for all the thick, unmanageable emotion inside, climbing now to a higher, more dangerous level.

Ivan caught up with her in the cedars. She turned to him, his strong fingers tight around her forearm. On his moonlit face, a flare of something fierce and unfamiliar. He kissed her hard, then dropped her arm. "It's not that I don't believe in fighting, because I do. I believe in fighting for truth, for justice, for eggs that come over easy when you order them that way. But not for a lover. I'm tired of waiting, Phoebe. That's just a fact. And here's another. If we get together, you need a better reason than *why not.*"

She reached out for him, but he backed away and left her leaning against a cedar trunk. Soon after she heard the studio door close, all the lights went out. She wondered if he'd be able to sleep. She knew she wouldn't. And she wondered if he fell into the same category for her as compliments: something nice she didn't believe she deserved. And if that was true, was it too late to change?

The one certain thing was that she owed Ivan better. He was right, issuing his ultimatum. "Ultimatum." Another misheard word from childhood. She had understood it as "old tomato." As in, He threw the old tomato at me. It felt a little like that with Ivan, a little like being pelted offstage with rotten fruit. Or maybe she herself was the old tomato—which would be plain to see now that Ivan had Marieke, a young ripe one, at his side every day.

It seemed her whole world had turned into an advanced geometry exam like the one she'd failed long ago, when she miscalculated all the angles between her, Whit, Dinah, Mitchell, and Joe. Only now she had double the number of impossible triangles to resolve and no time to study.

Phoebe rubbed the jewelry beneath her sweatshirt as her eyes began to fill.

17

"Welcome to Parisgrad," Joe said as he drove Whit and Phoebe down Saint-Paul Street in Old Montreal. Even though Phoebe had never been abroad, the looming stone edifices they passed *did* seem better suited to the banks of the Volga than the Seine. Old? *Oui.* But Parisian? *Non.* Then, leaving behind the broad boulevards along the St. Lawrence River, they turned onto narrow, curving, cobblestoned streets with smaller, friendlier buildings. Here it became possible for Phoebe to imagine Kiki wandering past facsimiles of Montparnasse street signs, kiosks plastered with posters for costume balls and cabarets, outdoor café tables, vintage cars parked against curbs. She squeezed Whit's arm in excitement as they stepped out onto the sidewalk. He closed his left eye, boxed his hands to frame doorways and storefronts, and then, squinting up at the clear blue sky like a vampire hauled out of his coffin to salute the sun, he said, "We might as well be shooting in Reseda. Get me clouds, Irving. Get me rain."

"Don't worry, Meyer. We'll make some if we have to."

Since there weren't many exterior scenes in the movie, indoor locations would matter more, and the places in Plateau Mont Royale chosen to become studios, bedrooms, and nightclubs were all fine. A rented warehouse in a drab industrial neighborhood contained a replica of a Parisian café that was nearly complete. Whit put his hands on Phoebe's shoulders. "Recognize it?" he asked.

"Oh yes."

"The Dôme come to life."

"It's amazing."

"Only it's La Rotonde, darlin'."

Phoebe flinched a little. Ever since their night with Dinah, the undercurrent of Whit's scrutiny had grown stronger and the sense of falling short struck dread in her heart. She tried to shrug off this aspect of him, dismiss it as her own guilty invention. Whit might have angled for a threesome, but she was the one who made it happen. That must be why they hadn't once discussed Dinah since she left them alone in the Chateau Marmont bungalow, her breezy "Thanks for everything" hanging in the air. Meanwhile, the knowledge Whit acquired by watching her and Dinah together spread to his hands, his lips. Maybe it was best to reframe it all as just another scene they concocted, just another instance of art bleeding into life.

"It's hard for me to tell them apart," Phoebe told Whit, "without the little awnings outside."

He smiled, swept Phoebe's bangs aside, and leaned down to plant a tender kiss on her forehead, easing what began to feel a little more like paranoia. "This is as good as it gets, you know. Right now, everything's possible."

"Time and money, Meyer," Joe said. "Our only limitations."

"Don't be such an Irving, Irving."

"You can do anything you want, pal. So long as it doesn't take more than twenty-eight days, eight hundred thousand American. If we had more, we'd be in Paris for real."

"Just let me dream for a few minutes, will you? Then you can play producer again."

Joe had set up offices in a suite at Hotel La Ville, where every significant imported member of the cast and crew would also be staying. Whit and Joe's desks were in one of the bedrooms; the company accountant and production manager's in the other. Phoebe's was in the living room, with the assistant director and production assistants. Now that the "bible" was finished there wasn't much for her to do, so she volunteered to plan the party scheduled for the night before filming began. She reserved a banquet room in the hotel, hired a caterer, booked a French-Canadian chanson band. Meanwhile Zoe, a p.a. from New York who looked like a young female Woody Allen, buzzed beside her. Until the shoot began, Zoe's job was to arrange plane tickets and airport pickups for all the actors soon to descend on the hotel. Including, of course, Dinah.

Phoebe and Whit shared a much smaller suite on the fourteenth floor, and as the film's start date drew near, she nested into that anonymous-feeling space with the urgency of a pregnant woman about to give birth. She replaced the ratty curtains and shiny synthetic bedspread with wooden jalousie blinds and a silk patchwork quilt that she found, along with antique French linen sheets and deco-style vases, at the Lesage Flea Market. Anticipating night schedules and odd hours, she supplemented the kitchenette's meager supply of cookware and staked out nearby butchers, fishmongers, and markets with the best fresh local produce. She seeded the suite with lavender sachets, filled vases with lilies, put candles on every available surface, then stuffed all the hotel's ugly oversized ginger-jar lamps into a closet.

On the day Dinah was to arrive, Phoebe drove Whit's rental car to the art department's shop to "borrow" stockpiled deco-style floor lamps that hadn't been assigned to sets. When she got everything she wanted out on the loading dock, someone said, "You're never going to fit all that junk in your car."

She turned to see one of the set carpenters having a smoke. He was built like the spike man on a volleyball team, tall with broad shoulders and thick, ropey thighs protruding from faded cutoff jeans. His cloud of nearly nappy red hair gave an antic, vaguely Bozo-ish air to what was otherwise a candid, serious, strong-boned face. What mainly struck Phoebe, though, was that he spoke to her in English, a respite from Canadian French with all its hard, trilled *r*'s and biting nasal sounds—a version of the language that, despite her proficiency in Madame Poiret's demanding classes, she could neither speak nor understand very well.

"I could use a hand," Phoebe admitted.

"You're with the movie?"

"I'm with the director."

"His assistant?"

"Girlfriend."

"Tell my boss. If he'll give me an hour, I've got a pickup to cart it all in."

His name was Mitchell, Mitchell Gentry, and his dusty red truck had California plates. To make room for Phoebe's stuff, he shoved aside an amp, guitar, and electric keyboard. "You're a musician?" she asked as they headed for the hotel.

"Nobody pays me much for it." He drove breezily, one-handed, using a brody knob on the steering wheel for turns.

"This your first movie?" she asked.

"Fourth."

"Joe hired you in L.A.?"

"Nope. The set designer's a friend. Coming here was as good an exit strategy as I could find."

"You're not interested in this movie?"

He shrugged. "I like berets. I like surrealists. I like naked women."

"It's just that I know nobody's getting paid that much."

"You can say that again."

"So I kind of assumed it was a labor of love."

"Hah," Mitchell snorted. "That's something only above-the-line people say, not below-the-line peons like me." Phoebe gave him a quizzical look. "Your boyfriend, all the producers, all the talent—they're above the line. Below-the-line people's hearts don't bleed when those guys say they're not making any money. Maybe they're not, compared to somebody like Kubrick. Compared to us, they're doing great."

Phoebe had agreed to go without a paycheck until production was under way, and even then, she would be earning a fee only for working on the script. Everything else she did was because she couldn't help but do it. That attitude was more in keeping with her *Children of Paradise*–spawned fantasy of filmmaking as some sort of wild, creative, communal carnival than with Mitchell's acidic analysis. "I see," she said.

"No you don't. You might if you hang around the set enough. Of course, since you're the director's girlfriend, nobody else would give you the poop straight as me. Everybody likes to talk up a new director. At first, anyway. But if he turns out to be a shit, that'll change pretty quick."

"He's not a shit."

"You don't work for him."

"I wrote the script with him."

"Really?"

"Yes. I mean, it doesn't say so yet. But it will."

Mitchell grinned. "Sorry, I've got a big mouth."

He didn't open it much more until after they'd made two trips from the hotel garage to the suite, unloading everything, and he spied Phoebe's Martin 000-28 lying across the couch. "Just like Clapton's. Mind if I try it?"

"Go ahead."

He strummed a few slow chords and then did a run of fast picking Chet Atkins style, with thumb and two fingers. "Amazing sound," he said.

"You're good."

"I'm just an Okie boy from Bakersfield. Raised on Buck Owens and the Stanley Brothers."

"I love the Stanley Brothers."

"Know 'Could You Love Me One More Time'?"

"I'm not sure. Give me the first line."

"Could you love me one more time?"

"No, sing it."

And he did, in a frayed, fragile tenor that brought the rest of the lyrics back to Phoebe. She sat with him on the couch to sing harmony, her voice fluttering around his, then, at Mitchell's nod, she took the lead on the second verse. It was nice, singing and being with someone her own age again. Someone she didn't have to worry about impressing. Though she clearly *had* impressed Mitchell.

"Interested in gigging while you're up here?" he asked on their return trip to Whit's car.

"Maybe. I'll let you know." Before they parted, she told him about the production party. "Below-the-line people are invited. See you there."

Phoebe ate a late lunch alone in the café adjacent to the hotel lobby, watching actors check in, privately pegging them to their *Kiki* roles. Dinah was supposed to have flown in from New York hours ago, but the hotel clerk said there were no messages from her. Dinah hadn't been in touch since Los Angeles. Phoebe felt a little ashamed of herself, for opening up her life so wide to someone whose interest in her could evaporate so quickly.

And a little stupid, too, not to wonder sooner if whatever had happened between them was for Dinah like the weight she put on to play Kiki.

Back in the production offices, Phoebe saw a stack of newly printed scripts on the desk next to hers. She picked one up. It looked different from the other scripts she'd seen, with their pages in four different colors to mark each revision—white, blue, pink, and green. Each color meant changes, cuts or additions, most of which she'd worked out with Whit. But these scripts surprised her with a chunk of yellow pages at the very beginning, a couple of scenes' worth. "When did these come in?" Phoebe asked Zoe.

"This morning."

"Who made the changes?" She imagined it must have been Joe, going over Whit's head.

Zoe blinked in surprise behind her rabbinical-looking glasses. "I got the new pages from Whit. You haven't seen them?"

Phoebe grabbed a script and went to Whit and Joe's office, but no one was there. She sat at Whit's desk to read. Instead of opening with Kiki as an impoverished child in the French countryside, spying on the bourgeois father who wouldn't claim her, now there was Kiki as a teenager in Paris, showing her breasts to an old man for three francs. That's how everyone would meet her? Why? So Dinah would have even more time on-screen? "Always count to ten," Joe had warned, "before you get mad on a movie set." And here she was, boiling already, without a single shot in the can.

Phoebe hurled the script across the office and into the bathroom, then followed it to splash her face with cold water. As she turned off the tap, the sound of Joe and Whit's arguing voices filtered in. "That scene *has* to be shot indoors," Whit was yelling.

"I told you, Whit. They won't let us shoot inside the mansion, and we can't afford to light it anyway."

Oh no, Phoebe thought. *Another favorite scene about to be wrecked.*

"It's a drunken party, Joe, and you want me to shoot it in broad daylight?"

That's dumb, Phoebe almost called out, but she was too upset to take Whit's side on anything just now.

"We'll make it a picnic," Joe said.

"And where are they going to have sex?"

"I don't know, in the bushes."

"Why do you keep telling me what I want can't work? Fix it!"

Then Dinah's throaty voice chimed in. "If I'm going to have sex in the bushes," she said, "it's not going to be in *this* dress."

One of the men, probably Joe, emitted a raunchy wolf whistle.

"Get lost, Irving." Whit's voice sounded lighter now. "Go *gevalt* me." Then, presumably to Dinah: "And what have we here?"

As they moved into the office, a lock clicking behind them, Phoebe nudged the bathroom door to a few inches from closed. Then, not knowing what else to do, she sat on the closed toilet lid and listened, clutching the script to her chest.

"All that lace," Whit said. "It's beautiful. Almost exactly like the dress she wore in those photos."

"I know! I was so excited, I had to come show you."

"It's spooky, how much you look like her now."

"And I hardly have any makeup on."

"Go ahead, take the pose."

"The pose?"

"You know, where she's lifting up the dress to show

her knickers." There was a long pause. "Didn't they get you knickers?"

"I told you I was excited. Come here."

Phoebe peered out to see Dinah sitting on top of Whit's desk, newly cropped hair slicked back behind her ears, wrapping her legs around his waist, unbuttoning his jeans, pulling him close for a kiss that he resisted for only a flash before giving in. Phoebe's muscles tensed with the sense that this wasn't the first kiss they'd shared alone. And there was nothing she could do about it, nothing at all, except announce her presence. Which she did by stepping back, flushing the toilet, and kicking the bathroom door open wide with the heel of her boot.

"Jesus!" Dinah gasped.

Whit was fastening his jeans as Phoebe stalked across the room and slapped the script with yellow pages down on his desk. "I hate what you've done," she said. "I hate it."

As a self-styled student of faery, Phoebe knew her magical creatures. Stirring up emotional extremes with whatever happened to be handy, that was all in a day's work for a nixie, a nymph, a sprite, an undine. Such a fairy might sink her teeth into creating the conditions for a jealous argument—but actually participating in one? Not her style. She'd be too sure, too sly to land on a lover with angry accusations when she finds him kissing someone else—especially if, in the course of exercising her wiles, she's kissed that someone else, too. But there was another kind of fairy, one not so crafty or cunning, who, when captured or exposed to light, melted into a pool of water. That's the kind Phoebe felt like now.

"I hate what you've done," she repeated when she and Whit were alone in their suite. "I hate the yellow pages."

Whit put his arms around her. "Guess you should have let your fingers do the walking."

"Not funny," she said.

"It's easy to stand back and snipe. What's hard is making it better."

"I liked the way it was."

"It was too literary, too many explanations. It needs to be more visual, more cinematic."

"Who says? Dinah, or her mother?"

"I wouldn't have agreed to anything I didn't think was a good idea."

"Like fucking Dinah in your office?"

"Don't be ugly, Phoebe."

"You don't approve? Well, I don't care, you're not my father. *Je suis comme je suis.*" She snorted back a head full of snot and backhanded her eyes. "You used to love me for that."

"I still do."

"Really? What sort of love would you say we have?"

"What almost happened isn't anything that didn't happen before."

"Except that before, you knew I was there."

"At this point, I barely know where *I* am from one minute to the next. Paris, Montreal, make-believe, reality. It's kind of crazy, what's between her and me. She's always testing, always pushing. And there's no way around it; it's part of the lunch."

"How about what's between *us*? I thought the way we were was special. Because of who I am. Because of who you are with me."

"This doesn't have to play like tragedy, sweetheart. Not unless you want it to."

"I don't see how what I want has to do with anything. This is about *you*—what *you* want. What sort of love? Seduction or courtship?"

"We're supposed to meet Joe for dinner. Maybe you should throw some cold water on your eyes."

"Not until you tell me." She sat on the couch and folded her arms. "What sort of love?"

Whit sighed and sank down beside her. "Well," he began, taking her hand in his, "I guess I'd have to say neither."

"Why?"

"Because," he whispered, kneading her fingers, "you're more than just my lover. I mean, as much as you excite me, my feelings for you go way beyond sexuality. So. It ain't seduction."

"Why not courtship?"

"That would imply I'm working for this"—he waggled her hand in the air—"in marriage."

"And you wouldn't want to do anything that traditional, would you?"

"Would you?"

"No," Phoebe said, qualification and doubt extending the syllable into a long, low note. Her answer would have been a lot more complicated if she hadn't been starving for some sort of guarantee.

"So it's not courtship either." Whit pulled her onto his lap, covering her belly with his tapered, elegant hands. "There's nothing I want that I don't want for you, too. We belong to ourselves, not to each other, if you want to get existential about it."

"I don't."

"You want to know what we've got, right?"

She nodded.

"What we've got is what I've always dreamed of having with a woman. I don't want to wreck it with analysis."

"So. I'm your woman."

"Woman, lover, daughter, teacher, wife, madonna, whore—you're everything, Phoebe."

Could she love him one more time? No question about it. No question at all.

Phoebe figured Whit wanted her to be as free as he was. He wanted her to detach from the work they'd done together and encourage *Kiki*'s evolution. But why would *she* want to do any of these things?

The answer was as terrible and entrenched as termites: to eliminate Dinah. Not as *Kiki*'s star—a pointless desire, beyond her powers anyway—but as a source of pain. This tough task grew even more difficult at the production party. From the moment Dinah arrived, she glued herself to Whit's side, drawing him into lengthy discussions that expanded only to include other actors, the ones playing Kiki's paramours. When the chanson band went on break, Phoebe and Mitchell took their places to sing two mournful duets—the Stanley Brothers song and an old Everly Brothers tune they both knew, "Crying in the Rain." Phoebe had planned this, had dressed for performing in a red silk off-the-shoulder minidress, had secreted her Martin in a corner, and had not shared her intentions with anyone but Mitchell.

As Mitchell strummed the last chord on Phoebe's Martin, his voice fading with hers, Dinah stood up on a table to lead the applause with a shrill, two-fingered whistle. Then she stamped her foot and whistled again. "How about some Kiki?" she shouted. In a cracked, raucous voice, Dinah began belting one of Kiki's bawdy songs, drawing everybody into the chorus. The chanson band's accordion player put down his whiskey to accompany her from across the room. Phoebe stared at Whit, willing him to come shower her with praise and affection. *If he does, I'll stay.* But Whit was fixed on Dinah, probably wondering whether he should shoot her on a tabletop for the movie.

"Too bad we only practiced two songs," Mitchell said. "We could've had them all night."

Phoebe turned to Mitchell. "Let's go upstairs." She grabbed the Martin and an open bottle of wine, then led him to the suite she shared with Whit.

They passed her guitar back and forth while singing enough songs for an entire set, a sweet, sorrowful trail that began with a Celtic lament, detoured through the Appalachian hills, and wound up in big-city, bright-lights heartache. "Christ," Mitchell said. "Better than sex."

Phoebe looked at him, considering. "How can you be sure?" She took the Martin from his arms, set it on the floor, and kissed him softly, parting his lips with her tongue. Her head twirled with drink and the sweet, sharp taste of him, like honeyed lemon.

"I don't know, Phoebe," Mitchell murmured, "I'm still healing up from something else. And you—"

"That doesn't matter. I want to."

"Here? Now?"

She slid her hand under Mitchell's shirt and over his belly. "Right here," she said. "Right now." He breathed in sharply, making room for her fingers to travel downward, beneath the waistband of his jeans to the tip of his erection. Mitchell slid Phoebe's dress down over her shoulders and she clasped her hands behind his neck. "Might be exactly what we both need," she told him.

Then, as if she'd just suggested that they sing in a different key, he said, "Okay, I'm with you."

It shouldn't have been romantic, their lovemaking, tangling together on the narrow couch, magnetized at the lips and hips. Clumsy creatures propelled by nothing so much as a compulsion to connect. That was how it started out, anyway, driving into each other so wildly Phoebe knocked a lamp over with her foot. It was such a paradox, what she wanted—to be in charge while losing control. Still, that was pretty much what she'd suggested, pretty much what he'd agreed to. No complications— not his, not hers. Just some simple flat-out fun. The kind that came from having nothing at stake, nothing to live up to. She was getting everything she wanted—liking it, too—until Mitchell wrecked it. Wrecked it by stopping her, stopping himself, just as their mindless pleasure peaked. Wrecked it by raising her chin and forcing her to look him in the eye.

"I want this to mean something good," Mitchell said.

Then everything shifted. To being somehow tender, somehow gentle, somehow kind. Things Phoebe didn't even know she'd been missing, she'd gotten so used to accommodating what Whit needed. And now here was Mitchell, filling the enormous gap inside that her compliance had created. In no time at all, he'd changed from a guy she'd decided to fuck on the couch because it wasn't as real a place as the bed, the bed she shared with her real lover, to someone whose empathic touch made her see how stupid she'd been. What had she been thinking, choosing Mitchell as a candidate for lighthearted, recreational, get-even sex? He was no good for that— not tonight, not with her. And now she had to convince him that's exactly what they'd done.

Mitchell touched her cheek. "Is that a tear?"

"Don't." She pushed him off to pull the top of her dress up from around her waist.

"Don't what?"

"Take this too seriously."

"How should I take it?"

"Come on, you probably sleep with somebody on every picture."

"Not the director's girlfriend."

"We got a little carried away."

"That's not why you're crying."

Before she could respond, someone pounded on the door. "Phoebe?" It was Joe's voice.

"Just a minute," she called. While Mitchell scrambled to put himself back together, Phoebe dried her face, smoothed her hair, stepped back into panties and shoes. Motioning Mitchell to his feet, she slung the guitar over her shoulder and went to answer the door. "We were working out some songs," she told Joe.

"Early start tomorrow," Mitchell said, his face flushed and shirttail hanging out the side of his jeans. "Better call it a night."

Joe nodded curtly. "Smart move." He turned to Phoebe as Mitchell left. "I've been looking all over for you. Whit was worried. Come on, let's help him wrap it up and get out of there."

When Whit saw her returning to the party, he clanged his glass with a knife. "To Phoebe," he said. "None of us would be here tonight without her." True. But his timing could have been better. By then the only remaining revelers were francophone technicians, who either didn't understand Whit or decided to treat his declaration as an opportunity to demonstrate they had no intention of responding to English on the set.

Early the next morning, Phoebe rode to the warehouse soundstage with Whit and parked herself behind the camera in the Rotonde facsimile while Ludvik's crew worked out the lighting. In this scene, the camera would discover Kiki having coffee at a table by herself, then register her response when a café regular, pointing out Kiki, asks the proprietor who the new whore is. Kiki calmly lights a match, blows it out, and looks into the mirror behind her to blacken her eyebrows. When the regular, who's an artist, receives only a shrug in reply to his question, he repeats it to Kiki. "So who's the new whore?" Then Kiki erupts, hurling insults, and the artist can quiet her only by suggesting that she pose for him. The way Whit had sketched it out in his storyboard, it was a complicated master shot—taking in the crowded café and swiveling around to Kiki, seen first in mirrored reflection, then dead-on as the ruckus begins.

While the assistant director arranged extras and other actors, Dinah arrived wearing the man's hat, plain dress, and worn cape that signified Kiki's ragamuffin days. Rehearsals stopped abruptly after Dinah, looking annoyed, gestured in Phoebe's direction and folded her arms. Whit called out in a voice loud enough that everyone on set, including Mitchell, could hear, "Move behind the camera, please."

As Phoebe swiveled around to see whom he was talking to—it had to be somebody else—the assistant director came over to usher her away. "You're in Dinah's sight line," he whispered. "It's an actor's thing. Unless you're working, they get distracted if they see you looking at them." Now that she'd been established as the cause of Dinah's snit, the target of Whit's command, she felt the sting of everyone staring.

The a.d. got her a seat by the soundman's rig at the rear of the set, and since she couldn't see anything from there, he gave her a headset hooked into the soundboard so she heard every word of dialogue once Whit called "Action." With the script coming to life, it felt all the more humiliating to be taking in only words. Bitter and acrid as the smoke wafting through the set, fanned by propmen. The smoke was there to create a mood. To soften the colors and light, give more depth, more warmth. On-screen it would be invisible to the viewer.

Like me, Phoebe thought. *Just like me.* What a dope, imagining she was so essential to *Kiki.*

"Remember what I told you about counting to ten?" Joe told Phoebe between takes. "He needs you close for courage. He's so naked out there."

"I know," she said. "You don't have to worry about me."

"Oh yes I do, sweetheart."

There were two more setups that morning, and Whit spent much of his downtime with Phoebe—drinking coffee, holding her hand, sharing his nerves and exhilaration, so attentive and affectionate that she took it as an apology for his earlier curtness, an assurance of her importance, and again she forgave him.

Lunch was served in a part of the warehouse decked out like a high school cafeteria, only the food was much better. Steak cooked to order, lobster rolls, omelets flipped on the spot. The way everyone settled into groups to eat was a little like high school, too, according to an unspoken protocol by which the coolest tables consisted of above-the-line talent. Joe sat with Dinah and other key actors; Whit with Ludvik, Sarah, the film editor, and Phoebe. Mitchell lunched with carpenters and electricians at the room's perimeter, studiously avoiding Phoebe's eyes. She couldn't tell if by doing this he was protecting her from discovery, or himself from feeling used.

She saw Mitchell again back on the set, unhinging a wall in preparation for a camera move. When the assistant director called for quiet—first in English, then in French—Mitchell put down his tools and watched, standing a few feet from Phoebe. Dinah was stationary in this shot, so they could be near without triggering another snit.

Whit positioned himself across the café table from Dinah, feeding lines for her close-up. On almost every take, Whit flubbed the lines. It didn't matter; a dreamy shot of Dinah was all they were after here, something to help the audience fall in love with her. Still, Whit enlarged on his mistake while the makeup woman took the shine off Dinah's nose. "I don't know why I can't say those lines. I mean, I *wrote* them."

"No you didn't." Phoebe spoke so softly nobody but Mitchell heard.

"What was that?" Mitchell asked, his voice pitched low as hers.

"Nothing. First-day nerves."

"Fucker just pissed on your boots again, didn't he?"

Phoebe shushed him loudly enough that Whit and Dinah turned in their direction.

"Your singing partner's got a thing for you," Whit said later, on their way back to the hotel. "Not that I blame him."

She wanted to tell him then, to get it out in the open so she wouldn't have to feel secretive and cheesy. She'd done nothing Whit hadn't; she was pretty sure of that. What's more, he'd encouraged her to do it. But the same high-school-cafeteria caste system that minimized Mitchell in Whit's eyes and kept him from looking like a threat worked to silence Phoebe. "I know," she said. "He's sweet."

That night, Whit made such fervid love to her that she guessed Mitchell played into his desire. Hungry for the connection, hungry for the release, she responded in kind. But her heart was not full.

At Whit's insistence, dailies the next night were a community event, with Zoe hauling in wine, beer, and boxes of pizza. Anybody could come, just like the production party, and most people wore the black, short-sleeved

Kiki tee shirts Joe had handed out, which made them look like members of the same team. Still, they settled into screening-room seats bunched in lunchtime hierarchies. When Phoebe pointed this out, Joe responded with an edge, as though she'd spoiled a pep rally by blowing a raspberry. "It's not like this on most movies. Only a handful of people get to see dailies on most movies."

"He means *real* movies," Whit clarified. "Real movies with real budgets."

As the room darkened, the projectionist focused on a still photograph of Dinah as Kiki in "Noire et Blanche," Man Ray's image of her pale, sleepy-eyed face beside an African mask. Phoebe sat at the rear with Whit, by a tape player rigged through the screening room speakers. Like a cinematic deejay, he switched on tango music, controlling the mood with deft fade-ins and fade-outs as footage from the previous day filled the screen.

The first shot worked; it was long, economical, and lovely, repeatedly reflecting all the major players in café mirrors, lingering on faces bathed in seductive light. Applause filled the room. Joe shouted out, "Bravo, Ludvik." Phoebe checked Whit's expression and it was one she'd never seen before, simultaneously orgasmic and anxious, already anticipating the next shot. Working the script with him had been joyful and silly, ecstatic and deep. But it couldn't be more plain. This stuff was the drug, and he was hooked.

An hour later, with all the film shown, all the pizza eaten, all the wine drunk, Phoebe heard Dinah say, "Whit throws a good movie, doesn't he?"

Phoebe stayed in the screening room with Whit while he told Sarah which takes he wanted to use. When they left, Dinah was waiting by the door. "I could use a sit-down dinner."

Phoebe looped her arm through Whit's. "Not tonight, Dinah."

Whit elaborated in gentler tones. "We're going to grab a little something by ourselves and turn in early."

"Okay," Dinah said. "But you don't have to feel so guilty about Phoebe anymore, Whit. Haven't you heard? Joe caught her fucking the carpenter." Then, with the French accent she'd developed for Kiki: "Phoebe is oh so—how do you say?—*démocratique*."

They drove back to the hotel in silence, and when they got to their suite, it never occurred to Phoebe to deny it. To blame Joe for making false assumptions. To blame Dinah for having an ax to grind. Why should she, considering all Whit's declarations and directives?

But that was before Whit told her she ruined the movie.

She created a catastrophe, a disaster impossible for him to recover from.

She undermined him in the eyes of the entire production company.

She betrayed him.

She was a vengeful, unfeeling, idiotic slut.

No one had ever spoken to her this way, much less someone she loved. And Whit wasn't even speaking—he was shouting, his face a mask of hot, unappeasable anger.

"I don't have to listen to this," Phoebe told him. "Do you want me to say I'm sorry? All right, I'm sorry. I'm sorry you're so upset."

"Some apology. Why don't you just say fuck you?"

"I thought this was what you wanted. You *said*—"

"What I *didn't* say is the problem. What I didn't say is that you should be discreet. I didn't think I had to. I thought you were smart enough to know that."

He picked up the phone and called down to the front

desk. "Can you get me another room, please," he said. "Right away."

"No," Phoebe said, reaching for the phone to stop him. "Don't go."

He shook her off with such force that she reeled back against the wall, banging into it so hard with the side of her body that it felt like she'd dropped from a ladder to the floor.

"*You're* going," Whit yelled. "I have to work, I have to eat, I have to sleep. I can't accomplish any of that with you around." He hung up the phone, yanked their room key from her purse, and threw the purse at her knees. As she stooped to pick it up, he shoved her out of the suite, into the hall.

Phoebe stumbled into the stairwell, where she wept and rubbed the purple bruises beginning to bloom on her hip and shoulder. Then she went down to the lobby, where the night clerk gave her the key to a crummy little room looking out onto an air shaft.

Phoebe believed everything Whit told her. She had to believe him. If she didn't, that meant he'd never loved her. And if he'd never loved her, nothing made sense.

Curled into a ball on the bed, in the dark, she expected nothing but to cry herself to sleep like an abandoned baby. But sleep wouldn't come, not now, not inside this broken Circle of Magic. She turned on the lamp and stared at the phone, wondering whom, in her disgrace, she should call. Nobody she knew in-house, that was certain. They were all lost to the same dream. How could any of them restore *her* to reality? Someone who knew how to build things, someone who knew how to measure angles, how to make the pieces fit and, more important, last once they got put together—someone like that might be able to help.

"I want to leave," she said when she got Mitchell on the line. "I want to go home."

A few hours later she sat in the kitchen of the rented crew house where Mitchell was staying, staring into the cup of hot tea laced with brandy that he had given her.

"First thing you do tomorrow morning," he said, "is get your paycheck."

"Okay. Then I'll go home."

"Not so fast," Mitchell said.

She stiffened, expecting him to berate her, too—for entangling him in her mess, a mess that was sure to cost him his job. Now, like her, he'd have to get himself back across the continent, and he couldn't just fly away, not unless he sold his truck. But all he said was, "You keep talking about home like I know what you mean."

"I'm not sure that I even know what I mean. I used to think my home was inside me, but now I guess it's where all my stuff is. In my room. In Mount Jensen. I know it's just stuff, it's not who I am, but I really need to go get it." And then, because she hated the prospect of making such a sad journey alone, she blurted out, "Can you take me there?"

"I don't think so. "

"Oh. Okay."

"Because I still don't know where *there* is."

The next morning, after they arranged for their money at the production office, Phoebe went alone to the set. She needed Whit's room key to get her things—that was her professed reason. But what she really wanted was to give him a chance to be overcome with remorse and make everything right again.

The assistant director stood by the soundstage door, smoking a cigarette. Phoebe assumed he was on break, but before she could open the door he held out an arm to stop her. "Sorry," he told her. "Whit says you're not allowed on the set today."

At that, Phoebe snapped. "Well, you can tell Whit that's fine with me, and he can shove his goddamn movie up his Tennessee butt and get someone else to kiss it from now on."

Back at the hotel, a sympathetic maid let her into Whit's suite. Tossing all her things into a single suitcase, she came across her diaphragm, forgotten in the turmoil of the last few days. Good thing her periods came like clockwork. By her faulty reckoning, ovulation was still a safe days-away distance.

She felt a little like Wendy leaving Neverland. Only unlike Wendy, she had been banished. And instead of Peter, it was one of the Lost Boys taking her home.

18

As dawn drizzle gave way to balmy sweeps of sunshine, Phoebe wandered her garden, deadheading anemones, dianthuses, and the Shasta daisies that bordered a winding stone pathway. A feline hiss drew her attention and she turned to see Amelia's cat Smudge, locked in a stand-off with an owl perched on a low-hanging fir bough. It looked like a fair match. Eyes magnetized, the creatures glowered at each other, ignoring her. She moved closer to Smudge, ready to protect. Who had started this, the bird of prey or the once-feral white cat? Impossible to tell from their coiled, pounce-ready positions, though each, no doubt, had come looking for a nice juicy mouse or chipmunk. The owl broke first, lifting its wings with a low whoop and flapping over Phoebe's roof. Smudge rose from her crouch, stretched, and sauntered off for Amelia's, collar bell tinkling. Breakfast time, and she wasn't on the menu. Not today, anyway.

Breeze-blown evergreens, wood smoke, wispy clouds that looked light as thistledown reflected in the full, still, slack-tide bay water below. A shame to waste such a fine autumn morning indoors, and after last night's memory flood of Montreal, Phoebe required earthy things to ground her.

Still wearing the pearl and the wedding band next to her skin, she went to the garage for bags of mulch and a shovel. Once she established a solid, steady working rhythm, it was Mitchell breaking through from deep inside—remarking on how the garden had grown since they'd first dug it out, wondering what kind of seed she'd put in the feeder to attract so many goldfinches. Sometimes, when Laurienne was quite young, Phoebe would report the substance of long, imaginary conversations with Mitchell, who would appear when something new and scary loomed—kindergarten, booster shots, a piano recital. But therapeutic as Phoebe had thought these encounters were for her daughter, she herself had never experienced anything like them until now.

This Mitchell of Phoebe's had more on his mind than flora and fauna. He had opinions about the way she'd been with Whit in Seattle. *Got a chance to play the same scene twice, didn't you? It's not like I don't see the draw. Could have turned out different this time. But you blew it, just like I was afraid you would. Remember?*

On her last morning with Mitchell, Phoebe nursed Laurienne and scanned the Seattle paper. A short article in the arts section mentioned that *Kiki* would be premiering at the film festival next week. Funny how Laurienne's birth had not only expanded Phoebe's world but shrunk it, too. There was no room for tracking *Kiki*, much less the film festival schedule, and anyone who knew her well enough to bring it up must have thought doing so would be unwise. Ever since she and Mitchell decided to marry, neither mentioned Whit. It took news of the premiere for Phoebe to risk breaking that silence. "I'd like to go," she told him.

He looked up from the high chair he was assembling. Laurienne was too little for it, but he was the kind of parent who enjoyed planning ahead. "Is it the movie you want to see," Mitchell said, "or him?"

Laurienne mewled while Phoebe closed one nursing-bra flap and opened the other. "I don't know. Both, I guess."

Mitchell stared at her in disbelief. "Phoebe, where's your pride? You should be guest of honor, with an engraved invitation to this thing."

"He doesn't know where I am." Even now, they avoided speaking of Whit by name.

"Bullshit," Mitchell said. "If he wanted to find you, he could. What bothers me is you showing up like some poor relation, begging for recognition."

"That is *not* what I'd be doing."

"That is exactly what you'd be doing. And you know what he'd do? Piss on your boots again. Only this time, it's not just you who'd get wet. It'd splash all over me and the baby."

"That's silly," Phoebe said. "He doesn't know about Laurienne."

"He would if you went. She's practically tethered to the tit."

"I could pump some milk for her. Anyway, he wouldn't want a baby."

"Not to take care of. But a beautiful little girl who might have half his genes? Don't kid yourself. Almost as good as looking in the mirror for a guy like him."

"That is not the point of this for me."

"It is for me. He'd wonder if she's his."

"That's what really bothers you, isn't it? I guess we need to do something so you'll know for sure. A blood test, maybe."

"Great, we'll do a blood test. I have a pretty good idea how that'll go. But even if I'm wrong, even if it's not me, I'm still her father and I still don't want you going down there for this."

"I wasn't asking permission. I wanted to have a discussion."

"If you go, I go. Laurienne stays with Jack and Helen. And you'll have to wear something so milk leaks don't show."

"That won't work. How am I ever going to resolve anything with him if you're standing there?"

"You want a resolution? I wonder what that would look like—you apologizing or him?"

Phoebe put Laurienne over her shoulder for a burp. "Don't yell; she's trying to digest."

Mitchell's forehead creased with effort as he lowered his voice. "I know what the movie meant to you. I know you've got loose ends. But you need to figure out some other way to tie them up."

"It's not like I can find him in the phone book or afford to fly out to wherever he is. This is happening right in my backyard. It's the easiest way."

"The dumbest, too."

"Oh, I get it. No wonder it's so hard for you to trust me. You think I'm stupid."

"Only when it comes to him."

It wasn't a knock-down, drag-out fight. They went on with washing the breakfast dishes and bathing the baby and spreading gravel for garden paths. But a chill lingered as they left to run errands in Mount Jensen. Phoebe had made out their list, and she could still remember some of the items on it (talcum powder, steel wool, motor oil), and how eagerly Mitchell took Laurienne from her arms when she offered to drive the pickup—she'd done it to please him, to soothe his irritation—then told her to wait while he went back inside for the baby's floppy blue sun hat.

On the highway, before the Impala forced them off the road, she chewed over their argument and decided

Mitchell's trepidations were mainly a cover for jealousy. It wasn't as though she never had dark thoughts about Whit, but somehow they had more to do with how terrible he had made her feel about herself than with him. Because she'd loved and trusted him so much, and because he was so much older and presumably wiser, she could only guess that to inflict so much pain on her, he must have suffered even more than she. Well, there was still a little time before the premiere. She would figure out a way to do what she wanted and appease Mitchell. That was her plan, the one she never got the chance to execute.

Whit didn't cause the accident, of course. But Phoebe's confusion over how he'd treated her was surely a factor—a piece of how she ended up with the scar he'd found so moving the other night, how she lost her husband and voice both.

Now it was Mitchell's voice in her head again. *Do you know what's wrong with you?* Always a dangerous beginning. Defenses spring up so quickly at the sound of those words. What follows doesn't really register. But now she remembered the wrong thing about herself he brought to her attention that day. *You don't know a predator when you see one.*

Well, why should she?

Don't let any bad dreams in, just let in good dreams. Don't let anything in except mommies and daddies and kitties and bunnies and fairies and lambies and pretty things.

Not a dangerous animal in the bunch. But that, of course, was Pearl.

When Laurienne was little, it was tempting to re-create the Magic Circle for her. Phoebe had felt like a failure because she just couldn't—it was too piercing a reminder of loss. Now this omission seemed like a blessing. Still, abandoning the idea of her Magic Circle as something unequivocally comforting and wonderful and loving was another blow, another cause for weeping, another cause for anger, too. Lots of anger.

She got angry after Laurienne called, without a word of apology for never getting back to her in Seattle. All Laurienne wanted was permission to bring Cliff up to the island this weekend. Which meant, Phoebe supposed, that they'd have the house as a launching pad for other adventures, with her to feed and clean up after them. And Phoebe had agreed.

She got angry after Amelia called and asked to come over with Dennis, the new boyfriend. All Amelia wanted was for Phoebe to check him out, as per Jasmine's instructions, before she slept with him again. And Phoebe had agreed.

She got angry after Jasmine bumped into her on the beach, this time pinning her down for a reading, which felt like taking a justified gut punch. And Phoebe had agreed to that, too.

But nothing made her so angry as when she passed through the cedars for no good reason at all and heard Ivan and Marieke laughing as they unloaded his new kiln.

Just as Phoebe predicted, skippers home from Alaska soon swamped Westerly Webs with damaged nets. What she couldn't have predicted, though, was how ordering the day's jobs would slowly chill her rage. At least here there were problems she could force herself to face, problems under her control. The kinks in her stomach dissolved, so that she managed to get some food down and start bringing Vincent, her new employee, up to speed.

While Brian, Kristin, and Sophie worked on complicated repairs, Phoebe hung up a simple job and called
Vincent over. "See how the fixes they made at sea start
out so nice?" she said. "They're like good little Boy
Scouts here, matching the meshes one to one, cleaning
all their knots." She pointed to a place farther down.
"Then oops, it rips again, and now they do a coozy."

"A coozy?"

"A coozy's what happens when they quit doing it
right. They just grab a bunch of netting, lace it together
with sloppy, spotty hitches, never mind the mesh, and
the knots are a mess, twine sticking out all over. All they
want to do is throw the thing back in and catch more
fish. From here on out, every fix is a coozy. The net's like
a chart of their frustration."

"Geez," said Vincent. He looked bewildered, the way
everybody did at first, before they understood the pro-
gression of repair. "Where do I start?"

"Tear out all their lacing, clean the knots, and trim the
holes."

As she stood by, watching him work the knife, she
considered her own torn-apart places. The first rip, with
Pearl, she sutured by leaving home, claiming indepen-
dence. The rip with Whit she closed with a new man, a
new baby, a new home, a new means to make her way in
the world. Next rip, with Mitchell, and the coozies start
coming, spaced out so far apart for so long that everything still holds together okay. But lately there's just one
on top of the other, a nest of coozies so thick you might
as well give up on mending and start over from scratch.

Later, as Phoebe finished showing Vincent how to fix
his mistakes, Angus walked into the shop. "Here you
go," he said, handing her a tall latte from the Terminal
stand.

An odd thing, Angus bringing her a four-dollar coffee,

since he lived up to his Scottish name by being famously tightfisted. "What's this?" Phoebe asked.

"What the hell do you think? Told the boy to keep all his double-this, skinny-that mumbo jumbo to himself and just make it the way you like."

He motioned for her to try it and verify that his orders were followed, which she did with a nod.

"My fourth man broke his leg cleaning a gutter," Angus said. "Won't be able to go out with us, so I'm looking for somebody else. Could you spread the news?"

"For a latte? Sure."

"My guy was a great on-deck mender. It'd sure be sweet to get somebody else quick with a needle. Maybe you'd like to come, Phoebe," he teased. "You won't have to do a thing but mend and tell bedtime stories and tuck us in, I promise."

"Thanks, but I wanted to be Peter, not Wendy."

"Who?"

"Wendy, from *Peter Pan*."

"I'll take your word on that."

"Come on, Angus—you had kids, you eat peanut butter. It's not like I'm quoting Shakespeare here. Anyway, I don't have an immersion suit, and you're too cheap to buy me one."

"True. Besides, you know me. I'm scared of girls."

"So was he, I think."

"Still talking about that brat?"

"Yeah," she said, wondering why.

When she got home, Phoebe unpacked all the groceries she'd bought for Laurienne and Cliff's visit, forced herself to eat a salad, then poured a glass of wine, took it to her study, and pulled off the shelf a copy of *Peter Pan* that she had found in an antiquarian bookstore when Laurienne was little—filling an obvious hole in her col-

lection. Laurienne had not been enchanted by J. M. Barrie's droll prose, and Phoebe, with so little time for reading then, never finished the book on her own. Tonight
she did, wrapped in a knitted afghan on the fainting
sofa, looking for answers from this fairy-tale character
who had been her first love.

All the differences between the spirit of the book and
the play, let alone the Disney version, astounded her.
This Peter was such an arrogant, heartless little guy—
caring for no one, really, but himself. By the end, when
Peter kills Hook and takes over his ship to play at being
pirate captain, it struck her that Hook was almost exactly what Peter would have become had he ever dared
to grow up and find his own ageless boy to envy.

Phoebe remembered what she'd told Angus earlier—
how she had wanted to be Peter, not Wendy. And that
was true, basically, once. She had wanted a fairy of her
own; she had wanted to soar. But somehow when Whit
came into her life, she was happy to play not only Wendy,
coming up with stories for him, but Tinker Bell, too,
providing endless supplies of the magic dust that let him
fly. And when she ran away from him, where had she
ended up but on her own enchanted island—hardly an
Indian princess, à la Tiger Lily, but she did settle on
tribal property. And now her heartless man-child was a
neighbor.

Then there was the matter of Tink drinking poison
meant for Peter. Hadn't she done something similar for
Whit? And unlike Peter, he didn't even bother to clap her
back to life—unless he thought fucking her again years
after the fact would do the trick. Peter's lost shadow also
seemed suspect now, the way he grabbed all the clever-
ness credit after Wendy sewed it back onto his body.
Phoebe remembered how she first introduced herself to

Whit on paper, all but promising to be *his* long-lost shadow. If he obliged by using a film to project his darkest parts on her, well, wasn't that the bargain?

Too galvanized by this backward treasure hunt for sleep, Phoebe reached for a second unread book, a biography of Barrie that Jack had given her as a birthday present. Only a few pages in and more nuggets: Barrie wrote his play long before the book (no wonder the tones were so different), and Peter—not Hook—was meant to be the villain. "A demon boy," in Barrie's words. Hook bagged the bad-guy part only after audiences went crazy for him in a bit role. Wendy was Barrie's designated heroine, but she turned out to be a foil at best. Still, there was some small comfort in the notion that nobody cared much about girls who were too pure and flawless. And onstage, anyway, Peter ended up a heroine after all, always played by women. An adventuress in disguise.

It sparked Phoebe, digging in the soil of make-believe again. Her analytic mind hummed with new insights. But if these were "tools," as Margaret would call them, she didn't know what to do with them. How could she know, when nothing seemed to be as she had once thought? To sustain any kind of anger at Whit, she had to abandon the notion of him still loving her, mailing packages over the years to prove it. And that she couldn't do. So she dangled, hanging on by her fingernails, afraid to look down, afraid to see how far she'd fall if she let go.

Jasmine's reading was set for nine o'clock the next morning. Phoebe would rather be having a root canal. At least then she'd be numb while someone poked at her insides.

"Oh, my," Jasmine said as she opened the door to her office, "don't look so grim. This won't hurt; I promise. Not with a chart like yours. Come on in; I made some tea. Amelia's mugwort—it's supposed to sharpen intuition."

"Yours or mine?"

Jasmine laughed while she poured from a thermos into small ceramic cups. "I hope it works for the both of us."

Her office was pretty much as Amelia had described—sisal rug, framed woodcuts, a rough-hewn table that gave off the scent of cedar. More like a monk's meditation room than a fortune-teller's lair. Jasmine lit a tiny piece of incense and a spiral of smoke reached Phoebe's nose. Ylang-ylang, if she wasn't mistaken. Then Jasmine popped a cassette into her portable machine, hit the red record button, and laid on the table an ink drawing that looked like a pie cut into twelve wedges, dotted with symbols and crisscrossed with multicolor lines. "The planets are in black and gold," Jasmine said, "and I make colored lines for the aspects between them."

"Sounds complicated."

"Not so very. It's just a map of the sky at the moment of your birth. This line through the middle is the horizon. Only a few of your planets are above it—you're a pretty internal girl. Astronomers always slam astrology, but the map is astronomically correct. You might want to frame it. A lot of my clients do."

Just what Phoebe needed—another crazy map on the wall to confuse her.

"I'll start with your rising sign," Jasmine went on. "Whatever sign's rising on the horizon when you pop out into the world, that's the energy people pick up on from you right off the bat. It's the personality you wear when you're running the regular Phoebe show. As opposed to, say, coming from your deeper consciousness. Okay, so that's the first order of business. Then I'll talk about the significance of each planet and its purpose in your soul's evolution."

With that, Jasmine was off to the races. It seemed Phoebe's role here was just to take her seat in the audience and pay attention. She noticed how Jasmine's demeanor changed. It wasn't as though her eyes rolled up into the back of her head, or she spoke in a different accent. That would have been beyond the beyond for Phoebe. But Jasmine did pitch her voice lower now, and her focus switched to somewhere around the top of Phoebe's forehead. Was she performing, or accessing her deeper consciousness? Maybe Phoebe would know if she could cauterize the wound that kept her wondering what it was like for this woman, being married to Whit. And vice versa. Thoughts that only stoked her bad conscience.

Phoebe shifted forward and propped her chin in hand, concentrating on Jasmine's words. The best way, it seemed, to endure them.

"Think of your chart," Jasmine said, "as the result of a celestial board meeting you had with your guardian angels before you were born. And the agenda you signed on to was meant to maximize all the talents that you came into this life with—or brought along from your last life, if the idea of reincarnation doesn't creep you out. Lots of obstacles along the way. But obstacles are good; they're your pipelines to power. And power's what it takes to solve your numero uno predicament: trusting other people, but relying only on yourself."

How generic could you get? If Jasmine were a fishing boat, she'd be a factory trawl with a huge net. "I guess that means I'm pretty much like everyone else," Phoebe said, sipping her tea.

"Not at all." Jasmine went on to describe in detail Phoebe's particular gifts of sensitivity, creativity, and critical thinking. Which only made Phoebe's stomach squirm, hearing such flattery at such great length from a woman whose husband she'd just fucked.

As Jasmine finished her planetary rundown, the recorder clicked off on the first side of the tape. Jasmine opened the machine and flipped the cassette over. *Oh God,* Phoebe thought, *another thirty minutes of this.*

"Okay," Jasmine said, "that's the lay of the land. The B side will be all about what's going on now."

Watching Jasmine pour more tea, Phoebe had to admit to herself that Whit's wife wasn't a ditz at all. She wasn't even so ethereal, when you got right down to it. Somehow, "street-smart" seemed a more accurate description. But now they'd come to the part Phoebe had been dreading—Jasmine jabbing at her with personal information culled from who-knew-where. The chart, Amelia, Whit, Phoebe's very own brain waves. Each possibility worse than the last.

"Let's begin," Jasmine said, "by talking about your mother."

"My mother?" As Phoebe straightened in her chair, Jasmine reached across the table to lay a hand on her arm.

"Hold on, you need to hear this. Gotta get the mom stuff straight with a moon-ruled chart like yours. What's her name? I'll bet it's one of those earthy, elemental names."

Phoebe withdrew her arm and wrapped it around her ribs. "Pearl."

"Did Pearl check out early?"

Phoebe looked at her, puzzled.

"I'm sorry, let me phrase that better. Did Pearl die when she was young? When you were young?"

"Yes."

"Well, that always takes lots longer to process. But I'd

say you're just about ready to turn the corner on Pearl's death. Maybe other ones, too, because you've got so much good stuff waiting to happen. Only first you'll need to clear the decks. That means coming to terms with your Neptune squares." Jasmine pointed to a pair of thick red lines on the chart. "With squares there's always a battle, and you, you've got an adult dose, a two-for-one double whammy. Not only does Neptune square your Venus—that's the planet of love and beauty—it also squares your moon, the planet of emotional needs. Neptune brings dreams and visions, but what you've got to watch out for are the delusions."

Jasmine put down the chart, folded her hands, and fixed Phoebe with a toothy smile. "That might sound woo-woo to you," she continued, "so I'll boil it down. Neptune rules the kind of guys you pick for lovers."

"Is that supposed to go for everybody?" Phoebe asked.

"No, it goes for you, specifically. The only men you let near are Neptunian—artistic types. Which is great, but only so long as they know how to ground themselves, because you don't know how to do it for them. Let's face it, when it comes to lovers you've got as many delusions as ideals. Who's best for you could be right under your nose, but you just don't see him. Does that ring any bells?"

Phoebe nodded, feeling queasy and set up but in no position to object. What could she possibly say? *I was his fairy girl, only one foot ever on the ground. What we did together was fly.* Jasmine couldn't be interested in that sort of disclosure. "I take your point," Phoebe told her.

"Sorry. Looks like I broke my promise, doesn't it?"

"Territorial rights—fair warning and all that. You don't have anything to be sorry for."

Jasmine laughed. "Don't be so sure. There's no such thing as a clean break with my guy."

If Jasmine didn't know for certain, she certainly suspected. Just as Phoebe had certainly imagined. But what she didn't anticipate was how withering it would be, hearing her past with Whit so blithely minimized by his wife. It made her feel stupid. Maybe she was, not to see it coming.

"This seems like a good place to finish up," Phoebe said, bending for her bag.

"Sure." Jasmine punched the stop button on her recorder. "Remember that day I saw you in the Co-op? I was so hoping we'd be friends."

"Looks like we've got a little too much in common for that."

"Not really. My background's totally different from yours. Totally."

"How do you know?"

"The astrology's a prop," Jasmine said, "but it works. Your kind of chart doesn't come from getting born to Mike and Linda Price over at the feed and seed store. Mine does."

Phoebe met her crackling gaze and nodded. "I don't suppose Jasmine is your real name. He called me Dolores."

"Oh. Dolores. As in con Cuervos." It was a statement, not a question. Phoebe could see she'd broken Jasmine's composure. But it wasn't very satisfying—almost as bad as saying "I made a baby with your husband; you haven't." And so near to what might be literal truth that she regretted going there.

"Anyway," Jasmine said, "I'm friends with one of Whit's old lovers. An actress. You'd know her name if I told you."

"Not Dinah," Phoebe said.

"That was your era. Dinah's not so busy anymore. You know how it is for actresses over forty."

Not a bad little actress herself. Jasmine spoke as though she found the plight of actresses over forty a shameful thing upon which all women possessed of finer feelings could agree.

"Well," Phoebe said, "whomever you mean, I doubt you're best friends—the kind you went on about to Amelia? Even if that were possible, he would hate the idea of women comparing notes about him."

"That would depend on what they said, wouldn't it?"

"Are you telling him about this?"

"Not unless I need to." Jasmine reached for the red record button and pressed it again. "Just one other thing I want to get on the record," she said. "I got a great hit on that guy you were with in the Tavern. This was before I had any reason not to trust you, so it was a clean one. Quit underestimating him. Clarity, that's your new mantra, Phoebe. Remember, you heard it here first."

Now she sounded like Whit. Not surprising. He was a contagious sort of person.

It could have been worse, Phoebe supposed on her way to the net loft. Jasmine might have poked at some unexpected tender spots—Ivan, Pearl—but at least she hadn't come close to Laurienne. What continued to stun, though, was how sanguine Jasmine had seemed about it all. Why was that? Margaret's description came to mind. *She knows him like an ant knows an aphid.*

"I've got a client soon," Margaret said when Phoebe called. "Why don't you come over for lunch?"

After one look at Phoebe's face, Margaret pulled out some chilled white wine to go with the vegetable curry she ladled into bowls.

It was a long while before Phoebe could get words past the weight on her chest, the lump of emotion in her throat. And then, after a headlong rush of explanation that covered her recent night in Seattle with Whit, her reading today with Jasmine, she slid into tearful despair. "I just want to run away."

"You've been doing enough of that, don't you think?"

"I know, I know. Why can't I think straight when I'm with Whit?"

"I'll tell you why," Margaret said. "If you did, you'd have to take him on. Only when it's time to stand up for your rights with a guy like that, he'll try to make you lie down. And if that doesn't work, he'll have you sit down—sit down and examine your wrongs, toward him. Kind of like someone who nicks his finger stabbing you in the back and then, while you're on the floor bleeding, the dagger still stuck between your ribs, he expects you to get up and go find a Band-Aid for him."

"You make him sound so awful."

Margaret shook her head. "You do."

"Maybe I shouldn't." Phoebe's face contorted as she reached for the box of tissues Margaret had placed between them. "I was right there with him in Seattle," Phoebe told her, "every step of the way. I've been dreaming about him for years; the dreams just never stopped. If he sent me all those packages, the same thing must've been going on with him. And there he was, apologizing again. Wanting me again. Loving me again."

Margaret waited for Phoebe's sobs to subside. "Okay, so in those dreams, honey, what part of you do you think he represents?"

"Leave it to you to say that. I knew you would. I even figured out the answer. He's my creative masculine energy, right? I was only ever in love with something in him that I needed to be myself, right?" Phoebe, calmer now, grabbed another tissue and blew her nose. "But that's not what the dreams mean to me. I dream about him because he's still inside me. I never put him out of my heart. But now I have to, don't I?"

"You're human, you made mistakes."

"Doesn't that apply to him, too?"

"I don't care about him," Margaret snapped, rising to clear dishes. "He's got enough people caring about him."

As Phoebe finished helping Margaret clean up, she noticed a magazine left open on the counter—*The Modern Jungian Journal,* with Margaret's name beneath an article title that read, "The Significance of Spider Women." Phoebe wiped her hands dry and read the opening paragraph:

Consider the different connotations accorded to the archetype of spiderlike women in fairy tales and myth. On the negative side, they weave webs of intrigue and evil. On the positive side, their steady, repetitive work quiets internal chatter and frees the spirit to fashion a decidedly feminine psychic web—out of memories, fantasies, hopes, dreams. Their process is a vital one.

"Take that copy," Margaret said. "I've got extras. Not a bad time for you to be reading this, come to think of it."

"Why? Because I'm one of those negative spiders now?"

"Because your web is stronger than you think."

"What's great is that you're published again."

"Don't change the subject," Margaret said. "That was a compliment. I meant it."

"Thanks, but I can't see much good about myself right now. Out of all the stuff Jasmine told me, the one thing I remember is that I don't have what it takes to ground Whit."

"Well, she would say that." A blast of steam came pouring from Margaret's espresso machine and she grabbed a pitcher to froth their milk.

"That's Jasmine's job," Margaret continued as they returned to her long, polished pine table. "She's his emotional grounding wire; he can't do it for himself. The narcissist and the hysteric—that's who they are. A common couple in my world. All those nasty things that asshole said back when you had your fling? I don't care what's on his birth certificate, every narcissist's middle name is projection."

Margaret's labels bothered Phoebe, as usual (such tidy little categories, not unlike Jasmine's), but "narcissist" came close enough to last night's revisionist reading of Peter Pan, of Whit, to bother her more. Then she remembered how Margaret had described Jasmine the last time she'd come here for comfort. "You said all her power was from Whit. But if she grounds him, doesn't that give her power of her own?"

Margaret shrugged. "Some. Enough to keep him, maybe. Not enough to keep him faithful. Sneaking around's a lot hotter than the home fires burning."

"Jasmine might be a little dippity-do, Margaret, but she's not hysterical."

"Don't take the term so literally. What I mean is more like histrionic—just a whole lot of emotion and drama. Maybe you don't see it, but I'll bet he sure as hell does. You'd think a guy in his business would get enough of that stuff at work, but all her performing is focused on him. On being this emotive, hyperfeminized female for him and him alone."

"That could be Kiki you're talking about," Phoebe said. "That could be a really negative definition of what a muse is."

"I suppose. Or a geisha. Or you—when you were with him, anyway."

Phoebe sat silent for a while, considering. "But he really cared about me when I was young," she said. "I came after him harder than he did me. I threw myself at him, if you want to know the truth. You're not looking at my part in all this."

"Your part? Your part was seduction—that's where your takes-two-to-tango model works. And if someone like him didn't exist, you'd have had to invent him. But what he did to you? That's a different kettle of fish. Maybe it doesn't get much press, but muses end up raped and pillaged all the time."

"Raped and pillaged?" Phoebe's mouth puckered as though tasting the words.

"Not physically. Creatively. Spiritually."

"I hate how that sounds. Like I'm a victim."

"You were, Phoebe. You've got to get clear on that. Otherwise you'll just keep punishing yourself."

Phoebe pushed back from the table. Her hand went to her throat as she took one labored breath, then another.

"What's the matter?" Margaret said.

"It almost feels like I'm choking," she managed to spit out.

Margaret took Phoebe's arm, walked her to the couch, and arranged cushions for her to lie against. "It's okay, you'll be all right. Close your eyes. Try and focus on your breathing."

But the stranglehold was still on, even tighter than before.

"It's just a feeling," Margaret said, "that's all. It's not good or bad."

Phoebe rasped and gasped over and over again before anything like a full breath passed. Gradually, the back of her throat loosened. Her face relaxed a little as she sank deeper against the cushions.

"Just let it move through you," Margaret told her.

Behind Phoebe's closed eyelids a purplish dot appeared and pulsed, spreading into a spherical shape—the sum of all her loss and damage, it seemed, all that had been suffocating her, translated into color and form. The contents of her own personal Aunt Dora's box? Maybe that, too. Such a pretty vision for such a mess. If she made it all her fault, then she could fix it all, wipe it all away. But her throat constricted again, her body screaming *No, that won't work anymore.* And with her next deep breath came tears unlike any she had ever cried in her life, a strong steady stream let loose without sobbing, without wrenching her stomach or clenching her muscles, just flowing past her ears and down her neck, a quiet, necessary thing. Not so much one feeling but many, needing only to exist without fighting her for control.

When she opened her eyes again, the neck of her shirt was still damp but her face was almost dry. *Raped and pillaged?* The words came back to her, this time only as definitions of something that had occurred, not of her.

"Better now," she told Margaret. "Calmer, anyway."

"Anything come to you?" Margaret sat in a chair close by, not hovering or anxious, but interested, attentive.

"Yeah. I think so. Hard to explain. The difference between pity and compassion. For myself, I mean."

Margaret smiled. "That's good. You know what they say—charity begins at home."

"Except it's already slipping away, and what I'm wondering is how Whit can imagine that I'm the one who rejected him. Strange, don't you think?"

"Not strange at all. You bolted without waiting to be dismissed."

"I thought I *was* dismissed."

"No, no, no. He wasn't done with you yet. You left orbit without permission. Same thing as rejection in his book."

Phoebe nodded. "I guess that makes sense."

"It's hard to see when you're stuck in the wrong paradigm."

"You lost me there."

"Not everyone has a conscience—at least, not as you or I might define it. Look at the way you blame yourself for Dinah. I'll bet Whit just saw a three-way as an interesting experiment, no worry over the effects on a young girl."

Phoebe sat up and dropped her head to knead the back of her neck. "I'm exhausted. And I haven't even told you everything."

"Try to get some rest," Margaret said. "And come stay with me if it's too tough on your own."

As Phoebe gathered her things to leave, one of Margaret's south side neighbors rang the doorbell—Walter, a retired dentist. "Did you open your mail today?" he demanded.

"Yes," Margaret said, "but now is not a good time."

"You can say that again. If I'd known they were going to monkey around with our leases like this, I would have nixed the Christmas trip to Hawaii. Now it's too late."

"I'll call you, Walter," Margaret told him.

Phoebe had picked up her own mail today, but hadn't examined it. "I heard that," she said after Walter left. "What's going on? If it's bad news I'd just as soon not be alone when I get it."

"It's not as important as what you're going through."

"Spill, Margaret."

Margaret went to her desk and returned with a letter printed on tribal stationery. "The rates on our leases are going up," she said. "By a lot more than usual. There's also an assessment."

Punchy now, Phoebe barked a lunatic little laugh. "Can we blame Whit for that, too?"

"Well, he does have a way of tearing people apart, doesn't he? I suppose it was bound to happen, though. Only fair that the tribe gets closer to market value for their property. Nobody's sold here for so long it wasn't on their front burner. But a celebrity paying big bucks for a modest cottage? Just made it hit sooner rather than later."

Phoebe took the letter and read.

Dear Tenant:

The Owl Island Land Trust's contract with Owl Island lessees contains a clause stating that economic expediency allows for the adjustment of lease rates apart from regularly scheduled increases. Such an expediency now exists due to the sharp discrepancy between present lease rates and current values for comparable waterfront property. In addition to lease increases that will begin in January of 1997, a special assessment will cover the costs of maintaining water and sewerage lines in accordance with environmental regulations.

Please examine the accompanying schedules for a detailed breakdown of individual tenants' costs. Questions and concerns will be addressed at the annual Owl Island Tenants meeting, after tenants receive copies of their new leases.

Respectfully submitted,
Carl Brown

"Ivan was right," Phoebe said. "That's why the B.I.A. sent Amelia's new boyfriend."

"When you got here today, I thought maybe this was what brought things to a boil."

Phoebe shook her head. "Somehow," she said, "I don't think Amelia's going to be seeing her guy tonight. They were supposed to come by for drinks."

"Knowing Amelia, she'll say the screwing she got wasn't worth the screwing she got."

An accurate prediction, as it turned out.

Not only did Amelia cancel, but Laurienne left a message at Westerly Webs saying that since she and Cliff would be working late, and had yet to pack, Phoebe shouldn't wait up for them. Which left Phoebe with extra time to go over the new schedule for lease hikes and assessment payments. Everybody else on the Road must have been similarly occupied or the phone would have been ringing nonstop. Her north-side neighbors had to feel especially hard hit.

A lot for Phoebe to process, on top of everything Margaret had said today. Jasmine, too. Difficult to grasp that such different perspectives applied to the same single person, much less herself.

And now it was Ivan's voice stuck in her head. *Here we are again, back at confused.*

At least she had a good excuse to talk to him, and about something other than his "old tomato." She put on her jacket and walked to his studio, wanting only to measure his reaction to Carl's letter.

"Ivan went into town," Marieke told Phoebe when she arrived. "I'm not sure when he'll be back." With Marieke was a nice-looking, rumple-haired, bespectacled man who appeared to be in his thirties. Her boyfriend, Phoebe found herself hoping. But Marieke introduced him as Matthew, a glass artist from Seattle, there to loan the burnished vessel that Marieke was busy cataloging for Ivan's show. In color and shape the piece was not unlike the sphere Phoebe had envisioned while with Margaret.

"I remember when Ivan was making these," Phoebe said. "About ten years ago, wasn't it?"

"That sounds right," Matthew said. "But I keep terrible records. I was just telling Marieke she'd have to get the date from Ivan."

"I'm Phoebe, by the way. Phoebe Allen."

"You're Phoebe Allen?" Matthew said. "*The* Phoebe Allen, with a Port Pritchard P.O. box?"

Phoebe looked at him, perplexed. "That's me."

"Did the hummingbird's nest make it okay?"

"What?"

"Ivan gave it to me before I left for Guanajuato. Had one hell of a time figuring out how to pack it so it wouldn't get crushed, or so customs wouldn't confiscate it. Although I don't know why an empty little bird's nest would upset them. Bugs, maybe. You can probably tell, I'm the nervous type, that's why—"

"Wait a minute." Phoebe's eyes widened. "Ivan gave the hummingbird's nest to you?"

"Oops. Maybe I wasn't supposed to tell."

"And he asked you to send it to me from Mexico?"

"I knew it was a surprise," Matthew said, "but I thought that by now—"

"He would have told me. Or I'd have figured it out."

"Yeah. Sorry."

"It's all right," Phoebe said. "I'm just a little slow. Do me a favor, though—don't let on to Ivan that I know."

"Sure."

"And thanks, Matthew."

"For what? Blowing Ivan's surprise?"

"Your package. The nest got here fine."

Marieke had evidently caught the entire conversation. "I love that kind of present," she said. "Mighty dear of Ivan, don't you think?"

"What it is," Phoebe said, "is fucking incredible."

She left for the beach without another word.

Perched on a flat-topped stump close to the rising tide, Phoebe recalled all the Mystery Packages she'd received. The red-dirt salt, the unset rubies, the child-sized clogs, the rusted clock. Twelve, once she got through counting. Only now could she discern how each and every treasure had Ivan written all over it. At some point, he had been to Kauai—the salt. Once he went to Turkey—the rubies. Holland—the clogs. But these objects never arrived near enough to his journeys, some of which had occurred before she even knew him, for her to form the connection. Other objects, like the clock and the nest, he could have collected closer to home and handed off to former students, friends, fellow artists like Matthew. It seemed the enterprise was an ongoing art piece—or could be, if the items were all assembled and displayed alongside a history of their peregrinations. Receiving that hummingbird's nest on the very day she'd saved the life of one wasn't the stunning slice of theatrical time she had mistaken it for, but a piece of magic much more solid, more connected to who she really was. Like Ivan himself.

Not Whit. Never Whit.

Ivan all along.

What an idiot, not to see it sooner.

If only she believed in astrology—then she could attribute her delusion to Neptune squares instead of her own thickheadedness. Here she was, sitting on a stump and feeling herself to be its intellectual inferior. And she hadn't just been dumb about Ivan but also patronizing, superior, thoughtless, and cruel. She was tempted to camp out at his studio until he returned, then shower him with accolades, appreciation, apologies. But that wouldn't fix how she'd shoved aside everything deep and true he had to offer and gotten lost instead in her little land of make-believe. She didn't trust herself to go to him, to make another move. Even if she deserved him, which she doubted, all she'd do was screw that up, too. Anyway, it was too late. He was fed up with her and had Marieke to appreciate him now. Ivan might be slow to make a decision, but he was damned immovable once he did.

Clarity—that's what Jasmine said her mantra should be. But it seemed more like blinding vision, seeing how little Whit's loving her had meant when he never, ever cared about what he might be doing to her. Never. Ever. Even waiting until she was eighteen before they met, which had always seemed romantic, was most likely self-protective. All of his sorcerer's attributes were so glittering, so mesmerizing, that she couldn't tell he was feeding on her. And he was too frightened and empty at his core, too trapped inside himself, to be aware of operating that way. Which was probably why it worked so well. Oh, he wanted to be found, all right, but not found out. And missing the distinction, she'd heard only an irresistible cry for help.

No wonder he liked playing the director, hiding behind the camera while he probed the other, giving back nothing—unless you counted an image thick with his fingerprints. That was all she got from him. An image. A version of Phoebe distant from her own, but too dazzling to be dismissed. Easier to stay in the trance, where Whit felt like her lover and friend, than to register the deception's magnitude and what it implied. About him, yes, but especially about her.

She didn't want Whit back.

Jasmine could have him, and good luck.

What she wanted back now was all the time she'd wasted—tying her value to his opinion; measuring other loves by his; believing, as he had taught her, that she wasn't his match. Impossible, of course. There was only one way to evict him from the place he'd occupied in her imagination for so long, and that was to believe, really believe, that all the joy he ever stirred up there was something independent of him, a force for her to master.

Phoebe stood up as though rising on the strength of that resolve, but dropped back down again at the skin-crawling notion that Whit could still be Laurienne's father. Then she'd *never* be free of him. She clenched her hands as if squeezing the life out of that possibility, reminding herself that nobody else knew, nobody else suspected, and if it was up to her, Whit would never even meet her daughter.

19

Laurienne threw her duffel bag into the back of her old Volvo and set out with Cliff for Owl Island at ten thirty—late enough that there wasn't much traffic on the Interstate. The speed limit rose to seventy after Everett, but Laurienne stuck to the far right lane and held the Volvo steady at sixty-five. "You could go faster," Cliff said.

"I don't want to push the engine."

"You're way too cautious, Laur."

What really bugged him, she knew, was her refusal to speed ahead with cashing in her BioIngenious options. They'd been tussling about it for the past thirty miles. Ever since his lunch with the gaming executives who'd last rejected Lexie, the two of them had reversed positions. Now Cliff was the one who wanted to sell, to use the money for finishing Lexie on their own, and *she* was reluctant—though not from fear of failing, as he'd been. For what seemed the first time, she had a serious moral dilemma of her own, not a friend's, to resolve: whether or not to take profits from a fishy patent.

"I just don't feel right about it," Laurienne said. "We could finish the game, but wouldn't the game be tainted?"

"This is our fuck-you money. We could own the game ourselves; we wouldn't have to sign away rights to anybody else." Cliff held his hand over an air vent. "Doesn't the heat work?"

"We're supposed to be taking a break, having a good time," Laurienne said, turning up the fan. "Do you think that'll be possible?"

"The point is, it's a smart gamble. Anyway, if you follow your logic all the way down the line, we're already tainted, taking a paycheck from them."

"Oh, that makes me feel a whole lot better."

"You've only ever seen that one gene patent application, Laur, but they all work the same. It's not like you'd be insider-trading, fleecing the people who buy your stock."

"I would be to my way of thinking."

He released a long, aggravated breath. "Okay, let me put it to you like this. The patent application's not classified information. Selling won't make the stock drop. If anything, the stock will keep going up for a while. Sell low and you're not taking advantage. If you're sticking it to anybody, it's the robber barons. Exercising your options is a vote against them. Understand?"

"I'm not stupid. I'm just not sure it's what I want to do."

"If word got out we were dumping now, they'd all think we're traitors. But they'd mainly think we're idiots for not riding it up."

Laurienne nodded. "That's pretty much what Whit said."

"Whit? You saw him again?"

"No, he's running some stuff by me—on the phone."

"What kind of stuff?"

"Computer stuff, screenplay stuff. I don't see why he bothers you so much."

"It takes a guy to get that."

"Oh, please."

"I'm serious. Girls don't understand the code of fucking the way guys do."

"That is *not* what's interesting about him to me," she huffed. "Besides, he's married and he knows I'm with you. He invited both of us for lunch tomorrow."

"I'll bet you said yes."

"Yeah," Laurienne admitted. "I just thought it would be fun—a nice place up on Chuckanut Drive. It's pretty there, and his treat. Kind of a thank-you for my help."

"Is his wife coming?"

"Yes."

"Well, you go. I'm not interested. You're the one he wants to bonk."

"Come on, Cliff. It's not a cock fight."

He laid a hand on her thigh. "Don't be mad."

"Principles aren't a bad thing," she said, brushing his hand away.

"But you're so naïve about the options—guess it got me going global. Sorry."

"I don't need your seal of approval, but it would help if you at least tried to understand my position."

"Okay, okay. Calm down; you're almost going eighty."

She checked the speedometer and lightened her foot on the accelerator.

"It's our motive that counts," Cliff went on. "That's all we can keep lily-white here. Sometimes you just gotta roll the dice, even if they are a little dirty. Remember Myst? Sixteen million games at thirty bucks a pop."

"Do you really think we'd hit it that big?"

"Say we only hit it semi-big—even semi-demi-big. You'd still make enough to fight the power. A whole lot better than just wringing your hands over something that won't make any difference."

Laurienne reached into the bag of barbecue potato chips between them and chomped for a while. "I want to go over it with my mom. Maybe Ivan, too."

"Okay," he said. "It's a big step. Just let me talk to them if they've got a problem."

He put his hand on her leg again and grinned when she gave him a sideways glance, letting it stay.

By the time they reached Spit in the Wind Road, Phoebe had already gone to bed. While Cliff scratched Lily's belly, Laurienne read the note Phoebe had left on the kitchen table. "Well," she told Cliff, "looks like you're sleeping on the couch."

After they pulled out the convertible sofa and tucked in all the sheets and blankets, Laurienne unbuckled Cliff's belt. "What are you doing?" he said.

"Putting you to bed."

They made love teenage style. Whispery, giggly, stealthy, and all the more exciting for what, in her mother's house, was surely a bogus idea—that they'd be in some kind of trouble if discovered. After dozing for a while, Laurienne slipped out of Cliff's arms. "Where are you going?" he mumbled.

"Upstairs." She kissed the tip of his nose. "So I can pretend I've been there all night."

Lily stayed on her cushion by the woodstove, as if determined to keep a wary eye on this sleeping stranger. But when Laurienne returned to Cliff early the next morning—after her shower, before Phoebe was up—she found Lily snoozing with her head pillowed on his hip. That was a first, having a boyfriend who'd also slept with her dog. Her laughter woke Cliff.

Opening one eye, he said, "What?"

"Coffee time." Laurienne handed him a mug.

"No Coke?"

"Nope. Give Mom a chance to like you before she finds out you're white trash."

After a few sips he put on a pair of Levi's and a thick,

cabled red sweater. Laurienne grabbed binoculars and they took their mugs down to the beach, Lily trailing behind.

In the distance, Mount Baker's frosty cone wore a collar of clouds. The tide was out, exposing a wide swatch of air-hole-pocked flats, but coming in fast. High on the beach, set upside down on parallel logs, were an aluminum canoe, a blue fiberglass kayak, and a wooden rowboat painted red and gray. Cliff ran his hand along the rowboat's hull. "Nice shape," he said.

"It's a Gloucester Gull."

"My folks used to have a cabin on a lake. My rowboat was dinky compared to this."

"Ivan made it for me when I was in high school, so I could keep up with rowing in the summer."

"Guess you had to fill the swimming pool to do that."

"The tide'll be all the way up in a few hours. We'll have to come back. The beach is so pretty then."

"Can you explain to me why people out here think rock yards are beaches?"

She grabbed him by the neck and nipped his earlobe. "Punk."

Cliff pointed at a bald eagle gliding over the bay. Laurienne imitated the big bird's chittering call and it swooped closer, tipping wings like a stunt pilot saying howdy.

"Cool," Cliff said. "I didn't know you could speak eagle."

She handed him the binoculars and pointed out Heron Island, beyond the neck of Little Pritchard Bay, and then, closer in, tiny Dead Man's Island—her destination point when she rowed on the Brookland team, almost exactly three hundred yards across, perfect sprinting distance.

"Why's it called Dead Man's Island?" Cliff asked.

"Because when tribal people lived here, that's where they'd take their dead."

"What's there now?"

"Nothing much. But when I was little, I thought it was a great place to go exploring."

They walked for a while, Laurienne drawing Cliff's attention to a cormorant, a hawk, a seal. She turned over a large, barnacle-covered rock to show him skittering little crabs, then cracked open an oyster with his Swiss Army knife. "Want to eat it?" she asked.

It took Cliff a while to make up his mind.

Phoebe had lain in bed awake after Laurienne and Cliff got up, just as she had lain in bed awake when she heard them first arrive at the house. Last night she wasn't in the mood to be sociable—talked out after conferring on the phone with Margaret and some north-side neighbors, their only resolution being to gather for more discussion at Phoebe's house. This morning her excuse for staying in bed was that she wanted to get herself caffeinated, showered, and dressed before meeting Cliff. He might be accustomed to seeing Laurienne bathrobed and bleary-eyed in the morning, but *she* didn't want to make his acquaintance that way. As soon as the two of them left the house, Phoebe threw back the duvet and stretched.

The only boys Laurienne ever brought home before had been part of a group. No romantic gestures or physical displays of affection with that bunch—not, at any rate, when a parent might be around to witness them. Laurienne's college crowd didn't seem to date so much as congregate, and Phoebe could surmise that sex came into the equation mainly from a profound lack of alternatives. Why else did they use the words "boyfriend" and "girlfriend" to refer to each other? It wasn't about mating but merging to drive the same highway for a while. This thing with Cliff already seemed different. Going about her morning business, it was almost as if Phoebe could hear the house hum, finally happy to have a pair of real lovers in it again. Wistfulness on her part, probably, since having a real lover again seemed beyond her ability.

In the kitchen, cracking eggs into a bowl, Phoebe looked out the window and spotted Laurienne and Cliff walking through the garden, arms looped around each other's waists, his short, mussy dark hair close to her auburn curls. Phoebe wiped her hands on a dish towel and went to open the door for them, sweeping Laurienne into a hug and then finding herself swept up into a hug by Cliff, as if it were the most natural thing in the world for him to do.

"Thanks for having me," he told her. "This is such a great place."

"He's just buttering you up," Laurienne said. "He called the bay a swimming pool, and the beach a rock yard."

"But I made up for that by eating an oyster," Cliff said.

Phoebe wrinkled her nose. "Before breakfast?"

"Yeah." Laurienne looked at Cliff as though he'd scaled a glass mountain to win her favor. "To commemorate a historic event."

When Phoebe asked what event that was, Laurienne laughed.

"Go on," Cliff said, "I dare you to tell her."

Just a little playful banter, surely not enough to account for the sudden surge of good feelings Phoebe had about Cliff. What on earth was going on? Then it hit her. Laurienne had never really known Mitchell, and still she'd picked someone close to him in his broad-

shouldered build; in his open, even, good-humored man-
ner; even in the twang of his accent—almost as if she
knew exactly what she'd missed and needed. Maybe she
did. Maybe Mitchell really was inside her. If Phoebe had
been a practicing Catholic, she would have crossed herself at the thought.

Laurienne insisted on making breakfast so Cliff and
Phoebe could talk. Which they did, nonstop. Mostly
about the island, the house, her business. He was so full
of questions that Phoebe had no time to ask any of her
own before the phone started ringing again. She let the
answering machine pick up. It was Sophie. "I'll be there
at ten thirty with extra coffee and doughnuts," Sophie
said. "If we don't figure *something* out today, Charlie's
gonna put the house on a flatbed and haul it off somewhere."

Phoebe got up to set the answering machine to one
ring and turn down the volume on messages. The calls
kept coming, and most of breakfast was spent with her
explaining the new lease situation.

"*You're* not going to move, are you?" Laurienne asked.

"I doubt it," Phoebe said. "But everything is kind of
up in the air right now."

"What about Ivan?"

Yes, what about Ivan? "I don't know," Phoebe said.
"I'm worried about him, too." So worried, in fact, that
she didn't trust herself enough to call him about this
morning's meeting, and had asked Amelia to do it for
her. But she didn't mention that to Laurienne and Cliff.

After breakfast, they went to Port Pritchard in separate
cars. Phoebe gave Cliff a tour of Westerly Webs, then
walked the Terminal docks with him and Laurienne,
pointing out her trawlers.

"Will you be back for lunch?" Phoebe asked when it was time for them to split up.

Laurienne said no, but at the same time Cliff said yes, and she shot him an irritated look. "I'm trying to talk Cliff into lunch on Chuckanut Drive," Laurienne offered.

"Whatever you do is fine with me," Phoebe said. "There's plenty of sandwich stuff at home."

Phoebe went to the Pioneer Market to pick up some extra half-and-half. As she lifted a carton from the dairy case, someone tapped her on the shoulder. "Well," Carl Brown said, "are *you* going to speak to me?"

"Why wouldn't I?" she countered.

"You know. The leases."

"You could have given us some warning."

"And lost my job."

"If you say so, Carl. Look, I've got to run—a few people are coming over soon to talk about it."

"Well, a word to the wise. What we've got here is the opening salvo, but it's not an attack."

"Just what the hell is that supposed to mean?"

"Find the best points to haggle. They're there, I promise. But remember—I never said a word about it to you."

"Why say anything at all?"

Carl smiled and stroked his beard. "Isn't that obvious? I live there, too. Then there's your basting sauce. I figure the more points I score with you, Phoebe, the better my chances for getting the recipe."

More people came than Phoebe had expected. Not just north-siders—Sophie and her husband Charlie, Amelia, Ivan, a half-dozen others—but Margaret showed up with three of her south-side neighbors in tow, including Walter. "We just thought everyone ought to pull together now," Margaret said.

Ivan looked especially glum, which tore at Phoebe's heart. She felt worse for him than she did for herself, having this to deal with on top of his show, on top of her bad behavior. "Glad you could make it," she told him.

He just shrugged and took off with Amelia to haul extra chairs from the garage, as if small talk was more than he could manage.

When everyone was settled around the dining room table, Charlie said, "What if we took the tribe to court?"

"A waste of money," Sophie told him. "The facts are in their favor. Besides, who wants a legal hassle? Nobody would be able to sell."

"I need to sell," Amelia wailed, "but I don't want to."

"I'll have to dip into my savings big time." This from Willis, a guy who worked a steady construction job. "What about you, Ivan?"

"Just signed on to Angus's boat for a winter trip." He cut his eyes at Phoebe. "That ought to get me through next year okay."

Willis nodded. "Most money for the least time. Sensible."

"Sensible?" Phoebe gripped the table's edge, thinking of Mitchell, how frightened she'd been whenever he went out. "Have you lost your mind?" she shouted.

Everyone stared. Phoebe pinched her voice to a furious hiss. "You haven't been winter fishing for years, Ivan. It's too dangerous up there."

Again, Ivan shrugged. "I've heard drowning is a good way to go."

Phoebe shut up and glanced at Margaret, whose expression told her she'd caught all the implications.

"I've got an idea," Margaret said in a changing-the-subject tone. "Instead of charging the same lease rate for every property, it would be more fair to phase in the hikes according to length of residence. And why not pay based on a home's market value? That would be just like property taxes, and the tribe could step it up from there."

A south-sider saying south-siders ought to pay more? With her neighbors nodding in agreement? Everyone seemed surprised. But Ivan looked as though Donald Trump had just turned over his tower to the homeless.

"It's for the common good," Margaret added. "What could be more boring than an island where everybody's the same demographic?"

It occurred to Phoebe that Margaret's suggestion meant Whit would take a big hit—maybe the worst clobbering of all, depending on how fancy his remodel job was. Just the thought sent a slow, delicious rush of revenge through her body. But more significant was that Margaret had made a smart, valid point, and if anything could keep Ivan off Angus's boat, it would be a barrage of smart, valid points. Phoebe pulled herself together to voice one of her own. "The assessment's the real killer," she said. "Instead of one lump fee, we should negotiate for them to amortize it."

"Amortize?" Amelia asked.

No wonder Gabe went to Wharton—he couldn't count on Amelia to show him how the world worked. "Spread it out over time," Phoebe explained.

"I don't think anyone on the north side built or bought with bank loans," Ivan said. "But if we can get the lease language fixed so banks would approve, maybe that could happen, too."

Willis got out a calculator and started running numbers. Sophie took notes on a yellow legal pad as more suggestions flew. And in the middle of all this, Cliff arrived, alone.

"Don't mind me," he said after Phoebe introduced him. "I'll just make a sandwich and take it to the beach."

"Where's Judge?" Ivan asked.

Cliff frowned. "Judge?"

"Laurienne's nickname," Phoebe told him.

Cliff nodded as if he thought it suited her all too well. "She's meeting people for lunch."

Phoebe wanted to ask more questions, but quizzing Cliff in front of a roomful of strangers would be rude. Besides, talk at the table had already turned to organizing an agenda for the annual tenants' meeting.

Later, with the agenda nailed, Sophie helped Phoebe ferry dishes to the sink.

"Why don't you see about finding us a sport nets distributor," Phoebe said to her. "Looks like time to branch out."

As Phoebe started to load the dishwasher, she glanced out the window and noticed a rowboat that looked a lot like Laurienne's two-thirds of the way to Dead Man's Island. Someone in a red sweater was rowing. Cliff, of course. Without a life vest. Which she would have insisted on his wearing had she known he planned to take the boat out. And he probably would have ignored her, just like Laurienne did before Ivan busted her for rowing without protection and used gruesomely vivid accident accounts to drill all the imperatives of water safety into her head. Knowing Ivan, he'd be the first to zip into an immersion suit if anything went wrong on Angus's boat. But Phoebe's fears were too wild on that score to be calmed by reason.

At least Cliff wasn't beyond her sight, caught in some terrible Alaskan winter storm. He looked like he knew what he was doing, too.

Then a big tourist cruiser cut across the bay to circle Dead Man's Island, and instead of angling over the wake, Cliff hit it head on. The boat rocked hard, slapped down off-center, and tipped over. "Oh, God!" Phoebe screamed. But no sooner had the words left her lips than she switched into the urgent, clipped efficiency of emergency mode.

"Ivan," Phoebe said, "Cliff's flipped the Gull."

Phoebe raced down the hillside, Ivan behind her, both of them carrying towels and blankets. Charlie had Ivan's dory halfway in the water when they reached the beach.

"Go back to the boat," Charlie was shouting at Cliff, swimming now for Dead Man's Island.

Phoebe jumped into the dory after Ivan, and Charlie shoved them off. She knew the water wasn't freezing. Still, it was cold enough that without a vest, Cliff would have inhaled some from the gasping shock when he went under, then lost more body heat swimming. Even with help so near, so quick to come, it would take no time at all for hypothermia to set in.

Ivan started the motor and opened the throttle. Although Phoebe sat in the boat's front end for ballast, they were going so fast the dory's prow lifted clean out of the water.

Ivan drew parallel to Cliff, who was hanging on now to the Gull's hull, then angled across, killed the engine, and held out an oar for him to grab. Phoebe slid to the opposite side of the boat while Ivan hauled Cliff in, then helped him pull off Cliff's sweater, tee shirt, jeans, briefs, and socks. The shoes were already gone. "We have to keep him prone," Ivan said, "or the cold blood'll go to his heart." After they wrapped Cliff in blankets, Ivan started the motor again.

"Sorry," Cliff kept saying, through blue lips and chattering teeth.

"Shush," Phoebe said. "Don't talk. Don't move. Don't do anything." She reached to grab his jeans. Good thing Cliff wore them tight—his wallet was still in the back pocket.

"How's his breathing?" Ivan shouted over the motor's roar.

"Steady," Phoebe yelled, holding her hand on Cliff's chest. She remembered the Fates, those spiderlike goddesses mentioned in Margaret's article who spin the thread of human destiny. Silently, she petitioned them. *Let him be all right; don't let this happen to my daughter like it did to me.*

Back on shore, Charlie waited with Willis to land the dory and help Ivan carry Cliff up the hill, handling him like a fragile child. "He's conscious," Charlie said. "That's good."

"Yeah," Ivan told him, "but past the warm-bath stage. Let's take him to the ER—it'll be quicker than getting medics out here."

"I'll call ahead," Charlie said, "make sure they're ready for him."

Up at the house, Sophie was waiting with two flannel-wrapped hot water bottles and Laurienne's down sleeping bag. *If I ever have to be saved from drowning,* Phoebe thought, *these are the people I'd want around me.*

They laid Cliff in the back of the Explorer. Phoebe climbed in to follow Sophie's orders, placing one hot water bottle on Cliff's chest, the other over his groin. Then they zipped him—still shivering, blankets and all—into the sleeping bag.

Charlie put a piece of chocolate in Cliff's mouth and handed Phoebe the rest of the bar. "For energy," he said.

As Ivan sped them off island, Phoebe alternated feeding Cliff bits of chocolate and rubbing her hands together for heat, then placing them on his chilled cheeks. Not a tiny hummingbird to revive this time, but a full-grown man. "Stay with us," she said, and Cliff nodded, eyelids fluttering.

Ivan swerved into the drive at Pritchard Valley Hospital. "Good thing you saw him," he told Phoebe.

Tears stung her eyes, and a wave of gratitude overcame her. "Good thing you were there. Good thing he's still alive."

"Damn good thing," Cliff mumbled. Then he passed out.

20

The emergency room doctor, whose name tag read "Al Heller," motioned for Phoebe and Ivan to follow him past the admission desk, through a set of swinging doors, and into an examining room, where the two male nurses were easing Cliff off a stretcher and onto a flattened hospital bed.

Heller hovered over Cliff for a minute, fingers on his carotid artery. Then he raised his head, with its nimbus of salt-and-pepper curls. "He didn't pass out. He just fell asleep."

"Is that bad?" Phoebe asked.

"Better than passing out." Heller checked Cliff's temperature, shone light in his eyes.

Still wrapped in his cocoon, Cliff gave a shuddery groan. "No picnic," he mumbled. "Sandwich overboard."

He became even less intelligible when Heller strapped a clear plastic mask—connected to something that looked like the chubby little robot from *Star Wars*—over his mouth and nose.

"Cliff," Heller said, tousling his hair, "it's not that I don't want to hear what you have to say. It's just that you'll be more eloquent after I warm you up a little."

Phoebe felt another rush of gratitude, wishing Heller were a regular doctor so he could be not only hers but everybody else's she once loved, did love, would love in the future. Over-the-top, but then so were the circum-stances. Limbs gone rubbery, she dropped into a chair. "He'll be all right?"

"At worst, we're only looking at moderate hypother-mia. How long was Cliff in?"

"Maybe ten minutes," Ivan said. "No protection."

Heller nodded as if that was a guy for you. "It's a plus he's so young and strong."

"Ivan thought we better bring him in," Phoebe said.

"Ivan thought right. You'd be lucky to get a medic with one of these machines on board. Coast Guard Rescue's got 'em. They've pulled out men in immersion suits who've been treading water for hours—critical cases. Still, they're stable after twenty minutes' inhala-tion warming."

"His color's better already," Ivan said.

"Yep," Heller agreed. "Not nearly so cyanotic. You're pumping with oxygen now, aren't you, Cliff? Don't try and answer, that was a rhetorical question." He glanced back at Phoebe and Ivan. "You folks relatives, or Good Samaritans?"

"He's my daughter's boyfriend." Phoebe's heart gal-loped at the thought of Laurienne, and how she'd take the news of Cliff in the same hospital where Mitchell had been dead on arrival. Phoebe checked the wall clock. For all that had happened, it was only one fifteen. "I don't want Laurienne hearing about this from anybody else," she told Ivan.

"Do you know where she is?" Ivan asked.

"No, but there aren't many places on Chuckanut. It won't be hard to check them out."

"Go," Heller told them. "I'm throwing you out now anyway. If I were a betting man, I'd wager on Cliff being home for dinner."

*   *   *

Phoebe fished Cliff's health insurance card out of his wallet and left it with the admission clerk. When Ivan offered to drive the Explorer again, she was quick to agree.

They passed two restaurants on Chuckanut before coming to the one where she'd eaten her first raw oyster— once Oyster Cove Inn, now reincarnated as Oyster Shoals, with a fancier menu and prices, but cantilevered like always over a rocky beach by the first hairpin turn going north. Phoebe spotted Laurienne's car in the lot. "She's here."

Ivan slowed to a stop, switched on the left-turn signal, and waited for a break in oncoming traffic. "Want me to come with you?"

"Both of us? That might scare her."

"True. But the worst is over."

"It is if you don't go fishing with Angus. I've got to tell you how weird it was, Ivan—standing at the window, watching Cliff out there. Right before he flipped, I was thinking about you, imagining you getting tossed into the Gulf."

"That's not going to happen."

"Good. You've changed your mind."

"Didn't say that, did I?"

"You should, though." But she saw that for him to trust her again, to value her opinion again, she would have to do more than set herself straight, or recite better reasons than why not, or marvel over his Mystery Packages. She would have to hold him closer than she could now imagine doing.

Close enough to risk another loss.

Close enough for him to examine not just the scar on her throat, but how it got there.

Ivan drove across the highway and stopped by the

restaurant entrance. "I'll wait here," he said. "I'd just as soon Laurienne not drive. Let's take her to the hospital with us."

"Okay."

As Phoebe walked inside, she heard an old Chet Baker song. Her father had been right, all those years ago. He *did* sound strung out. "Can I help you?" the hostess asked, leaning over her hostess lectern.

"No thanks, I'm here for my daughter." Phoebe walked down three steps into the crowded bar. A waiter with perspiration beading his face slipped past with a tray full of drafts, oyster samplers, and chowder. From the bar, Phoebe scanned the L-shaped dining room, where view tables covered with white cloths were arranged against a bank of casement windows. At the farthest end, she spotted Whit.

It seemed she'd fallen into a time warp, watching Whit drink brown-bagged Pilsner Urquells with her in this very place, before it got so sophisticated. But no, he had a wineglass in his hand now, and he was leaning toward an auburn-haired companion, looking at her as though she were the only person in the world who mattered.

It couldn't be Laurienne.

Laurienne was meeting *people,* that's what Cliff had said.

Her lunch date was plural, not singular.

But there was only one redhead in the restaurant, and judging by the tilt of her head, the slope of her shoulders, she was intrigued—if not captivated.

Phoebe grabbed the rail beside her, paralyzed by the implications. Not just a violation of her creativity this time. Not just her intelligence. Not just her body. But the whole existence she'd built since her first escape from Whit. He was inside her life, just as he'd been inside her not so long ago, only now she could measure the jeopardy as it occurred. It felt like a nightmare, menace blistering the air while she stood frozen in place, sick with fear, unable to move. But she had to move, she had to act, she had to protect her daughter—from someone who might or might not be her father. Two equally awful alternatives, each the more terrible for Phoebe's not knowing how far things had gone.

Phoebe willed herself to walk, and at last her legs responded. When she was halfway to the table, Whit noticed her, with a startled, questioning look, but Phoebe was so focused on Laurienne that she only caught it from the corner of her eye.

Laurienne took a spoonful of crème caramel before following Whit's gaze to see her. "Mom," she said, pushing back from the table. "What's wrong?"

"Mom?" Whit repeated.

Even glancing sideways Phoebe could tell that he hadn't known of her child till now. He hadn't so much as suspected. Someone else in his position might behave like a cornered rat, but this was Whit. Two women swirling around him, each vibrating with emotion? Phoebe could almost see him squint, framing them through an imaginary lens.

"Sweetheart," she said, leaning down toward Laurienne so that her back was turned on Whit. "Everything's all right, but Cliff had an accident in the Gull. They're stabilizing him at the hospital; he'll probably be released in a few hours."

Reassuring words, voiced with every ounce of comfort Phoebe could muster, but she couldn't quite hide her shock over Whit, and Laurienne, grabbing hold of her hand, seemed to seize on Cliff's condition as its cause. "Are you sure he's okay?"

"Positive."

"I shouldn't have come without him."

"Don't worry about that now."

"I wouldn't have let him go out—not by himself."
Laurienne's cheeks splotched with color as she tightened
her grip on Phoebe's hand. "He's only ever rowed on
some dumb little lake."

"It's not your fault," Phoebe told her. "I'll bet he'll say
so himself, first thing. He knows we've come to get you.
Ivan's waiting outside."

Laurienne swiped at her eyes and spoke to Whit as she
rose from the table. "I'm sorry," she said, "but this is my
mother—"

"So I gathered," Whit said, standing himself.

"I know exactly who he is," Phoebe told Laurienne.
"You don't have to introduce us."

"That's right," Whit said. "Your mother and I are old
friends. Very old friends. In fact, she wrote my first fan
letter."

"And it was all downhill from there," Phoebe shot
back. Laurienne took in the tone and knit her eyebrows,
but Phoebe put an arm around her waist and swept her
away, saying, "Not now—Cliff needs you."

"Mom," Laurienne said, stopping before they stepped
out the restaurant door. "Whit's wife was supposed to
come, but she caught a cold and I'd rather you not mention it to Cliff—he's got this thing about Whit."

"Yes. I can just imagine."

All during the ride to the hospital, Laurienne asked about
nothing but Cliff, wanting all the details of his accident,
his rescue, his condition. Phoebe let Ivan do most of the
talking, chiming in with information of her own just to
keep from seeming upset. When they arrived and Lauri-

enne ran ahead of them, Ivan took hold of Phoebe's shoulders and turned her to face him.

"You're white as a sheet," he said. "What's going on?"

"Nothing." She tried for a laugh. "Maybe I better talk to Dr. Heller, tell him I need some oxygen, too."

"Don't tell me nothing just happened back there, Phoebe. Something just happened. What was it?"

The concern in his voice was unmistakable. Still, he looked prepared to turn her upside down and shake her till the truth fell out. "I'll tell you," she said, "but not till after I go through it with Laurienne."

Laurienne was practically in bed with Cliff when Phoebe and Ivan returned to the room where he was recovering. "I think we're past the point," Heller was saying to Laurienne, "where your body heat's going to do him any good."

"Hey," Cliff said, pulling the inhaler mask away from his face, "don't knock a good thing." No longer flat on his back, he sat halfway up now, wearing a hospital gown and covered only by a few blankets.

"I'm serious. If somebody else had been naked in that sleeping bag with you, you wouldn't have needed the inhaler." Again, Heller checked Cliff's temperature and pulse. "Now you're nearly normal."

"Thank God," Laurienne said.

From Cliff behind the mask, muffled words: "Thank your mom and Ivan."

In a flash, Laurienne was in their arms. Phoebe wanted to believe her intensity meant that Whit was at worst a harmless infatuation. But at this point, she couldn't afford another mistaken excursion into the Land of Make-Believe. What sort of story would that be, anyway? Oh, easy answer: Whit only took her daughter back to Chuckanut the way Peter Pan took Wendy's daughter back to Neverland—after Wendy grew up and couldn't go herself, that is—wanting nothing more than a few bedtime stories and a little spring cleaning.

Phoebe motioned Ivan into the hallway. "I've got some things to do at home," she said.

After Ivan dropped her off and returned to the hospital in his own car with extra clothes and another pair of shoes for Cliff, Phoebe set out on foot for Whit's, running, cloud shadow at her feet.

How sweet it would be to banish Whit, as Glinda did the Wicked Witch of the West. "You have no power here! Begone, before somebody drops a house on *you*!" But much as she'd like to drop a house on him—his own, preferably—she had no magic wand. And satisfying as revenge might feel, it wouldn't serve her daughter. Shuffling through dried leaves and pinecones, her feet beat out a tattoo of if-onlys. If only Mitchell had lived and they had found out for certain who Laurienne's father was. If only the truth hadn't always seemed too impossible to tell her daughter. If only Whit had never come back. But each if-only came with its own built-in, unhappy dead end, leaving her daughter still at risk for the uncut version of Whit.

Enough. She had to do for Laurienne what she could never do for herself where Whit was concerned—demand answers, set boundaries, assume an authority over her life greater than his. She had to be exactly the kind of woman for whom he had no use. Was that why she hadn't done it sooner?

The wind picked up as she climbed the ridge on the edge of Whit's property. A new high cedar fence surrounded his place, shielding the house from view. Phoebe opened the gate, closed it behind her, and walked up the drive. Only one Range Rover parked in the carport, the black one that was his.

She continued up steps to a wide deck that wrapped around the house. The deck was studded with huge clay pots full of autumn blooms. Jasmine's work, no doubt. Whit wasn't earthy enough for gardening, even in containers. Alongside the front door was a tall, narrow strip of glass through which she could see the foyer. A vase of out-of-season irises sat atop a burnished tansu. She rang the bell, waiting only a minute before she rang again and pounded the door. That brought him, with an annoyed frown. He had a black roam phone at his ear, and spoke into it as he opened the door. "Looks like I've got a messenger here, I'll call you back."

Whit clicked off and before Phoebe could say a word, he shook his head with a grin and said, "I don't suppose you'll go away if I tell you I gave at the office."

"We have to talk," she told him. "Right now."

"I think you missed your calling, Phoebe. You'd have made a great Jehovah's Witness."

"Oh, I'm a witness, all right. Are you going to ask me in, or do you want to come outside?"

"I'm working, Phoebe."

"I know, you're a very busy guy these days, aren't you?"

"I don't think I like your tone."

"Too bad. Well?"

He checked his watch. "We've got ten minutes before Jasmine's here."

Inside, the house smelled of lavender and orange. The thick wall-to-wall carpeting, avocado appliances, and pine paneling that Phoebe remembered from the Miller place were all gone, replaced by wide-plank floors, gleaming aluminum, and walls painted a pale terra-cotta. She barely glanced at the view, stunning in this cloud-tossed, buttery afternoon glow, but she couldn't help feeling as if she were on a set Whit had ordered up, one of his requirements being that no direct lighting would fall on his face. It all came down on hers.

She sat on the edge of a sleek, scallop-backed sofa while Whit perched on the arm of a leather club chair—one foot on the floor, ready to push off again. "I assume this is about Laurienne," he said.

"Yes."

"She's a fascinating young woman."

Phoebe kept her voice low and steady. "I have to know just how involved you are with her."

"This is starting to sound like 'Hell hath no fury.' You're not jealous of your own daughter, are you?"

Phoebe shook her head. "You *would* do that—take a protective mother for a woman scorned."

"Not a pretty picture, maybe. But understandable."

"Of course, because it keeps you center stage. But there's only one person in the spotlight for me, and that's Laurienne."

"Don't forget, I just found out today that she's yours. So you'll have to forgive me if I can't decide who you think you're doing here—Mother Courage or Mildred Pierce. We met because her car broke down and I helped her out. Counting today, I've seen her twice since. Did she tell you?"

"I wasn't about to discuss you with her until I knew for a fact how far it's gone."

"Strange, isn't it? I mean, it's not every day you find out you're involved with two generations of women."

She recognized the look on his face. He was afloat, in such an intoxicating bubble of theatrical time that he'd barely heard a word she said.

"Maybe I knew subconsciously," he went on. "My

script's building up to exactly this kind of thing. I was just telling Joe about it when you got here."

"Your script? Screw your script, and Joe, too. This is my daughter we're talking about."

"I wonder why you never mentioned her before. I'd be shouting it from the rooftops if Laurienne were my daughter."

"You're right, she's very special." Phoebe rose to look him in the eye, standing head-to-head with him. "And now that you mention it, there's a chance she *is* your daughter."

That stopped him cold. But she could see her revelation only enlarged, instead of burst, his bubble. She wished it could sail out over the bay with him inside, higher than eagles flew, then evaporate.

"A chance," Whit said. "What kind of chance?"

"Fifty-fifty."

"You don't know who her father is?"

"You or Mitchell. Mitchell Gentry. Sound familiar? His name got cut from the *Kiki* credits, too. He died before we could find out for certain. How far, Whit?"

His eyes went distant and diffuse as he sank into the club chair and laced his long, tapered fingers. "My sister Becky was a redhead. The one who died."

"That doesn't prove anything. So was Mitchell, so was my mother. I have to know, Whit. I'm not leaving until you tell me."

When he spoke again, each word seemed careful, considered. "It's always difficult, defining a bond— especially one that's so new. But don't worry. There's been a paternal tone all along between Laurienne and me. And if I'm her father, I imagine it's just going to deepen."

Phoebe's insides wadded up with resentment at the sight of him savoring the situation, all its newfound power and control. He consulted his watch again. "Two minutes, Phoebe."

Impossible to tell if he was threatening her or punishing her or just sharpening his claws on her hide. She'd bet money he didn't know himself.

21

In the aftermath of Cliff's accident, Laurienne's sense of time didn't so much melt as elongate. It began when she entered the hospital—the same hospital she used to drive by holding her breath, taken by dark undercurrents of thought: *Here's where my mother was when she found out my father died. Here's the start of her getting so cautious, so defensive.* And what about herself? She could have lost Cliff, the way Phoebe lost Mitchell. But she didn't. Nothing had been lost, except for Cliff's shoes. And instead of contracting the way her mother had, she felt herself stretching out, too.

She remembered Phoebe saying fairy tales had their own reality. That's how things seemed now, full of their own reality, not unlike a fairy tale, the kind she'd always raised logical objections to as a kid. She could almost hear herself doing it. *Wait, wait, wait—why did that girl leave her sweetheart alone when they're supposed to be in love?* She'd made a mistake there, no doubt about it. But nobody died because she screwed up. And without her mistake, the spell wouldn't be broken. The spell she hadn't even been aware of operating under before, though now it seemed obvious. Maybe the headaches would go away, too. Another one had crept up on her going to the hospital, but it disappeared without any Coke, without any Advil. From sheer happiness, it appeared. Although it didn't hurt hearing from Dr. Heller that baby migraines like hers had nothing to do with brain tumors.

She ran the Volvo's engine for ten minutes before Cliff got in, wanting to get the car good and hot for him. "Did your life flash before your eyes when you were in the water?" she asked.

"No," he said. "Just a fish. A big silver one. Sorry I broke up your lunch."

She laughed. "No you're not."

"I am sorry, though—sorry I didn't go with you. Mr. Wonderful's not so bad compared to almost drowning."

"His wife had a cold; she didn't come."

"Why am I not surprised?"

And that was it. Her conscience was clear, without any further suspicions or snarky remarks from Cliff. She knew why. Alone with him in the hospital, she had finally done it—come out and said she loved him. Not once, but three times.

It was sweet, having Ivan and Phoebe with her at the hospital. Like a real family. Another blessing from the accident, teaming them up again. And Cliff was astounded by all the visits and phone calls from people along the Road who needed to know he'd be okay. "No wonder you get homesick," he said.

She fussed over Cliff, settling him into her bed upstairs and bringing a tray of soup and crackers and the Coke over chipped ice that he craved.

After Ivan went home, Phoebe came with extra pillows and some magazines. "Can I borrow your girlfriend for a while?" she asked Cliff.

"Anything for you." Then he turned back to Laurienne and whispered, "Have you told your mom about the options yet?"

"Not yet. I will."

"No time like the present."

"You must be feeling pretty good if your head's into the game again."

As Phoebe led her downstairs, Laurienne chattered non-stop. "Would it be okay if I stayed with him tonight? I want to be there in case he needs anything."

"Yes, that's fine."

"Good. Anyway, the extra blankets still have that icky wet-wool smell. Maybe cold Coke isn't the healthiest for him right now, but it's his thing and the caffeine . . . well, Cliff could sleep through a tornado. And just so you know, Mom, that wasn't any big secret we were whispering about up there. It's our stock options. We're thinking about cashing in to quit and finish Lexie. I wasn't sure I wanted to, on account of this Peter Pan gene patent."

"Good Lord," Phoebe said.

"Oh, right. Peter Pan—that's your guy."

"Not anymore."

"Yeah? What happened?"

"Never mind." Phoebe sat at the dining room table. There was no way to make this job of hers easy, but it might help if Laurienne weren't quite so blissful. Which only meant that much more she'd be destroying. "I need to talk to you about Whit."

"Is that what's bothering you? Relax. I already told Cliff about lunch; it's not a problem. It was just a pissing contest, nothing serious."

"That's not it."

"Okay, okay, let's talk about Whit." Blithe as ever, Laurienne went to the refrigerator and poured a glass of mineral water. "It's so cool you two know each other. I wouldn't have met him if my car hadn't died—out on Hobson Road; I waited there forever. He kind of annoyed me at first, but now I think my favorite thing about him is how he's so funny and fascinated by everything. I didn't think a famous person would be like that."

"It was kind of a shock for me," Phoebe said, "when he bought the Miller place."

"The Miller place?" Laurienne slid back into her chair with a low whistle. "I mean, I knew he lived around here, but I figured it must be somewhere fancier than Owl. Wow. This sort of stuff must happen to him all the time—almost the first thing he told me was he didn't believe in coincidence. But he's a neighbor? That's one for the books."

"Honey, I need to begin at the beginning with this, okay?" Laurienne nodded with a mystified frown on her face. "Mitchell and I got married in Port Pritchard," Phoebe said, then reached for Laurienne's glass and took a sip.

"Yeah, I know."

"What you don't know is we met each other in Montreal. I was there with Whit. He was making a movie that kind of came out of our relationship. His first one. *Kiki.* It's about—"

"I know what it's about; I saw it on video." Laurienne had the same look on her face she wore when matching jigsaw puzzle pieces. "It was at Gramps's house, in his collection. I picked it out. He seemed kind of worried about me seeing *Kiki*—on account of the sex, I thought. But now I guess it was really because of you."

"Probably."

"So what are you telling me? You and Whit were in love?"

Phoebe dug at a piece of candle wax on the place mat in front of her. *We were in love with the people we imagined we were*—that's what she wanted to say. But this territory she was crossing had land mines buried everywhere, all the consequences of not recognizing sooner who Whit was. She had to watch her step. "Yes."

"Why the big secret?"

"It was a hard time for me."

"Wait, this doesn't make sense. Why would you write Whit a fan letter if you were with him for *Kiki*?"

"That was before. He had a radio show I liked on KARP when I was in high school. He wrote to me, too. For years, until we finally got together."

"But I thought you met my father singing," Laurienne said.

"Not exactly. Mitchell was a production carpenter; I ran into him on the *Kiki* set. After that, we played music together."

"So Whit knew my father, too?"

Oh, it was so easy to read the excitement in Laurienne's green eyes: *Another human with memories of Mitchell, and someone special to boot.* "Not really," Phoebe said. "But we were all in Montreal for the movie. You see, I worked on that movie like you've worked on Cliff's game. I guess that's what made me so crazy when you first told me about it. Because I didn't take very good care of myself, but I took terrific care of him."

"Who?"

"Whit."

"Oh. I thought you meant my father."

"Mitchell took care of me. After things blew up with Whit, we quit the movie and drove out west together."

"And that's when the two of you fell in love?"

"That's when I really got to know him, yes."

"Then you moved to Owl Island and had me."

With that segue of logic, that demand for sense and safety, Phoebe heard a plea for "The End." But she had to go on. "I'm not exactly sure which one's your father, Laurienne."

"What?" Laurienne folded her arms tight against her chest. "What do you mean? How can you not be sure?"

"I went from Whit to Mitchell around the time I got pregnant. It could be either of them."

"You lied to me my whole life?"

"I didn't want you growing up confused, not about a thing like that. That would have been terrible for you."

"Confused? Do you think I'm not confused now? How old am I? And you've waited this long to tell me?"

"I understand why you're upset, honey. But I was trying to protect you."

"How were you protecting me?" Laurienne's soft voice flamed.

"If Mitchell had lived, we could have found out for sure when you were little. But he didn't, and I had to decide the best way to handle things by myself."

"How were you protecting me?" Laurienne repeated.

"From the beginning? By choosing Mitchell. I knew he'd be the best father—he wanted me, he wanted you. And after he died, I protected you from Whit because, well, I didn't want to expose you to someone who might not be best for you."

Laurienne shook her head. "Who were you really protecting, Mom?"

"I was protecting my daughter!"

"No you weren't." Laurienne's hand slammed the table like a gavel. "You didn't want to share me. You didn't want me out of your control."

Phoebe reached an arm around her shoulders. "Control? Oh baby, how could you think that?"

Laurienne squirmed away. "You're only telling me now because you have to."

"I was scared. Maybe too scared to make a good decision. You're the one who knows how to weigh things and do what's right—you're the judge, Laurienne. But it was my job to keep you safe, and no matter what you think, that's what I was doing."

"Did Mitchell know?" Laurienne asked in a cold, clipped way.

"Yes. He would have loved you anyway, but your hair convinced him."

"It didn't convince you?"

"My mother was a redhead, remember?"

"Does Gramps know?"

"No."

"Does Whit?"

"I told him today."

"Did he believe you?"

"Yes."

Laurienne went into the kitchen and pulled out some drawers—Phoebe couldn't see which ones, the cabinets blocked her view—then she rushed to the closet and grabbed her jacket.

Phoebe leapt to her feet. "Where are you going?"

"Where do you think?"

"That is not a good idea, Laurienne," Phoebe said, racing after her. "You don't understand the situation. I don't want you doing anything until you calm down."

Laurienne, halfway out the door, sounded furious again. "Don't you get it, Mom? I don't care what you want."

"I'll go with you."

"No."

"I know how charming Whit is, but Laurienne, you've got to be careful. He's not anything like Mitchell."

"Yeah, he's alive."

When she slammed the door, Phoebe heard the crash of shattered trust.

*   *   *

Dully, dutifully, Phoebe checked on Cliff and found him dead asleep—Laurienne knew her man. She turned out the light and took his tray back to the kitchen, where she shook the last of her Nats out of its box.

Outside, as she exhaled smoke, words from Pearl's journal came back to her. *I wanted to give you a life free of my troubles, free of my losses, free of my pain.* No doubt Pearl believed it. Well, didn't Phoebe believe what she'd told Laurienne? Still, Laurienne's question dug at her: *Who were you really protecting?* The implication being that there was only one correct answer: myself. And she had only to imagine asking the same of Pearl to see its truth. But the tougher questions remained. Why? From what?

When Lexie Shields cracks the code on an alien homing device, she penetrates the aliens' alternate universe to discover that her father isn't dead after all but trapped there, a situation where Lexie's extraordinary powers are no help—she captures just a one-way vision of her dad. So she dives into battle with her terrible longing and rage, photon gun blazing, because not only did she have enough years with the guy to make a positive ID, but the antimatter glop that sucked him away had altered her DNA so that she could materialize anywhere on earth with the ease of subatomic particles. No sappy entrances, no stupid explanations, no sloppy exits slowing her down. Lucky Lexie.

Whereas Laurienne was stuck on Owl Island. Maybe with her father—was that the good news?—but definitely with her mother, and that was the bad. Nowhere to go after storming out of the house with *her* longing and rage but to the one place where she might find an answer. Or at least the beginnings of an answer.

As she drove to the old Miller house, light rain began

to fall. Laurienne turned on her wipers. The blades were old and just smeared water around on the windshield, making it hard to see anything but blurred trees and mailboxes. Slowing to a crawl, she realized that if Whit was her father, she'd have to figure out how to be not only some man's daughter, but some well-known man's daughter. And if it was Mitchell? Weird, but she was afraid that somehow he would be more dead to her than ever, for having slipped into a realm of possibility where no blood ran between them, where he had saved her life but not given it.

Laurienne gulped down air, stoking the anger that fueled her now. The only straightforward thing here was her mission. Once she stopped the Volvo at the end of the Road and threw it into park, she put on her imaginary supersuit and charged up the hill.

A creamy-skinned woman with black hair came to the door, a cloth napkin in her hand.

"Hi," Laurienne said. "You must be Whit's wife."

"Who is it?" Whit called out.

"Sweetie, she hasn't had a chance to tell me yet," the woman called back.

"Sorry to interrupt your dinner." Before Laurienne could say more, Whit was by the woman's side.

"Jasmine, this is Laurienne," he said. "My computer whiz."

"Oh." Jasmine opened the door and motioned her inside with a hesitant, but beautiful, smile. "Hi."

"She's been helping with my script software on the phone," Whit went on, "but we couldn't figure out how to change the margins. Her boyfriend had a little accident, so she didn't make it over this afternoon. How's he doing, kid?"

"Fine, but he's not getting into a boat without me anytime soon." From the foyer, Laurienne saw the candlelit dining area and heard the same kind of smoky saxophone jazz that Whit was playing in his car when they met. "Do you have a minute now? What I need to do shouldn't take long."

"Sure, we were just finishing up."

"I'll make some tea," Jasmine said. "You're welcome to stay for a cup, Laurienne."

"Thanks, but I better get back to Cliff."

"Okay," Whit said, "we'll skip the tour, then." He led her straight to his study and closed the door. It was a tidy place, with a small stereo system on the bookshelves, an old typewriter sitting on a stool, and the computer set up on a long wood table, stacked pages and an ashtray beside it. "Well, that was weird. I was probably a little clumsy back there—you took me by surprise."

"My mother says—"

"Hold on." Whit turned on the stereo. More jazz, piano now.

Laurienne lowered her voice. "She says you might be my father. I need to know." She pulled a popsicle stick from her pocket and advanced on him so quickly he looked frightened. "Open your mouth."

"The answer's not in my teeth," he hissed, shrinking from her.

"But it is in your spit. Open up."

"Are you sure you know what you're doing?"

"Don't you want to find out?" She pulled out another stick and one of several stashed Baggies. "All I need is a couple of swabs. I can do it, or you can do it for me."

"Tell me first—would you like me to be the one?"

"I just want to know who my father is."

"It's all right, nothing to cry about."

"I'm not crying."

"The way your face changed, you were about to. Listen, it might be something to be really happy about, who knows?"

"So you'll help me find out?"

"What do I do?"

"Scrape the inside of your cheek, get as much on each stick as you can, and bag them."

"I'll do it in the bathroom. Easier than making a deposit at a sperm bank, I guess."

Laurienne obliged him with a weak laugh.

"Meanwhile, there's something you can do for me." He went to his computer and turned it on. "That margin problem's for real. Could you make them wider on the dialog? I've got too many pages; I need to cheat."

"I'll try."

While he was gone, she bagged a roach from his ashtray and a green wad of chewing gum, too. She might not know exactly what Lyle would do with these specimens in the lab, but, she figured, the more the better.

Whit's laptop was on, but the lid was closed. She opened it and up popped a screenplay file called "Watertight," page 15 out of 120. A chunk of words jumped out at her.

> NICK
> I feel like I conjured you.

> KATE
> I knew you'd say that.

> NICK
> Yeah, well, the same guy still
> writes all my material.

> KATE
> Did you know I was here?

NICK
Here, there and everywhere—
isn't that your address?

KATE
Not for a long time.

Laurienne felt a little creepy, as though she were read-ing his mail, so she quickly punched up the dancing camera and typed "margins" into the dialog box.

In the car again, a trickle of sweat slid between Lauri-enne's breasts. Tense as she'd been back there, Whit's fib hadn't escaped her notice. Well, what was he supposed to say—"Honey, this young woman might be my daugh-ter?" He was in a spot, too. Still, he didn't mention lunch. And Jasmine didn't sound—or look—like she had a cold.

22

Laurienne barely spoke to Phoebe after she swept back into the house, and made clear her reluctance to expend each word. She had plenty to say to Cliff, though—behind her closed bedroom door, where Phoebe heard their voices hum.

If Phoebe couldn't learn from Laurienne what happened at Whit's, she might as well forget about engaging her in conversation about who it was she'd really been protecting all these years—though enough ideas on that score did occur over a largely sleepless night to have sparked discussion at breakfast, if only Laurienne hadn't been in such a hurry to leave. "I'm grabbing a shower," she said while finishing a bowl of cereal at the kitchen sink. "Then we're off."

After Laurienne went upstairs, Cliff gave Phoebe a smile that somehow managed to be all at once loyal, rueful, and sweet. "She's pretty pissed."

"I know."

"But she's going to find out for sure if it kills her. Which it won't. I mean, it ought to be relatively easy."

"How?"

"Laur got some spit off him last night."

Phoebe shook her head, wondering if he might be delirious again.

"Saliva samples," Cliff explained, "for testing. This guy

in our lab will do it—he owes me a favor. Takes a while
to get results, though."

"How long?"

"Lyle says less than a week."

"I'd like to know what they are. God, what am I saying? I'm desperate to know. But Laurienne might not
want to tell me."

"I'm your ace in the hole there," Cliff said. "Not to
brag, just that I wouldn't be around if I'd drowned.
Once she cools down enough to get her scales of justice
out again, that'll make a difference."

Phoebe wasn't so sure. Especially when the lone hug
she got as they left was from Cliff. Oh, Laurienne thanked
her, but in a perfunctory, remote way, avoiding her eyes.

Only when you're tormented by your own blunders in
raising a child do you begin to develop some real compassion for your parents. Or so it seemed to Phoebe with
Sunday stretching out before her, and everything that
mattered spinning somewhere beyond her control. With
Laurienne in charge, she felt all the more ineffective. Just
what did she suppose she would have done if weeks ago
Whit had said yes, he knew about Phoebe's daughter,
and might she be his? Difficult to imagine herself putting
him off while she surreptitiously gathered samples and
hired help, getting the answer to her dilemma before
anyone else knew of it, and deciding how to proceed
from there.

She ought to try and do something to lessen the sick-
ening undertow of it all.

Still in her nightgown and robe, Phoebe went to the
garage, this time for Pearl's red notebook. It was in a
box all its own, along with the oil portrait of Pearl
painted by Hans in Holland, the color of her eyes and
hair so like Laurienne's. Since that distant day when

Phoebe skipped school and rode the ferry with Pearl's journal, she had never once opened it again. The part she did read was seared into memory, but she'd avoided finishing the last few pages, telling herself it wasn't worth the risk of plunging back into all the old grief. But the truth was, those pages represented a chance to see Pearl again, hear her voice, and it was a comfort having the possibility before her. She hadn't wanted to lose it, not until now.

Phoebe removed the notebook and took it back to bed, bringing along a pot of spearmint tea. Rain sprayed the windows as she read.

Bill Champlain, that was my first husband's name. It was less a marriage than a wartime romance, since we had only a few nights together before Champ shipped out to the Pacific, where the bomber he piloted went down. But he did end up taking care of me, with a war widow's pension.

True to her promise, Hannah paid only for my first year of college. With my pension, though, I had money enough to finish school and go on for my master's degree. I worked, too, so there was even extra to buy a few prints by Morris Graves and Mark Tobey, which later became valuable enough that Daddy and I sold them for the down payment on our house. A house of my own, with my own study, my own garden, husband, and child! A dream almost as big as Pearl the college girl. Sometimes, though, I wish I'd kept the prints. Think of what they'd be worth today. Or even in a few years, when Daddy gives you this to read. But then, recognizing the worth of what was mine never came easily to me. It almost seems as though it's taken a tumor to drive me to it.

You know that Buddhist secretary in Daddy's de-

partment? She gave me a book of spiritual stories the other day (for comfort, I suppose), and there's one about a man in ancient times who spends his life struggling to make his fortune, never aware that all along, a jewel precious beyond measure was sewn into the hem of his robe. A wealthy friend did the deed while the man slept, not wanting to disturb him. Though if you ask me, the real favor would have been to put the thing in his hand. (Like Jimmy Stewart tells that angel who says they have no use for money in heaven—"It sure comes in handy down here, bub.") But the story had a different lesson, and a good one, too.

When I met your father, one of the most attractive things about him was that he didn't care about my past. It was our future that mattered, our lives together. We would have been happier, though, if I hadn't locked quite so many doors behind me. Now that we're making our peace, there's nothing I can't tell him, and almost nothing he doesn't seem to understand. Apart from leaving you, that might just be the bitterest thing of all to accept. So much time spent in the dark, with the curtains drawn.

I got so used to pain with the headaches that it seemed nobody could ever help me, so I waited too long when I got sick with this. Now I'm not brave enough to refuse these damn treatments and the extra time they might mean. I may not have the mind or energy to write much more, but Daddy can fill you in on things from our time together, and as a family. Don't be mad at him if he needs someone else when I'm gone. He'll never learn how to drive; I can promise you that, and he wasn't meant to live alone.

Advice is pretty useless when you're young, and mistakes must be made. But I love you so much that *it seems only right that I try to leave you with some wisdom, and the very best I can do is lay my own mistakes before you to judge as you will, and to say, keep <u>your</u> house open, honey. You are the jewel in the hem of my robe. And if there's any power given me in what's to come, you can bet I'll be tucking away as many jewels as I can for you. If you don't find them in your robe, check the clouds, check the garden, check where hummingbirds lay ivory eggs no bigger than bumblebees. (I found a nest like that once when I was pregnant with you—the most delicate thing I ever saw.) But the best place of all to look might be in the eyes of someone who sees you, really sees you, for the treasure trove you are.*

Phoebe closed the notebook, but she wasn't ready to let it go. How different might all the preceding pages seem to her with this last part still throbbing inside? She rolled over on her side, opened the notebook again, and read it straight through. Then, instead of succumbing to grief, she fell asleep with the sense of Pearl's arms around her, stronger and more fearless than they'd ever been in life. It was the soundest sleep she'd had for months, lasting long, dreamless hours.

Later, lying in a tub filled with rosemary-scented water, she remembered the days when Jack would take her away, as if he sensed how helpless having Pearl struggle in the dark made her feel, and how he sweetened those times with movies, with music—the only medicine he knew to give. It worked. He might have been able to make Pearl happy, too, if only she had let him.

Phoebe dressed and went to her jewelry box to take off the pearl and the wedding band she'd been wearing. The necklace, like the journal, had done its job. Now *she* had to do the first job she could see her way clear to finishing.

"Daddy," she said when Jack answered the phone. "I miss you."

The next morning, Phoebe put Sophie in charge of the shop and—with Lily in the back seat—took off for Seattle, hoping just to feel like a daughter again herself.

After dropping Lily off at Jack's house, she headed down to the UW campus to pick him up for lunch and a matinee at the Harvard Exit. Her father, as Pearl had predicted, never did learn to drive.

Phoebe parked the Explorer and walked past crowds of class-changing students to the small office the university had granted Jack as an emeritus professor.

"Hi, hi," he said when she opened the door.

She wished she had been able to park closer to his building when she saw how he huffed after climbing a hill, how much slower his step had become in the time since she'd last seen him. His interests were the same as ever, though—as established by the canvas sack he had given her to carry to the car, filled with their time-honored means of sparking conversation. Music tapes he thought she might like to hear, books she might like to read, videos she might like to see. If she let him, he would talk about nothing but these things meant for her pleasure all through lunch and until the theater lights dimmed; then, when the lights came up again, he'd have the sure-to-be terrific movie to savor. But she wasn't about to settle for connecting through third-party creations, not today.

"I'm sorry it's been so long," she said as they settled in at his favorite seafood grill.

"No, no," he said. "Not a problem. I've had Hiram's letters to keep me busy."

She knew the letters he meant—all written by Hiram Johnson, California's progressive Depression-era governor. Jack's postretirement project was organizing them into an archive and writing his own passages of commentary. A lot of work, but she didn't want Hiram getting her off the track. "It's just that when Helen died it reminded me too much of when Mother died," she said. "It's nobody's fault, but I need to talk about her with you."

Jack's eyebrows, which extended over his glasses in a thick, bushy white shelf, rose now in a startled peak. "Well, well," he said.

Phoebe wondered about this new habit of doubling his words. Maybe he had suffered a minor stroke and she was too late in coming to him for what she needed. But he relaxed once he understood she had no wish to relive anything but Pearl's particularity—with details only the two of them could remember, each adding to the other's stories with his or her own private knowledge until it almost seemed as if Pearl were sitting there with them.

At first Phoebe felt selfish, plunging Jack back into his first marriage with the loss of his second wife more recent, but this was the wake neither one of them had ever been prepared to have. "Do you think her secrets killed her?" she asked.

"No, the tumor did."

"You know what I mean, Daddy."

"Everybody who's had any kind of life keeps a few secrets. It wasn't the secrets. It was how she couldn't get past them."

Phoebe had already figured that out for herself. What moved her was the complicity of having him affirm it.

* * *

Lunch lasted so long that when Phoebe signaled for the check, servers were readying all the empty tables around them for dinner. After stopping by the house to walk Lily, they went to an early evening show instead of the matinee. Afterwards, Jack chose not to revel in the terrificness of the Australian movie they'd just seen, which surprised her—he was a huge Judy Davis fan. Instead, he brought up Whit. "Isn't your friend about due for a new one?"

She was driving him home, heading north on the Ave. "Whit's my neighbor now. He bought a house down the road from me."

"You don't say. My, my."

"But you know what? He's not my friend. He was my lover, he was my playmate, he was my mentor, and in a way he was even my father. But he was never really my friend, and I doubt he's ever going to turn into my friend, because he doesn't know how to be anything but an imaginary one, and to tell you the truth, it hurts when you call him my friend, so I wish you would just stop doing that."

"I see." Then, after a long pause: "He should make more comedies. My favorite movie of his was a comedy. The one about the advertising man with amnesia." Jack chuckled, as if remembering a stellar scene.

All that explanation for nothing. Here she felt as though she had just swum the English Channel and he didn't even notice her hair was wet. He didn't have a clue about her feelings after all. "Your favorite's not *Kiki*?"

"Oh," he said, "I don't consider *Kiki* his movie. I consider *Kiki* yours."

Phoebe drove awhile in silence, wishing he had said this years ago, when they first saw *Kiki* together, then wondered if he had; nobody's opinion of the movie but

Whit's mattered to her at the time, and *he* wasn't talking. Only now did she have the ears to hear her father's words, the heart to tell the emotion behind them.

He spoke to her in the shorthand they used for talking about cultural things. "What's that Alice Faye song? From that Barbary Coast movie—"

"*Alexander's Ragtime Band.* Alice Faye and Tyrone Power, a whole bunch of Irving Berlin songs, she sang—"

"No, later—during the war. Still San Francisco, though."

"*Hello, Frisco, Hello?*"

"That's the one. But the song?"

"Oh geez, what is that song? The same one Scorsese starts his movie with—where Jodie Foster's a wiseass kid, Ellen Burstyn's a waitress, *Alice Doesn't Live Here Anymore.*"

"Yes! An Alice Faye song for his own Alice. Nice touch."

Words came to match the notes in Phoebe's head. "I've got it—'You'll Never Know.'" She pitched her voice low, so as not to exceed her range, and sang the first verse to him, a sweet pair of you'll-never-knows—how much I miss you, how much I care. It was one of those don't-you-get-it? songs that she had always been partial to, with the three little words saved, like a treasure, till the end. Jack joined in on the last verse and finished it out with her—the first song they'd sung together in a very long time. The closest she could come, as a grown woman, to sitting in her father's lap.

Neither of them spoke again until they pulled into the driveway and Jack unbuckled his seat belt.

"Sleepy?" she asked.

"Oh, no," he said. "I'm much too stirred up for sleep."

"Me, too."

They went inside to share an omelet, and while they ate she told him about how she'd left *Kiki* with Mitchell, the situation with Laurienne and Whit. Just as Pearl's journal seemed to promise, he understood. Maybe he didn't hate emotional messes so much as he just never knew what to *do* about them. Still, Phoebe couldn't help asking, "Why didn't you try and stop me from going with Whit?"

"Well," he said, "I was afraid of losing you. Like you were afraid of losing Laurienne, I suppose. Your mother would have known how to handle things."

Phoebe shook her head. "I was pretty stubborn."

"All I heard when you came back from Montreal was that you fell in love with somebody else. I was sorry you didn't finish school, but you know how much I liked Mitchell."

"You liked Whit, too."

"I liked some of his movies. It's not the same."

"Well, you did only meet him once."

"That was enough, I think. More tea?" It seemed he was changing the subject and she didn't blame him, not after the colossal mess she'd put before him. Then he said, "At my age, you get a bigger perspective on things. I'm sorry for how bad you feel, Phoebe, but it's not the end of the world. I have a lot of faith in you, and Laurienne, too."

It was too late now for driving home. Phoebe washed their dishes, kissed Jack's cheek, and went upstairs to her old bedroom, which Helen had refurnished for Laurienne's Brookland years. She would be sleeping not in her own old bed, but her daughter's. Some small, unexpected comfort in that while she tucked on clean sheets, but she fell asleep fearful. What if Whit only aggravated Laurienne's alienation from her, diminished her further in her daughter's eyes?

That night she dreamed of going to a conference room where Whit sat waiting for her to join him. It was no ordinary conference room; it had a bar. And though every wall was mirrored, she saw only her own reflection. "You're so short," he said, just as he had the first time they met in front of the Port Pritchard post office. At the bar she found glasses of ruby liquid, labeled "Drink Me," for them both, and as they drank she told him why they were never friends and never could be. When they both got up from the table, she was so much taller that he barely reached her chest.

What an Alice dream that was, she thought on awakening. Alice of Wonderland, Alice Prin of Montmartre, Alice Faye, Alice Doesn't Live Here—she could feel all their energies inside it. But she wished the dream had shown for sure whether Whit was Laurienne's father. It seemed likely as not that somewhere in her body—her womb, maybe, where the melding had occurred—there lay the verdict, certain as any that would come from a laboratory test, and the only way her body might speak to her would be through a dream.

Not this one, though.

Hard as she probed, the answer wouldn't come.

Phoebe drove all the way home without playing the radio or any of the tapes she kept in the Explorer for highway trips. The whole while, she thought of nothing except what she had to tell Ivan.

He sat down with her at the kitchen table that night and listened for a long time without a word. When he scooted his chair closer to hers and put his arms around her, she wept on his shoulder.

"At least you're looking at what's really there now," he said. "So am I."

She raised her head, unsure of his meaning. "And what do you see?"

"Why you've been so twisted up. He's the kind of guy who could put you in a place like that."

Looking into Ivan's pale blue eyes, she could tell how much saying this had cost him. No, that wasn't right. His words were another gift, and what she had caught a glimpse of were the huge reserves from which it came.

23

"I think it's wonderful," Jasmine told Whit after she read his finished script. "The best thing you've ever written."

"You always say that."

"And I always mean it." Then Jasmine got that look in her eyes, as if she were seeing something he couldn't. "But this one's different. Big-time different."

"Big-time? You must be on Steven Soderbergh's wavelength. So did you buy it when the girl turns out to be his daughter?"

"Oh yes."

"I'm worried it's too melodramatic."

Jasmine shook her head. "With somebody else, maybe. Not how you'll shoot it."

Right away, he had Jasmine FedEx the script to Joe, who called back so early the next day he must have read it in one sitting. Joe's verdict was essentially the same as Jasmine's, only more meaningful for coming from a pro. "This thing has tremendous potential, Whit, just tremendous. Great parts, big canvas, killer ending. But it'll cost to do it right."

"You sound like that's a bad thing."

"No, no. Just more budget than we ever got for you before, that's all. Tell you what, let me call in a couple favors, get some overnight reads on this."

"From who? Your Seattle moguls?"

"Forget them—we can go to real people with this one. And if I'm right, you can color us green by week's end."

Money was what he meant, and Joe never kidded around about money. In Whit's mind, it was almost as good as in the bank—a major payday, the kind he'd never had before. He hung up the phone flooded with optimism. Some divine intelligence must have led him back to the Northwest, to exactly the sort of script he needed to write, to all the pieces of his past gathering strength, to not just a comeback but a resurrection. And like his detective, it looked as though he had a grown daughter to boot. Life imitating art, as it so often did with him. Funny, how almost from the first he could imagine working with Laurienne. She was so different from Phoebe, yet with the same quick intelligence, empathy, and smarts about things that sparked his imagination. So reminiscent of his sister Becky, too. Without Becky in the house, he never would have grown into who he was.

When would it be official? When would Laurienne receive her confirmation? He called both her office and her apartment, getting only voice mail and her answering machine. Since she and Jasmine had met, he supposed it was all right now to leave his home phone number with Laurienne. He'd deal with how to break the news to Jasmine later. It shouldn't be difficult, especially since she was so crazy about the script. She knew how much of himself went into these things.

Next he called Howard, his business manager in Los Angeles, and told him to find out what Phoebe's fee would have been if she'd been credited for the *Kiki* script. Whit would even throw in a bonus. That ought to smooth over matters between them, pull her back to her real feelings for him. Which seemed necessary, now that they almost certainly had a daughter in common.

Arranging the money took a little maneuvering. Joe's assistant had to track down Phoebe's social security number. Howard had to call the Screenwriters Guild to ascertain fees for such an old script, and then Whit doubled the amount. Thirty thousand dollars was what it came to—not much by Hollywood standards, but a nice chunk of change for Phoebe. No need to go into fine-print particulars with her, quantifying his generosity with estimates of interest and residuals. And why bother changing the credit unless Phoebe brought it up again? She probably wouldn't. This wasn't her career; she didn't belong to a union. If what she'd wanted to be was a writer, surely she'd have become one by now.

Whit wanted her check to look official, for tax purposes, so he told Howard to cut it on the Handheld Films account he kept for business expenses. It would come to Phoebe with a letter from Howard saying "Whit Traynor has directed me to issue this retroactive payment and bonus for writing services on *Kiki*." Though for his own records, Whit directed Howard to apply the outlay for Phoebe as *Watertight* research, so it could be written off against Whit's sure-to-be-hefty earnings on the film.

Howard put up a fuss. "There's not enough cash in the Handheld account to cover it," he said.

"I'll have my broker wire the money," Whit told him.

"I wish you'd wait until you get paid."

What could you expect, with an accountant's mind like Howard's? No vision there, and Whit wasn't about to explain himself, not to someone who worked for him. "Just wait a few days, then overnight it to her," Whit said while he looked in the phone book for Phoebe's business address.

With that settled, Whit called Brad, his broker. "I want to sell my BioIngenious shares."

"How many?" Brad asked.

"Every one."

"But you just bought them," Brad said. "Sure you want to dump it all?"

"Yeah, the whole ball of wax."

The amount equaled Phoebe's fee almost to the dollar. Whit knew full well he was breaking the first rule of filmmaking: Never use your own money. But when had he not broken the rules?

Two days later, Howard called about a letter from the tribe that had come to his office, where all Whit's bills were delivered—something about sizable lease-rate hikes and assessments.

Whit exploded. "That bastard," he said, meaning Carl Brown. "He promised rates were fixed for five years!"

Then, that evening, the blonde woman from Carl Brown's party showed up at his door. She had to remind him of her name—Margaret.

"I hate to bother you," Margaret said, "but we weren't sure if you knew about the tenants meeting coming up." She extended a lengthy outline in Whit's direction. "Thought you might like to look over the agenda some of us put together."

"Why would I want to do that?"

"Oh, I don't know." She shrugged. "So you can see what some of your neighbors think is the best way to handle the situation? So you can make objections, suggestions? Be part of the community?"

"Well, thank you very much," Whit said. "I appreciate your concern. But I really don't have the time now for community activities." Let Margaret recycle the paper herself.

"Suit yourself," Margaret told him. "I gather you usually do."

What in the hell did she mean by that? Jesus, when did

people around here get so rude? Just this morning, while he was filling up his tank, that waitress from the Tavern had looked up from screwing on her gas cap and glared at him. Then, on his way home, neither of the neighbors he passed on the Road seemed as glad as usual to see him. They didn't even raise a palm from the wheel in the obligatory island wave.

That afternoon, Joe called.

"First the good news," he said. "Three different studios are slobbering over this baby of yours." He told Whit who had read the script—major players, every one. "We've got a bidding war going on here; it's unbelievable. You're the belle of the ball; the script's a slam dunk."

"So what's the bad?" Whit asked.

"There's no sweet way to put it, so I'll just tell you flat out. Nobody thinks you can direct this up to potential."

"You're kidding, right?"

"You've never had a budget big as what they want to throw at this one. They're scared you'll get in over your head, fuck it up."

"Listen, I did my part. Convince them I won't. Isn't that your job?"

"Sorry, Whit. Not this time. And don't give me any crap about Hollywood loyalty, because I've stood by you longer than anybody else in this town would. You can always shop it on your own, but when you're done dicking around you'll come to the same conclusion I have. Bottom line? You've got a choice. You can scrape the financing together, make some cheap version that nobody'll see, and pay yourself peanuts."

"Or I can go to the whorehouse with you."

"Right, and earn more than you got for your last three movies combined."

"Since when did this get to be just about the money?"

"Lemme see, what time is it? Oh, right. Since now."

"I'll talk to my agent."

"Okay, talk to your agent—he'll have an orgasm. I'm already assuming we'll get you on board as a producer, tack on another fee there. But you'll queer the deal with too many demands."

"Like sole screenplay credit?"

"Yeah. Like that. Think about it. I need your answer fast."

Whit slammed down the phone. So that's how it was. Those pricks would sign up some hot young director who'd hire somebody else to rewrite the script, somebody with a big box office track record—the kind of hack who endorsed that screenwriting software. By the time they were done writing and shooting, Whit would be lucky to recognize anything of himself in the movie. He'd just be the guy who drew up the first blueprint, the one who spat out a script that begged for a more successful director's vision to transform it. He'd just be one of the screenwriters, and in the end, screenwriters always got fucked. Always, always, always.

24

It was rare enough for Westerly Webs to receive a FedEx delivery that Sophie came bounding up the stairs and stood waiting in the office for Phoebe to open it. "It's from Los Angeles," Sophie said. "Might be a referral from that sport net distributor."

Phoebe checked the return address—some firm she'd never heard of—then ripped the envelope tab. As she pulled out the letter inside, a check fluttered to the floor.

"Are you all right?" Sophie asked as Phoebe studied the letter.

"It's personal, Soph," Phoebe said, picking up the check and putting it on her desk. "Nothing to do with work."

"Did somebody die?"

"No. Somebody's trying to make good on a bad debt."

"Lucky you. I mean, we can all use a little extra these days."

Phoebe grabbed her anorak, wound a scarf around her neck, and slipped the check into her pocket. "I've got a few errands to run," she told Sophie.

Outside, traffic lights and shop signs swung in the wind. Sylvia, a south-side neighbor who owned the Magic Whisk Cook's Shop across the street, waved a corn husk at Phoebe from the display window before going back to her harvest-time tableau of dancing turkeys. The air smelled of salmon smoking at the seafood store, hops from the Brew Pub, and caramel cooking at the place that sold candied apples. Phoebe crossed the Fishermen's Terminal lot and walked straight out to the farthermost dock.

What was Whit up to now? Her mind raced as she sat on a stack of tethered crab pots under a moody, darkening sky. How did he arrive at this amount, and what did he expect she would owe him in return? Could the check really be compensation for *Kiki,* or was it a clumsy stab at assuming paternal responsibility? If Laurienne had punished her by telling Whit first how the test turned out, then he'd know something she didn't. But that was too indirect for her daughter, no matter how angry she still was at Phoebe. Still, easy to believe Whit assumed his DNA would beat out anybody else's.

Oh, imagining what compelled him was such a familiar routine she could go on like this forever. Did he mean to make a generous gesture? Was he so loaded as to be only tossing crumbs her way? Maybe he was afraid of what she might tell Laurienne about him, or what she might tell Jasmine, in which case the check was hush money. She even wondered if he was worried about her being able to pay the new lease rates and fees, but that was wandering in the Land of Make-Believe again. What mattered were *her* intentions.

Only a few things to be done with a check: cash it, tear it up, or frame it. Framing it would be unbelievably sappy, as if she needed to advertise her connection to Whit. Ripping it up wouldn't be satisfying at all. But cashing it? That felt funny—moneygrubbing and reckless somehow, as if she'd be consenting to whatever he had in mind for her. As if she had a price.

Phoebe pulled the check from her pocket for another look. She held it between her thumb and forefinger, daring the wind to take this light but laden thing away from her. And it did, blowing the check against a pile of netting ropes. She stared at it lying there for so long that the wind changed direction, lifting the check and skittering it back across the dock toward her. She nailed it easily with the heel of her boot. And then it was as if the hand of some strict, impatient, unseen teacher thumped her on the head, asking, *And* now *do you get it?* No reason to go chasing after this check's meaning the way she'd always chased after some notion of Whit—who he was, how he felt, what he needed. What she had here was just a piece of paper, endorsed by her footprint, meaning nothing about her character, her intelligence, her worth. Meaning nothing about her at all.

The wind died down as the first drops of rain fell and she picked up the check. Then *poof*—Whit flew out of her head, disappeared from her considerations, leaving no shadow this time.

25

On the same day Laurienne brought her labeled Baggies to Lyle, she sold her options and gave two weeks' notice. So did Cliff. When the saliva samples finally ripened, Lyle called to arrange a middle-of-the-night rendezvous. No one else but security guards was moving through the building as Lyle ushered her and Cliff to the only lit corner of the lab, the place where he would run his final tests.

The tests that would reveal who Laurienne's father was.

And wasn't.

She felt like a nervous father herself, the corny kind who paces and chain-smokes until the baby pops out. Only this seemed more like anticipating her own birth—from twenty-two years' fast-forward distance.

"I didn't bother with the roach," Lyle told them. "The last thing I need around here are illegal-substance traces. But I got juicy hits off everything else." He pulled six glass slides from a drawer. "Three are yours, and three are his."

"Show me who's who," Laurienne said. She just wanted to be sure *he* knew. "What now?" Cliff asked after Lyle obliged her.

"Now," Lyle said, "now we make magic."

"I hope that means an answer," Laurienne said. "I can't stand any more waiting."

"Alchemy takes time," Lyle said. "If you could do this at home, kids, you wouldn't be here. But hey, if you'd rather spend a thousand bucks for a paternity test from Poppa Whosis, fine with me; my feelings won't be hurt."

"Sorry," Laurienne said. "I'll be good."

Lyle put on a pair of thick magnifying glasses and picked up a vial as if he were a television chef, compelled to talk his audience through every step of the recipe. "Microscopic gold beads. State-of-the-art stuff, you won't find these at Daddy Dearest." He reached for a tiny glass pipette. "When I spill beads over a slide, they match up with specimen DNA. Then I dip the slide into a photographic solution and presto, change-o—here's where it gets sexy. At this very moment, even as I speak, silver ions in the photo soup are bonding with each and every little invisible-to-the-naked-eye gold bead. Now they're turning into black beads that are hundreds of thousands times bigger."

"Like sperm and eggs," Cliff said. "Cool."

Lyle repeated the process for each slide, then put them through a photo scanner, one by one. For every slide, the scanner spat out a sheet of black-dotted patterns. Lyle stacked them as they came out of the machine.

"Now what?" Laurienne asked, breath suspended.

"Now we look for matching patterns. If this guy's your father, half your DNA patterns will match his."

Cliff reached for Laurienne's hand while Lyle spread the patterned sheets out on a table, Whit's on the left and Laurienne's on the right.

Lyle folded his arms and nodded. "Well," he said, "there you are."

But for Laurienne the dots all meshed and swirled off the paper into big black globs and the only conclusion she could reach was that she must have started life as a tar baby, not a real person at all. "What?" she cried. "What do you see?"

"Can't you tell?" Cliff asked, pulling her close and putting an arm around her.

"No!"

"It's pretty plain," Cliff said. "Your patterns and his— they don't match at all."

Laurienne burst into tears and buried her face in his neck.

"It's okay, it's okay," he said, stroking her hair. "I know how you feel."

It wasn't the first time since last weekend that she had cried, and it wasn't the first time he had told her this, either. But it *was* the first time she believed him.

"Want your samples back?" Lyle asked after Laurienne recovered enough to thank him.

She shook her head.

"How about the slides—want to hang on to those?"

"I don't need souvenirs."

"Then can I keep them?"

She frowned at him, puzzled. "Why? What do you want my DNA for?"

"Not yours, his. He's got this cool anomaly on the gene we're working. Be fun to play with it."

The Peter Pan gene, no doubt. As a scientist, she liked the idea that something bigger might come out of this exercise, justifying that stupid patent. A medication, a vaccine, a cure. But as a human being, her only choice was to shove everything into her backpack and get the hell out of there.

For the first time, Laurienne let Cliff stay at her apartment. She'd slept alone there ever since coming back from Phoebe's, thrashing her way through troubled dreams.

Last night's scenario—that was how she thought of her dreams since Lexie came into her life, as scenarios—had her picking oysters on the shore when a giant wall of water came roaring across Little Pritchard Bay. As she scrambled up the hillside, shouting to warn everyone, she kept slipping back down onto the beach. Then, just as the tsunami curled overhead, a rich, throaty voice entered her dream, sounding like the women who narrate feminine hygiene commercials. *I'm sorry, Laurienne,* the voice said. *This is not your dream. This dream was sent to you by mistake.*

How terrible, she thought on awakening, *to be someone with mistaken dreams.* But now the dream seemed funny—prophetic, even.

Brushing her teeth, she watched Cliff circle the bedroom, examining her things. He picked up the framed photograph on her nightstand, the only family portrait she had, blown up from an old snapshot. She was fat and gummy-grinned in a pink sunsuit, sitting in the crook of Mitchell's muscular arm with a hank of Phoebe's long black hair wound around her fist. Laurienne especially liked the shot because Mitchell was the only one of the three without a hat or sunglasses, smiling directly into the camera. "That's your father?" Cliff asked.

She rinsed out her mouth and came to look at the photo with him. "Yep," she said. "That's my dad."

She had been wrong about how it would be, learning from a test that she was in fact Mitchell's daughter. It wasn't so much like losing him all over again, the way she'd feared, as getting him back inside herself, where he belonged. Holding on to him the way he had held on to her.

Falling into bed with Cliff, Laurienne felt light, exhilarated—freed of more than doubt about her father's identity. Another, much older burden was gone.

Not so much a spell as the sheer weight of her mother's past; sorrows only suggested, never defined, but decoded to mean that since Phoebe couldn't create her own happiness, it was Laurienne's job to do it for her. An unconscious, underground kind of job, neglected in recent years, but a job all the same. Well, that was one thing her anger had been good for. Taking off the weight.

Laurienne turned out the light and curved her body around Cliff's. It seemed so luxurious, spooning naked in a comfy, adult-sized bed without being drenched in sweat. No computer-generated heat here; chilly air through a cracked-open window had a discernible effect. Her poufy comforter felt delicious, a cozy cloud of insulation covering them instead of Cliff's thin, damp sheet. This was what sleeping with your lover on a near-winter Northwest night was supposed to be like.

"Cool," she whispered in Cliff's ear. "Like sperm and eggs." And as he laughed, she pulled him over to make slow, sleepy, satisfying love.

Only later, as Cliff's breathing grew deep and even, did she remember the messages from Whit she hadn't returned. The idea of telling him he wasn't her father got her pulse hopping. "I can't do it," she said aloud.

"Do what?" Cliff mumbled into her neck.

"Call Whit."

Cliff rolled over and turned her with him, reversing their spoon. "The one you need to call," he said, "is your mother."

26

Phoebe worked into the evening Friday, doing the payroll with Sophie. Just as they were finishing up, another storm blew in, a fierce one from the north. "How much you want to bet the island's dark when I get home?" Sophie said.

"Not much." They always lost power in wind storms, for long enough to justify emergency candle supplies, but not to spoil food in the refrigerator. Phoebe didn't mind. In fact, the idea of going to bed in candlelight tonight pleased her, since she didn't expect to be alone.

After Sophie left, Phoebe took a quick shower in the office bathroom and dressed for dinner in clothes she'd brought from home. A crushed-velvet skirt, slit to show a lot of leg when she walked, and a V-neck linen sweater in the rusty shade of orange Ivan liked on her so well. She dabbed pure Parisian amber oil on her neck and wrists, and was sliding in the posts to a pair of dangly aquamarine earrings when someone called her name from downstairs. Whit, with a plaintive note in his voice. She stepped into her heels and went to the door. "Up here," she called out.

His hair was wet, plastered to his forehead, and she got a sense of manic energy propelling him as he charged upstairs. Twenty minutes till she had to be at the Black Swan for dinner, but she felt no urge to be tit-for-tat rude and time Whit the way he had her. Especially not now, with all her confusion vanquished. A reward, it seemed, for exiting the low, mistaken road she'd been traveling with him.

"Va-va-voom," Whit said, looking her over.

Phoebe stood back, motioned him in, and exhaled audibly, preparing herself to deliver Laurienne's news. A job she'd been given earlier today, at the end of a terse, matter-of-fact phone call: "You tell him. I can't."

"Whit, I know why you're here," Phoebe began, but he shook his head.

"No you don't. You couldn't possibly. I mean, it's unreal what's happening to me now, beyond fucking belief."

Phoebe went to her desk, settled into her office chair, and poured out the last cup from a pot of Earl Grey tea she and Sophie had been sharing. Here he was again, her old imaginary friend, the Whit Show, live and in person. "I'm listening," she said.

"I told you how much you had to do with this new script, right? Well, it turned out great. So great, in fact, that they're doing everything they can to steal it from me, and my good buddy Joe—remember Joe? The one who whipped up all that trouble between us? Joe's driving the getaway car."

It seemed Whit had a new intro song now—not "Talk to Me of Love," but "Talk to Me of Betrayal." While rain pounded the windows, he went on and on with all the ways he'd been victimized, pacing in front of her Mystery Package display shelf, oblivious to all its precious objects. Mostly he raged about his movie, with a brief detour into his tribal lease, as if he were the only one on the island affected.

Phoebe breathed the scent of bergamot in her mug. It couldn't be plainer what Whit required of her, what run-

ning the maze of his dilemma this time would mean. He
wanted her to share his outrage for a good long while
before telling him to go ahead, take those stupid people's stupid money for his script; he'd have the last
laugh, there were plenty more scripts where that one
came from—just as good if not better. That was the kind
of service his check was meant to guarantee. But she
was done feeding this insatiable creature. "Gee, Whit,"
Phoebe said, "how awful. What are you going to do?"

You'd think from his stricken expression that she'd
pounded a stake through his heart. Well, in a way, she
supposed, she had.

"You're still mad," he said, "aren't you?"

She could see how much he'd prefer anger to indiffer-
ence, but she wasn't going to give him that satisfaction.
"No, not at all."

Whit pulled Sophie's chair around and sat leaning
toward Phoebe, angling an elbow on her desk. "Good,
because we can't just think about ourselves here. We
have to look at things differently now, we're Laurienne's
parents." He inhaled near her ear. "You smell wonderful."

"Well," she said, sliding her chair back from his, "yes
and no."

"Yes and no? What do you mean?"

"Yes, we have to look at things differently now. And
no, we're not Laurienne's parents. That is, I am her parent. But you're not. She called with the test results today."

Whit swept back his damp hair with the heel of his
hand. "Are you sure? Because you're not exactly the
most reliable source, Phoebe. You never would have
told Laurienne the truth if I hadn't come along, and
you've lied to me before. I mean, I knew you never went
to Paris, and this is a lot bigger than Paris. God only

knows what you've been telling all your friends on the island about me. You've betrayed every ideal I thought we shared, every single one of them. How am I supposed to trust you?"

Phoebe shook her head. "Better talk to the guy who writes your material, Whit," she said, "it's slipping. I'd explain if it would do any good. But it won't because you can't get outside yourself long enough to understand what anybody else goes through. It's not just me— even strangers sitting in the dark with their popcorn can feel it." Oh, that was nasty. But he had someone else to suture all his wounds now, someone glad for the full-time job.

Phoebe stood to get her raincoat. "I have to go."

Whit muttered as she ushered him down the stairs. "Everybody's a liar, everybody there is. Exceptions don't exist, they only prove the rule."

Phoebe got out her keys and held the shop door open for him. "Do you know what you should do, Whit?" she said, patting his back a few times until he stepped out onto the sidewalk. "Go home and be happy with Jasmine. I'll bet she's worried about you."

She raised her raincoat overhead, and after she dashed down and across the street and stopped beneath the Black Swan's awning, she saw that he was still standing where she'd left him, not so much looking at her as in her direction, no doubt imagining what kind of equipment he'd need to shoot what just happened, to replicate the wind, the rain, the ethereal streetlamp light. "Shoo," she said out loud, knowing he couldn't hear her. She swished her hand in an actual shooing gesture, though it might have been interpreted as a wave.

Maybe he waved back, maybe he didn't. She didn't wait to see.

*   *   *

The Black Swan maître d' took Phoebe's coat, and when she found Ivan at their table, he pulled out her chair. "The storm hold you up?" he asked, pressing his cheek to hers.

"What held me up is that I just landed this really big fish." She raised her face for a kiss. "But once I got a good look at the sucker, I had to open the net and throw him back in."

"A fish story, huh?"

"I'll give you the blow-by-blow later, but right now I think I deserve some champagne."

After their bottle came and the waiter poured, Phoebe clinked Ivan's glass. "To wonderful surprises," she toasted.

"Speaking of which," Ivan said. Then he reached down beside his chair and came up with a shoe box. He took off the lid and pulled back tissue paper to reveal three neat, even stacks of fifty-dollar bills. "Never would have guessed that fifteen thousand dollars would fit into a shoe box with so much room to spare."

"Looks like you've got a patron."

"Patroness is more like it," Ivan said. "Size seven-and-a-half feet. Guess I don't have to tell you this came by messenger today. From an anonymous sender, the guy said."

"Really?" Phoebe leaned across the table, chin in hand. "In my experience, the most valuable things arrive that way. It just takes some people way too long to figure out where they're coming from."

"Well," Ivan said, "at least they made some people happy enough to keep them. That was the real point."

"I hope you're listening to yourself."

"What's going on, Phoebe?"

"Don't worry—it's not a loan, it's not anything obligating you to anybody."

"That covers what it's not. How about what it is?"

"An investment. I'm investing in you, Ivan. Banking on the future, for a change. A little windfall blew my way and now it's split, between you and Laurienne."

"You didn't send hers in a shoe box, I hope."

"No, that's our tradition."

He sat smiling at her for a while under slightly raised eyebrows. "So it's yours, free and clear?"

"Of course it is. I mean, it was. Now it's yours."

"Okay. But if it's all right with you, I'd like to invest a little differently."

"How?"

"Hope you're not in a rush, because I figure this is going to be a long conversation." Ivan moved the tabletop candle closer for another inspection. "Are you sure it's not counterfeit?"

"Got it from the bank myself."

"I should probably get it back there Monday morning. Never made a cash deposit like this before—they'll probably think I robbed somebody."

"No, they're expecting you. But what will you do with it in the meantime?"

Ivan shook his head with a mystified expression. "Hide it under a mattress, I guess."

"Great idea," Phoebe said. "Yours or mine?"

27

When the morning of the second Sunday in August rolled around again, marine fog shrouding Little Pritchard Bay promised warm, sunny weather for Phoebe's barbecue. This year, though, she felt more like the barbecue's custodian than its hostess, which didn't bother her much— probably because of all the practice she'd had lately in enjoying things beyond her control.

Ivan saw to the salmon, Amelia orchestrated salads and side dishes, Laurienne delegated desserts, and Carl Brown handled beverages. All Phoebe had to do was prepare her basting sauce. As she assembled the ingredients, Ivan sat at the kitchen table talking to Jack, who'd come up for his first barbecue ever toting a bag of freshly made sausages from a Bavarian delicatessen in Seattle. Laurienne and Cliff were out on the deck, churning up ice cream while Lily lay at their feet, gnawing a T-bone from last night's dinner. Phoebe yawned and poured herself a second cup of coffee. She was still a little jetlagged.

"Judge!" Ivan had cried when he spotted Laurienne at the airport the other morning, come to meet their plane. Phoebe was surprised to see her, too. Laurienne wasn't nearly so guarded as when they'd last spoken, with a wariness on Laurienne's part that made Phoebe wonder if they'd ever rediscover their old easy harmony. But it couldn't be more clear what her daughter's real excitement was about: Cliff, and the custom-made engagement ring she wore, with a circle of tiny cultured pearls surrounding a gold inlay in the shape of something Phoebe couldn't quite identify. "A bunch of grapes?" she guessed.

"No, a blackberry," Laurienne said. "And the pearls are for oysters. That's what we ate together right before our first kiss. I picked them after the barbecue last year. Remember?"

Oh, Phoebe remembered, all right—so well she didn't need any snapshots to remind her what she was wearing, discussing, or thinking. After all, last year's barbecue marked the end of an era. Or the start of a new one. What kind of time did historians wedge between the two? Her father would know.

Now, standing by the kitchen window, Phoebe watched as sunlight angled over cedars, piercing the fog. Then she measured out a cup of tamari and threw in a piece of packaged kelp and a handful of dried tuna flakes—the stuff that made her sauce so rich and smoky, the ingredients no one else had ever managed to guess right. Another secret no longer worth the bother of keeping. In *The Owl Island Community Cookbook,* a copy of which had arrived in the mail while she was gone, her recipe was there for the taking.

While Phoebe rinsed out her cup, Cliff came inside. "Laurienne went down to the beach," he said. "Why don't you join her?" Phoebe read other thoughts in his eyes: *Yeah, she's still pissed, but if you do your part, I'll do mine.*

When Phoebe caught up with Laurienne, only a single strip of fog remained, a long gauzy layer hovering over the water that made the mountains above seem airborne. Laurienne stood at the shore, her hands filled with a small collection of smooth gray rocks.

"Let's see," Phoebe said. Each rock had at least one quartz stripe running all the way around it—wishing stones, they'd always called them, not easy to find. "Oh, Laur—you've got some real beauties there."

They walked awhile, Phoebe holding her tongue so Laurienne would have room to say what needed saying. At last she spoke. "Maybe what you did made sense when I was five. You were really selfish, though, not telling me sooner."

Phoebe fought back all the self-justifying words that bubbled up and didn't let herself respond until Ivan-like language came to her lips. "I can certainly see why you might think so," she said. "Mothers and daughters—they're a tough act."

"That sounds so across-the-board, Mom. I don't know anybody else who's been in a situation like mine. Like ours."

"You're right. It's just that I can't help thinking of my own mother, how I used to believe that if only she'd told me more, I would have understood her better. Myself, too. Now I'm not so sure. Seems like the biggest thing I needed was time. Can you give this time?"

"Maybe." Laurienne's next exhale puffed out her cheeks. "I think so."

Farther down the beach, Laurienne stooped for another quartz-ringed stone and handed it to Phoebe, who rubbed it in her palm for the rest of their walk. When they got back to the house, she put the rock in a small saucer of water to bring out all its subtle gradations. Then she went upstairs and placed the saucer by her bed.

Residents of the island's north and south sides didn't mingle just at Phoebe's barbecue anymore. Enough friendships formed in the wake of everyone's working out their leases and assessments that islanders took over the Tav-

ern to throw Ivan a party after his April museum opening. Women from up and down the road brought pot-
luck to meetings for their newly formed book club. And
Amelia met the dapper Evan Hong, who ran an organic
green-bean farm in Stanwood, at one of Carl's dinners:
at last, a boyfriend who didn't require precoital clearing.

Still, Phoebe's barbecue was the summer season's big
event, and the big topic of conversation was Phoebe
herself. Margaret, Amelia, and Sophie arrived early to
hear her news of Paris, Holland, and Italy. Since it was
Phoebe's first trip abroad, her report counted for more
than Ivan's.

After opening presents (Murano glass earrings for
Margaret, a Provençal tablecloth for Sophie, an antique
Belgian lace nightie for Amelia), they took chilled glasses
of beer out to the garden, thick with all the sunflowers,
zinnias, dahlias, and delphiniums that Amelia had been
tending. Phoebe popped open a cherry-red umbrella
over the table where they sat. Even in the shade, even in
her ginger-colored linen sundress, she could almost feel
her pores opening in the heat. She knew the kind of
things her friends wanted to hear—more personal than
what she'd scribbled on their postcards.

And so Phoebe told them about Paris—the cozy Left
Bank apartment a French landscape designer had loaned
them, the nearby theater playing a retrospective run of
version originale Ernst Lubitsch comedies that she went
to alone every afternoon. She told them about Holland—
the distant Blume relative she met who had survived the
camps as an adolescent and remembered Pearl; now he
was an architect, a jovial man who became their Amsterdam tour guide. And she told them about Italy—the
Tuscan estate where Ivan taught as part of an American
university's graduate arts program, and how Phoebe
amused herself there by sitting in on a memoir work-

shop, doing exercises that spun her off into writing something the instructor liked so well he took her aside to discuss it. "I hope you thanked your unconscious," he said.

"For what?" Phoebe asked.

"That piece about your rock-and-roll childhood. You already feel like a mature writer to me."

From then on, she was a full-fledged member of the group.

"Oh, honey," Margaret said. "That was *your* graduate program."

When Ivan and Jack swept by with the first platters of salmon and sausages off the grill, everyone but Phoebe followed them up to the house. She lingered in the garden, cutting flowers to fill the vases she'd set out and hoping what Margaret had said about her trip was true. But the other night she'd dreamed her airport dream again, the one where she races for a plane headed somewhere fabulous, then dumps out all her luggage in a futile search for her ticket. When she awoke in a panic, Ivan was sweet, holding her till she fell asleep again. But the dream lingered, warning that some essential thing was still missing. But what? The question hummed in her head.

No it didn't.

The humming she heard was the sound of tiny wings.

Phoebe cut her eyes and saw a green-throated creature suspended in the air, close to her ear. Her own personal hummingbird, every bit as good as a fairy, sipping nectar.

Among the next guests to arrive were the new neighbors who had bought the old Miller place. That's what everyone still called Whit's house, despite all the improvements he'd made. If Whit had bothered to show his face at just one community meeting, maybe Phoebe's neighbors would still be nursing their collective crush on him; she'd had nothing to do with how quickly it evaporated. As little as Whit may have wanted a new best friend on the island, he hadn't come here to be invisible. Once people stopped fussing over him, it wasn't long before he put his house on the market and bought a new place in Ojai. So much for celebrity neighbors.

Laurienne was serving up her blackberry ice cream when dusk fell and a big, buoyant moon rose on the horizon. Phoebe went inside for a shawl and a box of matches. Lighting candles along the deck, she saw that Margaret and Jack were sitting together. Phoebe hadn't heard Jack double a single word since he got here, and now he was making plans to attend a lecture series at the university with Margaret.

Only the parents with small children went home before midnight. Everybody else stayed so late there was talk of a sunrise breakfast on the beach, but that was just a last rally before the party folded.

"A moon like this always stirs things up," Ivan said as he and Phoebe lay in bed, watching it disappear from view.

Later, Phoebe dreamed her airport dream again.

Only this time, after pawing through the contents of her wallet, her purse, and three pieces of luggage, she thinks to check the pockets of her clothes. So many pockets, and they all prove empty until she reaches inside her blazer to find her ticket, tucked away next to her heart, where it had been the whole time. The flight attendant waves her on, and she dashes through the empty Jetway to find her seat, next to Ivan's.

"There you are," he says. "What took you so long?"

"Where are we going?" she asks, falling breathless into her seat. She still doesn't know where this plane is headed.

But the dream ends there, before he can answer.

Acknowledgments

Because this novel came to completion with the help of some remarkable people, it is a privilege to express my gratitude. Given my reliance on Jack Remick's impeccable eye and ear, it was surely just another piece of my good fortune in knowing him that the waitress at the café where we worked pages every week turned out to have Kiki's violin tattooed on her back. I am grateful to my Oregon editor, Barbara Sullivan, for her brilliance at key junctures, and to Kent Carroll, the publisher whose advice and generosity were extraordinary gifts to the process.

Sara Lee Skamser, the mistress of Foulweather Trawls in Newport, Oregon, educated me in the intricacies of her business. There are other water folk to thank for sharing knowledge of and enthusiasm for what they do, including Steve Patterson of Net Systems; Marcia Dale, the Bristol Bay salmon-net queen; and Lori Swanson of Groundfish Forum. My dear friend Beverly McDevitt allowed me to borrow limitlessly from her store of psychological wisdom. Ara Condas illuminated the job of computer programming, and Beth Hailey of Dona Flora Herbs & Flowers was another valuable resource.

The encouragement of my husband, Nick Fennel, is something I cannot imagine writing without. Much of my experience of Northwest splendors came from his painterly sensibility and his insistence on turning a floating cabin off the Puget Sound into our weekend retreat. There I had the pleasure of dockside visits with Allen Moe, a neighbor who often paddled by on high tides with amazing creations in the hold of his kayak, pottery pieces he had made from fish heads, chicken-foot skin, or a deer's stomach.

My mother, Bette Lee Coburn, is the other visual artist in my family with a sharp literary eye, and her loving support was crucial. Thanks to the staff of Hedgebrook, the Whidbey Island retreat for women writers, for allowing me a return visit in which to work on the novel. And to Valerie J. Brooks, my longtime Hedgebrook "sister," for not only arranging our writing trips to the Oregon coast but offering feedback as treasured as her friendship. Another gifted friend, the playwright Silvia Peto, provided notes for which I am grateful, as did Jack Mackie, Kimberly Carnethon, and Sherry Kromer Shapiro.

The publication of this book comes exactly thirty years after I first set foot in Washington state and met Libby Burke, to whom I am most happily and forever indebted for sharing her spacious heart.

Finally, I would like to extend boundless appreciation to my agent, Suzanne Gluck, and her assistant, Erin Malone, for being such consummate professionals, and to Linda Marrow, the editor I feel blessed to be working with at Ballantine.